The Tapestry of Grace

The Tapestry of Grace

A Novel

KIM VOGEL SAWYER

WATERBROOK

THE TAPESTRY OF GRACE

Scripture quotations are taken from the King James Version and the Luther Bible. Used by permission. All rights reserved.

Italics in Scripture quotations reflect the author's added emphasis.

This is a work of fiction. Names, characters, places, and incidents are the products of the author's imagination or are used fictitiously. Any resemblance to actual events, locales, or persons, living or dead, is entirely coincidental.

Published in the United States by WaterBrook, an imprint of Random House, a division of Penguin Random House LLC.

WATERBROOK® and its deer colophon are registered trademarks of Penguin Random House LLC.

LIBRARY OF CONGRESS CATALOGING-IN-PUBLICATION DATA
Names: Sawyer, Kim Vogel, author.
Title: The tapestry of grace / Kim Vogel Sawyer.
Description: First Edition. | [Colorado Springs] : WaterBrook, 2023.
Identifiers: LCCN 2022048816 | ISBN 9780593194386 (Trade Paperback) | ISBN 9780593194393 (Ebook)
Classification: LCC PS3619.A97 T36 2023 | DDC 813/.6—dc23
LC record available at https://lccn.loc.gov/2022048816

Printed in the United States of America on acid-free paper

waterbrookmultnomah.com

2 4 6 8 9 7 5 3 1

First Edition

Book design by Virginia Norey
Wheat grass art: huhehoda/stock.adobe.com

In honor of my grandmothers whom I never got to meet, *Elizabeth Klaassen Voth* and *Lillian Miller Vogel*, and my wonderful step-grandma who filled their role in my life, *Helen Hawk Vogel*—you were generous, loving women of strong faith, and I know you'll be part of my welcome-home party someday.

Let us therefore come boldly unto the throne of grace, that we may obtain mercy, and find grace to help in time of need.

—Hebrews 4:16

The Tapestry of Grace

Chapter One

Alexandertol, Kansas
April 9, 1897
Augusta Dyck

Augusta stood just inside the Alexandertol Mennonite
Church and scanned the crowded benches on the women's
side of the sanctuary. *Ach,* every woman in town must have
come to tonight's meeting. Was everyone so interested in the
new women's club, or did they only mean to enjoy an hour of
escape from their overly excited children? If the latter, Augusta
wouldn't blame them. As much as she loved teaching the youngest children residing in or near Alexandertol, the last day of
school was always a difficult one, with children too eager about
beginning the planting season to pay attention.

Weariness from the long day—and her typical end-of-the-
session doldrums—tugged at her. Maybe she should have stayed
home, after all. But she needed something on which to spend
her hours until school began again in late fall. A women's benevolent society, briefly mentioned by Reverend Hartmann at
the close of last Sunday's morning worship service, seemed a
worthwhile pastime. She wanted to know more about it.

On the dais at the front of the church, Martina Krahn noisily
tamped a stack of pages on the pulpit. The woman was older
than Augusta by only five years but already mostly gray haired
with deeply imbedded frown lines forming a V between her eyes
and framing her thin lips. She clearly wanted everyone quiet so
she could begin. Augusta should take a seat.

She rose on tiptoe and searched for an open spot. Of course, all the back benches were full. Walking to the front would garner the notice of every woman in the room, and especially Martina's. Something Augusta preferred to avoid. Martina had a way of withering others with her stern glare. Augusta—nearly forty years of age, a seasoned schoolteacher and mother to an eleven-year-old daughter—shouldn't be intimidated by the other woman. But she was. Based on how a hush had fallen following the sharp *clack-clack-clack* of paper against wood, she suspected she wasn't the only one cowed by Frau Krahn's authoritarian demeanor.

Augusta hurried up the center aisle to the second bench from the front and seated herself. Martina's frowning gaze flicked in her direction, and it seemed as if the V in her brow pinched even tighter. Then her dark eyes swept across the entire group. A tiny facsimile of a smile relaxed her ordinarily tense features.

She swept her arms open in a graceful gesture. "Welcome, ladies, to the first meeting of the Alexandertol *Frauenverein*."

Augusta drew back slightly. Had she misunderstood the preacher's announcement? Or had she missed a previous gathering when the decision to form a group had been made? She hadn't realized this was an official meeting. A murmur rolled through the room, and Augusta looked over her shoulder at the others. Several women stared at Martina, their confusion evident.

Elsie Weber shot to her feet. "Frau Krahn, I came to learn more about what this ladies' club is about. If this meeting is for members, I should leave. I always consult my husband before making commitments to clubs and such."

A few other women nodded their agreement, and all across the benches, pairs put their heads close together and whispered to each other. Augusta had no husband to consult. Her dear Leopold lay at rest in the Alexandertol cemetery, gone for over five years now. But she preferred to pray about the things to which she committed time and energy, to be certain they were God's will for her. She hadn't addressed her heavenly Father even once yet about joining a Frauenverein.

Martina waved her hands at the group, frowning again. "Ladies, ladies, you remind me of a coop of clucking, nervous hens. Of course we aren't an official club . . . yet. But is this not our first meeting to discuss the possibility?"

Augusta contemplated Martina's opening statement welcoming them all, and she swallowed a chortle. In Martina's mind, this club was already established. Most likely with her serving as leader. Martina headed up every quilting bee, every church picnic, and every wedding party. She'd even tried to organize the school Christmas pageant last year, but Herr Elias, the teacher for the older children, tartly informed her that he and Augusta were capable of the task and sent her scuttling. Martina hadn't attended the program.

Although Herr Elias had gloated about putting the strong-minded woman in her place, Augusta took no pleasure in squashing Martina's quest for leadership. She and her husband were the only childless couple in town, which probably left Martina with extra time on her hands. But Herr Elias had been right that he and Augusta were better suited for organizing the school pageant.

As for this organization, wouldn't the minister's wife, gentle Berta Hartmann, make a more personable leader for a benevolent club? Augusta didn't have nerve enough to voice the question aloud, but a couple others attending the meeting might. If they challenged Martina, there very well could be a fight for control of the coop. Augusta hoped she wouldn't see feathers fly in the sanctuary of the church this evening.

"Please have a seat, Frau Weber, so we may continue," Martina said, her voice sweet but her gaze narrow.

Elsie plopped back onto the bench and folded her arms.

Martina cleared her throat, and the whispers ceased. "Perhaps I should begin tonight's meeting by sharing where I found the idea of starting our own Frauenverein." She lifted a strip of newsprint from the pulpit and held it out with much pomp. "I cut this article from a recent issue of *Der Grütlianer,* which is published in New York City, New York, and mailed to Gerhard each month from his cousin. The article tells about the impact the local Frauenverein has had in comforting those who became widowed or orphaned during the voyage from Germany to America, helping them feel at home in their new land, and meeting their needs for shelter, food, and friendship."

Martina's eyes shone as she spoke, and some of Augusta's weariness lifted in light of the woman's sincere passion.

"The first Frauenverein, established over forty years ago, limited itself to reaching out to members of its own congregation. But, eventually, it expanded as needs arose and extended its benevolence to the sick, infirm, or otherwise suffering or needy. I believe we should start the same way, reaching out to the widows"—her gaze briefly slid to Augusta—"and orphans in our own community. Later, if we become aware of people outside of Alexandertol who need a helping hand, we could extend it."

Lucinda Klein, one of the older members of the church, rose from her seat. "Frau Krahn, exactly what kind of 'helping hand' will we extend?"

"Food supplies, clothing, or medical care." Martina answered so promptly it seemed she had a script ready for recitation. "Perhaps housecleaning, gardening, or tending to children."

Tending to children? Augusta's heart skipped a beat. She knew a family who had need for this type of benevolence.

"Are these not the types of acts family members perform for one another?" Lucinda dabbed her face with a wrinkled handkerchief. "Is there truly a need for such a club in our community?"

Elsie Weber stood again. She nodded so enthusiastically the frilly brim of her bonnet bounced like butterfly wings. "Oh, yes, there is need. While I don't know of any orphans living in Alexandertol, we do have several older widows who often need firewood cut or lack the provisions to carry them through the winter months. My Franz has taken unsold bolts of cloth or wilted vegetables from our store shelves to these women on many occasions. He's also sent our oldest boys to do chores for them."

Lucinda's forehead furrowed. "If someone's already seeing to these needs, why start a club? I hope no one asks me to chop firewood. And I don't want to sound petty or selfish, but I need the vegetables from my garden to feed my husband and me. At my age, it's all I can do to grow enough for the two of us."

Now Berta Hartmann stood, leaned forward, and tapped Lucinda's shoulder. "Frau Klein, maybe we could put you and your husband on the list to receive benevolence, since your boys both moved to the city and you don't have someone else to look in on you."

Lucinda's mouth fell open. "Heinrich and I have no need for charity."

Agnes Bauer, who'd been sitting on the very back bench, strode up the aisle to Lucinda and put her fists on her hips. "Frau Klein, there is no shame in accepting help." Then she turned to Martina and held her hands out in a gesture of defeat. "But her attitude is common. Most people are prideful. They don't want to admit that they need help. Even if we start this club, will we have an opportunity to serve anyone? I, for one, don't have time to waste searching for people who need help if those people won't accept it when we offer it."

More mutters broke out.

Augusta watched Martina look from one speaker to another. The woman's normally stern expression changed from consternation to confusion and then dismay. Augusta felt as if she was witnessing the fading of a treasured dream. Although she couldn't admit to a great deal of fondness for Martina Krahn, her heart rolled over in compassion. She understood the pain of crushed dreams.

On impulse, she stood and blurted, "Frau Krahn?"

Every woman hushed and shifted her attention to Augusta.

Having a roomful of children intently gaze at her was very different from capturing the focus of a group of adults. Augusta's face heated, but she drew on her classroom demeanor and squared her shoulders. With her gaze fixed on Martina's startled face, she said, "I know who could be the first recipient of benevolence from the Alexandertol Frauenverein."

Martina's eyes sparked with interest. "Oh? Who?"

Augusta raised her chin, triumphant. "Herr Rempel and his sons, Folker and Walden."

Martina Krahn

Herr Rempel? Martina pressed her palm to her suddenly jumping stomach. Of course Augusta meant well. Of course she couldn't know about— But Martina couldn't possibly— She shook her head slightly, attempting to shoo the rattled thoughts from her brain. Then she gathered her dignity and forced a stiff smile in the schoolteacher's direction.

"I think you misunderstand the purpose of the Frauenverein, Frau Dyck." My, how calm and sensible she sounded when her nerves jangled like the bells on a fire wagon. "What does it say in James 1:27? 'Pure religion and undefiled before God and the Father is this, To visit the fatherless and widows in their affliction.' The Frauenverein will seek to honor this biblical instruction. We will minister to the widows and orphans in our community."

Surely, somewhere—if not in Alexandertol, then in a town nearby—there was an orphaned boy who needed her as much as she and Gerhard needed him. Would this club finally lead her to the son for whom she and her husband longed?

Augusta was still standing, her fine brows pinching together in either puzzlement or obstinance. Martina didn't know the woman well enough to be certain which. Either way, she needed to squelch this idea of ministering to the widower Rempel. She shifted her attention to the group at large.

"Now that you know what the Frauenverein is about, who is interested in becoming a member of such a club?"

It seemed every woman in the room turned into a statue. They sat, hands clasped in their laps, staring straight ahead at Martina with uncertainty etched into their faces.

Unexpectedly, anger swelled in Martina's chest. What was wrong with them that they had no desire to help their fellow citizens? Guilt swallowed the burst of anger. Who was she to judge them when her motivation was far more selfish than selfless? Still, she couldn't run this club all by herself. She needed members for it to be a real Frauenverein and not just a desperate woman's attempt to satisfy her husband's need for a son to raise.

She formed a sentence of encouragement in her mind, then opened her mouth to deliver it. Augusta Dyck raised her hand. Hope ignited within Martina's soul. "You wish to be part of the club?"

"I do."

Martina clapped her palms together. "Wonderful!"

"And I also wish to discuss Herr Rempel's need for benevolence."

Mercy, wasn't this woman determined? Martina assumed her sternest frown. "Frau Dyck, it is kind of you to think of Herr Rempel, but we must remember that this club will minister to *widows* and *orphans*. Why, you should be on the list of possible recipients given that you are a widow and your daughter's a half-orphan." She shook her head. "No, I'm sorry, but ministering to men could lead to impropriety."

Someone in one of the back pews—probably Agnes Bauer, the town's most prolific gossip—tittered, the soft sound seeming to shout speculation.

Augusta's face flamed pink.

Martina hurriedly added, "We must limit our assistance to those mentioned in the verse in James." Then she scanned the faces again. "Who else would like to join?"

Martha Gotwals stood. "I'm interested, but I need to speak to my husband first. How often will we meet, and how much time will it take to be part of the club? He'll want to know these things."

Martina had already thought these details through and answered without hesitation. "We will meet on Friday evenings here in the church, as we've done tonight. When we meet, we will discuss possible recipients. If there is only one need, one person can volunteer to meet it. If there are several, we can divide them amongst members or, if necessary, recruit helpers outside of the club. But I don't believe membership will require more than an hour a week for meetings and perhaps another hour or two for service."

"Thank you." Martha sat.

Martina steepled her hands and pressed her fingertips to the underside of her chin. "All right, ladies, a show of hands, please. Who would like to be part of the Alexandertol Frauenverein?"

Hands went up from various locations on the benches. A smile burst in Martina's heart and found its way to her face. She felt it rounding her cheeks—a wondrous feeling. She bounced her smile over each of the women holding a hand in the air, silently counting, and she reached the twelfth hand. Which belonged to Augusta Dyck.

Martina's smile briefly faltered. "Thank you, ladies. Will those who raised their hands please gather on the front benches? We must assign the positions of president, vice president, secretary, and treasurer. Everyone else, you are dismissed, but please know you are welcome to join the club at a later time if you change your mind."

Martina inwardly rejoiced. She had a club. Now to secure the position of president. If her plan went well, by this time next year her husband would have his son. And she might regain her husband.

Chapter Two

Konrad Rempel

"Boys, it's time to settle down and go to sleep." Konrad had already given the directive twice since he'd tucked the twins into their bed an hour ago. Folker and Walden were always full of snips, snails, and wagging puppy dog tails, as their mother had often laughingly said, but tonight—the last day of school for the season—their tails were wagging too hard.

The pair of tousled dark-brown heads popped up. Innocent faces turned in his direction.

"We're settled down, Pa," Folker said.

"We're almost asleep, Pa," Walden said at the same time.

Their eyes shifted, peeking at each other, and matching grins twitched on their lips.

Konrad held his firm expression although he battled the urge to chuckle. His boys were such comics, always making their father laugh. They'd saved him from sinking into a sea of melancholy when their mother died in childbirth three years ago. What would he have done if he hadn't had his little boys to look after? Yes, they gave him a reason to live. But now he needed to rest, and their antics prevented it.

He pointed at them. "This is my last time to come in here with only words. If you don't go to sleep and I have to come again . . ." He let the sentence dangle. They were smart enough to understand the unspoken meaning.

They flopped onto their pillows and chorused, "*Ja,* we will sleep."

Konrad stood in the doorway, observing them shift onto their sides, back-to-back. He couldn't see Walden's face since he'd rolled toward the wall, but Folker's eyes slid closed. The boys did nearly everything alike, so Konrad trusted that Walden's eyes had also closed. He waited another few minutes, squinting across the shadowy room. Neither boy wriggled, snickered, or sneaked a look toward the doorway.

Satisfied they'd finally succumbed to slumber, Konrad clicked the door closed and returned to the sitting area of his little house. The cup of coffee he'd poured before trudging to their room yet again had grown cold, but he drank it anyway. He'd become accustomed to cold coffee. To cold suppers. To cold nights alone in his bed. And he didn't really mind. Cold was better than the searing heat from his forge.

Without thought, his hand rose and rubbed the rippled skin below his jaw. His beard grew thick on the left side of his face, sparse on the right, but he'd never shave it off. Even though his *Vater* always warned that facial hair was a hazard near a forge. He'd said, *"What if your beard catches fire? Then what?"* Konrad never defied his father, except in this. The beard and the hair on his head, which he grew longer than most men, helped hide the scars. But of course, no beard or head of shaggy hair could mask the scars he carried on his soul from the teasing and name-calling he'd endured during his growing up because of the marks on his face.

Folker and Walden were often ornery. Or high-spirited, their mother had said. But he'd taught them never to ridicule another, especially for things over which the person had no control. His heart swelled with pride again, recalling the notes the boys' teacher, Frau Dyck, had put on their end-of-the-year report. Certain words—*helpful, kind to everyone, cooperative*—paraded through his mind. If Frau Dyck wrote them down, then they were true. She and his Hannah had been good friends until

Hannah's death, and he knew her to be an honest woman. So, yes, they were good boys. Good-hearted boys. But oh . . . such busy boys.

Now they were out of school until September, when harvest would be complete. More than five months stretched in front of him with the twins at home all day, every day. Shouldn't it be easier, the bigger they got? That's what fathers at church said. The older the children were, the more responsibilities they could carry. Put them to work, the fathers told him. Putting them to work would keep them out of trouble, they said with confident nods. But those fathers were farmers and storekeepers. They could put their boys to work without endangering them.

The blacksmith shop was no place for active boys. Hadn't this been proven by the accident he had when he was only a year older than the twins were now? He would never forgive himself if one of his little boys hurt himself on an anvil, burned himself on red-hot iron, or—worst of all—fell into the forge and bore scars for the rest of his life.

Konrad drained the last of the coffee from his tin cup, then carried the cup to the dry sink. He dropped the cup on top of the other dishes left over from supper. He'd wash them tomorrow, after breakfast. Or maybe he'd have the boys wash them. They were eight years old. Plenty old enough to wash dishes for their pa. That would keep them busy for a half hour. Maybe a little longer.

But then what would he do with them?

Martina

Martina hummed all the way home. She couldn't recall the last time she'd felt this light in spirit, this filled with hope. She was now the president of the Alexandertol Frauenverein. Even the women choosing Frau Augusta Dyck as the secretary and treasurer—*"Who would be better at recording our meeting notes and keeping accurate count of any funds we gather than a schoolteacher?"* the elected vice president, Frau Berta Hartmann, had insisted—couldn't dampen Martina's happiness. This club . . . it would be her salvation. She sensed it in her bones.

The tall oil lamp on the table in front of the window was burning, guiding her up the hard dirt walkway the way a lighthouse guided ships. She hurried the last several yards, clattered up the porch steps, and flung the screen door wide. It slapped against her backside as she twisted the porcelain doorknob on the front door and pushed. The door wouldn't open.

Locked.

A chill wended its way down Martina's spine. In Alexandertol, no one locked their doors. Why bother? Everyone knew everyone else, and they all trusted one another. There was no need for locked doors.

Unless someone had something to hide.

She tapped the door, leaning close to the oval window and straining to see past the lace curtain on the other side. "Gerhard?" She whispered her husband's name, silently berating herself for being so ridiculous. Would he hear her call for him if she didn't shout? But shouting would also notify the neighbors that she couldn't get into her own house. Herr Bauer from the east or Herr Zimmerman from the west might come to her aid. And then they might find out what Gerhard meant to keep hidden.

One person from town besides her already knew. Konrad Rempel. She couldn't risk anyone else finding out. So, no, she wouldn't shout. But what should she do? She couldn't spend the night on the porch.

After glancing up and down the street, she tiptoed to the

front window, where the lamp glowed bold and bright. She cupped her hands and squinted past the glare of light. Gerhard was in his favorite wingback chair, slumped as crookedly as a rag doll tossed on a shelf. She couldn't hear anything beyond the glass, but she knew from experience he was snoring as loudly as a rumbling train engine.

All the joy of the evening washed away on a mighty wave of disappointment. One evening. Not even two hours. She'd left him for such a short time and he'd chosen to spend his alone hours doing *that*? Her husband, a leader in his church and a respected businessman, couldn't be trusted on his own.

But it isn't really his fault, is it?

She flinched as if someone had slapped her across the face. Oh, how she hated the voice that whispered accusation to her in these moments. She already knew the truth of why Gerhard did what he did. She was to blame. Did she need the reminder? Of course she didn't. She wanted that voice to hush and never speak to her again.

She stomped off the porch, deliberately smacking her feet down so hard the impact stung her soles. She groped her way around the side of the house. It was dark behind these windows, and the moonlight didn't reach into the narrow gap between houses. But the soft glow from lamps behind the neighbors' windows offered a tiny bit of illumination. Branches from the newly budding spirea bushes growing along the foundation scratched her hands and snagged her dress sleeves as she went, but she couldn't worry about it. She needed to get inside before someone noticed her wandering around in her own yard in the dark. She silently begged God to let the darkness hide her from the neighbors' sight.

And with every step, she prayed that Gerhard had forgotten to lock the back door. If it was unlocked, then it meant he hadn't planned to use his evening doing *that* but had only gotten caught up in it as an afterthought. Although it still pierced her to know what he'd done, she could bear it more easily if he hadn't plotted to do it.

Their back door had no porch, only a square stoop in front of it. The older she got, the more she wished for a porch with a railing she could use to help her climb up. Tonight, propelled by humiliation and guilt, she mounted the crooked limestone steps as nimbly as a mountain goat and nearly leaped onto the stoop. She grabbed the doorknob, sucked in a breath, and twisted. The door eased open on squeaky hinges.

Relief sagged her spine. She staggered into the little enclosed porch, shut the door behind her, then leaned against it with her eyes closed and heart pounding. She'd made it inside without a neighbor seeing her and asking if all was well. Her prayer had been answered.

But what a selfish prayer, one to let you hide your shame.

Her eyes popped open and she pressed her palm to her aching chest. God answered this prayer, but how many selfish prayers would He grant before He grew impatient with her and stopped listening to her altogether?

She couldn't contemplate the answer to that question now. She had to get Gerhard to bed. He might slide out of his chair onto the floor and hurt himself. Again. How many times would the doctor believe that Gerhard had tripped over his shoes or slipped on stairs? The bed was a safer place for him to sleep off the effects of what he'd done tonight. She started through the kitchen, and as she passed the window she glanced out. There, on the other side of the narrow yard between her house and the Bauers' house, Frau Agnes Bauer stood framed behind her kitchen window. She sipped from a glass, but her spectacle-rimmed eyes seemed to peer straight at Martina.

Martina came to a stop and stared back. Could Agnes truly see her, or was she only looking out at the night? Then Agnes's thin lips formed a smile. She lifted the glass slightly, as if offering a wave of greeting—or was it a mocking toast?—and took another sip.

Martina forced her hand to rise and gave a brief wave of acknowledgment. Then she scurried on. God might have affirmatively answered her prayer about the back door being unlocked, but He might have chosen a no regarding her being seen by neighbors. If Agnes had witnessed her sneaky passage past the spirea bushes, she would be full of questions. She wouldn't ask them of Martina, though. She'd voice them to other women in town, couched in concern. But Martina knew better.

By morning, she must come up with a logical reason for her front door to be locked. She'd need to share it with Agnes in a way that didn't sound like an excuse or an outright fib. She stifled a groan. Keeping secrets was so much harder than she'd ever imagined. But if all went well with her plans for the Frauenverein, she would be able to redeem herself and rescue Gerhard from his melancholy. Then there'd be no reason for him to do *that* anymore, and all would be well.

Chapter Three

Augusta

Augusta could have slept late the morning after the meeting about the Frauenverein. After all, today was Saturday—not a school day. And even if it wasn't Saturday, school was now finished for the season. There was no pressing reason for her to rise before dawn. But she awakened at her usual time of half past five and couldn't fall back asleep, so she got up.

She lit the hand-painted oil lamp on the stand next to her bed, then opened the handcrafted *Schrank* in the corner of her bedroom. As she selected a floral cotton frock from those hanging on hooks in the wardrobe, she couldn't help thinking how differently she dressed now than when she was growing up in the Russian village of Alexanderwohl. And the loose-fitting plain-colored dresses she'd worn in Russia were different from the clothes worn by her great-grandmother, who'd grown up in Germany.

As she fastened the buttons of the trim-fitting bodice, she pondered why her ancestors, after leaving Germany more than a century ago by invitation of Russian leader Catherine the Great, had held on to many of their German customs, farming techniques, and language yet adopted the Russian style of dress and house construction. Now she lived in America, the land where freedoms were built into the country's government so they could never be taken away, as they'd eventually been trampled in Russia, prompting so many from her family's village to leave. The solid-color babushkas and belted sarafans had all been replaced with wide-brimmed bonnets and full-skirted dresses, both in lovely patterns.

Her Schrank held an amazing assortment. Six work dresses, five school dresses, and three church dresses should have made for a tight fit, but the wardrobe was a full six feet wide and more than two feet deep—a massive piece of furniture. She closed the door and couldn't resist trailing her fingers over the grain design on its center raised panel. The detailed lines were so realistic, if Leopold hadn't told her they had been painted on with feathers, she would have thought they were the wood's natural grain.

For a moment she stood and gazed at the solid poplar Schrank. Leopold had never hesitated to spoil her with fine furniture, dresses, jewelry, or whatever else captured his fancy. She was the only woman in Alexandertol with a Florence sewing machine. And indoor plumbing! Leopold had put in an underground line that pumped water directly into her kitchen wash basin—a convenience nearly as rare as the treadle sewing machine. She owned a total of six ornately jeweled music boxes and at least two hundred leather-bound books. So many books that Leopold had added a designated library to the front of their house. Each time he brought her a new volume, he'd say, *"Für meine liebling Gelehrte,"* with a smile that spoke of pride and affection. How proud she'd been to be called his dear scholar. Especially since her father believed book learning was a waste of time for a girl.

The very last book Leopold had bought her, before the hunting accident stole his life, was a collection of writings by Robert Browning. When he gave it to her, he pointed out the opening line in one of the poems, titled "Rabbi Ben Ezra," smiled tenderly at her, and said, "See here? 'Grow old along with me! The best is yet to be . . .' This is my dream for us, Gussie." Ah, what a precious memory. She cherished the book and, even more so, the sentiment. Her dream, too, had been to grow old with Leopold.

No, Leopold had never withheld gifts or tender words of affirmation from her. Thanks to his lucrative fur-trapping business in Russia and his success as a buffalo hunter when they arrived in Kansas, they'd been able to build this beautiful two-story house and fill it to the brim with the finest furnishings. She was blessed beyond measure with material things many others lacked and some envied. But she would give away every bit of it if doing so would bring her Leopold back to her.

With a sigh, she turned from the Schrank. With a puff of breath, she extinguished her lamp. Carrying her shoes, she tiptoed down the staircase that separated hers and her daughter's bedrooms, unwilling to awaken Juliana so early on her first day of school vacation. In the kitchen, Augusta sat and donned her shoes, then slipped out the back door.

Melodious birdsong serenaded her as she crossed the grassy yard beneath a dove-gray sky to the outhouse tucked between a pair of apple trees. She never approached the little building without marveling at its resemblance to a child's playhouse. There, too, Leopold had lavished attention, adding fish-scale siding beneath the roof peak and painting the structure to match their house—pale yellow with trim colors of purest white and robin's egg blue. He'd even painted its inside walls, something for which he'd received much good-natured teasing from some of the men in the community. But he insisted the bright-white interior made him feel less closed in. Leopold had never cared for close spaces, a leftover effect from being accidentally locked in a cellar when he was a small boy. Empty lots stretched on either side of their home. Leopold needed "breathing room," as he'd put it.

As she left the outhouse, she considered, not for the first time, selling this property and moving into a smaller house on a single lot. The reminders of Leopold everywhere she looked were ofttimes painful. Would it be easier on her heart to start anew with Juliana in their own place? But as quickly as the idea flitted through her mind, she shooed it away. This tall, lovely house, constructed as a gift by her husband who'd doted on her, was home. Not as much as it had been when Leopold was living, but still . . . it was the only home Juliana knew. She wouldn't take those memories away from her precious daughter.

Augusta hurried the last few yards and returned to the kitchen. She began her usual morning routine of building a fire in the stove's box, heating water for coffee, and selecting items from the cupboards to prepare breakfast. As she measured flour into a mixing bowl for pancakes, one of Juliana's favorites, she heard the patter of feet on the stairs. Seconds later the back door slammed, and Augusta caught a glimpse through the window of Juliana, still attired in her ruffly nightgown, racing barefoot across the yard to the outhouse.

As the frying pan heated, she stirred vanilla-scented batter and cast occasional glances out the window. When Juliana emerged from the outhouse, Augusta crossed to the window and observed her daughter pause and send a lingering look skyward. Was she filling her lungs with morning air, as her father had done each day, or trying to identify the feathered singers? After nearly a full minute of intense observation, she gave a little hop that set her feet into motion, and she half skipped, half danced her way to the house.

Augusta returned to the stove, a fond smile tugging at the corners of her lips. From where had Juliana inherited her agility? The child never merely walked. In fact, at times she almost seemed to float, so nimbly and effortlessly she traversed from one point to another. If they lived in a big city, she might grow up to be a ballerina who performed on stages, enthralling audiences. But here in tiny, conservative Alexandertol, learning ballet was not a possibility.

Yet Augusta couldn't be sad about the lost opportunity. Perhaps Juliana wouldn't grow up to be a ballerina, but the solid biblical principles that guided the people of this community would give her daughter a strong base on which to build her life. To consistently grow in God's grace was the most important thing Juliana could learn.

Juliana entered the house, letting the screen door slam into its frame behind her as she always did, and came to the kitchen. She wrapped Augusta in a hug from behind, her cheek pressed between Augusta's shoulder blades and her arms tight around her rib cage.

Augusta gave her daughter's hands a little pat. "Good morning, *meine Waldnymphe.*" She deliberately used the nickname Leopold had chosen for their little girl when she was only a toddler. He'd said her lithe frame and delicate movements were more indicative of a wood nymph than a human child.

Juliana's musical laughter rang out. She released Augusta and moved aside. "Mother, may we go to the mercantile this morning after breakfast?"

"What do you need at Weber's?" Augusta poured pancake batter into the ready pan and spoke above the sizzle it made when it met the bubbling lard.

"Yesterday Herr Weber drove his wagon to the Marion railway depot to pick up a shipment for the store. He expected to receive a full crate of books." Her daughter's eyes, the same sky blue as her father's, sparkled. Juliana had her mother's red-gold hair, but Augusta was always glad God had seen fit to give her child Leopold's beautiful eyes instead of Augusta's hazel ones.

She raised her brows. "How do you know this?"

"Laura told me."

Of course. Augusta should have surmised as much, given how close Juliana and the Webers' middle daughter were. While opposite in appearance—Juliana's long-legged and slender frame compared to Laura's pudgy one—they shared a love for learning and both possessed tender, giving hearts. Augusta couldn't have chosen a better best friend for her daughter.

Juliana leaned in slightly, clasping her hands beneath her chin. "May we go check if they've been put on the shelves already? Laura said he ordered some of Stevenson's newer titles."

Augusta carefully flipped the pancake, then watched until the bubbles around the edges disappeared. She lifted the pancake from the pan and placed it on a plate. As she poured more batter, her daughter continued talking with her head tilted in a beguiling pose.

"My copy of *Treasure Island* has become tattered I've read it so many times. It looks absolutely sad in the bookcase. I wouldn't mind having a replacement. I've heard the latest version has full-color illustrations. And perhaps, if Stevenson's new short-story collection came in the crate, we could purchase a copy?" Her expression turned dreamy. "There's a perfectly placed limb in the larger apple tree for settling in to read."

Ah, so that's what her daughter had been considering before returning from the outhouse.

Juliana sighed. "I could spend hours there, with the right book to engage me."

Augusta turned the cake, giving herself a moment to form an answer. Always, her first impulse was to grant Juliana's requests, whether for new books, new frocks, or a sweet. Mostly because she knew that Leopold would have done so and Juliana had no siblings to entertain her. But was it wise to give a child everything she asked for? Juliana hadn't shown signs of becoming selfish or ungrateful, but Augusta didn't want to invite such behavior by overindulging her.

"I tell you what," she said as she added the pancake to the waiting plate, "fetch the syrup jug from the pantry and have your breakfast while these cakes are hot." She plucked a fork from the crock on the nearby breakfront cupboard and pressed it into Juliana's hand. "Then get dressed for the day and see to your chores. When we've finished our work for the morning, we will take a walk to town and see what books have been added to the mercantile's shelves."

A squeal of delight showed Juliana's approval. She rose on tiptoe and planted a kiss on her mother's cheek, then scurried off with the plate and fork. Augusta fried two more cakes and joined her daughter at the table. By then, Juliana was already finished eating.

Juliana pushed back her chair and rose. "Since we'll likely go to town, I believe I'll wear a school dress today but add a work apron to keep from soiling it." Her musing tone and crinkled brow, as if the day's ventures required great deliberation, tickled Augusta. "But when we're back from town, and especially if we purchase a new book . . . or two . . . I'll change into a work dress before climbing the tree. I won't want to tear one of my nicer dresses."

With effort, Augusta maintained a serious countenance. "A chore dress will be fine for whatever activities we pursue today, Juliana."

Juliana's fine brows dipped inward.

"Besides . . ." Augusta couldn't stop the grin from growing on her face. "Changing clothes will only take time that could be spent reading."

Her daughter's bright smile returned. "Such sound thinking, Mother. Perhaps that is why you are the teacher and I am but a student." Her dimples flashed, and she moved to the dry sink with a little bounce in her step. "I'll don a chore dress, and my first task of the day will be seeing to the breakfast dishes, so please leave yours in the wash basin when you've finished eating." She clattered her plate and fork into the tin washtub, offered a quick wave of her fingers, and darted around the corner.

Because they'd awakened so early, they finished their standard Saturday chores before noon. Augusta drew a shawl around her shoulders and retrieved her largest shopping basket. Juliana's face lit at the sight of the basket. Augusta quickly cautioned, "I don't intend to fill it with books, my wood nymph. I have need of other items, too." Perhaps fabric. Why hadn't she noticed until now how short Juliana's dresses had become? The girl must have grown two inches in the past year.

Juliana affected a teasing pout, then she shrugged and headed for the front door with her typical grace.

Augusta and Juliana followed the sidewalk to town. Augusta's nostrils filled with the scent of rich, moist earth. Last week's rains had turned the dormant grass bright green, and already tiny buds dotted the slender limbs on flowering shrubs. By the end of the month, the street would be alive with colorful blossoms. She was always grateful for the foresight of the earliest arrivals to plant trees and bushes that would provide bright splashes of color.

When she and Leopold, newly married, first arrived on the Kansas prairie in 1872 along with about twenty other immigrant families, she bemoaned the drab appearance, so different from their sweet village along the Molotschna River in Russia. The group of newcomers deliberately chose to plot their little town near a river, even though the size and scope of the Cottonwood River seemed a mere trickle when compared to the Molotschna. But over time, as the town grew, it became less and less lackluster until now she enjoyed every aspect of the community's appearance. The bank of the Cottonwood River was her favorite picnic spot. Perhaps she and Juliana would take their supper to the riverbank that evening as a reward for completing their chores so efficiently.

Other townsfolk were also visiting the businesses this noonday. Juliana smiled and waved at every passing wagon, called hello to those they met on the street, and paused for a brief chat with elderly Frau Warkentine, who rested on a bench in front of the little post office. It warmed Augusta's heart to see how openly everyone responded to her daughter. Augusta enjoyed teaching, sharing her knowledge with youngsters, but she always felt shy around grown-ups. Perhaps because her father had always been so stern with her? She sent up a prayer of gratitude that Juliana held no such inhibitions. Her daughter was at ease with all, old or young—a trait that would benefit her as she matured into womanhood.

They entered the mercantile, and Juliana darted to the back corner of the sizable store where three shelves attached to the wall with brackets held the entirety of the book selection. Trusting her daughter to be respectful of the merchandise, Augusta went to the bin of seed packets near the front door. Some of last year's flowers—black-eyed Susans, marigolds, bachelor's buttons, and daisies—would reseed themselves, but she hoped to grow some pansies. Pansies grew prolifically in front of Berta Hartmann's porch. She loved their cheerful faces.

While Augusta placed packets of pansy and various vegetable seeds in her basket, she made a mental note to talk to the Schmidt boys after worship service tomorrow about preparing the winter-hardened ground in her garden plot. She had hired them each year since Leopold's untimely death, and although they were still young, they did a fine job.

She added a second packet of pea seeds to her basket, then turned, planning to check on Juliana. But two of her students blocked her pathway. Delight filled her, and she returned the matching smiles on Folker and Walden Rempel's faces with one of her own. Her hand automatically reached out and smoothed a wayward strand of Folker's pecan-colored hair into place. "*Guten Tag*, boys. How are you this fine Saturday?"

"*Wir sind gut,*" they chorused.

Augusta always marveled at how often the twins seemed to function with one mind and voice. She gave a nod. "I am glad to hear you're both fine." They seemed happy, although their hair was uncombed and a greasy smear with a few crumbs caught in it—from breakfast?—decorated Walden's cheek. When Hannah was alive, the boys were rarely so disheveled. Augusta's heart panged in loneliness for her friend. If she missed Hannah, how much more did Konrad and these grinning waifs miss her? Herr Rempel did his best with the boys, but surely they would benefit from a woman's attention. She needed to convince Frau Krahn to spend some of the Frauenverein's benevolence on the motherless as well as the fatherless.

Augusta glanced around. "Is your father shopping?"

They shook their heads in unison. "He took some horseshoes to the hardware store to sell," Folker said.

Walden added, "We were waiting in the wagon, and when we saw you, we decided to come tell you hello."

Worry nibbled. "Did your father instruct you to wait in the wagon for his return?"

They exchanged a glance, sucking in their lips.

No words were needed. As she had suspected, the pair wasn't supposed to be in the mercantile. She turned Folker toward the door, signaling Walden with her firm frown to do the same. "Well, then, it's best that you climb back into the wagon right away. Your father will worry if he comes out and doesn't find you there."

The boys released heavy sighs, their shoulders slumping, but they scuffed in the direction of the door. Augusta followed them onto the boardwalk. Across the street, the Rempel wagon and team of horses stood in front of Duerksen Feed & Seed. She moved to the edge of the street and looked both ways. A wagon was coming from the north. The driver was twisted on the seat, his chin on his shoulder, seeming to examine something in the bed.

She turned to the twins. "Boys, please wait for—"

Just then Konrad Rempel came out of the Feed & Seed.

Folker grabbed Walden's elbow. "There's Pa!" Both boys dashed into the street.

Augusta dropped her basket and cried out, "Boys! Stop!"

Chapter Four

Konrad

Augusta Dyck's shrill cry, full of alarm, stopped Konrad in his tracks. He turned toward the sound, and his heart seemed to leap in his chest. There were his sons, standing as still as a pair of tree stumps in the middle of the street. Two mighty horses pulling a wagon bore down on them.

Konrad raced into the street, scooped each boy around the middle, and by whirling in a half circle, flung them toward the boardwalk. Then he dove after them the way he'd dive into the river. His hands hit the ground and flipped him into a neat somersault.

The farmer driving the wagon yanked back on the reins and hollered, "Whoa!" The horses came to a halt, snorting and stomping their front hooves against the ground. As Konrad pushed to his feet, the man stood and glared down at him. "Herr Rempel, what did you think you were doing? I could have killed all of you."

Konrad trotted to his twins, who lay in a heap at the edge of the boardwalk, and crouched next to them. Their chins quivered, but neither wailed. He ran his hands over their heads and frames, wincing with each contact against his scraped palms. Neither boy seemed hurt, thank the good Lord. Only scared. As they well should be.

He rose, took each boy by the hand, and crossed to the side of the wagon. "I am sorry, Herr Hiebert, that we frightened you and your team."

"Herr Rempel!" Frau Dyck scurried around the back of the wagon and to Konrad's side. "Are you—are they—" Her hazel eyes, wide with worry, fixed on the boys. The pair pulled loose of Konrad's hold and buried their faces against her waist. She stroked their hair and aimed her attention at Konrad. "When I told them to stop, I meant for them to come back to me. They—they obeyed so promptly. I didn't mean for them to stay in the middle of the street. I'm so very sorry."

She had no reason to apologize. If the boys had obeyed his directions and stayed in the wagon, then— He shook his head. No, he couldn't blame the twins. He shouldn't have left them for so long. He knew how active and curious they were. If he'd taken them inside with him, then no one—not Herr Hiebert, Frau Dyck, the boys, or him—would have received such a fright.

Konrad took hold of the boys by their shoulders and pulled them to himself.

Herr Hiebert's gaze shifted from twin to twin, and his fierce scowl softened. He dropped onto the wagon seat. "*Nein,* I am the one who is sorry. I should have been looking forward instead of into the back. My shepherd dog is in the bed with her litter of puppies, and their whining distracted me."

Suddenly Konrad recognized the odd sound he was hearing. "They must be very young yet."

"Less than two weeks old. I am taking the dogs to my son's place. His wife will see to them until they're big enough to fend for themselves. It's planting season and the sun shines. I don't have time to nursemaid a mama dog and her pups."

The boys turned eager faces to their father. Walden tugged Konrad's sleeve. "May we see the puppies, Pa?"

"Please, Pa?" Folker begged with his eyes wide.

After just scaring him half out of his wits, they were very brazen to make such a request. "*Nein,* you may not."

Both boys hung their heads.

Herr Hiebert gruffly cleared his throat. "Ja, well, I am grateful I looked in time to see you. Are you and your sons all right?"

"I think we are." Konrad might discover bruises tomorrow, but he was certain they'd all escaped with no broken bones or serious injury.

Herr Hiebert took up the reins. "Then I will leave you."

Konrad moved to the side of his wagon, drawing the twins with him. Frau Dyck kept pace with him. He waved the farmer on, then turned to the schoolteacher. "Don't blame yourself. I did not mean for them to be so long untended. My business inside took more time than I expected." He'd never had to quibble with Duerksen over the price of his horseshoes before. Why had the Feed & Seed owner decided fifteen cents a set was too much? "If I'd known, I would not have left them in the wagon." But then, would he have wanted them listening in on the disagreement? Nein, he would not.

Tenderness replaced the worry in her eyes, and she aimed the caring look at the boys. "Well, no harm's been done. That's the most important thing." She quirked her left brow. "And perhaps Folker and Walden have learned it's wise to do as their father says and stay put, ja?"

Both boys nodded, their heads bobbing in beat with each other. "Ja, Frau Dyck," they said together, then Folker said, "The next time we see you, we will only wave." Walden nodded at his brother and added, "We won't come to say hello." They chorused, "Unless Pa says we can."

The woman's lips twitched as if a bumblebee fought for escape behind them. She quickly lifted her gaze to Konrad. The humor dancing in her eyes almost enticed him to smile. She glanced toward Weber's General Merchandise. "Speaking of leaving children untended, I left Juliana in the mercantile by herself. By now she's probably selected an entire shelf of new books. I should retrieve my basket and check on her."

Konrad glanced toward the mercantile and spotted a basket lying on its side on the boardwalk. Small squares of paper—seed packets, he realized—lay scattered all around it. "Wait one moment, please, Frau Dyck." He lifted the boys into the wagon bed one at a time. He pointed his finger at them. "You stay in there. I'm going to walk Frau Dyck across the street, and"—

"Oh!" A soft gasp escaped. "That isn't necessary, Herr Rempel."

—"then we'll go home." He pretended he hadn't heard her protest and offered her his elbow. "Come, Frau Dyck."

She hesitated, worrying her lower lip between her teeth. Maybe he should have considered how it would look for him to escort her across the street. When Hannah was still living, the women's friendship would have made such a gesture seem commonplace. Now? It could be misconstrued. But it was the gentlemanly thing to do. And it wasn't as if they had no interactions at all. She'd been the boys' teacher for the past three years. He'd sat in front of her desk twice each year for reports on the twins' progress, and of course they attended the same church. If people read something verboten into him escorting her across the street, then it was their problem, not his.

A little sigh left her throat. She gave a slight nod, as if agreeing with herself that it was all right to accept his offer, then she gingerly placed her hand in the curve of his elbow. He looked right, left, right again. Certain no peril awaited them, he ushered her forward. The moment they stepped onto the boardwalk, she released his arm and moved aside.

He crouched, gathered up the seed packets, and placed them into the basket. Then he stood and held the basket out to her. "Thank you for your kindness to my boys." He grimaced. "I dare not think what might have happened to them today."

She curled her slender fingers around the basket's woven handle and rested the basket against her skirt. "I praise the Lord neither they nor you were injured." She tipped her head slightly, peering intently into his eyes. "Are your hands all right? It seemed you landed pretty hard on them."

His face heated, and he imagined his scars glowing bold red behind his whiskers. He looked aside and shoved his hands into his trouser pockets. "Just roughed up the skin a bit. They'll be fine." He backed up one step. "I need to take the boys home. Have a good day now, Frau Dyck."

"Herr Rempel!"

He turned his head, startled by the insistence in her tone. "Ja?"

"What happened today with Folker and Walden . . . Something similar could happen again unless they have supervision."

The heat flowed from his face downward until every bit of him sizzled underneath his skin. Embarrassment and, yes, even indignation rolled within him. Did she think him completely inept as a parent? Within his pockets, he balled his hands into fists. "Frau Dyck, I appreciate your concern for my boys. You are a good teacher to them and they like you very much." As had his wife. "But I will thank you to keep your opinions about how I see to them to yourself."

Her mouth fell open and her eyes widened.

He turned away from her astounded expression and strode across the street.

Augusta

He had spoken firmly yet kindly to her. Even so, Herr Rempel's stiff shoulders and the stern set of his boot soles against the ground screamed displeasure. Augusta gazed after him in both dismay and remorse. Her intention had been honorable. Her concern for the twins' safety prompted her comment. But clearly she'd chosen the wrong words.

She stayed on the boardwalk until Herr Rempel's wagon, with the pair of dark-haired boys sitting like bookends on either side of their father on the wagon seat, rolled out of town. Then she entered the mercantile and went to the book corner. Juliana was sitting cross-legged on the floor with an open book snug in the nest her skirt formed.

She looked up when Augusta stopped in front of her. "Oh, Mother, this book is wonderful!" Eyes alight, she held up the maroon leather-covered volume.

Augusta bent down slightly and admired the gold-filigreed stamp with the title centered on the cover. "*A Child's Garden of Verses?*" She sent Juliana a curious frown. "Is that not too young for you?" Juliana was, after all, growing very rapidly into a young lady, only five years younger now than Augusta had been when she exchanged marriage vows with then-thirty-year-old Leopold and crossed the ocean to America.

Juliana shook her head, making her thick, red-gold braids bounce. "No, the verses are delightful." She hugged the book to her chest. "May I have it, Mother, please?" She then glanced at a stack of three books resting on the floor beside her. "I'll put one of these back, if you prefer."

Augusta straightened, smiling. If only all her students were as interested in reading as her daughter was. "If you don't ask for another new book for the entirety of the school break, you may have all four books."

Juliana's happy squeal echoed from the mercantile's high tin ceiling. Still holding the volume, she bounced to her feet and embraced her mother. The spine poked Augusta's flesh, but she didn't mind. She placed a quick kiss on top of her daughter's head and gently shifted her aside. "But pick them up from the floor, please, and let's pay for these items. The apple tree beckons, does it not?"

Juliana's bright smile offered enough of an answer. She gathered the books and followed Augusta to the counter, where Frau Weber tallied their purchases on a little notepad, then showed the amount to Augusta. The woman never spoke amounts out loud, protecting her customers' privacy. Leopold had found it an odd practice, but Augusta appreciated it. It was no one else's business what she spent on books or anything else.

She put the books in the basket, with the exception of the poetry book, which Juliana cradled in her arms, then followed her daughter to the door. As they were leaving, Martina Krahn entered, also with a basket on her arm.

Still thinking of the scare she'd received when Folker and Walden dashed into the street a few minutes ago, Augusta reached out and stopped the woman. "Frau Krahn, may I speak with you for a moment?"

Juliana stopped but fidgeted in place, impatience pulsing from her lithe frame.

Augusta gave her daughter a smile. "Go on home. I know you're eager to explore your book."

Juliana's dimples flashed. "Thank you, Mother." She scurried out.

Augusta turned to Martina again. "Do you have time for a brief chat?"

The other woman's lips pursed, but she nodded.

Augusta escorted her to the corner, where she felt secure no other shoppers would overhear them. "Only a bit ago, right in front of the store, there was a near tragedy." She divulged the harrowing event involving the Rempel twins and their father. "I know you have qualms about the Frauenverein ministering to men. I don't wish to disregard your feelings, but I am gravely concerned about Folker and Walden. We intend to reach out to the orphaned, ja?"

Martina's head bobbed in a brusque nod.

"Well, are not these boys motherless?"

Another nod, even more brusque, acknowledged Augusta's query.

She laid her fingertips on Martina's arm. "This makes them half-orphans. The same as my Juliana. In good conscience, can we overlook their needs?" She waited, searching Martina's unsmiling face for signs of softening.

The grim lines framing Martina's mouth and marring her forehead remained in place. She moved aside a few inches, separating herself from Augusta's light touch. "Frau Dyck, I appreciate your taking so seriously the purpose of the Frauenverein. But—" Her spine went erect. Her eyebrows shot up. A tiny "Oh!" escaped her parted lips.

Augusta frowned. "Frau Krahn, are you all right?" It seemed as if a sudden pain had gripped her.

Martina closed her mouth and nodded, this one slow and thoughtful. "I am . . . thinking." She stared at Augusta for a few seconds, her graying brows pulled into a reflective V. "Frau Dyck, when we have our next meeting, will you share this story about the Rempel twins with the other women of our club? Perhaps we can find a means of keeping the boys safe during this long break from school."

"Of course I will." Augusta couldn't hold back a smile of delight. "*Danke,* Frau Krahn."

A faraway look entered the woman's eyes. "Nein, thank you, Frau Dyck. Seeing to the needs of the motherless is as important as seeing to the needs of the fatherless. I should have realized it myself." She gave a little jolt, and her typical unsmiling countenance fell over her face. "And now, I must see to my shopping. Guten Tag, Frau Dyck." She hurried off.

Augusta left the mercantile and walked home. As she went, an uncomfortable thought settled in the back of her mind. Had she spoken too soon? Herr Rempel hadn't seemed keen on hearing ideas about how to keep his boys safe. But Martina showing eagerness to reach out to the Rempel family after such opposition seemed God inspired. Surely it was meant to be. Or was it only wishful thinking on her part?

She cringed, pondering again Herr Rempel's reaction to her concern. Perhaps he'd felt at ease being so frank with her because they knew each other fairly well. To her knowledge, he had no friendly connection with Martina Krahn. Thus, he might take greater care in what he said to her. Oh, how she hoped so. Augusta wasn't prone to argue with people, but Frau Krahn was both brash and not one to be denied. If he responded similarly to her when she approached him about his boys, an unpleasant disagreement might ensue. Had she cracked open a door to trouble?

Chapter Five

Martina

M artina entered her house through the back door. The trapdoor for the cellar was open and leaning against the wall, as it had been when she'd left a little more than a half hour ago. Gerhard must still be down there.

She hurriedly deposited her purchases on the pantry shelves beside the cellar opening, then leaned over the hole and called, "Gerhard?" She received no response, but odd, metallic clanks sporadically sounded. She called again, louder this time. Only the strange *plink-plink* replied.

With a sigh, she pinched her skirts out of the way and crept down the dirt stairs. Ugh, how she disliked the cellar. Damp, dark, smelling of mildew, and lurking with spiders and crickets. But when storms came, she was grateful for its shelter. She also appreciated its coolness. Their milk and butter stayed fresh down there, and of course it was the perfect place for fermenting shredded cabbage into sauerkraut. She only wished Gerhard didn't use it for fermenting things other than cabbage.

She reached the bottom. A set of floor-to-ceiling unfinished pine shelves, laden with crocks, baskets of foodstuffs, and assorted items they didn't often use stretched nearly the full width of the dirt-walled space and divided the cellar in half. A lantern glowed from the other side of the shelves. "Gerhard, are you back there?"

"Ja, I am." His grunting answer stung her. She missed his

cheerful voice and the sweet tunes he used to whistle when they were both young.

She had no desire to go to the other side of the shelves, to the deeper, danker part of the cellar. Maybe she should wait until he came upstairs to talk to him about the idea she'd hatched while visiting with Augusta Dyck. But no, if she waited, she might lose her nerve. It was best to address him now.

She sucked in a breath of fortification, then inched her way past the shelves and to the section of cellar where Gerhard's workbench and personal paraphernalia were set up. He had his back to her, and the glow from the lantern on his workbench cast a halo around him. Like an angel. But she knew, far too well, Gerhard— as much as she loved him—was not angelic. Not anymore.

Fearful of what she might discover him doing, she moved up beside him. To her great relief, he was only matching nuts with bolts and dropping them into a bucket. She smiled and tipped her cheek against his shoulder, a tiny gesture of affection so far removed from how she'd greeted him in their early years of marriage. But then, they weren't the same people they'd been twenty-five years ago. Would they ever find themselves again?

Her gaze on his thick, strong fingers deftly moving, she sent up a quick prayer for favor and spoke softly, as she'd learned to do on days following one of his spells. "Gerhard, I wondered if I might ask you a question."

He shrugged and dropped a set in the bucket with a tinny *ping*. "I suppose."

"Have you ever considered apprenticing a youngster? Teaching him the wainwright trade?"

His fingers kept twisting a nut on a bolt, but his frowning gaze shifted and settled on her upturned face. "Hiring an apprentice? Nein. Why would I do such a thing?" He tossed the set into the bucket.

Martina chose a nut and bolt and methodically screwed them

together, needing something to do. "Well, you're very good at your craft. But"—she coughed lightly into her fist—"we aren't getting younger. The older we get, the more difficult physical labor becomes. Having help from a younger person would benefit you, and it could benefit the entire community. If you teach a boy how to build good, sturdy wagons, then the people who live around here will always have a fine wainwright to see to their needs, even when you're no longer able to do so."

His ability as a wagon builder was what had prompted him to uproot them from Russia and come to this country. The changes in leadership that brought changes to their village, the most disconcerting one being a requirement for young men to serve in the military, hadn't affected them personally given they had no sons who would be forced into duty. But Gerhard had insisted they pack their bags and go, too, to benefit the new community, which would need someone with his skills. She'd been proud of his desire to serve people and also hopeful a fresh start in a new land would bring change for them, too.

"Maybe I don't want someone else in my shop." He spoke so brusquely Martina winced. But not only because of his tone. Fear niggled. Sometimes he did things he shouldn't here at home. Was he also doing something out there in his shop that he didn't want someone else to see?

She swallowed the knot of sadness forming in her throat and forced a little laugh. "I know you like your quiet and privacy when you work. That is why I don't bother you when you're in your wainwright shop. But wouldn't it give you a sense of pride to pass on the knowledge you possess? It could be your . . . legacy to Alexandertol."

He dropped the bolt and nut he'd picked up and swished his palms together. Then he turned and leaned his hip against the workbench, staring hard into her face. "Have you already picked out an apprentice for me?"

"Of course not. You would need to make the selection your-self." But, oh, how she hoped when she suggested apprenticing one of the Rempel twins, he would be amenable. The boys were still young, barely old enough for apprenticeship, but that was why she wanted one of them. At such a tender age, it would be easy for the boy to form an attachment to Gerhard. And for Gerhard to grow affectionate, even fatherly, toward the boy.

Of course, it was still too soon to plan. Maybe even too soon to hope. But didn't it seem providential that a boy right here in Alexandertol might need Gerhard as much as Gerhard needed him? Of course, Konrad Rempel would have to agree, too. If he knew what she suspected he knew, he wouldn't approve sending one of his sons to Gerhard's shop.

But did he know? Or did she worry needlessly? Weeks ago, he had delivered a few flattened iron bands to their home after not finding Gerhard in his wainwright shop. Gerhard was home be-cause he was not fit to work. Martina had been certain Herr Rempel grasped the reason for Gerhard's flushed cheeks and slurred speech, but he'd never said anything to indicate he knew. If he had, Agnes Bauer would have made sure Martina heard about it. Agnes's silence on the subject encouraged Mar-tina. Maybe she should trust that he did not know. That he would agree to send one of his boys to spend the daytime hours with Gerhard. That he would discover how much easier it was to raise only one by himself. That, eventually, Gerhard and she would—

"Martina?"

She gave a start and peered into her husband's face. His thick, graying brows met in the middle, and his dark-blue eyes nar-rowed. She licked her lips. "Ja?"

"What is wrong with you? You are trembling from head to toe."

She was? She glanced down at herself and realized, yes, it was

true. Even her full skirts quivered. She hugged herself and released a nervous laugh. "It is cold down here." In the first years
of their marriage, if she said she was cold, he had warmed her
with an embrace.

"Then go upstairs." He turned his attention to the scattered
pieces of iron on the workbench. "We can discuss your idea
more later."

Hope ignited in her breast. She eased backward, still hugging
herself, smiling broadly. "Ja, Gerhard, we will talk about it again.
Later." She whirled and darted through the gap between the
shelves and the wall, not even caring that her skirts brushed the
damp wall and carried away a streak of dirt.

Upstairs, she collapsed into a kitchen chair and laughed for
the sheer joy of it. Soon, so very soon, her dearest wish could
come true. And they hadn't even held their second club meeting
yet! This idea must be blessed by God. Her deliverance was coming.

Konrad

In his forty-one years of living, Konrad could only recall a dozen
times he had not attended Sunday morning service. Over the
years, various illnesses and, once, a bad snowstorm had kept
him home. Then there was the weekend his dear Hannah died
while bearing their stillborn daughter, and the weekend after,
when deep grief from laying Hannah and Baby Girl—they hadn't
decided on a name and he couldn't bring himself to choose
without Hannah—to rest held him captive. He didn't like counting those Sundays, but they were part of his life's tapestry, too,
and they'd shown him how much his community cared about
him. How many visitors came after he missed those services?
Not only the preacher, but several concerned neighbors, too.

When he didn't appear at the church building this morning, would visitors come? The thought almost propelled him out the door. He shouldn't alarm his friends and preacher. But the soft snores coming from the twins' room—evidence that they were soundly sleeping—convinced him to stay home. That, and the remembrance of the schoolteacher's stinging comment.

"Something similar could happen again unless they have supervision."

How many times would her warning play through his mind before he forgot it? He hmphed. He was fooling himself. He would never forget her words. Because they were true.

He scuffed to the little table where his Bible lay open to the book of James, the book he tended to read when he was uncertain what to do. He wasn't a learned man. Only a simple man. But God's Word, his parents had taught him, provided whatever he needed, including wisdom.

Sinking into his chair, he scanned the text. Verse 3 from chapter 1 seemed to leap out at him. He underlined the text with his finger and read aloud, "'. . . *und wisset, daß euer Glaube, wenn er rechtschaffen ist, Geduld wirkt.*'" His scalp tingled in response to the statement that the trying of one's faith worked patience.

He believed the words. He'd seen evidence that testing resulted in stronger faith. These few years after losing Hannah, leaning completely on the Lord for companionship, had drawn him more deeply into fellowship with his Father. Not that he hadn't known God intimately before Hannah's death. He had walked with the Lord for more than half of his life now after asking the Lord Jesus Christ to forgive his sins and become his Savior when he was a teen.

He'd never forget the sense of freedom and relief that followed his decision, nor his parents' joy when he was baptized. He would also never forget the schoolteacher's kind yet somber expression and heavyhearted tone when warning about his boys' well-being. He wanted to believe that his sons would be fine. He wanted to fully trust that God watched over them and protected them from harm.

As always happened with such thoughts, his hand rose and rubbed his scars. His father had trusted that his sons would be fine . . . but sometimes accidents happened despite God's watchful eyes on them.

For the last two school breaks, he'd only worked during the day while the boys napped and then again in the late evenings after he put them to bed. His business had suffered with him spending so few hours in his blacksmith shop. And now the boys were too old for naps. Could he look after them all day and still work late at night? Maybe for a few days, but not for weeks at a time. Not only the business, but his health, too, would pay a price.

He jerked his hand away from his face, and his finger slid to verse 5. He read silently, *"So aber jemand unter euch Weisheit mangelt, der bitte Gott, der da gibt einfältig jedermann und rücket's niemand auf, so wird sie ihm gegeben werden."* Gratitude filled him.

Wasn't God a loving Father? If one lacked wisdom, he could ask of God who gave it without reproach. How he needed God's wisdom for keeping his business in full operation and his boys safe during these next months.

He closed the Bible and linked his hands on the worn black leather cover. With his head bowed and eyes closed, he petitioned the One who never slumbered and begged Him to not only grant wisdom but to let him forget the schoolteacher's words. He sensed he would never be at ease in her presence again unless her warning was erased from his mind.

Augusta

During corporate prayer time Sunday morning, Augusta asked
God to redeem her hastily uttered words to Herr Rempel about
Folker and Walden. As the boys' teacher, she cared about them.
But she wasn't their mother, and those days of friendship with
Hannah were long past. Her caution, while stated in sincerity
and concern, was inappropriately given. She also asked God to
help her make amends to Herr Rempel. As she finished praying,
she decided she would seek him out and ask his forgiveness as
soon as church was over.

When the minister released the worshipers from service, she
rose and turned from her normal place near the front of the
women's side and scanned the back area of the men's section,
where Herr Rempel always sat with his two wiggly boys. But the
father and sons weren't there.

She frowned. Had they left already? Considering their seat so
near the door, they could quickly go to their wagon. If she hurried, she might still be able to catch them.

Eager to set things right with the man, she touched Juliana's
arm. "I'll be right back." Then she eased past people gathering
in little groups to chat, excusing herself as she went. She exited
the church and pattered down the porch steps, scanning the
rows of wagons. The Rempel wagon, easily recognized by the
block letters *Rempel Blacksmith* painted on its side, was not with
the others. She cupped her hand over her eyes and searched the
road leading in the direction of the Rempel home. No wagon
was rolling away from the church, either.

She put the details together in her head and came to a worri-
some conclusion. The Rempel family had not attended service.
What had interrupted their usual faithfulness? Had one of the
boys, or Konrad Rempel himself, been injured after all in yesterday's escape from the wagon?

"Mother?" Juliana came up beside Augusta. She held both of their Bibles against the bodice of her rose-colored dress. "You didn't come back, and everyone was leaving." Her brow crinkled as she gazed into her mother's face. "Is something wrong?"

Augusta took her larger Bible from Juliana's arms. "I'd hoped to speak with Herr Rempel, but apparently he and the twins didn't come this morning."

"Oh." Juliana angled her head. "What did you want with him?"

Her daughter's tone only held its usual curiosity, but heat still filled Augusta's cheeks. What would people think about her standing out here in the churchyard, seeking Herr Rempel? Especially if they'd witnessed him escort her across the street yesterday. She would set the town gossips' tongues wagging if she didn't exercise caution.

She forced a smile and slid her arm across her daughter's slender shoulders. "Nothing that can't wait. Let's go home, hm?"

They started up the sidewalk, Juliana waving at passersby and softly humming one of the hymns they'd sung that morning. By the time they reached their house, Augusta had decided that if Herr Rempel didn't come to evening service, she would seek Reverend Hartmann's advice. But for now, she would keep her concerns between herself and God.

Chapter Six

Augusta

To Augusta's great relief, Herr Rempel and the twins attended the evening service. When it was over and people lingered in the yard, enjoying the mild twilight of their day of rest, the twins raced to her, as did several other of her young students.

Augusta welcomed each of them with a hug and a few kind words. Although she'd never received formal training as a teacher, she had strong memories of those under whose tutelage she'd learned. She'd borrowed the most effective techniques and put them to use in her classroom. One thing she remembered well was how much more quickly and confidently she grasped new concepts when she believed that the adult at the front of the classroom cared about her. Those teachers who'd reached her heart made the greatest educational impact. So she made certain her students knew she cared.

The other children darted off after receiving their hugs, but Folker and Walden stayed near. She smiled at the pair. "I missed you two this morning." One of Walden's suspender straps drooped toward his elbow, and a tuft of Folker's dark hair stuck straight up, but she resisted the urge to fix either issue. Only a few yards away, Agnes Bauer observed the three of them. Augusta wouldn't give the woman fuel for speculation or invention.

"We slept too late." Folker crinkled his nose.

Walden's bright-blue eyes sparkled. "Uh-huh. Pa took us fishing yesterday afternoon, and we got all worn out."

"You must have had a grand time." Augusta bounced a smile over both upturned faces. "How many fish did you catch?"

"None," the twins said at the same time. Then Walden laughed. "Folker and me aren't very good fishermen. Pa says it's because we wiggle too much and scare off the fish."

Augusta hid a grin behind her hand. She was familiar with the boys' squirming at their double desk. They wouldn't fidget any less on a creek bank.

Folker shifted from foot to foot, proving his inability to be still. "But Pa caught a whole string. We had a mess of catfish for our supper last night." Both boys rubbed their bellies and licked their lips.

Augusta almost licked her lips, too. Was there anything better than fresh-caught catfish dredged in cornmeal and then fried crisp? She thought not. She hadn't dropped a line in the water for a couple of years at least, but maybe the next time she and Juliana went to the river for a picnic, she would try her hand at bringing home some fish for their frying pan.

She nodded at the pair of look-alike boys beaming up at her. "Well, now that school is out of session, perhaps your father will teach you how to sit still and catch fish."

The pair shrugged in unison. "Maybe," they chorused, then smirked at each other. Folker said, "As long as he catches some, I guess we don't have to. Bye, Frau Dyck!" They dashed off, their shoelaces flopping.

Affection flooded Augusta as she gazed after them. She wanted the best for all her students, but she confessed to an extra amount of tenderness toward the Rempel twins. Their motherless state invited compassion. Thank the Lord that Martina Krahn now recognized the need to bestow compassion on the motherless as well as the fatherless.

If someone from the Frauenverein approached her about ministering to Juliana in some way, how would she respond?

Her first inclination was to claim her daughter had no needs. After all, Leopold had left them well-set financially. Their house was paid for, and she had a sizable amount in an account at the bank. The small fund she received from the county for teaching covered her and Juliana's expenses. She would most likely turn away any offer for assistance.

The same way Herr Rempel would probably turn away offers for assistance.

She searched the grounds for the widower and his sons. Her gaze encountered Walden and Folker rolling in the grass like a pair of puppies behind their father, who visited with a few men. Just beyond them, a mother separated her sons who'd been wrestling and brushed the bits of grass from their clothes while mildly scolding. A realization crept over Augusta. Children received different kinds of instruction from mothers than they did from fathers.

Mothers clothed the children, fed them, nurtured them, kept them clean, and taught them manners. She could do all that for Juliana without difficulty. But fathers guided them, taught them necessary life skills, gave an example of the heavenly Father in how they led the family. Juliana lacked that kind of instruction. So many times the Rempel twins came to school with unwashed faces or wrinkled clothes, making them stand out from the children who'd been tended to by their mothers. As Juliana grew toward womanhood, would not having a father's guidance negatively affect her and make her stand out from those who did have a father in the home? The thought didn't set well.

Such a kind, attentive, loving father Leopold had been. Perhaps his age—forty-three—when he became a father for the first time impacted his tenderness toward his only child. She and Leopold both had felt God gave them a miracle when Augusta conceived a dozen years past their wedding day.

Her own father was nearly that old when she was born, the youngest of five living children, and years of labor had hardened him into a gruff, authoritarian figure who'd frightened Augusta with his stern frowns and barked orders. She would always be grateful for how much Leopold had lavished affection on both her and Juliana, and she would forever mourn his premature departure from their lives.

At the far edge of the churchyard, Herr Elias, who taught the older children at the Alexandertol school, was hitting baseballs for boys to catch. A flutter of possibility winged through Augusta's heart. Next session, Juliana would move to the older students' classroom. Having Herr Elias as her teacher would give her a man's influence. Would it help fill the void Leopold's passing had created? She would pray so.

Then she released a little gasp. Why hadn't she considered such a thing before? If Herr Elias could be a fatherly influence for Juliana, why couldn't Augusta be more than instructor to the Rempel boys? Couldn't she provide a motherly influence for the twins? Of course she could.

From the corner of her eye, she spotted Agnes Bauer and her husband ambling to their wagon. Augusta's pulse gave a little leap. If the woman was leaving, she wouldn't be able to observe Augusta asking Herr Rempel for a moment of his time. She still needed to deliver her apology and ask his forgiveness for her hastily given warning. She would do so, and then on Friday when the club members for the Frauenverein gathered, she would present her idea to the group. Who better to supervise the boys during the summer months than someone they already knew and trusted? In her imagination, she already saw herself tending to the boys over the next months. Such a perfect solution.

With a smile residing in her heart, she crossed the churchyard and stopped a few feet from the circle of visiting men. As soon as Herr Rempel turned from the group, she would speak to him. Receiving his forgiveness would relieve a great burden from her heart. And it could very well open him to receiving her offer to assume responsibility for the boys during the school break.

The first week after closing the school for the season, Augusta hardly found time to breathe. She and Juliana spent all day Monday and Tuesday at the two-story brick schoolhouse, cleaning out desks, taking down papers from the walls, scrubbing the chalkboards and floors, and repairing then sealing books in crates to protect them until school started up again.

On Monday, Herr Elias was there, too, closing down his classroom. He joined them for lunch at Augusta's invitation, and she observed her daughter's interactions with the older children's teacher. Ordinarily gregarious, Juliana seemed shy around the man, but Augusta surmised she would relax when she got better acquainted with him.

At breakfast on Wednesday, Augusta told Juliana she could fritter away her day since she'd been such help at the school. She expected her to ask to visit friends, but after they finished eating and cleaning the kitchen, the girl put several books and various snacks in a basket and went to the apple tree. Augusta couldn't help but chuckle at her little bibliophile.

With her daughter cheerfully occupied, Augusta sorted the frocks in Juliana's wardrobe. A few dresses had enough fabric in the skirt that Augusta could lower the hems, but others needed to be replaced. She spent the remainder of the day at her sewing machine, lengthening the too-short dresses.

Thursday, she and Juliana walked to town, and Augusta allowed her to select fabric for three new dresses. Elsie Weber clicked her tongue on her teeth while adding up the cost for the fabrics, ribbons, buttons, and lace. "Augusta, you'll spoil her by giving her so many things. Just last Saturday, she got how many books? And now you're making new dresses for her . . ." She glanced up, her face pinched into a disapproving frown. "Although Franz and I own this store and could shower our children with gifts, we make them earn the things they want. Since your Juliana has no father in the home, it will be very easy for you to indulge her. I advise you to exercise caution."

Defensiveness stirred in Augusta's chest, and at the same time, worry nibbled. Juliana spent a lot of time with Laura Weber. Had Elsie or Franz witnessed troublesome attitudes or behaviors in her daughter? "Do you think Juliana is spoiled?"

Elsie waved a hand in the air. "Nein. Not yet. But . . ." She gestured to the stack of dress goods and frippery. "It could happen."

Augusta released a soft chuckle. "I appreciate your sage advice, but I can assure you, being the only child in the home, she has many responsibilities to carry out all by herself. She has earned these dresses. The dear child helped me ready my schoolroom for the summer break and even cleaned the potbellied stove, inside and out!"

Elsie's eyebrows rose. "Ach, such an unpalatable task. My boys complain mightily when I ask them to see to the stoves or fireplaces."

Augusta opened her purse and counted out the amount of money needed to pay for her purchases. "Besides, she's growing so fast. I can't have her wearing dresses that are too small, can I?"

A small smile played at the corners of Elsie's thin lips. "Of course you can't. And I suppose, a teacher who works with many children can recognize a child who's been overindulged."

And those who were underindulged. "Ja, I can, and it isn't pretty, which you already know. I will guard against inviting a selfish, spoiled attitude in my Juliana."

On her walk home, she repeated Elsie Weber's comment in her mind and fought another wave of defensiveness, which she made herself squelch. She should appreciate the woman's candor. She now could better understand Herr Rempel's sharp response to her voiced concern for his sons. No parent wanted to hear criticism about their parenting.

Thank goodness the twins' father had accepted her apology, which had removed a great weight from her shoulders and seemed to relax his stiff bearing, too. Forgiveness benefited both the giver and the receiver. She inwardly forgave Elsie, even though the woman hadn't asked, and hummed the melody for "Blest Be the Tie That Binds" as she completed the distance between the mercantile and her home.

She kept the sewing machine humming all Thursday afternoon and evening, and started again on Friday morning. Juliana asked to spend the day with Laura Weber, and Augusta granted permission. But she put her hand on her daughter's shoulder and gave her a stern look. "Remember, the Webers have a business to operate. You mustn't disturb them. Be on your best behavior."

Juliana blinked in innocence. "Of course I will be, Mother. Laura asked me to have dinner with her, too. May I?"

Augusta smiled. "You may if you promise to help clean their kitchen afterward."

"I will." The girl sighed. "It's such fun at their house, Mother, with so many children talking around the table. Laura sometimes complains that there is never a quiet moment, but I envy her many brothers and sisters. It must be grand to be part of such a group." Juliana kissed her mother on the cheek and skipped out the door, wearing one of the dresses that Augusta had modified for her changed height.

Augusta gazed after her only child, her heart aching. Ja, she and Leopold had given their daughter many material blessings, but despite their desire, they'd not been able to provide a brother or a sister. And now it was too late. But nothing could change that now, so she shouldn't moon over it. Didn't her Bible advise her to give thanks in all things? She would be thankful for the gift of her daughter and for the precious memories she carried of her dear husband. Her Father God did not neglect her.

By working diligently in the quiet house, Augusta finished one of the new dresses by the time Juliana returned in the late afternoon. They had a simple supper together, then Augusta retrieved a pencil and lined notepad from the desk in their library to record notes for the evening's Frauenverein gathering. She gave Juliana instructions to stay inside until her return, then set off for the meeting.

When she arrived at the church, she found the women's door standing open. Lamplight glowed behind the windows, and women's chatter carried on the breeze. She was the last arrival again. As an officer, she needed to be early from now on. She hurried inside and took a seat on the front pew, where she'd sat the week before.

Frau Krahn was already at the preacher's podium. She aimed a quick moue at Augusta and then cleared her throat. "Since we're all here, let's get started, shall we? Would someone like to open us with a word of prayer?"

Martha Gotwals raised her hand. "I will." She bowed her head, and Augusta followed suit. Martha offered a simple prayer of thanks for all who'd come and asked God to guide and direct them to those they were meant to serve. "Amen," she finished, and several echoed the word.

"Thank you, Martha." Martina bobbed her head at the woman, then turned to Augusta. "Please take roll now, Madam Secretary."

Augusta quickly recorded the names of each of the women in attendance. She hadn't realized the club would be formal enough to require a roll. She silently planned to leave the next page blank and write the members' names alphabetically before their next gathering. When all twelve names formed a neat column, she said, "I'm finished."

"Then you are ready to record our conversations, ja?"

Augusta turned to a fresh page, wrote *April 16, 1897* at the top of the page, and then looked up. "I am."

Martina scanned the group. "Does anyone have a concern to bring before the club?"

Attendees exchanged glances, but no one offered a suggestion.

Augusta raised her hand, and Martina called on her. Augusta laid aside the notebook and rose. "I would like to bring before the club the name of a family in need of assistance—Herr Konrad Rempel and his sons, Folker and Walden."

Charlotte Osborn raised her hand. "Frau Krahn, I thought you said last week that we would minister to widows and the fatherless. You said it would be unseemly for us, as women, to minister to men."

Martina pursed her lips. "Ja, I did say such a thing. But I think I was too hasty. Frau Dyck helped me see that the motherless have needs as well. Please listen to Augusta's reason for mentioning the Rempel family." She bobbed her chin at Augusta. "Go ahead."

Augusta briefly recounted the boys' near catastrophe. No one seemed surprised by the tale. Alexandertol wasn't a large community. There were few secrets and not much excitement. Herr Hiebert had probably told the story numerous times.

When Augusta finished divulging the details, Martina shook her head in a sad gesture. "Herr Rempel will have a difficult time seeing to his responsibilities in his blacksmith shop during the months of planting and harvesting with two little boys underfoot and no wife to keep them safe and occupied. Therefore, I believe we should consider making the Rempel family the first recipients of benevolence. Does anyone object?"

The women glanced at one another, but no one spoke.

Augusta raised her hand again.

Martina frowned. "You object?"

"Nein, not at all. I have a suggestion for helping Herr Rempel."

A smug smile curved the woman's lips. "As do I. But please share your idea first."

Augusta shifted slightly to address the group. "I'd like to offer to have the boys stay with me each day. They know me since they've been my students for the past three years, and my Juliana is old enough now that she doesn't need constant supervision. In fact, she's old enough to help keep watch over them. I believe the boys will be safe and happy with me."

Several women nodded, smiling their approval.

Augusta's heart turned a happy somersault. She aimed her gaze at Martina, and a stone seemed to drop into her stomach.

Martina's mouth hung open, her eyes wide with dismay. "You— They—" She closed her mouth and swallowed. Then her eyes narrowed, and she shook her head. "Nein, Augusta, that is not a good idea."

Chapter Seven

Martina

Martina inwardly groaned. Why hadn't she shared her own idea first instead of letting Frau Dyck speak? It had taken nearly the whole week, with carefully phrased comments perfectly timed in their delivery, to convince Gerhard that one of the Rempel twins would make a fine apprentice for his shop. His agreement was nearly miraculous. But now this schoolteacher could take it all away.

The woman remained standing, staring at Martina in confusion. "Why is it not a good idea? The boys need tending. I've offered to tend to them. Does it not solve the problem?"

Martina's thoughts raced. Augusta's idea itself wasn't bad. It only derailed Martina's idea, which made it bad in her mind. But how to say so? She forced a little laugh that came out more like a cough. "I apologize. I didn't mean to say it was a bad idea. I only meant we should explore many ideas before settling on one, ja?"

She faced the group. "Does anyone else have an idea about how to help Herr Rempel's motherless boys?" Her pulse pounded, and she held her breath as she waited for comments. Although the women exchanged glances, no one offered anything. She eased the breath from her lungs, then forced her stiff lips into a smile. "I have a suggestion, too. My husband is interested in hiring an apprentice to learn the trade of wagon building and repair. If he hires one of the Rempel boys, then not only will the boy be occupied during these break months, he'll also learn valuable skills that could benefit him now and be of service to our community at a later time."

Agnes Bauer raised her hand. "Martina, are you saying Gerhard would take only one boy into apprenticeship?"

"Ja, that is correct." Martina had anticipated the question and was prepared to answer it. "By having one apprentice, Gerhard can give the boy his full attention. We had thought that assuming responsibility for one of his sons would make things easier for Herr Rempel, too. One boy underfoot is less of a burden than two." Perhaps Augusta's suggestion held more merit than Martina originally thought. She tapped her chin, thinking aloud. "The same reasoning applies to Frau Dyck, as well. It would be less taxing for her to oversee one boy instead of two. And with both boys away during the day, Herr Rempel could work completely free of distraction."

Now Sallie Bair stood, shaking her head with adamance. "Separating the twins might benefit those who provide supervision, but it could be harmful to the boys. I have twin brothers. They never wanted to be apart when they were growing up. Even now, as adults, they live on plots of ground next to each other and work their joined fields together." She folded her arms over her chest. "Twins have a bond that the rest of us don't understand. If our goal is to help the Rempel family, then I vote for a way that is best suited to the twins' needs, not easier for the helpers."

Several women nodded, and panic filled Martina's breast. "Thank you for sharing your thoughts, Sallie." Her voice emerged strained and higher pitched, proving her inner turmoil. She gruffly cleared her throat. "Of course we want to consider the twins' needs. But, as Augusta expressed, the most crucial need is supervision. It may not be practical to expect someone to assume responsibility for two active boys."

Sallie flapped her hand in Frau Dyck's direction. "But Augusta already offered to take both boys. Why don't we allow her to do so?"

Because then Gerhard won't have a boy with whom to bestow his attention, and he will continue drowning his sorrow.

Thank goodness Martina possessed enough control to hold the comment inside. She gripped her hands and pressed them to her pounding chest. "Because we are still discussing possible solutions to Herr Rempel's need for help with his twins. We should discuss many ideas and then choose the best one. Now, I think—"

Sallie released a snort. "Martina, since the need is Herr Rempel's, why not let him decide what is best? After all, he knows the twins better than any of us do."

More nods and a few murmurs ensued. Martina gritted her teeth. Only their first meeting, and she couldn't control the club. All the planning she'd done to present their first project, all the anticipation of rousing approval, was crumbling. She snapped her attention to Augusta Dyck, praying her frustration didn't show on her face. "Madam Secretary, please record both suggestions given this evening. Add that I"—she would accept no argument on this point since she was president of the club— "will pay a visit to Herr Rempel and present the offers to help. As Frau Bair wisely suggested, we will allow him to decide what is best for his sons."

Oh, such a painful concession. But what else could she do? She waited, watching Augusta's hand make marks on the page. When the woman set the pencil aside, Martina faced the group again. "I'll ask again, has anyone encountered a need our group could address? Anyone who is sick? Who has need of a meal brought in? Who needs help with chores?"

Only a few sideways glances or shrugged shoulders offered a response. Martina took the gestures as a desire to end the meeting. She drew in a breath and sighed it out before delivering her planned ending for the meeting. "Very well, then, we will come together again next Friday. Remember, keep your eyes, ears, and hearts open to those around you, just as F-Frau Dyck did this past week." She hadn't realized how hard it would be to add that part. She swallowed. "Let us strive to be the hands and feet of Jesus to those living in and around our community. You are dismissed."

Women rose and ambled toward the doorway. Except for Berta Hartmann. The elected vice president came straight to the edge of the raised platform. "Martina, when do you intend to visit with Herr Rempel about the twins?"

Martina remained on the dais and gazed down at the woman. "Perhaps tomorrow afternoon. Perhaps Sunday, at the close of service. I haven't decided yet. Why do you ask?"

"Well . . ." A blush filled the woman's face. "If you choose to go to his home tomorrow, please take someone with you. Either Gerhard"—

Gerhard wouldn't come. He liked his Saturdays at home.

—"or one of the club members. As you pointed out in our first gathering, ministering to men could be misconstrued." The blush in her cheeks darkened, creating two red splashes. "William never calls on widows, or on wives whose husbands are away, by himself. Having someone else along protects his reputation as well as theirs. I would be happy to accompany you if Gerhard is not available."

Martina agreed that the minister was wise to guard his reputation. She should guard hers, too. But if she took someone with her, there would be a witness to what she told Herr Rempel. Not that she would tell him untruths. She would mention both options. She had no choice. In a town of this size, word would eventually spread about their meeting and what was said. People would know if she left out Augusta's offer. But if Martina went alone, she could give her own idea greater emphasis, hopefully swaying the man to apprentice one of his boys to Gerhard. He could do whatever he pleased with the other—keep him or send him to Augusta Dyck.

Berta placed her hand on Martina's arm. "Please let me know what you decide. I am available all day tomorrow, and of course I'll be at service on Sunday."

Sunday there would be countless people listening in. Tomorrow, at Herr Rempel's place, would be best. Martina gave a firm nod, her decision made. "I'll go tomorrow afternoon. At two." Well past dinnertime yet also far from suppertime. A good time to call on the man. "If you'd like to accompany me, please be at my house by a quarter 'til two."

"Should we also take Augusta with us? After all, she is also an officer in the club, and she is the one who brought the concern to our group."

Martina narrowed her gaze, heat rising in her chest. "Nein. Two of us going will be sufficient. We needn't overwhelm the man." She pasted on a smile and stepped down from the platform. "Come now, Berta. I'll help you extinguish the lamps, and then we can go home."

Konrad

"Pa? Pa!"

The noise from the raging forge almost covered the call, but Konrad's ears were tuned to hear his sons' voices. He laid aside the tongs with the short steel rod still caught in its grip and took a step away from the forge. He swiped the back of his gloved hand across his forehead. He had hoped to finish a half dozen long-handled kitchen spoons while the twins weeded the garden, but their constant interruptions—first there was a garter snake sticking out its tongue at them, then they were thirsty and needed help bringing up the bucket from the well, and then Folker was upset that Walden gave him the hoe with a nick in its blade—made him work so slowly that he had only two spoons made.

He turned and looked toward the wide opening to the barn. This time it was Walden seeking his attention. The boy stood just outside the doorway. He rocked in place, digging his bare toes into the soft dirt.

"Ja?" Konrad snapped out the query, impatience to finish his work overwhelming him. "What is it now?"

"There's a buggy coming up the street."

Konrad frowned. "So let it come. What is that to us?" He shouldn't be so brusque. Hannah would frown at his tone if she were listening. But he'd been in his shop more than an hour and had so little to show for the time.

His son shrugged. "It's coming up *our* street."

Suddenly Konrad understood. "You mean it's coming up our lane?"

Walden nodded. He glanced over his shoulder, then shrugged again. "It's here."

Konrad tugged off his gloves and tossed them onto the workbench on his way to the yard. When Hannah was alive, they frequently received friends, and sometimes her brother and his family from Durham came to call. But these days, visitors were usually people seeking his services as a blacksmith. He shouldn't begrudge them. He needed customers to keep his business going. But he hoped whoever this visitor was wouldn't request anything too difficult to craft or didn't need something quickly. He wouldn't be able to promise delivery. Not until the boys were back in school.

He flicked his hand at Walden. "Go back to the garden, Son."

Walden scowled his displeasure, but he trudged off.

The buggy had stopped halfway between the blacksmith

shop and his house. He recognized the single mare pulling it. He'd fitted shoes for the horse a few times over the years. But usually Herr Krahn brought it. Seeing Frau Krahn and the minister's wife on the leather seat both surprised and concerned him. Was something wrong with Herr Krahn?

His leather apron prevented Konrad from jogging, but he walked as quickly as possible to the buggy's driver side. He squinted up at the women. "*Guten Nachmittag,* Frau Krahn and Frau Hartmann."

Frau Krahn set the brake and then wrapped the reins around the brake handle. "Good afternoon, Herr Rempel." She smiled down at him, but her lips trembled.

Ja, something must be wrong. He braced himself to receive bad news.

"I am sorry we're taking you away from your work." Her gaze flitted to the barn and then seemed to scan Konrad's leather apron. "We thought, since it is Saturday, you might not be in your shop."

"Most generally I am not." He slipped his hands behind the apron's bib. "But things are a little different when school is out. I work when the boys are otherwise occupied."

Frau Hartmann sat forward and seemed to search the area around his house. "Where are your boys?"

"Chopping the weeds from our garden plot." Konrad shrugged. "They're probably almost finished by now." Which meant his time for getting anything done in the shop was nearing its end. He didn't want to be ungracious, but he didn't have time to spare. He cleared his throat. "Is there something I can do for you, ladies?"

The pair exchanged a look that reminded him of when the twins had been up to mischief and weren't sure how to tell him what they'd done. Frau Krahn squared her shoulders and lifted her chin. "Herr Rempel, we've actually come to do something for you."

He unconsciously took a small backward step. "Oh? What is that?"

Her lips formed a quivery smile. "Are you aware that several women from church have formed a Frauenverein here in Alexandertol?"

So the murmurs about a women's club starting in the community held merit. He gave a slow nod. "Ja, I heard something about it."

Her smile brightened. "*Sehr gut.* We know you are trying to run a business here. Having your boys home all day now must be a hardship for you. Thus, the members of the Alexandertol Frauenverein want to help."

Konrad scrunched his brow. "Help me . . . how?"

Frau Hartmann sat forward again. "By providing supervision for your twins while you work."

Frau Krahn shot the woman a frown, and Frau Hartmann settled back on the leather seat. Frau Krahn turned to Konrad. "Frau Hartmann is correct. My Gerhard wants one of the twins to spend days with him. He will teach your son the wainwright trade. A *gut* idea, ja? And Frau Dyck has made herself available to keep the other boy."

Konrad's hands behind the leather bib curled into fists.

"With both boys occupied elsewhere every day," Frau Krahn went on in a cheerful voice, "you will be free to work your usual hours. Your business will be unaffected during these break months." She tilted her head, her expression smug. "So now you need only to decide which twin will go where."

Chapter Eight

Konrad

Last Sunday evening when he offered forgiveness for what Frau Dyck said to him the day the twins ran into the street in front of the wagon, he'd thought the subject was done. But apparently it was not. The woman was still worried, and she'd set the Frauenverein ladies on him the way he would set a dog on an intruder. A sour taste flooded his mouth—the flavor of bitterness.

Frau Hartmann sat forward again. "Herr Rempel, Frau Krahn must have forgotten to mention that Frau Dyck is willing to have both boys spend their days with her."

The frown Frau Krahn turned on the woman was as scorching as the flame in Konrad's forge. Frau Hartmann didn't seem to notice. She went on, "You can rest assured that with either Frau Dyck or Herr Krahn, they will be well supervised."

Ja, they probably would be. Frau Dyck was a fine teacher who cared about his boys. Herr Krahn, although childless and therefore without experience in dealing with young boys, had never given Konrad reason to think he would be unkind or inattentive toward a child. But the idea that these women—nein, that one woman in particular—still held concerns about his ability to keep his boys safe rankled.

"Ladies, I . . ." He pulled one hand free of the stiff apron and rubbed his scarred cheek. "I don't know what to say to you right now." He would shock them if he said what he was thinking.

Frau Dyck is making mountains out of molehills and should prove her apology by not speaking of my boys' reckless act again.

"Well, you need not answer right away." Frau Krahn's smile seemed strained. "After all, the opportunities we've presented are vastly different. One twin will be in a working environment, and the other will have a fairly carefree day. You will want to choose the twin best suited for the place he will spend his days." She unwrapped the reins from the brake handle and gripped them in her fist. "Please think about it this evening. Pray about it, too. Then tomorrow after church you can tell Frau Hartmann or me what you've decided." She unlocked the brake handle, and the buggy rocked in place, its wheels squeaking. "We will see you in service in the morning, Herr Rempel. Enjoy the rest of your day."

Frau Hartmann waved. "*Auf Wiedersehen*, Herr Rempel."

Konrad waved, too, his hand shaky.

Frau Krahn snapped the reins over the mare's back. The animal strained forward, and Konrad stood in the patch of sunlight and watched the buggy turn a neat half circle and roll down the lane. As it turned onto the street, the twins pounded up behind him, both hollering his name. They skidded to a stop and glared at him with sweaty faces.

Walden pointed at his brother. "Pa, Folker whacked me across the bottom with the hoe handle."

Folker aimed his glare at Walden. "Because he poked me on the back of the head with his hoe." He turned an innocent look on his father. "He started it, Pa. He said I wasn't working, but I was."

Walden huffed. "You were not either. You were crouched down staring at a worm."

"I was making sure I hadn't chopped it in half." Folker's voice turned shrill. "Worms have feelings, too."

"Sometimes you are so dumb, Folker." The boys lunged at each other.

"Folker, Walden—enough!" Konrad caught them by their suspender straps and pulled them apart. He gave them each a shake before he let go. He frowned at the pair. "What is the matter with you two? Why are you fighting with each other?"

Walden folded his arms over his chest. "He was playing and I was doing all the work. He made me mad."

Konrad resisted rolling his eyes skyward. "Poking your brother with the hoe was wrong, and you need to tell him you're sorry."

Walden's mouth fell open. "But he—"

Konrad shook his head. "I am not finished." He turned to Folker. "And, Folker, you need to say you're sorry for hitting your brother. You know better."

Folker looked aside, his lips set in a sullen line.

Konrad gave each boy a little nudge on the shoulder. "Go ahead. Apologize to each other."

They held their gazes askance, but they muttered, "I'm sorry."

Konrad sighed. He would talk to them again later and insist on a more heartfelt apology, but they were still too aggravated to be truly sorry. But what to do with them now? He couldn't send them both back to the garden patch. Not with resentment still smoldering.

"Folker, you finish weeding." He curled his hand around the back of Walden's neck. "And you come with me. You can sweep the floor under the anvil and gather up all the metal shavings." The anvil was far enough from the forge that the boy shouldn't be in danger.

Both boys' eyes widened. "But, Pa!" they chorused.

Konrad pointed at them by turn. "And no more arguing today, do you hear me?" He waited until each gave a nod. "Good. Now do as I said."

The boys darted in opposite directions. His heart heavy, Konrad followed Walden. Every day this past week, he'd broken up skirmishes between the twins. Nothing as serious as using hoe handles to hurt each other, but petty arguments over who got to ride the rope swing first or who would wash and who would dry the dishes. For some reason, neither of them wanted to dry. Konrad solved that problem by making them take turns, but they snapped at each other the entire time they washed dishes.

What was happening to them? They'd always been close, the best of friends, and he didn't like the change since school released. Maybe . . . His feet slowed to a stop, an unpleasant thought taking shape. Maybe they were together too much now. When they were smaller, they were more like two halves of one whole. But as they got older, unique personalities were emerging. They were growing into individuals, and of course differences would arise.

Konrad stared in the direction the buggy had gone, remembering the women's offers and his less-than-enthusiastic response to them. Maybe they weren't such bad ideas after all. Well, one of the ideas. He didn't intend to send either of the boys to Frau Dyck. But letting the boys have some time apart might be good for them. And not having both boys with him all day should let him get more work done. Especially since the one left behind wouldn't have anyone with whom to argue. His ma always told him and his brother that it took one to start a fight but two to continue it.

Walden was waiting outside the doors in obedience to the boys' rule about never entering the blacksmith shop without their father. Konrad needed to stop thinking and get back to work. He set himself into motion, his strides as long as the bulky apron allowed. Inside the structure, he gave Walden a stiff-bristled broom, and he returned to the forge.

As he reheated the end of the rod, he pondered the opportunities presented by Frau Krahn and Frau Hartmann. Learning a trade wouldn't do either of his boys any harm. Even if neither chose to become a wainwright when he was grown, the skills needed to build wagons could be useful for other jobs, too. Ja, he would let Herr Krahn teach one of the twins.

He glanced at Walden, who was diligently guiding the tiny bits of metal into a pile next to the anvil. Maybe it was time to share what he knew about blacksmithing, too. Having only one boy in the shop would be safer than two—easier to keep an eye on one. Then both boys could spend their break learning.

He blew out a heavy sigh. Such a week it had been. A time of relaxation would do him some good. It wouldn't do any harm to the twins, either. He hollered over the forge's roar, "Walden!"

His son paused and looked at him.

"Go tell Folker to gather up as many worms as he can from the garden plot. When we've finished our chores, we'll go fishing."

Augusta

Augusta hooked the picnic basket on her arm, then smiled at her daughter. "All right, I'm ready. Do you have everything you need?"

Juliana bounced the pair of fishing poles on her shoulder and held up the cracker tin containing dirt and worms she'd dug from the alley behind their house. "Everything except the fish."

Augusta laughed. "Then let's go catch some."

The two left the house and headed for the north edge of town, which butted the Cottonwood River. After their busy week, Augusta looked forward to a relaxing picnic on the riverbank. Ever since the Rempel twins mentioned the catfish their father had caught, she'd been craving catfish fillets. As she and Juliana meandered side by side on the dirt street through dappled patches of sunshine and shadow, she tried not to get her hopes up too high. After all, she hadn't gone fishing since Leopold was still alive. But surely fish hadn't changed. They would still take hold of a worm on a hook, wouldn't they?

She glanced at the pair of poles bobbing on Juliana's shoulder. Leopold had purchased the bamboo poles from a store in McPherson, and the lines and hooks were the same ones he'd affixed to the slender lengths of wood. Using the old poles felt a bit like taking Leopold with them. He'd been a good fisherman. Of course, he'd been good at nearly every outdoor activity. If Juliana had inherited more than his gregarious nature and blue eyes, she would be good at catching fish. Maybe they could take Folker and Walden fishing when the boys spent days with them. The thought made her smile, and she even imagined she heard the twins' chortling laughter.

But was she only imagining it? She tipped her ear toward the line of cottonwood trees hiding the river from view.

At the same time Juliana turned a smile on her. "The Rempels must be fishing or swimming. I hear Folker and Walden."

Augusta nodded. "Me, too. I hope they won't mind sharing the river with us."

Juliana shrugged, then shifted the poles a bit. "It's not the biggest river in Kansas, but it's certainly big enough for all of us."

They left the road and eased through the break in the thick brush growing at the base of the scraggly, towering trees. When they emerged on the other side, Juliana pointed. "We were right, Mother. There they are."

Roughly a dozen yards upstream, Herr Rempel and the two boys sat on the sloping bank with their bare feet aimed at the water. About ten feet of space separated them, and Herr Rempel sat in the middle. The boys were jabbering past their father to each other and swinging their poles. Only Herr Rempel seemed focused on his line's cork bobbing on the surface of the water.

Augusta knew the moment she and Juliana were spotted, because Folker released a yelp and bounded to his feet. He tossed his pole aside and started in their direction.

Herr Rempel glanced up, and his eyebrows rose. He put out his arm. "Nein, Son. Stay here."

The man's quiet command startled Augusta. He'd never stopped either of the twins from greeting her before. Why would he do so now?

Folker sighed and returned to his pole. He picked it up and tossed the hook into the water, but he gazed longingly in Augusta's direction. Walden, too, sent peeks at her. Neither boy called out to each other anymore.

Regret smote her. For whatever reason, Juliana's and her arrival at the river had spoiled the Rempels' enjoyable afternoon. She turned to her daughter. "Sweetheart, maybe we should—"

Juliana held a wiggly worm aloft, her face bright. "Look at this one, Mother! See how fat it is? It should entice a nice fat fish to take hold, don't you think?"

The sight of that squirming worm did funny things to her middle. Or was it Herr Rempel's icy reception causing her stomach to churn? She couldn't be sure, but she wouldn't squash her child's delight. They'd come to fish, so they would fish. But a little farther downstream, where they wouldn't disturb the blacksmith.

She forced herself to smile. "I think you're absolutely correct. But wait just a moment before baiting your hook. There's a shaded, flat spot beyond that fallen log. Let's get settled there."

Juliana's fine brows pinched. "But this is our regular picnic spot."

"I know." She glanced at Herr Rempel. He stared at the water, the thick, dark whiskers on his jaw seeming to bristle. She lowered her voice to a whisper. "I think Herr Rempel is worried we'll distract the twins from fishing. They probably want fish for their supper. Let's move so the boys will pay attention to their fishing poles."

"I don't think they were paying much attention before we got here," Juliana whispered back. Then she shrugged. "But if that's what you want to do, we can go to the other side of the log."

Augusta released a little sigh of relief as Juliana tossed the worm back into the tin. They crossed the damp clay bank to the fallen log, gingerly eased over it, and laid out the things they'd brought with them on the ground.

Juliana sat cross-legged on the bank and baited her hook, concentration creasing her face. She tossed the line into the water and sent a sideways grin at Augusta. "You don't have much confidence in us catching fish, do you?" Although she didn't whisper, she kept her voice low.

Augusta speared a worm with her hook, grimacing at the unpalatable task. "What makes you say that?"

Juliana nodded toward the picnic basket. "You brought sandwiches along."

Now Augusta laughed. "I never planned to eat the fish this evening. Whatever we catch, I'll clean at home"—would she remember how Leopold had readied the fish for the frying pan?— "and soak the fillets in buttermilk overnight. We'll have them for our Sunday dinner."

"Ohhh." Juliana nodded wisely. "In that case, may I have a sandwich, please? Fishing makes me hungry."

They'd hardly had a chance to work up an appetite yet, and they'd both just handled worms, but Augusta set aside her motherly cautions and peeled back the checked-cloth cover on the basket. "Ham or cheese?"

"Ja."

Augusta blasted a laugh, then slapped her hand over her mouth. Hadn't she said they didn't want to disturb Herr Rempel? She rose up slightly and peered past the log. She gave a little start. The bank was empty. Herr Rempel and his boys had apparently gone home.

Chapter Nine

Augusta

"Come, Frau Dyck." Martina Krahn lightly gripped Augusta's elbow and guided her across the churchyard toward Konrad Rempel's wagon. Berta Hartmann followed on their heels.

Augusta wished she could wriggle loose and go home instead of talking to Herr Rempel. His strange behavior at the river yesterday afternoon troubled her and had interrupted her sleep last night. Sometimes women could be moody, swinging from friendly to frosty, but she'd known the twins' father for years—even before he'd become a father. She'd always seen Konrad Rempel as an even-tempered person. Now she couldn't help but wonder if the forgiveness he'd offered wasn't sincere. She didn't like thinking such a thing about someone she'd always viewed as kind.

Martina had told her before the service started that the three officers for the Alexandertol Frauenverein would briefly visit with Herr Rempel afterward. When Augusta said she needed to get home and put a meal on the table, the woman insisted that as the secretary for the club, she needed to hear Herr Rempel's decision about whether or not to accept their assistance in supervising his sons for the school break so she could record it in the book. So, against her desire, her stomach whirling in nervousness, she advanced upon the man standing beside his wagon.

As they neared the wagon, Herr Rempel took a few long

strides forward and met them. The twins waved at Augusta from their spots on the wagon seat. She sent them a small smile and nod, inwardly praying the silent acknowledgment wouldn't upset Herr Rempel. When he hadn't allowed Folker to run to her yesterday afternoon, it had hurt her feelings and, she suspected, Folker's, too. She didn't want the boys hurt again.

"Herr Rempel," Martina said in her usual authoritative tone, "have you prayed about what is best for your boys?"

He nodded, his gaze unwaveringly aimed at the Frauenverein president's face. "I have, and I spoke with the boys, too. Walden wants to learn about being a wainwright."

Martina released a happy gasp and let go of Augusta's elbow. "Oh, my . . ." She clasped her hands beneath her chin, tittering. "Gerhard will be so pleased. Thank you, Herr Rempel."

"Thank you for making the opportunity available." He adjusted his hat brim. "At what time should I have Walden at your husband's shop tomorrow?"

"Gerhard opens his shop at eight o'clock each morning. A few minutes before would probably be best."

"I will see that he's on time." He turned toward his wagon.

Berta Hartmann let out a little squeak. "Herr Rempel?"

He turned back, his blue eyes skimming past Augusta. "Ja?"

She held her hands outward. "What of Folker?"

"Folker will stay with me and learn about blacksmithing." He spoke so tersely that Augusta unconsciously drew back. "This way, both boys will spend their break learning." The skin behind his beard took on a pink tinge. "Thank you for your concern for my boys. I . . . appreciate . . . the chance given to Walden to learn new skills. *Guten Tag, meine Damen.*" He tipped his hat, turned on his heel, and strode to the wagon.

Augusta and the other two women remained in place until the wagon rolled past. The twins waved, and Martina and Berta returned the farewell. Augusta's arm refused to rise. Her heart hurt. The reason Herr Rempel gave for keeping Folker with him made sense, was even equitable since Walden would be working. But they were so young. Was it fair to make boys their age labor all day? Certainly, it wasn't uncommon in the big cities for children as young and sometimes even younger than the Rempel twins to work in factories. But here in Alexandertol, she knew of no children who worked beyond the standard chores required of family members.

Frau Krahn heaved a happy sigh and turned a smile on Augusta and Berta. "Well, I should say our first act of benevolence is a great success."

Augusta shook her head. "I'm not so sure it will be."

The woman's brows tipped together. "You wanted the twins supervised. They'll both be supervised. Is that not, then, a successful outcome?"

"They'll be supervised, ja." Worry niggled in the back of Augusta's mind. How could she make these women—especially Martina, who had no children of her own—understand? "But the type of supervision might not be appropriate for the twins. They are young yet and very active. The school day is shorter than a workday, and were it not for recess breaks where they could run off their excess energy, they would have struggled to stay on task during those hours. I'm worried they will—"

Martina snorted. "You are only jealous that Herr Rempel liked my idea better than yours."

Augusta gaped at the woman. Did she really think Augusta would be so petty?

"Maybe," Martina went on, a caustic bite in her voice, "he thought letting the boys stay with you would make you too attached to them. Then they would become teacher's pets. None of the other children like teacher's pets."

Berta touched Martina's arm. "You're hurting Augusta's feelings."

Remorse briefly glimmered in the older woman's eyes. "Not my intention." Her tone was kinder, but her lips still formed a stern line. "I'm merely trying to point out that Herr Rempel is the boys' father and, as Frau Bair told us in our last meeting, knows what is best for them. I am a little surprised he decided to separate them"—

So was Augusta.

—"but trust that he has sound reasons for doing so." She started toward the church, and both Augusta and Berta fell in step with her. "Frau Dyck, please be sure to record Herr Rempel's decision in the Frauenverein journal. You may give the report to the club when we meet on Friday evening."

By Friday, maybe Augusta could talk about Herr Rempel's decision without feeling as if she were rubbing salt into her own wounds. They parted ways, and Augusta walked home with Juliana. Her daughter talked the whole way, but Augusta paid little attention. She'd never liked being at odds with someone. Even when she was a child, her mother said she was more peacemaker rather than troublemaker. She'd always thought it a positive trait, but today she wished she could set it aside. Because everything within her wanted to restore peace between herself and Herr Rempel. Yet why did his perceived animosity bother her so much? Was it due to her old friendship with Hannah, or something more?

A Scripture she'd learned as a child tiptoed through her mind and found its way from her lips. "'If it be possible, as much as lieth in you, live peaceably with all men.'"

Juliana shot her a puzzled look. "What did you say?"

Augusta gave a little start. She offered her daughter a sheepish smile. "I was quoting a verse—Romans 12:18. I didn't realize I'd said it out loud."

Juliana laughed. "Well, you did. And it didn't make much sense to me, because I was telling you that Laura invited me to come over this afternoon and cut paper dolls from some magazines her mother gave her. May I go?" Her blue eyes pleaded.

They'd reached the walkway leading to their porch. Augusta slid her arm over her daughter's shoulders and escorted her up the rock pathway. "If it's already been approved by Laura's mother, then you may."

Juliana released a happy squeal.

"But first you must help me with the dishes."

Juliana's lips parted, as if preparing to beg off from the chore, but then impishness flooded her face. "All right. I'll live peaceably with you by helping before I go."

The simple, teasing comment lifted Augusta's spirits more than she could contain. She captured Juliana in a hug and kissed her temple. "Thank you, my wood nymph. Now, let's go inside and fry our fish. I'm hungry."

Konrad

Folker stood a few feet from the stove and rose on tiptoe, his gaze latched on to the catfish fillets sizzling in the hot lard. "I'm hungry, Pa. When's dinner going to be ready?"

Konrad used his hand-forged spatula to lift the edge of one of the strips of cornmeal-dredged meat. The bottom wasn't quite as browned as the top. He liked his fish good and crisp. "A few more minutes. Is the table set?"

"Ja. Walden set it."

Konrad whisked a frown at his son. "I thought I asked you to set it."

"I had to go to the outhouse, so Walden did it."

Folker's penchant for using the outhouse as an escape from chores was one of the things Konrad hoped to cure during this summer break. The Bible said even a child was known by his

doings, whether his work was pure and right. Pushing responsibility off on his brother was neither pure nor right and wouldn't
benefit him as he grew up.

"Since Walden set the table, it will be your job to clear it." He
checked another fillet, nodded in satisfaction, then shifted the
pan away from the hottest part of the stove. "By yourself." He
raised one brow for emphasis.

Folker set his lips in a pout and tromped to the table. He sat
across from his brother, propping his chin with his hands.

Konrad periodically glanced at Folker as he filled three plates
with fish fillets and scoops of the beans seasoned with onion
he'd left simmering in the oven while they were at church. He'd
told the Frauenverein ladies what he decided, which meant he
should be finished with the subject. But had he made a snap
judgment based on the boys' uncharacteristically fractious
week and his own need for uninterrupted hours of work? Maybe
they weren't ready to be apprentices.

He balanced the plates on his arms and carried them to the
table. When he'd placed the plates in front of each of their
chairs, he slid onto his seat and sent a questioning look to first
Folker and then Walden. "Would either of you like to thank the
Lord for our food?"

The boys stared at each other across the table for a few seconds, then shifted their wide-eyed gazes on their father. Konrad
bit back a laugh. Over the years, it had become easy for him to
discern which twin was which even though their physical ap-
pearances matched. Little differences—such as the way Folker
crinkled his nose but Walden quirked his lips to the side when
they were thinking, and Folker's slightly higher-pitched voice
and Walden's larger feet—gave them uniquenesses. In that moment, however, the mix of surprise and uncertainty on their
sun-freckled faces was identical.

"Would you rather I prayed?" Konrad didn't need to ask. The answer was obvious. But it tickled him to see the pair nod in unison. He bowed his head and thanked God for His provision. A lump formed in his throat as he spoke to his Father in heaven. After Hannah died, he worried about how well he and the boys would get along without a woman in the house, but God always met their needs. Maybe he should trust God to continue to do so even without sending one of his sons to Gerhard Krahn.

He said "Amen" and picked up his fork. The boys dug into their food as if they hadn't eaten in days. The food smelled good and Konrad's belly rumbled in eagerness to be fed, but he had trouble swallowing. Had Frau Dyck and her daughter caught any fish yesterday afternoon? He cut fresh poles each time he went fishing. The wood for the poles the girl was carrying had looked dried out. Dry meant brittle. Had the poles snapped when they tried to bring in the fish?

Rarely did he withhold assistance from someone who needed it. He'd been taught from the time he was young to love his neighbors as himself. Brotherly kindness was a sign of godliness, his Vater always said. Neither of his parents had ever spurned an opportunity to help someone. Konrad had surely shamed them and himself yesterday by ignoring the schoolteacher and her child. Especially since the woman had been a close friend to Hannah and had given so much to his boys over the past years.

If he was honest with himself, she hadn't done anything wrong. She'd expressed concern and then acted on it. Was that not what God the Father expected His children to do? Nein, she'd done nothing more than bruise his pride. Because, deep down, he knew that sometimes there weren't enough hands, enough hours, enough eyes, enough energy to give both boys everything they needed every day. He did his best, always his best, as any loving parent did. But sometimes—he inwardly winced—he worried about how much Walden and Folker needed a mother.

How he missed the boys' mother. Hannah would have been very upset about the twins running into the street. Hannah would have said, loudly and clearly, that he should not have left them unattended in the back of the wagon for half an hour. And Hannah would have been right.

Frau Dyck had essentially said what Hannah would have said. But he still didn't want to send his boys to her house while the school was closed. They were with her enough when the school was open. She needed a break, too.

He stabbed a chunk of fish with his fork and put it in his mouth. As he chewed, he decided he would tell Frau Dyck he was sorry for his rude actions and thank her for her offer to supervise the boys during the school break. Once she'd accepted his apology, maybe he could ask her a favor. A personal one, too personal to trust to just anyone. But he could trust her.

He swallowed his bite, knowing he would need to swallow a great deal of pride to ask the favor. But he could do it. For his boys. They were more important than his pride.

Chapter Ten

Konrad

K onrad put his hand on Walden's shoulder and walked his son from the wagon to Krahn Wainwright & Wheelwright Shop. Walden sent apprehensive glances at him as they went, but Konrad stared straight ahead, a smile fixed on his face. He didn't dare meet his son's gaze lest the boy read worry in his father's eyes.

The large barn had been built in the center of a full block. No trees dotted the property, and morning sunshine glinted on the shop's many windows. On cloudless days, Herr Krahn probably never had to use a lantern. The sun God created to light the day would provide enough illumination for him to work. Big double doors were already slid open on their black iron rails, and the scents of turpentine and freshly sanded wood greeted Konrad's nose as he stepped into the opening.

On the far side of the neatly organized shop, Herr Krahn stood with his back to them, taking tools down from hooks on the wall and clanking them onto a long workbench. Konrad recognized some as products from his own shop, and it made him happy—secure, even—to think Walden would learn to use things his own father had crafted.

He waited a few seconds to see if Herr Krahn would notice them. When he didn't, Konrad called the man's name.

Herr Krahn made an awkward turn and faced the doors. His gaze landed on Konrad and then dropped to Walden. At that moment, Walden scooted close to Konrad, almost slipped behind him. Konrad tugged him forward and whispered, "Stand tall and proud."

His son's skinny back straightened and his chin came up, but he continued to bite his lip.

Herr Krahn strode toward them, crossing between two wagon beds propped on sawhorses. He went straight to Walden, put his hands on his hips, and looked the boy up and down. "So, you're my new apprentice, are you?" The question seemed to boom out and echo from the rafters of the large barn.

Walden drew back slightly. He blinked up at the man. For a moment, Konrad thought he might turn tail and run, but then he stuck out his hand. "I'm Walden James Rempel, sir." He nearly bellowed his greeting.

Although Herr Krahn's lips remained in an unsmiling line, his eyes glinted with amusement. He shook Walden's hand. "And I am Herr Gerhard Krahn. But since we will get to know each other pretty well, you may call me *Onkel* Gerhard."

Walden peeked at Konrad, as if seeking permission, and he gave a quick nod. Walden nodded, too, shifting his attention to the big man. "Yes, sir."

"And if you're going to work here, you need a uniform." He reached behind himself and pulled a tweed newsboy cap from either his pocket or waistband. It matched the one he was wearing. He slapped it onto Walden's head, pulling the little brim nearly over his eyes.

Walden giggled and shifted it into place. He grinned up at Konrad. "Look, Pa. I have a uniform."

Konrad nodded, his smile tight.

Herr Krahn turned to Konrad. "Since you brought him this morning, I'll take him home at the end of the day. Is that suitable with you?"

"More than suitable. Thank you." Konrad had expected to

both deliver and retrieve his son each day. Then he groaned and slapped his hand to his forehead. "I just thought . . . I should have packed a dinner pail for him." In the week since school closed, he'd gotten out of the routine of making sandwiches for the boys to carry off with them. He dug in his pocket, withdrew a few coins, and offered them to Herr Krahn. "This will pay for some cheese, crackers, and fruit from the mercantile. I'll send food with him tomorrow."

Herr Krahn frowned at the coins. "A growing boy needs more than cheese and crackers. He will come to my house at noon and eat with Martina and me." He arched one eyebrow and examined Walden, as if measuring him. "Do you like fried chicken, boiled potatoes, and gravy?"

Walden's face lit. He nodded hard.

Herr Krahn smirked at Konrad. "Don't worry about packing a dinner pail. Martina won't mind fixing him a plate every day." For a moment, a shadow seemed to fall across the man's face. But as quickly as it formed, it disappeared, and he pointed to the bench where he'd been arranging tools when they arrived. "Time we get our day started. Say good-bye to your father, and we'll start by learning the names of the tools. You'll need to know what to bring me when I ask."

Walden slung his arms around Konrad's waist. "Auf Wiedersehen, Pa."

Konrad returned the hug, adding a kiss on top of Walden's new cap. "Auf Wiedersehen. Be good and do what Herr Krahn—"

The man cleared his throat.

Konrad grinned. "Onkel Gerhard tells you to do. I will see you at suppertime."

Walden's arms tightened for a few seconds, then he let go and took a step away from his father. He looked so small and uncertain standing there next to the barrel-chested older man that

Konrad almost snatched him up and ran off with him. But he'd made an agreement. And he needed to be able to work. They had to give this arrangement a try.

He waved, then turned and hustled to his wagon. Folker remained on the wagon seat, gazing forlornly toward the barn. Konrad pulled himself up beside him and lightly bounced his fist on the top of his son's uncombed head. "He'll be all right." He said it for himself as much as for Folker. "He'll be home in time for supper, and you two will have much to talk about, ja?"

"I guess so." Folker didn't sound convinced.

It was best to let the subject drop. Konrad picked up the reins and flicked them over the horses' backs. The pair of brown-coated beasts pulled their wagon off the Krahn property and toward the Dycks' house. Surely by now Frau Dyck was up and could receive a visit on her front porch. He had everything he planned to say ready in his head. He hoped he would have the courage to say it all when he was facing her.

His usually talkative son said not a word as they rattled up the street. He pressed his palms together and slipped his hands between his knees, slouching forward like an old man.

Konrad nudged him. "Sit up, please. If the wagon suddenly stops, you could pitch forward onto the horses' rumps. You wouldn't like that, and I don't think they would like it much, either."

Folker huffed and slouched backward. "I don't like leaving Walden with that man."

Konrad sighed. "'That man' is Herr Krahn." It warmed him that the wainwright told Walden to use the title *uncle* for his name. The boys had uncles—Konrad's brother who still lived in Russia and their mother's brother in Durham—but they'd never met the former and rarely saw the latter now that Hannah was gone. Having an uncle right here in Alexandertol would be nice. "Walden will be fine with him."

"But he's not with us." Folker's lower lip poked out in a pout. "I don't like it when people go away, Pa."

Suddenly Konrad understood. He shifted the reins to one hand and pulled Folker against his side. "Walden isn't staying with Herr Krahn forever. He isn't gone for good. Not like . . ." He swallowed. It still hurt to talk about Hannah going away. "Not like your mother."

Folker peered up at him. Tears brightened his blue eyes. "It feels funny, Pa. Sometimes I can't even remember what Ma looked like or sounded like. I don't want to forget Walden, too."

Konrad gave his son a squeeze and let go. "He won't be gone long enough for you to forget him. And you'll be so busy helping me in the shop you won't have time to miss him."

Folker squinted up at Konrad. "Are you sure?"

"I'm sure." He hoped he sounded sure. At that moment, he wasn't sure of anything other than he wished his wife were still alive. Since that wasn't possible, he must seek the next best thing.

The Dyck house waited just ahead. He pointed to it. "I'm going to stop here for a few minutes. I want you to wait in the wagon, like you did at the Krahns'."

Folker wiggled. "But that's Frau Dyck's house. Can't I go see her, too?"

Guilt nibbled at Konrad, but he shook his head. "Not this time. I can't stay very long. We have work to do, remember?"

Folker sighed. "Yes, Pa."

Konrad parked the wagon, set the brake, then hopped down. "Stay put." He gave his son a firm frown. He hated being strict when Folker was so sad, but this conversation needed to take place without little ears listening in. Konrad waited until Folker nodded, and then he strode to the house.

Augusta

Augusta was pouring her second cup of coffee when she heard a knock on the front door. She glanced at the little clock on the kitchen shelf. A quarter past eight in the morning was an odd time for a visitor to call. But maybe the Schmidt boys, Jasper and Eldo, had finally come to ready her garden to receive seeds. If so, she would put them to work.

"Finish your breakfast," she told Juliana and left the kitchen.

Carrying her fresh cup with her, she went to the enclosed foyer. The lace curtain on the door's oval window shrouded a shadowy figure on the other side. The person was taller and possessed broader shoulders than either of the Schmidt boys, who were both at a gangly stage.

She opened the door and gave a little start. "Why, Herr Rempel, what brings you here this morning?" She peered past him to the wagon. Folker sat on the seat, swinging his feet and gazing at the sky. Hope rose in her breast. "Did you decide to let Folker spend the day?"

"Nein. Folker is staying with me."

Disappointment fell. "Oh."

He yanked off the leather cowboy-style hat he always wore and smacked it against his thigh. "Frau Dyck, I am sorry for how I behaved at the river when you and your daughter came to fish. I was angry. At myself, I know now, but I aimed it at you. It was wrong of me, and I hope you will forgive me."

She stared at him, processing his words, which had come out in a rush, as if he needed to purge himself. "Oh. Well, of course I accept your apology, Herr Rempel. I want no ill feelings between us." All at once, her knees felt a little weak, and she realized his animosity had bothered her even more than she'd imagined.

She stepped from the foyer onto the porch, closed the door behind her, and leaned against it, cradling the warm cup in her palms. "I know you and I are not friends, certainly not the way Hannah and I"—

Pink spread across his face. Should she have mentioned Hannah? But was it better to pretend the dear woman had never existed? She'd been important to both of them for different reasons. It was too late to take back her words, so she hurried on.

—"were friends. But considering the size of the town and the fact that Folker and Walden are my students, we will see each other and talk to each other frequently." She smiled, hoping it would put him at ease. "Those interactions will be much more pleasant if we aren't at odds with each other, don't you agree?"

He swished his hat against his pant leg and nodded. The rosy color faded from his face. "Ja, I do agree, and I appreciate your kindness and sensibility."

She released a little sigh of relief. "Sehr gut. Thank you for coming by, Herr Rem—"

"Frau Dyck, I have something more to ask of you."

A hint of desperation entered his tone and alarmed her. She took a little sip of her cooling coffee, hoping it would bolster her. "All right. What do you need?"

Now he gripped his hat two-handed against his chest, wringing the brim. "I am glad you mentioned Hannah. I've been thinking about her a lot these past days. Missing her quite a lot, not only for me, but for Folker and Walden. They . . . they are growing up without a mother, and that doesn't seem right."

Sadness weighted Augusta's chest. She'd had similar thoughts concerning Juliana growing up without a father. She offered a slow, sad nod. "I agree. Sometimes, life does not seem fair."

"Nein, it does not." He curled the worn brim of the hat, his knuckles growing white. "My children need a mother. And I . . .

I need what God created for Adam, a helpmeet. I'm asking this of you because you and Hannah were friends. I know you will want to do what is best for her boys."

An uncomfortable thought formed in the back of Augusta's mind. Surely he didn't intend to ask her what she thought he wanted to ask her. Her mouth went dry, and she took a slurp of the strong coffee. "Herr Rempel, what . . ." Her voice sounded scratchy. She took another sip. "What do you want from me?"

He was going to turn his hat into a tube if he didn't stop twisting it. "The Frauenverein . . . it is formed to help people get what they need, ja?"

Still uncertain where he was leading, she managed a jerky nod. "Ja, that is correct."

"Then will you talk to the club about maybe helping me find a wife?" He sucked in a breath and seemed to hold it, his cornflower-blue eyes piercing in their intensity.

Augusta almost laughed. She'd been fearful he would propose to her. But he would misunderstand her laughter, and she had no desire to explain it to him. She stifled the urge and cleared her throat. "Ja, I will bring it up at our next meeting."

His breath whooshed out, and his shoulders sagged. "Danke, Frau Dyck. I know I can trust you because you loved Hannah and you are so kind to my boys. Thank you for caring about them."

The affection she'd held for Hannah and the affection she continued to hold for Folker and Walden rose and couldn't be squelched. She reached out and squeezed his wrist. "You are welcome, Herr Rempel. I appreciate that you love your boys enough to want them to have everything they need, including a mother. I will pray for God to lead the Frauenverein to the woman who is meant to be your helpmeet and the boys' mother."

"She must be a woman who loves children. That is what my boys need."

"A loving mother . . ." Augusta nodded.

"But not already a mother."

The forceful comment caught Augusta by surprise. "What do you mean?"

He toyed with a scorched spot on the hat's brim. "I prefer a maiden, or a widow who is childless. A woman with her own children will not be able to help but show favoritism to them."

He was probably right. Augusta had carefully guarded against showing preferential treatment to Juliana in her classroom. She offered a slow nod.

"I don't want Walden and Folker to compete for affection in their own home. I also worry I would have trouble loving someone else's children as much as I love mine. And then . . . settling in as husband and wife will be difficult enough with two children under the roof. More than that? I am not certain."

"You've given this much thought."

He nodded. "I have. I want what is best for my sons, not only what is good for me."

He was a loving father, an unselfish man. She appreciated his concern for the twins. "I understand, and I will make sure the Frauenverein understands."

A grateful smile graced his face, and he slapped the hat over his dark, wavy hair. "Danke, Frau Dyck. Have a good day now."

He strode off, climbed into the wagon, and then the wagon rattled away. Augusta moved to the edge of the porch and watched after the father and son until their wagon turned a corner and moved out of sight. Then she remained in place, her mind's eye filled with the image of Herr Rempel's shy yet hopeful expression. Certainly Frau Krahn hadn't intended the Frauenverein to serve as a matchmaking club, but she had said they would strive to meet the needs of widows and orphans. Helping Herr Rempel find a wife who could mother his boys would satisfy the intent.

"Frau Dyck?"

The male voice startled her so much she almost threw her cup in the air. She turned toward the sound. Herr Elias was standing on the sidewalk in front of her house. Heat seared her face. How long had he been there observing her gaze up the street like a woman pining for her seafaring husband's return?

He removed his bowler and held it against his chest in a courtly gesture very different from the way Herr Rempel had been mangling his hat. "May I have a word with you?"

Chapter Eleven

Augusta

A ugusta set her cup on the plant stand near the front door and came down the porch steps. Herr Elias advanced up the rock walkway, and they met just outside the patch of shade cast by the house's tall structure. She glanced up and down the block. Two male callers on one Monday morning. She hoped none of her neighbors were watching. She aimed a smile at her fellow teacher. "*Guten Morgen,* Herr Elias. How are you today?"

"I am well, although a little disappointed." His deep voice held an element of sadness that stirred her compassion.

Herr Elias's height, at least eight inches taller than Augusta's, forced her to tip her head back to look into his face. She squinted against the sun shining bright behind him. "I'm sorry your day had a rough start."

"Come, Frau Dyck." He put his hat in place and took her elbow. He then shifted them both slightly to the left, his gaze boring into hers, until full shade blocked the sunlight.

Such a thoughtful thing to do. She thanked him with a smile. "What has disappointed you?"

"As you already know, for the past six years during our school break I've worked as a hired farmworker for the Schmidt family. This year, however, Herr Schmidt said their oldest boy, Jasper, will take my place in the fields, so my help isn't needed."

Augusta instantly understood his conflict. The teaching position paid an adequate amount during the school months, but no monies were given during the break. She was fortunate that, thanks to Leopold's financial success, she needn't rely on her teacher's salary. "I'm sure that's created a hardship for you. I will pray that you're able to find another place to work during the break."

He sighed. "I've asked all around town already, and there is no job available here in Alexandertol. At least, not for someone who doesn't intend to hire on permanently. I'm on my way now to the Feed & Seed to borrow a wagon and drive to Durham. I will talk to store owners and farmers there. I appreciate your prayers for favor."

Worry tickled her. "But Durham is almost three miles away. How will you get there each day when you don't have your own wagon and horse?"

"I will have to seek temporary lodgings close to my new place of employment." A sad smile lifted the corners of his lips. "I confess, I'm not keen on giving up my quarters at the Lange homestead. Bruno and Adele have become accustomed to my monthly payment for room and board, and I'm afraid they will seek to fill the room in my absence. If so, when I return for the school year, I'll need to locate new living quarters."

"In Alexandertol?" There couldn't be many options available to one in his position. Dismay filled Augusta. She'd grown fond of Herr Elias over their years of working together. The thought of him being homeless and without a means of support made her heart ache. Then something he'd said raised another concern. "Jasper Schmidt is working all day in the fields with his father?"

Herr Elias nodded. "Ja, that is what Herr Schmidt told me."

She sent a frown in the direction of her waiting garden plot. Could Eldo do it all by himself? Certainly not as quickly. Maybe he thought it was too much to do all on his own. Maybe Herr Schmidt had already put both boys to work at his own place. So maybe they didn't intend to come at all. That would explain why they were so late this year seeing to her garden.

Herr Elias's throaty chuckle interrupted her reflections. "Frau Dyck, what are you thinking?"

She jerked her attention to him. "Pardon?"

The outer corners of his eyes crinkled with his smile. "You drifted away for a moment. Where did you go?"

She released a self-conscious chortle. "I was thinking that Jasper Schmidt being in the fields with his father has inconvenienced both of us." She briefly explained the Schmidt boys' help each year since Leopold had died.

He angled his face toward the large plot of ground, his expression thoughtful. "When do you need it done?"

"Last week," she said with a laugh. "Truthfully, I'm ready to plant seeds whenever the ground has been prepared. If the boys haven't come by Wednesday, I will talk to Frau Schmidt at Bible meeting. Then, if necessary, I can ask the Frauenverein for help."

His eyebrows rose. "The what?"

Apparently he hadn't heard about the newly formed club. "Several women from the Alexandertol Mennonite Church have come together to perform compassionate deeds for widows and orphans in our community." She wished their first deed had turned out a little differently. She would have enjoyed having the Rempel twins' lively company. Juliana would likely have enjoyed it, too. But at least she and Herr Rempel had found their peace. She would be satisfied with that outcome.

"There's no need to trouble the Frauenverein for such a simple task." He reached out and placed his fingertips lightly on her upper arm. "I would be happy to turn the soil for you, as a favor for a friend."

Surprise rattled her frame. More at his touch or his offer, she couldn't be sure. "That's very kind of you, Herr Elias, but—"

"Or you could call it payback for the sandwiches and cake you shared with me last week at the schoolhouse." He withdrew his hand, his fingers tracing a line toward her elbow. "I enjoyed that hour of relaxation very much."

Something in his gaze had warmed up, and alarm bells clanged in the back of Augusta's mind. She forced a nonchalant shrug. "A few sandwiches are hardly adequate compensation for preparing a large garden plot. As much as I appreciate your offer, it would take time away from your job search. I think perhaps seeking employment is the more important task right now, don't you agree?"

For a moment, regret seemed to purse his narrow face, but he nodded. "Ja, you are right. But"—he assumed an unsmiling stance, the way he probably silenced unnecessary talking in his classroom—"if the Schmidt boys are unavailable and the Frauenverein is unable to find someone to help, I want you to call on me. I might be a schoolteacher by profession, but I am strong and unafraid of hard work. And considering our many years of serving together under the same schoolhouse roof, we know each other well enough to request or receive a favor."

Augusta sought an appropriate response to his statement. Before one formed, the front door opened and Juliana burst onto the porch. She pattered to its edge, then slid to a stop, her wide eyes settling on Herr Elias. Even though she stood in the shade of the porch roof more than a dozen feet away, the bold red climbing her cheeks glowed like a beacon.

Grateful for the interruption, Augusta held her hand toward her daughter. "Did you need something, Juliana?"

"I . . . um . . ." She came down the steps, her hands gripped at her waist. "I didn't know you were talking to someone. I'm sorry."

Herr Elias cleared his throat. "It's all right. We were finished." His words were solicitous, but his tone held a slight edge of annoyance. He turned his full focus on Augusta. "Please let me know if you need help with the garden. For now, I should be on my way." He tipped his hat first at her, then Juliana, and strode up the sidewalk at a brisk pace.

Juliana scurried to Augusta's side. "You were gone so long I thought you might be sitting on the swing. I was going to sit with you, but then I saw . . . I saw . . ." She glanced up the street. "*Him.*"

Was resentment glimmering in her daughter's eyes? "Ja, he stopped for a few minutes on his way to an important errand."

Juliana folded her arms. "Mother, may I tell you something?"

Augusta gently tugged one of Juliana's braids. "You may tell me anything."

The girl held her lips in a scowl for a few seconds, and then she blurted, "I don't like the way Herr Elias looks at you."

"W-what?" Augusta drew back and stared at Juliana.

"He *looked* at you when we ate with him at the school. And, just now, when I came out, he was *looking* at you again." Juliana's blue eyes sparked. "He likes you."

Augusta shook her head, rattling loose the shock her child had delivered. "Well, of course he does. We work together."

The girl rolled her eyes. "Nein, Mother, he *likes* you. I can tell." And she was jealous. The emotion was as evident as the pair of freckles dotting her nose.

Augusta put her arm around her daughter and escorted her to the porch swing. She sat, tugging the girl down beside her. "If you are right"—and she likely was, based on the friendly way the man had acted on her walkway a few minutes ago—"would that be so terrible?"

Juliana's mouth fell open. "If he likes you, he might ask to court you. If he courts you, you might decide to marry him. If you marry him, my stepfather would be my teacher! Ja, that would be terrible!"

Augusta burst out laughing.

"Mother, it isn't funny." Juliana huffed. "I've had you for my teacher all these years. I'm finally old enough to leave your room and not have a parent observing my every moment. Do I not deserve some freedom?"

Still laughing, Augusta threw her arms around Juliana. She rocked the swing and held her daughter close and allowed the merriment to lift her heart. When she released Juliana, she stopped the swing's motion, then cupped her daughter's rosy cheeks in her hands and smiled. "Sweetheart, for me to allow a courtship to take place, I would first need to like the man very much."

Juliana searched her mother's face. "*Do* you like Herr Elias very much?"

"We work well together at the school. He is a good man, someone on whom I can depend. Ja, I like him." Over the years she had come to view him as a younger brother—a comfortable relationship. She tapped the end of Juliana's nose and lowered her hands. "But I don't like him the way you think he likes me."

"So . . . you won't let him court you?"

The worry in her daughter's eyes pierced her. She took one of Juliana's hands and gently squeezed it. "If ever I like a man enough to welcome his attentions, I will talk to you first. After all, he won't be courting only me. He will be courting you, too, in a different way."

Juliana sat very still and quiet for several seconds, her serious gaze latched on Augusta's face. "Do . . . do you think it will ever happen . . . that you like a man enough for . . . that?"

Augusta sighed and rested her head on the swing's scrolled back. If Juliana were a little older, Augusta might share her deepest thoughts about marriage. About how her heart still ached in loneliness for Leopold. About how, despite her needs being met, she often longed for a man's strong presence, for tender attention, companionship, and even intimacy. But an eleven-year-old should not be privy to such details.

"Mother?"

Her curious child would not rest until her question was answered. Augusta angled a smile at her. "None except God knows what tomorrow will bring. So I cannot say what might happen. But know this . . . whether I marry again or not, I will love you forever and ever. No one can ever take your place in my heart."

Juliana leaned forward and placed a kiss on Augusta's cheek, then she bounded up. "I'll take your cup inside and wash the breakfast dishes. Afterward"—she tilted her head, her expression impish—"I will take my new Stevenson book to the apple tree . . . ja?"

There were chores waiting, but before long, Juliana wouldn't ask to climb trees and read books for hours. For as long as possible, she should be given some freedoms to be a carefree child. Augusta gave a nod of approval and then shooed her away with a flick of her fingers.

Alone on the porch, she contemplated the two different morning visits and the two different visitors. Was it possible, as Juliana stated and Augusta surmised, Herr Elias was fond of her? It was a flattering thought, but it was difficult to think of him as a potential suitor. She chuckled to herself. Maybe when she told the Frauenverein members about Herr Rempel's need for a wife, she would mention Herr Elias, too. He would make a fine catch for some fortunate young woman.

Chapter Twelve

Martina

"Would you like some more potatoes, Walden?" Martina scraped up what remained of the mushy potatoes in the bowl with the serving spoon. The boy had already eaten two mounds of potatoes smothered in gravy as well as two chicken legs and a wing, but he might still be hungry. She recalled her brothers having what their father called *bottomless pits* for stomachs when they were young. She wouldn't send Walden back to the shop until he'd had his fill, no matter if Gerhard was finished and eager to return.

"Nein, danke. I am"—he burped behind his hand—"full."

Gerhard ducked his head, clearly hiding a smile, and Martina thought her heart might burst. She should scold the boy for belching at the table. Manners were important, her mother always said. But how could she criticize something that so amused her usually stoic husband?

She put the spoon in the bowl. "At least finish your milk, please. A growing boy needs to drink lots of milk." Oh, how wonderful it felt to speak in a motherly fashion to this child. She met Gerhard's gaze, and the smile in his eyes nearly brought her to tears.

Walden grabbed the glass with both hands, tipped his head back, and drained it with several noisy gulps. Then he set it on the table and released an "Ahhh" filled with satisfaction.

"If you are finished," Gerhard said, pushing to his feet, "let's go back to work."

Walden stood, too, but more slowly than Gerhard. Weariness was etched into the boy's features. Martina stretched her hand to Gerhard. "Should he rest for a bit? After all, he isn't accustomed to spending his days laboring, the way you are."

Gerhard snorted and slung his arm around Walden's narrow shoulders. "Nonsense. He's a fine, strong, strapping boy." As Gerhard spoke praise, Walden's chin came up and he stood erect, pride shining on his face. "He's ready to go back to work. Aren't you, Walden?"

The child nodded, making his thick, dark bangs bounce. He needed a haircut. When Gerhard returned to the house for his customary midafternoon snack, maybe she would bring out her shears and give the boy's hair a trim.

The two of them left, and Martina cleaned her kitchen while little remembered moments from their meal together played in her mind. At first, Walden had seemed shy, flicking uncertain glances at her and hunching his shoulders as if he wanted to make himself as small as possible. But Gerhard—who usually aimed his face at his plate and didn't say a word until his food was gone—kept talking to him, asking him questions, drawing him out. And then, when he'd finished his first serving of chicken and potatoes, he looked at her and said, "May I have some more, *Tante* Martina?"

She paused in the middle of washing a plate and pressed her wet hand to her chest, her heart fluttering. The title *aunt* wasn't nearly as good as *mother*, but so much better than *Frau*. Aunt indicated a relationship. Only one day—one meal together!— and she was building a relationship with this little boy.

And so was Gerhard. Clearly the child was at ease with her husband. But hadn't she always known he would be a good father? Before they had left Russia, the village children visited Gerhard's shop because he crafted little boats and sets of blocks from leftover pieces of wood. His joy when, early in their marriage, she whispered to him that she was expecting a child was beyond measure.

Although he built wagons and not furniture, he'd crafted a beautiful little cradle. They kept it in the corner of their sleeping room as a promise of the wonder to come. But then she lost the baby. He put the cradle in their small attic space with a promise he would bring it out again when another babe was on the way.

Three times he brought it out.

Three times he put it back.

And when governmental changes in their country had become unbearable and they made the decision to go to America, they left the cradle behind. He told her there wasn't room in their trunk to bring it, but she knew the truth. He'd given up on her. Given up on making toys for neighboring children. Given up on smiling and laughing. Given up.

He still didn't know about the two losses she suffered since they'd settled in Alexandertol, and he never would. Why should he mourn so many babies gone when it was all her fault? She pressed both palms to her belly, rounded slightly but from food instead of a growing babe, and inwardly cursed its inability to hold and nurture a child to its full development.

Sometimes she wanted to curse the Giver and Taker of life, but she couldn't bring herself to do so. If Job, who had suffered in so many ways, refused his wife's instruction to curse God and die, then she could be strong, too. But it wasn't easy.

She plunged her hands into the tepid water, and her fingers encountered the glass she'd filled with milk for Walden. A smile tugged at the corners of her lips, sending the gloom of the previous reflections into the far corners of her mind. The Gerhard who'd sat at the table with her today was more like the Gerhard she'd known in Russia than at any other time she could recall for . . . years. Walden Rempel was working magic. She could not have chosen a better apprentice. Now to hold on to hope that someday, not too long from now, they would be able to claim this little boy as their son.

Konrad

"He's here! He's here!" Folker's excited shout startled Konrad so badly he almost dropped the mallet. But he couldn't be angry. He was happy, too, that Walden was home.

He laid aside his work tools and followed Folker to the yard. The boy danced in place, his huge grin aimed at the wagon seat where Walden sat next to Herr Krahn. The man set the brake, then gave a nod, and Walden leaped over the side. At once, Folker grabbed him and wrestled him to the ground, knocking off his cap. Folker's laughter rang out.

Walden pushed at his brother, his face screwed up in disgust. "Folker, get off me!"

Folker did as Walden asked. Confusion and hurt replaced the happiness he'd exuded only moments ago.

Konrad reached the pair as they pushed to their feet. He moved between them and snagged Walden in a welcome-home hug. The boy didn't return it, but neither did he resist. Konrad set Walden aside and stifled a chortle. Sawdust peppered him from head to toe. Then Konrad frowned. Was his head less shaggy than it had been that morning?

Folker stood a few inches away, staring at his brother. He touched his own hair, his gaze rolled upward, then gaped at Walden again. He pointed. "Did you get your head stuck in a saw?"

Walden snorted—a sound of disdain. He bent over, snatched

up the cap, and positioned it on his head at a jaunty angle. "Nein. Tante Martina gave me a haircut. She said only hooligans let their hair grow long."

Konrad's face went hot. It took great effort not to reach up and smooth his own too-long hair away from his forehead. He cleared his throat. "Walden, go behind the barn and brush the dust from your clothes before you go in the house. Folker, wash up at the pump, then set the table for supper."

The twins darted off in opposite directions. Even though they were only obeying him, Konrad got a funny feeling in his stomach. Their actions seemed indicative of what was happening in their lives. He pushed aside the uncomfortable thought and looked up at Herr Krahn. "How did Walden do today?"

Herr Krahn stared after Walden. "Quite well, I think. He follows directions and is very respectful. He and I, we got much accomplished." He shifted his head and settled his somber gaze on Konrad. "Was your day productive, too?"

Taking extra precautions to keep Folker away from the most dangerous areas in the shop had slowed him some, but he got more done today than he'd accomplished all last week when both boys were home. He nodded. "Ja, it was. I am grateful."

"Good." The man barked the single word, making it sound more insult than affirmation. Walden traipsed across the yard toward the house, and Herr Krahn followed his progress with his narrowed gaze. "I commend you, Herr Rempel. Walden . . . is a good boy. You've done well raising him."

Konrad's chest swelled. "Ja, well, neither he nor his brother are perfect, but I think they are good boys. I am blessed."

The man's hooded eyes lifted past Konrad again. "Ja, you are." Then he grabbed the brake handle and gave it a firm yank. "I will see you tomorrow morning." He made a clucking sound with his teeth, and his horses pulled the wagon into motion.

Konrad returned to the shop, removed his apron, and put

away the mallet and partially completed horseshoe on which he'd been working when Folker shouted that Walden was home. He glanced around the shop. Folker had abandoned his broom when he ran off to greet his brother, but considering the unexpectedly curt response he'd received, Konrad wouldn't scold. He put the broom in the corner, then headed for the house.

Inside, Folker was circling the table, putting spoons beside each speckled plate. Konrad glanced around. "Where is your brother?"

"In his bed." Folker scuffed to the cutlery crock and pulled out three forks. "He said he is tired and wants to be left alone." The boy turned an accusing glare on Konrad. "You said Walden and me would have a lot to talk about when he got home. But he doesn't want to talk. He doesn't want me to talk, either. And I want a haircut so we look like each other again."

Konrad crossed to Folker and wrapped his son in a hug. "I think your brother put in a hard day with Herr Krahn."

"Walden called him Onkel Gerhard." Folker's voice was muffled with his face pressed to Konrad's ribs, but Konrad heard hurt in his tone. "So I called him that, and Walden got mad. He said he isn't my Onkel Gerhard, only *his*. And when I asked if I could try on his cap, he said nein, it was *his*." Folker tipped his head back and looked up at Konrad. "How come we can't both work for Herr Krahn? How come Walden gets to go and I don't?"

Konrad had chosen Walden to serve as Herr Krahn's apprentice because he was the more studious and less impulsive of the twins. If he said as much to Folker, the boy might feel as if he was less important than his brother. But Folker had good qualities, too. He was quick to show affection and had a tender heart. Konrad chose his answer carefully. "Walden gets to go, yes, but you get to stay. Just the two of us, all day long. Did you not have a good day with me?"

Folker went still, gazing upward as if deeply thinking, and finally sighed. "Ja. I liked being with you."

Konrad nearly collapsed with relief. What would he have done if Folker said nein instead? He ruffled his son's hair. "I am glad. I liked being with you, too." He had. Even though he missed Walden, it had been nice to give one boy his full attention, something very rare since they'd arrived in the world together and, until today, had always been together in his presence.

When he had a wife again and she could keep one boy with her, he would plan time with each of his sons on their own. Maybe fishing by themselves, or searching for mushrooms, or hunting quail. Time for him to really get to know them, and for them to know him. It would be a good thing for all of them.

Of course, he would also want time alone with his wife. He still remembered alone time with Hannah, treasured memories. But he shouldn't be thinking about that when he needed to put food on the table.

He gently tugged Folker's arms from around his waist and turned the boy toward the kitchen. "We need cups. Please fill yours and Walden's with milk and mine with water. It smells like the stew I put on the stove at noon is ready. After I've sliced the last of the bread from the mercantile, we'll be able to eat."

He and Folker worked companionably, as they'd done earlier that day out in the shop, and soon supper was ready. Folker sat in his chair, and Konrad went to the boys' bedroom. Walden was curled on the bed, soundly sleeping. For a moment, Konrad considered letting him sleep, but the boy needed to eat, and Konrad and Folker needed time with him.

He smoothed Walden's shorter cropped hair, then gave his shoulder a little shake. "Walden? Supper is ready."

Walden's eyes fluttered open. He looked at his father, then made a horrible face. "Pa, I was dreaming."

Konrad chuckled. He'd been deeply sleeping. "Ja, well, you

can finish the dream later. Come and eat, and hang your cap on the bedpost on your way."

Walden grunted, but he swung his feet to the floor and followed Konrad to the table. Konrad asked a blessing for the meal, and he and Folker picked up their spoons and began to eat.

Walden sat with his hands in his lap and examined the food on his plate. "Tante Martina made fried chicken for my dinner today. It was so good." He closed his eyes for a few seconds, as if making a birthday wish. He opened them and looked at the stew again. "How come you never make fried chicken, Pa?"

Because stews and beans were easier for him to cook. He wasn't sure he'd even know how to cut up a chicken. Or clean one. If he raised them, which he did not. He swallowed a bite of stew. "Frying a chicken takes a lot of time and work. My work is in the shop. I don't have time to fry chickens." He folded a piece of bread and took a big bite.

Walden still didn't pick up his spoon. "Maybe you could ask Tante Martina to fry a chicken for us sometime."

After only one day, suddenly the food in this house wasn't good enough? Konrad grunted. "God provides our daily bread and we will be grateful for it." Walden's eyes widened, and Folker paused with his spoon halfway to his mouth and stared at his father. Maybe Konrad should have held back the scolding retort. He didn't want to argue with Walden after they'd been apart all day, but it seemed as if he'd come home dissatisfied with his brother and his father. He bobbed his chin at Walden's plate. "Tonight we're eating stew. Get to it before it's cold."

Walden sighed and picked up his spoon. He scooped a carrot dripping with gravy and carried it to his mouth. He continued eating without another word of complaint, but Konrad lost his enjoyment in the meal. Sometimes he, too, got tired of stews and beans. Hannah had been a very good cook, able to make fried grouse or roasted pork. She baked her own bread and cakes and pies—all things Konrad didn't know how to make. Should he have told Frau Dyck that his new wife needed to be able to fry chicken and bake bread?

Tomorrow, after he took Walden to work, he might stop by her house again and mention these things. If the Frauenverein was going to find the right wife, they needed to know everything he wanted.

Folker leaned over his plate, and his hair fell across his eyes. Konrad cringed. And on Saturday, he and Folker would visit the town's barbershop. When his new wife came, he couldn't let her think he and his sons were hooligans.

Chapter Thirteen

Augusta

As Augusta performed her usual Friday task of bread baking for the coming week, she reflected on the past five days. That particular Monday through Friday in April 1895 would likely remain the oddest week of her life. Two morning visitors on Monday, both of them men, had been strange enough. But then to have those same men return each morning—Herr Rempel adding to his list of "must haves" for the wife he wanted the Frauenverein to seek for him, and Herr Elias giving updates on his search for a job—added to the uniqueness.

On Wednesday evening, Frau Schmidt had confirmed that Jasper and Eldo were unavailable to prepare her garden plot. Herr Elias immediately volunteered to take care of it and had arrived early Thursday morning. She gave a start at his appearance. She'd never seen him wear anything except a suit, and the sight of his tall frame in a pair of brown duck overalls and cambric work shirt made him seem like a stranger. However, his work ethic in the garden was no less diligent than in the classroom. He did a fine job chopping out the weeds with a hoe and then making use of the hand cultivator from her shed until every clod was eradicated.

She offered to pay him what she would have paid the Schmidt boys, but he acted offended and rejected her money. On impulse, to make amends, she invited him to supper. He agreed without a moment's hesitation. Then he stayed well into the evening hours, seemingly reluctant to return to his room at the

Langes'. He finally departed when Augusta said it was past Juliana's bedtime.

Although Herr Rempel didn't come today, Herr Elias did. He told her in a solemn tone, "I'm driving to Marion today. I pray there is a job for me there." She assured him she would say a prayer for him, too. Then, as bashful as she'd ever seen him, he gave her a small box of chocolate candies he'd purchased at Weber's General Merchandise as a thank-you for Thursday's supper. She accepted it, too stunned to do otherwise, but she inwardly prayed that Elsie Weber surmised he had bought it for himself.

Nothing untoward had occurred between her and either of the men, but she feared that by now her neighbors' tongues were wagging. So much activity at her home in a short span of time. But what could she do? She wasn't unkind enough to tell either man to stay away. And she truly cared about their dilemmas. So she received her visitors, prayed over their needs, and hoped that once both were met, things would return to normal. Because even more troubling than the neighbors' curiosity was Juliana's reactions to the men's visits.

The girl found great amusement in the reason for Herr Rempel's early morning knocks at their door. To Augusta's chagrin, on Tuesday morning, her inquisitive daughter had listened from an open parlor window. She severely scolded her for snooping and Juliana quickly apologized, but the twinkle in her eyes indicated a lack of true remorse.

It bothered Augusta that Juliana could find something humorous in Herr Rempel's serious need. And her response to Herr Elias's visits could only be defined as resentful. Juliana would sit under Herr Elias's instruction for the next six years of her schooling. If she held animosity toward the man, her education might suffer. Augusta needed to change Juliana's opinion of Herr Elias.

After Herr Elias departed, Augusta had escorted her daughter to the garden plot and praised the fine job he'd done preparing the soil to receive seeds. Then she gave Juliana the responsibility of putting the beet, radish, and pea seeds in the ground. "While you're working," she told the girl, "consider how Herr Elias's kindness has made it so much easier for you to do your part."

Juliana's lips pressed into a thin line, but she nodded.

Indeed, the week confounded Augusta in many ways, but she thanked God for the opportunity to increase her time in prayer. Extra time with the Father was never wasted.

As she removed an aromatic browned loaf from the oven, the back screen door smacked into its casing and Juliana entered the kitchen. She sniffed the air and sighed. "It smells heavenly in here, Mother. May I have a slice?"

"Not until it cools." Augusta gave the same answer she always gave when Juliana begged to cut into a fresh loaf. "We still have a little left from last week's baking. We'll finish that before we slice into one of these new ones."

Juliana looked longingly at the steaming loaf of bread, but she didn't argue.

Augusta took the second loaf from the oven, then closed the oven door. "Have you finished planting already?"

"Ja, and I speared a packet with a stake and pushed it into the ground at the end of each row so we'll know what's growing there. I also cleaned the hoe, put it away, and sprinkled water over the planted rows."

Augusta smiled. "Thank you, sweetheart."

Juliana crossed to the sink. She pumped the handle and filled a glass with water. She guzzled the entire glass and then said, "Ahhh." She set the glass aside and angled a scowl at her mother. "While I was planting the peas, Frau Bauer came by. She said she'd seen Herr Elias here yesterday with the very same hoe I was using, and she wondered if you'd hired him as a gardener.

But seeing me working in the garden told her you probably hadn't, or you would have had him plant the seeds, too."

Augusta paused in adding another shovelful of coal to the firebox. "I hope you didn't say anything she could carry away and repeat."

Juliana rolled her eyes. "Everyone knows how she likes to talk. I didn't say anything except 'danke' when she praised me for being so helpful."

Augusta nearly sagged in relief. "Good girl." She dumped the coal and hung the shovel on its hook.

"I didn't need to say anything more. She did enough talking for both of us." Juliana leaned against the counter and folded her arms, her blue eyes spitting fire. "She said it was high time you remarried so there would be a man to take care of such things as the garden and lawn and trimming the trees. She said—"

Augusta held up her hand. "Hush, please, Juliana. I don't care to hear anything more from Frau Bauer's gossipy lips."

Juliana jolted away from the counter. "Nor do I. Especially not about you and a parade of men coming to call."

Augusta's mouth dropped open. "W-what?"

"Ja, that is what she said to me. She said people in town are happy you're finally receiving callers." The girl's face mottled with pink. "Why are people so nosy?"

Augusta could have pointed out that Juliana had been nosy when she listened in on her conversation with Herr Rempel, but she'd already reprimanded her for it. The Bible admonished parents not to provoke their children to wrath, and such a reminder would, at the least, stir resentment. Besides, she seemed to have lost the ability to speak she was so stunned by what her daughter had told her.

"I wanted to tell her there has not been a parade of men here." Juliana's voice quavered. "Two. Only two. And only one who truly came to call the way a suitor would. But even he isn't a suitor. You said so yourself."

Her fine eyebrows crunched into a deep frown. "I didn't tell her anything, but you should talk to her and make her understand why Herr Elias and Herr Rempel have made so many visits. Otherwise, she will keep talking to people all over town. I don't want my friends teasing me."

Augusta captured Juliana in an embrace. "I am very proud of you for staying quiet when Frau Bauer said such ridiculous things. Holding your tongue takes a great deal of self-control, and your doing so proves you are growing up." She released Juliana and toyed with the humidity-frizzed end of one of her braids. "The Frauenverein meets tonight. When I report the needs Herr Rempel and Herr Elias have shared with me, the women will understand why the men have come by here. That should put an end to the gossip."

Juliana huffed. "I hope so."

So did Augusta. Once the gossip wheels started turning, they could be hard to stop. She gave the braid a light tug and released it. "Wash your hands now and change out of your work apron. We'll have some sandwiches, and then you may spend the afternoon reading."

"May I go to Laura's instead? She is keeping watch over her little brother and sister, and I could help her. I like pretending I am their big sister, too."

Augusta's heart twisted in her chest. If only she and Leopold had been able to have more than one child. Then Juliana wouldn't have to pretend. Although Augusta worried the Webers might think Juliana came over too much, she granted permission.

Juliana went to the hallway wash basin, and Augusta slid the last two pans of dough into the oven. She wiped her hands on her apron and turned to the crock holding her knives. She chose the slender one for slicing bread, then paused. She should use up the remaining heel of last week's bread, but a sandwich on fresh-baked bread would brighten Juliana's spirits. After remaining silent in the face of Agnes Bauer's gossipy chatter, the girl deserved a treat.

Augusta laid one of the still-warm loaves on her cutting board and gently sawed. Sandwiches on fresh bread now, and—by the close of tonight's meeting—an end to the ridiculous speculations. Both should make Juliana feel better.

Martina

Martina had Frau Dyck take roll, and then she opened the third meeting of the Frauenverein with prayer. She'd had such a wonderful week with little Walden Rempel brightening her and Gerhard's lives, it was easy to praise God. She closed her prayer by saying a heartfelt "Amen" and sent a sincere smile across the women clustered together on the front two benches.

"Thank you for coming tonight. I will begin our meeting by sharing that our first action as a club, aiding Herr Rempel in supervising his twins, is a success." Her mind's eye flooded with images of Walden's milk mustache, Walden's bright grin, Walden's sawdust-spattered, fresh-cut hair. The sounds of his cheerful chatter and endearing giggle were sweet in remembrance. "Herr Rempel is able to work without interruption because one twin is apprenticed to my Gerhard, and the other serves under his father's instruction in the blacksmith shop. Let us give ourselves congratulations for serving the widower's need so well."

She started clapping, and the others joined her. When she stopped, they did, too. "And now please share needs of which you've become aware over the past week."

Agnes Bauer stood so quickly the bench popped. "Frau Krahn, are we able to minister to those who are members of this committee?"

Augusta Dyck was the only widow in the club. Or maybe Agnes wanted to do something for Augusta's daughter, who was a half-orphan. Martina offered a slow nod, avoiding looking in the widow's direction. "If a need exists, ja."

Agnes's expression turned smug. "Ja, well, I think our own Frau Dyck has need of someone to do work in her yard. Only this morning, I saw her daughter laboring in their large garden plot. Such a slip of a girl, all by herself out there. I—"

"Frau Krahn?" Augusta's firm voice carried over whatever else Agnes had intended to say. "I appreciate Frau Bauer's concern, but I can assure you, we do not need help with our garden. The difficult task of cultivation is already done, performed as a kind favor by my fellow teacher, Herr Elias. From now on, Juliana and I can take care of the weeding and harvesting." Although the woman maintained a pleasant expression, something akin to irritation glimmered in her hazel eyes. "Let us please put our attention on pressing needs in our community."

Martina held out her hands. "Agnes, you heard Augusta. Thank you for your concern, but she and her daughter are capable of seeing to their garden. So . . ." Martina scanned their faces. "Are there, as Augusta phrased it, other pressing needs to bring before the committee?"

Sallie Bair mentioned widow Rosa Schulz's leaky porch roof. "If it doesn't get fixed soon, the floorboards could rot. That would be dangerous for her." After a brief discussion, Elsie Weber stated she would bring the matter to her husband, who would likely provide the materials needed, and Martha Gotwals volunteered her oldest son to make the repairs.

Then Clara Knoll told them widow Alma Koch's cow had gone dry. The woman didn't intend to purchase another, but she did have need of milk each week and was willing to pay for it. At once, Annie Guenst, whose brother owned the only dairy farm in Alexandertol, said she would ask him to deliver a bucket of milk to Frau Koch each week.

Martina couldn't stop smiling. Things were going so well, with women discovering needs and others finding ways to meet those needs. Since her own deep desire for a child at her table had already been fulfilled, she'd considered stepping down from leading the committee. Now she was glad she hadn't. Witnessing these acts of benevolence was a gratifying experience—almost as exciting as Christmas morning when she was a child. She thanked both Clara and Annie for their kindnesses, and then asked, "Does anyone else have a need to share with the club?"

Augusta Dyck raised her hand.

Martina aimed a concerned frown at the woman. "Did you change your mind, Augusta, and you would like us to find a helper for your garden?"

She shook her head and stood. "Nein. As I said, Juliana and I are fine. I have another request, though, one that will benefit Herr Rempel."

Martina raised her eyebrows. What else could Herr Rempel need? "Oh? What is it?"

Augusta sent a side-eyed glance at Agnes, then met Martina's gaze. "As we all know, he has been a widower now for three years." A murmur, sympathetic in tone, rolled through the room. "Although he still misses Hannah and mourns her, he needs a helpmeet. Additionally, his boys are growing up without a mother. He believes it is wise for him to consider marrying again, not only for his sake, but for the twins' sakes, too."

Martina's pulse doubled its tempo, fear capturing her. Only one week. One glorious week. Now would the child who had brought so much joy and laughter to her life be snatched away?

She tried to rein in her scrambled thoughts and form a coherent response that wouldn't give away her selfish want.

"Frau Krahn, may I speak?" Isabella Zimmerman was holding her hand in the air.

Martina, still struggling to find words, nodded to her.

Isabella rose, her face pinched into a pitying frown. "I am not hard-hearted about Herr Rempel's needs. If something were to happen to me, Nicolaus would look for someone to be his partner and help him raise our children. But choosing a wife is a personal thing. Men and women are attracted to each other for different reasons. How does Herr Rempel expect us to know what kind of woman is suitable for him?"

Augusta removed a folded piece of paper from her pocket and held it up. "He gave me a list to guide us." She looked at Martina, her expression hopeful. "May I read it?"

Chapter Fourteen

Konrad

Konrad lay awake in his bed, his hands linked on his stomach. Dark surrounded him, and the night's music—crickets' chirping, frogs' croaking, coyotes' distant yips, an owl's occasional *hoot*—drifted through the open window in a soothing lullaby. He should be asleep. He was tired. So tired after a week of working twice as hard to do his job and also keep Folker occupied and safe. But his mind would not stop tormenting him. He feared he'd made a terrible mistake.

The Frauenverein met this evening. When Frau Dyck gave the ladies his list of attributes for a new wife, had they laughed? Frau Dyck hadn't laughed. But he'd known she wouldn't, or he wouldn't have trusted her with the request. Hannah had trusted her as a friend. He trusted her as his sons' teacher. Ja, he could trust her, but what about the other club members? Would they think he was foolish for asking them to help? Would they think he was foolish for thinking a woman would want to marry him and help take care of his boys?

His hand drifted to the scarred side of his face. Tomorrow he and Folker would have haircuts, but he wouldn't allow the barber to trim his hair short above his ears. Nor would he ask for a shave. He slid his fingers over the patchy whiskers that covered the rippled skin on his jaw and then touched his misshapen ear. He cringed.

Hannah hadn't minded his scars. She'd known him from childhood, even from before he'd fallen into Vater's forge.

Maybe she remembered the way he'd looked before his face got burned and that's why she wasn't bothered by his scars. But a new wife, one who'd never seen him before, would probably see nothing except his scars when she met him for the first time.

He slapped his hand down, inwardly berating himself. He should have gone to Frau Dyck's house this morning with one final request. That she remove the description *comely* from the list of necessary attributes. A woman who viewed herself as comely would want a man equally attractive. He would have been handsome were it not for his accident. He knew this because he looked like his brother, and girls had always flocked around Karl. But Hannah—sweet, tenderhearted Hannah—chose him.

A groan built in his chest. Why did she have to die? Death during childbirth was common. Too common. But she'd delivered twins without complication. It made no sense that delivering their baby girl would take her life. He knew all the biblical answers for situations like this. The number of every person's days were written in God's book before one of them came to be. God was the Giver and Taker of life. Because Hannah knew God's Son, she now resided safe and healthy and joyful with Jesus in heaven. All these things should comfort him, and sometimes they did, but other times . . . like now . . . they only taunted him. How he'd loved her. How could he even think of replacing her with another wife?

"Pa? Can I come in?"

The trembling whisper came from outside Konrad's door. He sat straight up. "Ja, *du kannst reinkommen.*"

The door creaked open and a shadowy figure crept to the side of Konrad's bed. Folker. His still-shaggy hair was standing on end. Konrad cupped his son's head, pressing some of the strands into place. "What is the matter? Did you have a bad dream?"

Folker nodded. "We were fishing, and the fish pulled me into the river. It pulled so hard it pulled me out of bed and woke me up."

Konrad gave a start. How had he not heard his son hit the floor? He must have been too deeply lost in thought. "Did you hurt yourself?"

"Nein, I am all right, but the covers came off the bed with me when I fell out. It woke Walden up and made him mad." Folker sniffled. "I don't want to sleep with him now."

The week apart from each other hadn't brought an end to his sons' spats, the way Konrad had hoped. Instead, it seemed to have created new conflicts between the boys. He preferred not to have wiggly Folker and his cold feet in bed with him, but he didn't have the heart to refuse. He lifted his sheets. "Sleep with me." Folker dove onto the bed. His forehead collided with Konrad's shoulder, and Konrad grunted. "But you have to lie still. If you keep me awake, I'll carry you back to your room."

"I'll be still." Folker wriggled onto his side, his knees against Konrad's hip. At least his feet were pointing away. "Danke, Pa. I won't have bad dreams in here. I'm safe with you."

Warmth flooded Konrad's frame. Such confidence his son placed in him. For a while after his accident, Konrad had lost confidence in his Vater's ability to keep him safe. He'd questioned God's ability to keep him and his loved ones safe, too, when Hannah died. But Folker still trusted. Konrad sent up a silent, heartfelt prayer that his little boys would always feel safe—would *be* safe—with him. If they trusted their earthly father, it would be easier for them to trust their heavenly Father.

Konrad placed a kiss on his son's forehead, then he, too, shifted onto his side, facing Folker. He stared at his son's peaceful face, pale against the night shadows. He loved his boys so much it sometimes made his chest ache. He had loved them since the first time he held them in his arms. Maybe even before.

But they were too big to be cradled now. Were they too big for a new mother to love them?

The troubling thought kept him awake long after the frogs and crickets gave up their chorus.

Konrad slid into the barber's chair in front of the big mirror. Behind him, reflected by the mirror, his sons sat quietly side by side on a bench. Sticks of peppermint poked like cigars from their mouths. Ben Warkentine, the kindly barber, gave a striped candy stick to any boy who stayed still in his chair. Only Folker got a haircut today since Frau Krahn had trimmed Walden's hair already, but when the barber gave Folker his treat, Folker broke the stick in two and offered half to his brother. Such a small gesture, but after the skirmishes of the past week and especially Walden's unsympathetic reaction to his brother falling out of bed, seeing Folker share his candy—a rare treat—gave Konrad's spirits a mighty lift.

Herr Warkentine snapped the protective cotton cloth over Konrad's shirt and tucked it into his collar. He picked up a comb and shears from the counter and angled them at Konrad's head.

Konrad caught his eye in the mirror. "Please leave it—"

"Longer on the ears and neck." The barber finished Konrad's sentence for him, grinning. "Ja, I've been cutting your hair long enough to know how you like it." He made the first snips. "But I'm wondering who else in town is cutting hair now. Someone did a pretty good job on Walden's head. Not as even as I would get it"—he winked at Konrad's reflection—"but pretty good."

Konrad held very still under the scissor's *snip-snip*. He'd had to get stern with Walden about leaving his cap at home, but maybe he should have let him wear it. Then the barber wouldn't have noticed the boy's haircut. "Walden has been helping at Herr Krahn's wheelwright shop. One day when he was over there, Frau Krahn trimmed his hair."

"Ah. I'd heard you had apprenticed one of your boys to Gerhard Krahn." He combed a strand on the top of Konrad's head straight up and trimmed a half inch from its length. The cut bits rained down on Konrad's shoulder. "I bet you didn't expect haircutting to be part of the bargain."

"Nein, I did not." And Konrad still wasn't sure how he felt about the woman cutting his son's hair. She probably meant it as a kindness, but it felt like an insult. As if he wasn't capable of seeing to it himself. "She saved me a quarter, though, so for that I am grateful."

The barber laughed, the sound merry. "Well, I am happy for you, then." He continued trimming the top, sending little pieces of hair flying. "She cuts Gerhard's hair. He never visits my barbershop except to buy a bottle of tonic now and then. I hope she doesn't decide to open a shop. This town isn't big enough for two barbers."

Guilt suddenly attacked Konrad. One of the things he'd put on his list for Frau Dyck was *Able to trim hair.* Hannah had always cut his hair for him. She'd cut the boys' hair, too. But he'd been coming to the barbershop for a long time now. Maybe Ben now depended on the six bits Konrad paid him every month for haircuts.

"Well, even if she does," Konrad said with more emphasis than he'd intended, "my boys and I will keep coming to you. You do a fine job."

The barber made one more *snip!* and then he yanked the cloth away. Bits of dark-brown hair scattered like confetti all around the chair. He grabbed a broom and began sweeping the hair into a pile. While he swept up, Konrad checked his reflection. Neatly trimmed on top, parted on the left, and combed away from his face. Longer sides hid the top half of his ears. The nape hair hung over his collar and covered the scars on his neck. Ja, Ben Warkentine knew just how Konrad liked his hair cut.

He pushed out of the chair and dug in his pocket for his money. He placed three twenty-five-cent pieces on the counter, then gestured to his sons. "Come now, boys."

The barber reached for the dustpan, and he laughed. He picked up one of the quarters. "Konrad, you're so used to me cutting everyone's hair that you paid me for three haircuts." He held the coin out to Konrad. "You had better take this back."

Konrad shook his head and settled his hat into place over his new haircut. "Nein, you keep it. Thank you for the good job."

Ben dropped the coin in a pocket on his apron. "Very well. You and your boys have a good day."

"Danke. You, too." Konrad ushered the twins out the door. On the boardwalk, he hesitated. He'd planned to go to the mercantile and purchase a few food items, but the store looked crowded with customers. The boys had been sitting for a while and were fidgety. They might not have the patience for shopping. Maybe he should run his other errand first. The most important one, even if it would be hard to do. His mother always advised getting the hardest tasks done first. She was a wise woman.

"Come, boys, let's get in the wagon." He swung Folker up first, then Walden, and climbed up behind them. The ride to Frau Dyck's house didn't take long, and the boys shared grins and bumped each other with their elbows when he drew the team to a stop in front of her house.

"Can we get down, too?" Folker gave his father a hopeful look. He was probably remembering having to sit in the wagon and wait while Konrad talked with Frau Dyck near her porch every morning after dropping Walden at the Krahns'.

"You may run and play in Frau Dyck's yard."

Both boys cheered.

Konrad put out his hand. "But don't go near the garden plot. There are little signs there that show what will grow in the rows." Hannah had done the same thing. "Nothing is growing yet, but you might trample the signs, and then Frau Dyck won't know what's planted there."

"Ja, Pa, we'll stay away from the garden," they chorused, and he gave them permission to hop down.

While they ran to the side yard, Konrad strode toward the porch. Halfway up the walk, he paused. Had she gone to town for shopping like so many others? Then he noticed the front door standing open. She wouldn't leave it that way if she wasn't home. He hurried the final few feet and knocked on the door's casing.

Her daughter, wearing an apron over her dress and carrying a feather duster, answered. She pushed the screen door open. "Guten Tag, Herr Rempel. Have you come to see Mother?"

They must be housecleaning. Should he intrude? He took off his hat and worried it in his hands. "Ja, but I will only stay if she isn't too busy to be bothered."

The girl turned and disappeared beyond the little enclosed foyer. Moments later, Frau Dyck came to the door. She, too, wore a work apron and had a scarf tied over her hair. A smudge of something marked her chin. Coal dust, maybe? Or shoe blacking? He couldn't help staring at it, the way most people couldn't help staring at his scars.

Then she smiled, and his attention was stolen by the welcome in her eyes. "Herr Rempel, I'm glad you came by. I'm sure you're eager for word about the Frauenverein's decision."

"Ja. Ja, I . . ." He shrugged. "I can talk to you another time, though, if you have work to finish."

She glanced over her shoulder, stepped onto the porch, and

then pulled the door closed behind her. "This is fine if you don't mind my bedraggled appearance. I was giving my fireplace its spring cleaning. The weather has been so pleasant I doubt we'll use it again until fall."

"Ja, that . . . that's probably true." Why was he tongue-tied? He hadn't been shy when he brought her his list of want-haves. "Did the women laugh at what I asked for?"

"Laugh?" Her eyes widened. "Oh, no, Herr Rempel. No one laughed."

He hadn't realized how much he'd worried over it until she answered. His spine seemed to wilt, and a huge breath wheezed from his lungs. "Good. That is . . . good."

Compassion flooded her features. "Everyone understood your need, but I'm afraid the vote didn't go in your favor."

He straightened. "Oh?" He couldn't decide if he was more happy or more disappointed in this report.

"One member in particular was concerned about the Frauen-verein being viewed as a matchmaking organization." Pink streaks formed on her cheeks. "I think she instilled worry in some other members' minds. So the decision was that we shouldn't take on such a task as a club, but—"

A burst of laughter erupted nearby, and Folker and Walden dashed around the corner. They pounded up the porch steps and slid to a stop in front of their teacher, still laughing. Folker tugged at her apron. "Frau Dyck, guess what?"

Konrad caught hold of Folker's shoulder and pulled him away from the woman. He scowled down at the pair. "Boys, can't you see that Frau Dyck and I are talking? You know better than to interrupt when grown-ups are talking."

Folker hunched his shoulders and offered a sheepish grin. "I'm sorry, Pa, but Walden—" He jolted and then gaped at Frau Dyck's face for a few seconds. He pointed. "What is that?"

Konrad inwardly groaned. Of course Folker wouldn't ignore the smear on the woman's chin. He leaned down and whispered, "Son, you're being very impolite."

"But she's got—"

"A little bit of dirt on her face, ja, I know." He glanced at Frau Dyck, offering a silent apology with his grimace, then glared at his bold son. "You and your brother, go play. We'll talk about your behavior later."

Folker grabbed Walden by the arm, and the two raced off.

Konrad stood upright and turned to Frau Dyck. "I'm sorry. I try to teach them better manners."

"Please don't apologize." She lifted her apron skirt and rubbed her cheeks. The effort did nothing to remove the smudge or the embarrassed flush. "Did I get it?"

He shook his head. "Nein. It's . . ." He tapped his own whiskered chin.

She scrubbed again. When she lowered the apron skirt, most of the smudge was gone. "Now?" Only a bit remained along her jawline.

He pulled his handkerchief from his pocket and held it up. "May I?"

The pink in her face brightened, but she nodded.

He was sure his face was flaming red, but he gently swiped at the dust. She stood very still, her eyes aimed at the blue-painted ceiling, her hands tangled in her apron skirt. His hands trembled. Was he really cleaning the teacher's face in broad daylight where anyone could see? He performed this duty for his boys countless times every week, but doing it for Augusta Dyck made his stomach flutter. Even so, he wiped the streak until her chin was clean. Then he shoved the handkerchief into his pocket and kept his hand in there, wadding the cloth in his fist. "There. All gone."

Her gaze flitted to his, and a shy smile curved her lips. "Danke,

Herr Rempel. Now . . . as I was saying, the Frauenverein voted not to take on the responsibility for searching for a new wife for you."

He nodded, the motion jerky. "I understand."

She lifted her slender hand to him. "But a search will take place."

Confused, he frowned. "It will? How?"

Her smile broadened, and she held her head at a proud angle. "Who better than I, who knew Hannah so well, to search for the woman who will be your helpmeet and your boys' new mother?"

Chapter Fifteen

Augusta

Herr Rempel stared at Augusta with his mouth hanging open. She couldn't discern whether his reaction meant he was happy. But shouldn't he be happy? She cleared her throat, covering a nervous chortle. "Herr Rempel? Is it all right with you if I begin a search for your new wife?" He didn't speak. She swallowed. "You do want a helpmeet, ja?"

His mouth snapped closed so abruptly, his teeth clicked. His entire frame gave a little jerk, and finally he nodded. "Ja. Ja, I do want—need—a helpmeet. I am just . . . I did not expect . . ." He pulled in a big breath and whooshed it out. "Danke, Frau Dyck. I knew I could trust you."

Unexpectedly, tears stung her eyes. Nothing could have pleased her more than him proclaiming she had his trust. Especially since Hannah had once confided how much he struggled with trusting people because of the way some reacted to his scarred face. Secure in his support, she shared the plans she'd made after last night's meeting. "I will start the search by placing ads in newspapers in some of the larger cities here in Kansas. If it is all right with you, I'll also ask Herr Elias to share the names of any unmarried women or young widows in Marion County with me."

Herr Rempel's forehead puckered. "Herr Elias, the schoolteacher? How does he know all the people in Marion County?"

She couldn't hold back a soft laugh. In her eagerness to help her dear friend's husband and sons, she was getting ahead of herself. "He doesn't yet. But he will. He came by earlier with the good news that he found a temporary job stocking shelves in the Marion Mercantile. Since most residents of the smaller communities near Marion go there to shop, he will likely encounter women of a marriageable age."

For a moment, doubt intruded. Would Herr Elias agree to help? He might prefer to seek a wife for himself instead of one for Herr Rempel. But the two men were so different they would probably be attracted to women who were different, too. She set aside the idle thought and returned her attention to the guest on her porch. "When I have names, I will personally contact the women, discern their interest in matrimony, and then conduct informal interviews to ascertain if any match the list of needs you gave me."

"Concerning my list . . ." He swallowed and fiddled with his hat brim. "You should take away the need for the woman to be comely. Her appearance . . . it's . . ." He glanced aside and then turned a self-conscious grimace on her. "Insignificant. What matters is the kind of person she is on the inside."

What a wise observation. She smiled and placed her fingers lightly on his elbow. "I agree that one's inside counts more than the exterior. I will remember what you said. And, most importantly, I will pray for God to lead me to the woman He has chosen for you. He knows the desire of your heart, and He loves you enough to provide it. You said you trust me, and I'm glad you do, but we can both trust Him—the One who created the very first helpmeet for the very first man—even more, ja?"

He offered a jerky nod, his eyes glimmering.

She lowered her hand. "Do you have any questions or suggestions?"

"Nein. Not right now. You've made a good plan, Frau Dyck. I

will wait for you to tell me if you find someone." He slapped his hat onto his head. "I thank you for your kindness. You . . . you are a good friend." He turned and hurried toward his wagon, calling for his boys to come.

The twins dashed from the side yard, waving to Augusta as they ran. Herr Rempel lifted them into the bed of the wagon, and then he climbed up onto the seat. As he gripped the reins, he glanced in her direction.

She raised her hand in farewell. He bobbed his head, his mustache lifting with his smile. He flicked the reins, and the wagon rolled away. Augusta sighed, happy with how well their conversation had gone. But now she should finish cleaning so she'd have time to prepare a good supper. She went inside and knelt in front of the fireplace.

Juliana breezed out of the library, swishing the feather duster against her skirt, and stopped beside her mother. "I dusted all the furniture, the tops of the baseboards, and the windowsills. And I swept the kitchen, library, and our bedrooms. But I can't sweep in here until you've finished making your mess."

Augusta laughed. "Cleaning the fireplace does make a mess, doesn't it? I will clean up after myself when I'm done."

Juliana's face lit. "Then I'm all done with chores?"

"Not quite." Augusta sat back on her heels and looked up at her daughter. "Would you please fetch some potatoes and carrots from the cellar and peel them for our supper? Six of each should do. I'll roast them with the cut of beef I bought at the butcher yesterday."

Juliana's brow furrowed. "I thought the roast was for Sunday dinner. Are we having our Sunday dinner early?"

"Ja, because we're having company for supper tonight. Herr Elias is coming over to eat with us."

Juliana didn't say anything, but her eyes narrowed slightly.

"We are helping him celebrate. He has been looking for a job to do during the school break, and he found one in Marion."

A sly grin formed on her daughter's face. "In Marion? That's fifteen miles away. Is he going to move there?"

Although she rarely discussed grown-up topics with her daughter, Augusta decided in this case, Juliana needed to know the details. Her imaginative daughter might misconstrue things otherwise, and sharing answers to prayer would help grow Juliana's faith.

Augusta caught hold of Juliana's wrist, stilling the swish of the duster. "Nein, he isn't moving there, but he will spend weekdays in Marion and return to Alexandertol for weekends. God was very gracious in providing not only a job, but a little room above the mercantile in which he can stay during the week and the use of a horse from the livery in Marion to go back and forth. This way, he will be able to keep his room at the Langes' and continue attending church in his own community." Not to mention he would be in the perfect place to meet marriageable women, one of whom might prove to be the answer to Herr Rempel's prayers. She gave Juliana's wrist a light squeeze, smiling. "Do not all these answers to prayer warrant a celebration?"

Juliana shrugged. "I suppose so. But why must he celebrate here? Doesn't he have any other friends?"

Augusta gasped. "Juliana, what an unkind thing to ask. Whether he has other friends or not doesn't matter. The Bible instructs us to rejoice with those who rejoice, and in this house we will do what God calls us to do."

Juliana hung her head. "I'm sorry, Mother. I didn't mean to sound rude. I just don't like giving people reasons to talk about us."

Augusta rose and embraced her daughter. "You're forgiven." Then she took hold of Juliana's shoulders and peered into her face. "Sweetheart, some people like to talk. It makes them feel important, I suppose. But we can't decide what we will do based on what someone else might do. We must do whatever is right, and I believe it is right for us to celebrate Herr Elias's new job with him."

"Because you and he teach at the same school?"

Augusta nodded.

The sly smile returned. "Good. That's what I will tell people if they ask why Herr Elias came for supper. Then they won't make up other reasons for him coming over." She stepped free of Augusta's touch. "I'll get the potatoes and carrots ready for the roasting pan. And then may I—"

A knock at the front door interrupted her. Juliana started in that direction, but Augusta intercepted her. "I'll see to it. You go peel the vegetables."

Juliana sighed, but she headed for the kitchen.

Augusta hurried to the door, shaking her head. Who could it be this time? She'd never before had so many visitors in one week. To her surprise, Martina Krahn was waiting on the porch. Augusta opened the screen door. "Why, Frau Krahn, hello. Please come in."

The woman crossed the threshold and stopped just inside the door. She set her unsmiling gaze on Augusta. "Augusta, I'm sorry to come unannounced, but I had such trouble sleeping last night. And all morning, I have battled worry. I couldn't put off this visit a moment longer."

Shivers rattled down Augusta's spine. "Is something wrong?"

"Ja, there is." Martina folded her arms. "This plan of yours to play matchmaker for Herr Rempel is destined for disaster. I must ask you to reconsider taking part in such an activity."

Martina

Everything within her wanted to beg God to make Augusta do what she asked. But God wouldn't honor such a selfish request. All she could do was hold her haughty position and hope she might be able to cow the other woman into giving up her pursuit.

A puzzled frown appeared on the schoolteacher's face, but she showed no signs of intimidation. "I'm sorry you're bothered by the idea of helping Herr Rempel seek a new wife, but I don't understand why it troubles you so much. The Frauenverein won't be involved at all, so you don't need to worry about people getting the wrong idea about its purpose."

Why must she be so stubborn? "But Agnes Bauer . . . and her wagging tongue . . ." Martina should kick Agnes out of the club. The only reason Agnes had joined was to be privy to what the other members were doing. The only reason Martina had allowed her to stay was so she would be with Martina on Friday evenings and not at home peeking out the windows at Gerhard. Martina huffed. "Can you imagine what she is probably already saying about what you're doing? And then others will talk, too."

An odd smile formed on Augusta's face. "I have learned in my years of teaching school that I will never make everyone happy. All I can do is what I believe in my heart to be right and pray that I please the One who put me to the task. The same applies outside my classroom. I'm not seeking a potential bride to upset anyone. I'm doing it to meet Herr Rempel's needs." She tilted her head slightly, her brow creasing. "You agreed to help him by asking your husband to apprentice Walden. It was kind of you, and it's certainly made Herr Rempel's days easier. But it can't fix the larger problem of his sons needing a mother's care."

"Ja, it can, if you'll leave things alone!" Martina sucked in her lips. She'd said too much. She should not have come here. She gave the screen door a push and took one step onto the porch, holding the door open with her backside. "I can see you are going to be *störrisch* about this, so there is no sense in me talking to you."

A glint of frustration briefly ignited in the woman's eyes. "Frau Krahn, I'm not being stubborn out of obstinance." She held out her hands in a gesture of futility. "And it's possible my search may fail. I can't guarantee that there will be a woman willing to come to Alexandertol and marry Herr Rempel. But I have to at least try. I vowed to help him and, in memory of my dear friend Hannah, I will honor my word to him."

"*'That which is gone out of thy lips thou shalt keep and perform . . .'*" How often had Martina recited the words from Deuteronomy 23 to herself on the most difficult days with Gerhard as a reminder of the vows she'd made before God to remain with her husband through good times and bad? She understood the desire to keep one's word and be found faultless before the Lord. But oh! If Frau Dyck's promise cost her the boy she was already imagining growing up under her roof, how would her heart survive?

Forcing a *hmph* of disdain, Martina moved away from the screen door and let it slam into its casing. "I still think you are going to create trouble and mar the Frauenverein's reputation, but you do what you deem best, Frau Dyck. Good day."

She stomped down the sidewalk to the street and headed for home as quickly as her feet would carry her without breaking into a run. As she'd pointed out to Augusta, people liked to talk, and a forty-five-year-old woman running through town would certainly stir speculation. She set her feet down with firm smacks against the ground, gritted her teeth, and pumped her arms, willing all the aggravation coursing through her to vacate her frame before she got home and faced Gerhard. He couldn't know what Augusta was up to. He couldn't know that Walden might not remain his apprentice. He couldn't know, or he would soothe himself.

She rounded the final corner, and she stopped so abruptly the soles of her shoes slid on the hard-packed ground. She caught her balance and stared at the woman on her porch engaged in conversation with Gerhard. Her heart pounded like a bass drum in her chest and perspiration broke out all over her frame. What was Agnes Bauer telling Gerhard? Was she frightening him with the prospect of a new wife for Herr Rempel, one who would assume responsibility for Walden?

Panic propelled her into a clumsy run. She huffed to a stop at the base of her porch steps and panted out, "Agnes? Did you need to see me?"

Both Agnes and Gerhard gaped at Martina. Then Agnes tittered behind her hand. "My goodness, Martina, was a skunk chasing you?"

Martina climbed the porch stairs, her chest still heaving. "Of course not. I was only hurrying home in case you needed something important." She flicked a worried frown at Gerhard and realized he was holding a bushel basket. "What do you have there?"

Gerhard glanced into the basket as if uncertain what he held. "Frau Bauer was cleaning out her cellar and found these apples. She brought them in case they could be turned into cider."

Suspicion clouded Martina's mind. "Cider? In the springtime?"

"Ach, ja." Agnes beamed. "I remembered how good the cider he made at Christmastime tasted, and remembering it made me wish I could have some now." She laughed again. "Of course, by now, if any of that cider remained, it would most likely be fermented."

She wrinkled her nose and then waved her hand at the basket. "Those are too far gone for me to use in baking. If they are too far gone for cider, go ahead and throw them out for the birds. Or feed them to your horses." She lifted the hem of her skirt and went down the porch steps one at a time, still talking. "If you make cider out of them, Herr Krahn, I hope you will share with me. You make the best cider I've ever tasted. Have a good rest of the day now." She crossed the yard to her house and went inside.

Gerhard still stood there, staring into the basket. Something in his eyes—a hunger?—sent chills up Martina's spine. She took the basket from him and set it on the bench in front of their parlor window. Then she forced a smile and aimed it at him even though he didn't move his gaze from the withered fruit.

"Those apples are as wrinkled as prunes. There can't be even an ounce of juice left in them. Agnes should have known they won't be good for cider." Had she really brought them for Gerhard to make a batch of cider? Or did she know that Gerhard deliberately fermented fruit juices and wanted Martina to know that she knew?

Fear pulsed through her veins, making it difficult to maintain a casual tone. "Do you think Daisy and Champ will enjoy eating them? Or should I, as Agnes suggested, throw them out for the birds?" She held her breath, waiting for him to acknowledge her.

Finally he shifted his focus to her, and the bleary look in his eyes cleared. He coughed out a short chuckle. "Save them for Daisy and Champ. When Walden comes on Monday, he can give the horses a treat. He'll enjoy that. Every time I turn my back on him, he goes to the corral and pets their noses. I wonder if instead of a wainwright or wheelwright, he'll become a farrier someday."

If he was still thinking about Walden coming every day, Agnes must not have mentioned Augusta's plan to find Herr

Rempel a new wife. The relief was so great her knees went weak. She sank down on the bench next to the basket of apples.

Gerhard stared outward, his expression now turned dreamy. "Would that not be something if he did? Maybe the two of us will work together—him with the horses and me with the wagons." A sweet smile of hope curving his lips, he crossed to the door and entered the house.

Martina stared after him, worry churning in her belly. Just as it had all last night. They'd gone one full week without Gerhard needing help to his bed at night. One full week of cheerful conversation around their table. One full week of Gerhard staying with her in the parlor every evening—staying clearheaded.

Nein, they could not lose Walden Rempel. They *could not.*

Chapter Sixteen

Augusta

When Augusta had put the two-pound cut of beef surrounded by chunks of vegetables into her oven to roast, she'd been certain there was enough food for Saturday's supper with leftovers for Sunday dinner. But now she gazed in astonishment at the platter on the dining room table. Only a smear of grease remained. The bread plate, on which she'd stacked six thick slices, was also empty except for a few crumbs. How had the three of them consumed so much?

On her left, Juliana placed her rumpled napkin on her plate and stood. "Would you like me to clear the table, Mother?"

"Thank you, my wood nymph. I would appreciate it." Although Augusta suspected her daughter was trying to hurry Herr Elias out the door, Juliana had given her the opportunity to speak to him privately. "Please wash the dishes and put them away, too."

Juliana nodded. "Ja, Mother." She stacked her bread plate and cutlery on her dinner plate and left the room.

Augusta picked up her cup and smiled at their guest. "Would you like to join me in the library? We can finish our coffee there."

Herr Elias swiped his mouth with his napkin and dropped it next to his plate, rising. "Ja, that sounds nice."

He followed her to the library, then stood politely while she settled into one of the wingback chairs across from the fireplace. He took the second chair and placed his cup on the round table between them, then leaned his elbow on the armrest and smiled at her. "I've had a very pleasant evening, Frau Dyck. Thank you for the delicious supper. You are a wonderful hostess."

The lamp on the table brought out the amber flecks in his brown eyes. His penetrating gaze locked on hers and made her wish she'd asked Juliana to join them, too. She took a sip of her coffee, then set the cup aside. "Danke, Herr Elias. I'm glad Juliana and I could help you celebrate the new opportunity you've been given in Marion. It truly is an answer to prayer."

"Ja, it is, and I am grateful." He continued staring into her eyes, as if nothing else in the room was worthy of his attention. "But I don't believe I would have taken the job if the mercantile owner hadn't told me I wasn't needed on the weekends. Being able to come back to Alexandertol every Saturday and Sunday will let me keep my room at the Langes', but—more important to me—will let me remain a part of this community. I wouldn't want to leave for several months and risk being forgotten."

His serious expression sent silent messages she didn't want to receive. Augusta released a short laugh, hoping to add some lightheartedness to the moment. "Herr Elias, you wouldn't be forgotten. Your work with the children of Alexandertol makes you an important person here."

"I wasn't only speaking of the children, Augusta."

The use of her name and the warmth in his gaze changed the atmosphere in the room and rendered her temporarily speechless. She didn't want to hurt his feelings—he was a good, kind man, and she liked him as a friend—but neither did she want to mislead him. Suddenly the next months when they wouldn't be in daily contact with each other seemed a gift. She should ask her favor quickly and end their evening.

"Herr Elias, I—"

"Won't you consent to calling me Dean?" He tipped his head,

and his lips curved into a hopeful smile. "We've worked together now for six years. Aren't the titles *Herr* and *Frau* a bit too formal when we're away from the schoolhouse?"

Augusta gave a tiny shrug. "I'm so accustomed to calling you Herr Elias, anything else feels peculiar. Since we do work together, it might be best to retain those titles so we don't accidentally use something less formal in front of the students."

His shoulders sagged for a moment, and he looked aside, but when he turned and faced her again, the momentary disappointment had vanished. "Very well. But it seems a shame that a lovely name like Augusta is so seldom heard." He leaned back and lightly drummed his fingers on the armrest. "Now . . . you were about to say something when I interrupted you. Please proceed."

What had she intended to say? She retraced her thoughts and remembered the purpose of this private conversation. "Danke. Ja, I was going to ask a favor of you. You see, the Alexandertol Frauenverein has received a very unique request. A local widower would like help finding a new wife."

"Are you speaking of Konrad Rempel?"

Augusta gave a start. She'd deliberately not mentioned his name, not to be secretive but to protect Herr Rempel's privacy. Had someone else been talking about it? She found the idea disconcerting. "Why do you ask about him?"

He chuckled. "Two reasons. It's a small community, and Herr Rempel is the only widower with young children still at home. It makes sense that he would want to marry again. Also, I noticed his wagon in front of your house several mornings this past week when I was driving out of town. I actually wondered if he might be seeking a courtship with you." A flash of jealousy lit his eyes, then faded. "If it is him you're helping, I find it somewhat of a relief that I was wrong in my suppositions."

But she wasn't wrong in her supposition about Herr Elias.

He was interested in more than friendship with her. She picked up her cup and took a sip of coffee, hoping to calm her unsettled nerves. It failed. "Ja, well, you have guessed correctly, but I would appreciate it if you wouldn't discuss this arrangement with anyone else in Alexandertol."

"I'd be proud to keep your confidence, Augu—Frau Dyck."

She swallowed another sip and held the cup between her palms. "Danke. Now, for what I wanted to ask of you—would you be alert to young women of marriageable ages who might be a good match for Herr Rempel? Please don't ask them about their interest, but simply record their names. I will contact them and make inquiry using the list of qualifications Herr Rempel shared with me."

His eyes sparkled with mischief, making him seem even younger. "Are you engaging me as a spy for the Frauenverein's cause, Frau Dyck?"

She didn't like the way that sounded. Mostly because it was too close to the truth, even though it wasn't really the Frauenverein's cause. "I . . . um . . ."

He laughed and reached across the table. His warm hand closed briefly over her wrist and then withdrew. "I'm only teasing you. If it will please you to help Herr Rempel find a new wife, then it pleases me to lend a hand. I will keep my eyes open to lovely young women of a marriageable age."

The statement Herr Rempel made on his visit that morning rolled through the back of Augusta's mind and spilled from her lips. "Lovely isn't necessary."

Herr Elias's eyebrows rose. "Are you sure? I don't know of any man who is interested in having a wife who isn't pleasant to look upon."

Augusta gave a firm nod. "I'm sure. Not all beautiful women are beautiful on the inside, and not all beautiful women possess faith. Strong faith, good morals, a kind nature, especially toward children, and a hardworking attitude—these are the most important qualities he's seeking."

Herr Elias stood. From his great height, he peered down at her, a slight smile lifting the corners of his lips. "And if she happens to be pretty, too, is that considered a bonus?"

Although her dear friend Hannah had been gone for more than three years, Augusta remembered her well. Hannah was everything she'd just described, and she'd also been lovely. Herr Rempel would not turn away from an attractive woman if she was a believer and of good character. "I suppose it would be."

He took the cup from her hands and put it on the table. Then he caught hold of her hands and pulled her to her feet. "And I suppose I am grateful that he has chosen to look outside Alexandertol for a new wife. It seems to me he has spoken every morning this past week to one who fits everything you said, plus possesses the bonus of beauty."

Fire ignited in her cheeks. She lowered her head slightly. "Herr Elias . . ."

He released one of her hands and hooked his finger beneath her chin. He lifted her face and smiled down at her. "I will gather as many names as I can from Marion. I will bring them to you when I return next Friday evening."

"I'll be at the Frauenverein meeting on Friday evening."

"Then I will bring them to you next Saturday. I won't want to miss seeing you when I make the delivery."

The warmth in his gaze, the gentle grip he maintained on her right hand, and the tapered finger still holding her face upward felt far too intimate. The library windows looked out over the street, and with the lamp glowing beside them, passersby would be able to see past the lace curtains.

She took a sideways step, slipping her hand free as she went. "That sounds fine, Herr Elias. Thank you for your willingness to help Herr Rempel."

He stood for a moment, his hand suspended in the air where her face had been only a few seconds ago. Then he lowered his hand and slipped it into his trouser pocket. "Thank you for the fine meal, the company, and"—he glanced around the room—"allowing me to spend some time in your beautiful home."

"You're welcome."

He gave a courtly nod.

She moved to the hall tree, and he followed. She stood aside while he took his coat from one of the hooks and shrugged into it. She lifted down his hat and held it out to him, but he didn't take it.

He cleared his throat. "The café in Durham is open on Saturdays. If I'm able to rent a buggy from Herr Duerksen, would you allow me to take you there for dinner next week? My way of thanking you for your kindness."

Augusta hesitated. If she said yes, would he read more into her agreement than she intended to say? If she said no, would she ruin their friendship? Such an awkward place to be.

"Oh, and Juliana, too, of course," he added. "She should come, as well."

Juliana had never eaten at a café. She should be given the experience. "Ja, thank you, Herr Elias, I think we would enjoy that very much."

A smile burst on his face. "Thank you. And for now . . ." He captured her hand and bowed over it, delivering a light kiss on her knuckles. "Good night." Then he took his hat, positioned it over his thick, dark hair, and strode out into the calm, cool evening.

She closed and locked the door behind him, then placed her hands over her still-warm cheeks. She should have considered the younger man's seeming infatuation with her before asking for his help in her wife-finding venture. Employing his assistance meant consistent contact with him. Consistent contact would certainly feed his affection. But how could she reverse it now? She couldn't. Not without losing Herr Elias's help, and Herr Rempel would then suffer the consequences.

She was stuck, as surely as if she'd stepped into a patch of quicksand.

Chapter Seventeen

Konrad

"Herr Rempel? Herr Rempel?"

The almost frantic call came from behind Konrad as he herded his restless boys to their wagon after church on Sunday. He turned and spotted Frau Krahn waving her hand and hurrying across the grass toward him. "Go on to the wagon, boys." He gave them nudges on their backs, then he waited for the woman.

She huffed up to him, her cheeks mottled red and perspiration dotting her face. "Herr Rempel, you nearly got away from me."

"*Es tut mir Leid.*" She hadn't mentioned she wanted to talk to him after service, so he shouldn't be sorry, but he still felt the need to apologize. Konrad had always found Frau Krahn somewhat intimidating. Walden spoke glowingly of the way she treated him, though, and Konrad appreciated her kindness to his son. "For what reason did you need me?"

A smile—a trembling one, as if her lips weren't accustomed to forming smiles—softened her usually austere features. "I put two fat hens in my oven to roast before leaving for church this morning. There is also stewed cabbage with tomatoes and boiled potatoes ready on the stove. I wondered if you and your sons would like to have dinner with Gerhard and me today. Unless"—she sucked in a little breath, as if something had frightened her—"you have other plans."

He'd planned to make sandwiches from leftover pork and the bread he purchased at the mercantile. *Able to bake bread* was on his list for a new wife, and he looked forward to the smell of baking bread in his house again. The loaves from the mercantile tasted good, but the fresh smell was already gone by the time he bought them. A house that smelled like fresh-baked bread smelled like *home*. He was willing to wager the Krahn house smelled like *home*.

"That's very kind of you." Why had she invited them, though? Other members of the congregation had occasionally asked Konrad and his boys to eat with them on Sundays, but not once had Frau Krahn done so before today. Maybe Walden had mentioned what a poor cook his father was and she'd taken pity on them. He didn't like the thought, but he couldn't deny that what she'd prepared sounded better than a cold sandwich. "Are you sure it won't be inconvenient? As you've probably figured out since Walden ate at your table all last week, my boys have bigger appetites than would seem possible given their sizes."

She laughed, and her eyes crinkled so merrily, Konrad couldn't help smiling in response. She gave his arm a light, teasing pat. "You are correct that Walden has a big appetite. I can assure you, I made plenty, and neither you nor your boys will leave the table hungry."

Her friendliness, coupled with a desire to get better acquainted with the couple who were spending so much time with his son, won him. "We would be happy to come, Frau Krahn. Danke for asking us."

She smiled even bigger, backing slowly away. "Sehr gut. I will see you at my house very soon." She turned and scurried in the direction of her waiting wagon.

When Konrad told the boys they were having dinner at the Krahns', Walden let out a cheer. He poked Folker with his elbow, licking his lips. "Wait until you taste Tante Martina's food. You will want to eat at her house every day for the rest of your life."

Folker rubbed a circle on his stomach and grinned, but jealousy filled Konrad's stomach. Folker had finally stopped asking why he wasn't allowed to go to the Krahns' with Walden each day. Would this dinner together make him dissatisfied again? The boys never went hungry, but Konrad's cooking wasn't the best. He hoped Frau Dyck hurried and found his wife so the boys would not only be fed but would enjoy the food at their table.

He followed the Krahns' buggy to their house, parked, and then stopped the boys from immediately leaping down. "We are guests, so be on your best behavior." He gave each a firm frown to emphasize his words. "Mind your manners when you eat, say 'please' and 'thank you,' and don't talk with food in your mouth."

They gazed back at him, innocence on their matching faces. Then Walden said, "Pa, we'll be too busy eating to talk. So will you. Her food is really good."

Konrad swallowed the chuckle threatening to erupt and nodded. "All right, then, get down. But walk to the house, don't run, and ask Frau Krahn if you can help set the table."

The boys didn't need to help set the table, because five place settings were already laid out, which made it clear the couple would have been disappointed if he'd declined the invitation.

Frau Krahn instructed the boys to take the bench on one side and Konrad one of the chairs across from them. Herr Krahn settled into the seat at the head of the table. He engaged the twins—both of them, not just Walden—in conversation while Frau Krahn carried out platters and bowls of steaming food. The aromas rising from the vessels made Konrad's mouth water. Even though he hadn't yet taken a bite, he understood Walden's excitement at being invited for Sunday dinner.

Frau Krahn took the chair at the foot of the table and nodded to her husband. Without a word, he bowed his head, and his wife and the twins followed his example. But Konrad couldn't close his eyes. His gaze drifted from Herr Krahn's humble pose to his boys, who sat so reverently, to Frau Krahn's steepled hands beneath her chin. The image was so perfect. So right. So similar to the scene at his table before Hannah had died. His heart ached with the beauty and simplicity of the grown-ups and the children bowing their heads together in prayer.

"Amen," Herr Krahn said, and everyone opened their eyes.

Frau Krahn picked up the closest bowl, which contained chunks of boiled potatoes dotted with glossy bits of onion, and held it to Folker. "Would you like one scoop or two, Folker?"

Folker glanced at his father, the corner of his lower lip clamped between his teeth. Then he hunched his shoulders and squeaked out, "I'd like three, please."

Konrad's mouth fell open at his son's audacity. "Folker . . ."

"What?" Folker blinked at Konrad. "I said 'please.'"

The boy's innocent comment broke the solemnity of the previous minutes, and Konrad laughed along with Frau Krahn. They passed the bowls, filled their plates, and ate. Konrad enjoyed visiting with the couple more than he'd expected to. They seemed relaxed and friendly here in their own home, and he set aside some of the notions he'd held over the past years about them being unsociable.

When they finished eating the well-seasoned chicken and vegetables, Frau Krahn went to the kitchen and returned with a cake covered in chocolate icing. Although Konrad's stomach was achingly full, he couldn't resist when she asked if he would like a slice. Both boys accepted large wedges, too. By the time they finished the dessert, the twins were nodding in sleepiness, and Konrad wondered if he would be able to walk without waddling.

He had intended to offer help with clearing the table and washing the dishes, but with his boys nearly asleep in their empty plates, it was best to take them home. He thanked the Krahns for their invitation, then helped the twins to their feet. They drooped against him, and he prodded them to tell Herr and Frau Krahn thank you for the good dinner.

"Tha . . . ank you." A yawn split Walden's words.

Folker blinked blearily and smacked his lips.

Herr Krahn covered his smile with his hand, and Frau Krahn tousled Folker's neatly trimmed hair. "Such sleepy boys . . ." Her tone held both melancholy and affection. "They seem too drowsy to even walk to your wagon, but they're almost too big to carry. Maybe"—she turned a hopeful look on Konrad—"they should stay here and nap this afternoon. You could take them home after this evening's service."

Walden already spent most of his daytime hours with the Krahns. Konrad wasn't willing to give up his weekends with him. "I appreciate the kind offer, Frau Krahn, but the boys rarely nap anymore. If they do, it's only for a short time. They would be up and intruding upon your quiet day if they stayed. I'll take them home with me."

The woman looked so crestfallen that Konrad felt as if he was being cruel to take his own children home. But he couldn't allow his sons to get too attached to Frau Krahn. Before long, they would have a new mother, and they needed to give that woman their affection when the time came. Growing accustomed to Frau Krahn's attention and then not spending time with her would be another loss for his boys. He would have to be cruel to the older woman in order to be kind to his sons.

As he'd done for years when needing to encourage them along, he cupped one hand on the back of each of their heads and aimed them for the door. Both Herr and Frau Krahn followed him into the yard and all the way to the edge of his wagon. Konrad lifted Folker up on the seat while Herr Krahn lifted Walden. After he'd climbed up with his sons, Konrad bid the couple farewell and urged the horses to carry them forward. He didn't turn around to look, but he sensed if he peeked over his shoulder, he would see the Krahns standing in the street, watching him leave.

That evening at church, Herr Krahn sat on the back bench with Konrad and the twins—something he had never done before.

Each day that week, Herr Krahn brought Walden home a little later until, by Friday, it was past seven o'clock before his wagon rolled up Konrad's lane. By then, Konrad and Folker had grown weary of waiting and had eaten supper by themselves. When Konrad told Walden to go in and have his supper, the boy said he'd already eaten with the Krahns—"Tante Martina made fried chicken. Since it's my favorite, she said I should stay and have some. You don't mind, do you, Pa?"

Konrad didn't trust himself to answer without a sharp tone, so he sent the boy to the house, then thanked the man for feeding Walden. He determined that on Monday, when he took Walden into town to the wheelwright shop, he would tell Herr Krahn he wanted Walden home for supper each night.

He let the boys stay up past their usual bedtime since Walden got home so late, and as he tucked them into their bed, he said, "Would you like to go fishing tomorrow afternoon?"

"Ja!" they chorused, and then Folker added, "With Frau Dyck and Juliana."

Konrad drew back in surprise. They'd always gone fishing by themselves. Even when Hannah was still alive and he'd taken the boys to the river to fish, she'd stayed home, letting him enjoy some time alone with them. Curiosity got the better of him, and he couldn't stop himself from asking, "Why do you want Frau Dyck and Juliana to come, too?"

"Because if we go together, Frau Dyck might say she'll our fish for us. Juliana says her ma is the best cook in the wo_

Walden nudged his brother with his elbow. Hard. "I bet Tan Martina is the best cook in the world." He angled a pleading look at Konrad. "Can we ask her and Onkel Gerhard to go with us instead? She'll cook our fish for us. I know she will, because she asks me every day what I want to eat for dinner, and I tell her, and she cooks it."

An uneasy prickle tiptoed across Konrad's scalp. He wanted Walden to be happy with their school-break arrangement, but it seemed he was becoming spoiled with the Krahns. He pulled the covers tight to the boys' chins and shook his head. "We'll go fishing by ourselves, like we always do, and I will cook our fish for us. Now, no talking. Right to sleep."

He paused long enough to watch their eyes drift closed, then he blew out the flame in their lamp and left the room. He poured himself a final cup of coffee and sat in the middle of the settee. Should he keep Walden home from the Krahns' from now on? They'd been very kind to Walden, and to him and Folker, too. He didn't want to hurt their feelings. At the same time, he didn't want Walden firmly attached to them. This was to be a temporary situation allowing him to work through the time of planting and harvesting. But maybe he was only feeling jealous, as if Walden was comparing Konrad to the Krahns and finding him inadequate. He'd not had to share his boys with anyone except their schoolteacher since Hannah died. Was he being overly sensitive?

He drank his coffee and allowed his thoughts to roam, balancing the benefits of Walden spending days with Herr Krahn against potential changes in the boy's attitude. Finally he decided he couldn't keep both Walden and Folker home. He'd get nothing done in the shop. He would continue to take Walden, with the stipulation that he be home for supper each evening.

And he would pray that Frau Dyck would quickly find a new wife for him. Once he had a wife in his house again, both boys could stay home all day, every day.

He swallowed the last gulp, then put the cup in the wash basin. Tomorrow might be too soon for Frau Dyck to have heard from anyone interested in moving to Alexandertol and marrying him, but he would go by her place after he took the boys fishing. It wouldn't hurt to ask if she'd made any progress.

Chapter Eighteen

Augusta

Augusta and Juliana waited on the porch swing for Herr Elias's arrival on Saturday morning, the second day of May. They'd each donned one of their nicest dresses, and Juliana had even pinned one of Augusta's hats over her braided hair. She looked so grown-up and beautiful that Augusta had a hard time not staring at her. Her little girl was growing up too fast.

A buggy with Herr Elias in the driver's seat pulled up to the house at eleven o'clock. Juliana shot from the swing as if fired from a slingshot, but Augusta rose more sedately. He disembarked from the vehicle and strode up the walkway, whistling a merry tune. They met him at the bottom of the steps.

Dressed in his Sunday suit with a fresh collar and his dark hair combed away from his smooth-shaven face, he appeared very dapper. He whipped off his bowler and bowed in front of them. "Good morning, ladies. You both look lovely."

"Danke," Juliana said with a little curtsy.

Augusta swallowed a chortle. Juliana had never curtsied before. She must have read about it in one of her storybooks. Augusta held her gloved hand to Herr Elias. "Danke. You look very nice, too."

He took her hand but, to her relief, only gave it a little squeeze rather than kissing it. He slipped her hand into the bend of his elbow and, tossing a wink in Juliana's direction, started toward the buggy. "The *Farmer's Almanac* predicted rain for today, but I'm glad to see a clear sky instead."

Augusta was grateful for the casual topic. She'd fretted that, after a week away, his affection for her might have grown. But so far he showed no hint of the romantic behavior displayed in her parlor last Saturday. She nodded. "Ja, it looks to be a beautiful day for a ride." The beautiful day was a blessing after a rather strained Frauenverein meeting yesterday evening. It seemed the women's ambivalence about her desire to help Herr Rempel secure a new wife was spilling over onto other suggestions for assisting neighbors, as well. They'd done more disagreeing than agreeing, leaving Augusta heartsore.

They reached the side of the buggy, and Herr Elias folded down a little step for their use. "Herr Duerksen only has this one buggy to lend out. There's no second seat, so it might be a tight fit for all of us. But it's less than an hour's distance to Durham and, as you said, it's a pleasant day for a ride."

Augusta hesitated. Should she have Juliana sit in the middle for propriety's sake? She turned to ask her to climb up first, but her daughter stared at the buggy seat with her hands gripped against her rib cage in a nervous gesture. Protectiveness swelled. Nein, she would not put Juliana between her and Herr Elias, no matter how much better it might look.

She allowed him to assist her into the buggy, and she settled on the tufted leather seat. He helped Juliana up, too. As soon as Juliana sat, Augusta urged her to shift as close to the seat's edge as possible. Then she moved close to her daughter, slid her arm behind Juliana's back, and gripped the curved iron rail that served as both backrest and armrest.

Herr Elias pulled himself up on the opposite side and sat, making the springs bounce. Juliana released a little giggle that stole some of Augusta's tension, and she smiled into her daughter's sweet face.

"Are you ladies ready?" Herr Elias released the brake and picked up the reins.

Juliana leaned forward slightly and smiled at the teacher. "I am."

"As am I," Augusta said.

"Then let's go." He flicked the reins, and the pair of bays drew them forward.

As they drove the dirt road leading to the small town of Durham, Herr Elias kept up a steady stream of queries, many of which were directed at Juliana. At first her daughter was shy, only answering "ja" or "nein," but eventually she opened up and offered a few peeks into her thoughts and opinions.

Augusta recognized what he was doing, and she appreciated him including Juliana so thoroughly. After Leopold's death, Augusta had briefly entertained the attention of a nearby rancher. He was a nice enough man, and she might have grown fond of him except for his tendency to act as if Juliana was invisible. How could she be happy in a relationship if the man treated her child so indifferently? Even though she didn't anticipate developing a courtship with Herr Elias, her heart warmed at his kind inclusion, and some of her worries about how Juliana would settle into the classroom with the older students next session melted away during that drive through the prairie beneath the midday sunshine.

When they reached Durham, Juliana sat up on the edge of the seat like an alert little sparrow on a branch and scanned the row of businesses. Then she pointed ahead. "There it is! There's the café, Herr Elias!"

Although the building was simple in appearance, Juliana's excitement was contagious. Augusta found herself sitting up in eagerness, too, and Herr Elias smiled at her as he drew the wagon to a stop at the edge of the boardwalk near the false-front clapboard building. Juliana clambered down on her own, but Augusta waited until Herr Elias offered her his hand.

He helped her down, then kept hold of her hand, preventing

her from joining her daughter on the boardwalk. He glanced toward Juliana, who was cupping her hands beside her face and peeking through the café window. "Juliana?"

She gave the teacher a quizzical look over her shoulder. "Ja?"

His fingers, curled around Augusta's hand, tightened their hold. "I need to speak very briefly with your mother. Would you like to go inside and ask for a table? We'll join you in only a minute or two."

To Augusta's surprise, Juliana bounded to the door and went inside without a moment's hesitation. During their ride from Alexandertol, she must have lost all apprehension about Herr Elias's presence. Or she was too excited about eating in a café to think about anything else. Whatever the reason, Augusta found herself alone at the edge of the boardwalk, holding hands with her fellow teacher. Her stomach flip-flopped in a discombobulated dance.

His eyes twinkled as he gazed down at her. "I thought it best to give you this while free of Juliana's curious perusal." He released her and reached inside his jacket. When he brought out his hand, it held a folded piece of paper. "As requested, names of prospective brides for your Herr Rempel."

Her face flamed at his choice of words. The man was hardly *her* Herr Rempel, but she took the page with nearly as much enthusiasm as Juliana had shown when darting inside the café. She unfolded it, and her delight faded. "Only two?"

He shrugged and straightened his lapels. "This week, ja. But that doesn't mean there aren't more. I spent the majority of my time organizing stock in the storeroom and came out on the floor when a shelf needed filling. Thus, I had few interactions with customers. These two"—he tapped the sheet with one tapered finger—"are half sisters, two years apart in age, who live with their widowed father. I would think either would be happy for the opportunity to care for her own home and family."

Or they could be too dedicated to their father to leave him. But Augusta wouldn't know until she sent them queries. She folded the paper again and tucked it into her little reticule. "Danke. I will send letters to them soon."

"*Bitte*—you're very welcome." He ushered her toward the café door. "Have you had any response to the advertisements you put in the Kansas City, Wichita, and Topeka newspapers?"

"None yet." But she wasn't disappointed. It would take time for women to write a response, and more time for the letters to make their way to Alexandertol. Even though Herr Rempel was eager to find a new wife, they would both have to exercise patience.

They stepped inside, and the scents of roasting meat and fresh bread greeted her nose—a very inviting aroma. Juliana had chosen a booth along the side wall, and she waved them over, her smile bright. Augusta slid in beside Juliana, and Herr Elias sat across from them. He ordered the daily special—two pork chops with dressing, applesauce, roasted root vegetables, and bread—for each of them. Augusta enjoyed the fine meal and also the conversation in which even Juliana participated.

They continued their easy camaraderie on the drive back to Alexandertol. Augusta's heart swelled in pride and gratitude when, without even a hint of prompting, Juliana reached past Augusta and thanked the teacher for the wonderful treat. He responded kindly, assuring her he'd enjoyed getting to know her better. Affection for the man flooded Augusta, and her thank-you for the fine meal and the pleasant drive emerged more warmly than she'd anticipated. And, apparently, more warmly than he'd expected, because his eyes lit and he took her hand.

"You're a lovely lady, Frau Dyck, and you're raising a delightful daughter. I cannot tell you how much this time of becoming better acquainted has meant to me." He released her hand, but his probing gaze continued to hold her captive. "Perhaps we can do this again someday soon . . . maybe next Saturday?"

As much as she'd enjoyed the day, she understood what two Saturday outings in a row would signify. "I'm so sorry, but I'm not able to accept that invitation." The disappointment falling over both his and Juliana's faces pierced her. Impulsively, she added, "But perhaps you'd like to have Sunday dinner with us."

His smile returned quickly, as did Juliana's. "I would like that very much. I will see you at church tomorrow." He got down, helped the two of them from the buggy, then climbed back up on the seat. Tipping his hat, he bounced a grin over first Juliana and then Augusta. "Good day, ladies." He departed.

Juliana danced up the walkway ahead of Augusta, and Augusta called after her, "Change into a work dress. We have chores to do."

"Ja, Mother, I know." She closed herself in the house.

Augusta had just reached the porch when she heard excited voices hollering her name. She stopped and looked toward the cries, and laughter built in her throat when she spotted Folker and Walden Rempel racing up the street toward her. A pair of fishing poles bounced on Folker's shoulder, and Walden swung a battered tin pail.

They came to a panting halt in front of her, Walden reaching up to adjust the brim of his tweed cap. Folker said, "Frau Dyck, guess what we did today."

She flicked the line on one of the poles he carried, pointed to the dirt-smeared tin pail in Walden's hand, and smiled. "I'm going to guess that you've been fishing. It seems you used up all your worms, but I don't see any fish. Were you not successful?"

"Ja, we were!" they said together, then Walden crowded in front of his brother. "I caught seven fish. Folker only caught six."

Folker pushed Walden aside with his elbow. "But mine were bigger than yours!"

Walden raised his pail as if preparing to whack Folker with it. Augusta quickly caught his hand and pressed it downward. "You should both be pleased with your catches. You're turning into very good fishermen."

"But Pa's the best." Folker's chest poked out. "He caught so many, we could invite the whole town to a fish fry and everyone would have plenty to eat."

Walden rolled his eyes. "Not the whole town. Or else everybody would only get a bite or two." He looked up at Augusta. "But there's enough for us plus some more, Pa said, so—"

"Boys?" Herr Rempel's disgruntled voice interrupted. He trudged up, a string of glistening fish hanging from his hand. "Why did you run off like that?"

Both boys blinked in innocence. Folker said, "We saw Frau Dyck and wanted to tell her about the fish we caught." He bobbed his chin at the string. "See there, Frau Dyck? See how many we caught?"

Augusta oohed and aahed, hiding her smile at the way the twins puffed up. "That's a very fine mess of fish, boys. You'll have a good supper tonight, and probably breakfast and dinner tomorrow, as well."

Walden shifted in front of his brother again. "But that's the other thing we wanted to tell you. Some of those fish are for you."

"For me?" Genuine surprise colored her tone. She looked at their father, expecting him to scold the boys for trying to give away some of their catch, but to her surprise, he nodded.

"Ja, we would be happy to share." Shyness colored his tone and showed itself in a rosy hue behind his whiskers, but his gaze bore steadily into hers. "It is the only payment I can offer for the . . . kindness . . . you are doing for me."

She didn't need payment, but how could she refuse the fish with the two boys beaming at her and their father looking so hopeful? Besides, there were few things tastier than fresh fish. They'd be delicious for tomorrow's dinner.

All at once, her tongue seemed to go rogue and spew words she hadn't completely thought through. "Why don't you and the twins come here after church tomorrow and have fish with Juliana and me?" And with Herr Elias. How could she have forgotten she'd already invited Herr Elias?

"Are you sure?"

Herr Rempel sounded dubious, but Augusta gave a firm nod. This wasn't a bad idea, after all. Having both men at her table at the same time would eliminate any townsfolks' speculation about courting. And Herr Elias was assisting in the search for a new wife. Becoming better acquainted with Herr Rempel might help him make better choices.

She smiled at the boys' father. "I have only one request." She glanced at the dripping string. "Would you help clean the fish you intend to leave with me? I don't mind frying them, but cleaning them . . ." She gave an exaggerated shudder.

To her delight, the man laughed. "That seems a fair exchange. Where would you like me to take them?"

She grinned and waggled her fingers. "Follow me."

Chapter Nineteen

Konrad

Being invited to Sunday dinner two weeks in a row might spoil him and his boys, but Konrad couldn't deny how much he enjoyed eating at Frau Dyck's table. While the food was simple compared to what Frau Krahn had served the week before, everything was flavorful and the company pleasant. Even after they'd eaten all of the fried fish fillets, wilted dandelion greens, and boiled carrots, he had no desire to hurry home.

Herr Elias poured himself another cup of coffee from the pot near Frau Dyck's elbow, then glanced at Konrad's empty cup. "Would you like some more?"

Konrad, like Herr Elias, had already drunk two cups with the meal. That should be enough. But he nodded anyway. Frau Dyck took the pot and filled his cup, then her own. The sight made Konrad smile. Apparently she wasn't in a hurry to send them all away.

Frau Dyck's daughter laid her napkin on her plate. "Mother, may the boys and I have some of the oatmeal cookies you baked last week? There are still quite a few in the crock."

Walden's and Folker's eyes lit. After all they had eaten, Konrad couldn't imagine them still being hungry, and he told them so.

Folker shrugged. "There's always room in my stomach for dessert, Pa." He raised his eyebrows and angled a pitiful look at their hostess. "We hardly ever get dessert at home."

Konrad cringed, but Frau Dyck laughed. "Spoken like a typical boy. Juliana, please put a dozen or so cookies on a plate and bring it in here. The men might like some with their coffee. Then you and the boys may take your cookies to the backyard. You can show them your favorite climbing tree."

The twins whooped and bounded out of their chairs. They clattered after Juliana, and Frau Dyck watched them, a fond smile on her face. When they'd disappeared beyond the doorway, she aimed the smile at Konrad and Herr Elias. "I'm sorry I don't have something more elaborate for dessert. Since the cookies are a few days old, they'll probably be hard."

"That makes them perfect for dipping," Konrad said, then wished he hadn't. Was dipping cookies in one's coffee a polite thing to do at someone else's house? His years of living with only the boys for company had stolen some of his manners. He needed to regain them before he took a new wife.

Frau Dyck took a little sip from her cup. "My Vater dipped nearly everything in his coffee—cookies, toasted rolls, even slices of cake."

Herr Elias's brow furrowed. "How did he dip cake into coffee?"

The woman laughed lightly. "Oh, he didn't dip the cake. What a mess that would make! He put the piece of stale cake in a bowl and poured coffee over it, then ate it with a spoon." The corners of her lips quivered, and her eyes went moist. "He wasn't one to coddle us children, but he always shared a spoonful of the soggy cake with me even though *Mutter* scolded that the coffee would stunt my growth." She sighed. "I'd forgotten about it until you mentioned dipping the cookies, Herr Rempel. Danke for the sweet remembrance."

While Frau Dyck was speaking, Juliana had quietly placed a plate of cookies on the table and slipped back out. Konrad took one from the plate and broke it in two. "You're welcome, Frau Dyck, and now . . . with your permission . . ." He suspended one half over his cup. She nodded, smiling, and he dipped the cookie, then put it in his mouth. The sweet cookie drenched with rich coffee was as good as any fancy dessert. "Mm, perfect."

Herr Elias followed Konrad's example. At his first taste, his eyebrows lifted in surprise, and he smiled his approval. The two of them ate cookies while they talked about local happenings, the farmers' hope for rain over the coming week, and Herr Elias's new job in Marion.

Suddenly Herr Elias gave a start. "There is something I should tell both of you. I think it will give you an idea of another place to seek a wife." He pushed his plate aside and rested his elbows on the table. "There is a notice on the mercantile window in Marion about a group of orphans coming later this summer."

Konrad had heard about train cars of orphans being sent from New York to farming communities, but to his knowledge none had been delivered so close to Alexandertol. While he found this information interesting, what did it have to do with him finding a wife?

"These orphans are sent in an attempt to give the children a better life than what the big city offers them," Herr Elias went on, "but children aren't the only ones who want a better life. There are matchmaking services in New York that send women out of the city to the western states to men who want wives. A lot more women of marriageable age probably reside in New York City than near here. You could find a wife very quickly by hiring a real matchmaking service." He cringed, sending a look of apology at Frau Dyck. "Not that I think you're incompetent. But if Herr Rempel is eager for matrimony, this could be a faster way of finding a match."

Frau Dyck turned a thoughtful frown on Konrad. "What do you think? Would you rather write to one of the matchmakers in New York? Herr Elias is right that they have a list of women who are interested in marriage. One could be sent by train to Marion." Her eyes widened, and she released a little gasp. "Why,

Herr Rempel, if you used a matchmaking service, it is possible you could be married by the end of this month."

Konrad's palms began to sweat. He swiped them dry on his pant legs, and a raspy chuckle left his throat. "That would be quick, wouldn't it?" Quick was good. His boys needed a mother now, and he needed a helpmeet. He would be able to end his arrangement with the Krahns if there was a woman in his home looking after the twins. But could someone who lived so far away know what kind of woman to send to this Kansas town located on a patch of prairie next to the Cottonwood River? Did he trust someone he'd never met to make such an important selection for him? But Frau Dyck knew what to ask. If she communicated those needs for him, the matchmaker could make a good selection for him.

"Of course . . ." Herr Elias's serious tone drew Konrad's attention. "Those services cost money. And they would want you to pay for the woman's travel to Kansas. So you need to consider that, too."

At the man's final comment, Konrad hung his head. He wasn't destitute, but he didn't have a large bank account. He might not have enough money to pay a matchmaker and buy a train ticket. "I think I will stay with what Frau Dyck and I have planned." Saying it out loud was like casting off a burden. He blew out a breath of relief and sat upright. "It might take longer, but I can wait for the right woman."

Frau Dyck nodded slowly. "The one for whom we're both praying, ja?"

Konrad nodded, too, and a sense of contentment flowed through him. "Ja, ja." He smiled at his Hannah's dear friend. "God knows who she is. With Frau Dyck's help, He will lead me to her."

Across the table, Herr Elias observed Konrad, and his gaze narrowed. He cleared his throat—a gruff *ahem.* "Ja, well, as long as you find her before school starts again. After that, Frau Dyck will be too busy teaching the children to be sending out queries for you."

Frau Dyck's fine eyebrows pinched. Her lips parted, as if she was going to speak, but then she picked up her cup and sipped from it. When she settled the cup in its saucer, the frown lines had smoothed away. "I have every confidence that God's timing will be perfect in bringing Herr Rempel and his new wife together." She rose. "It's been very quiet for a while. I believe I'll go check on the children. Please feel free to remain here and finish your coffee. I'll be right back." And she hurried out of the room.

Augusta

In all honesty, she wasn't worried about the children. She trusted Juliana not to do anything foolish or allow the boys to behave recklessly. She'd left the table to give herself a chance to recover emotionally from the unexpected feelings that had swept through her when Herr Elias mentioned the group of orphans coming to Marion.

She went to the kitchen window and looked into the backyard. The three children sat in the shade of Juliana's favorite apple tree. She was reading to the twins from one of her storybooks. They looked so sweet and content that Augusta battled another wave of mingled affection and sadness. She observed them for several minutes, memorizing the tender image. Then she turned away, biting her lower lip to hold back a sob.

If only she and Leopold had given Juliana siblings. Seeing her daughter with Walden and Folker, so at ease and happy, told her what a wonderful sister she would be. A sibling wasn't only a companion during childhood, but was someone on whom to depend as an adult. Juliana's father was already gone. Someday

Augusta would be gone, too, and then Juliana would be alone. The thought pierced her.

She closed her eyes against the stab of pain, and the picture of Juliana bent over the book, the twins leaning in with their heads almost resting on her shoulders, appeared vividly in her mind's eye. She had the financial means to support another child. If she chose a girl, the two could share Juliana's room. Juliana would welcome a sister into the family, Augusta was certain. Of course, she'd then be raising two children without a father's influence. But there were men in her life—Reverend Hartmann, Herr Elias, and even Herr Rempel—who could provide guidance. She should ask Herr Elias for the date of the train's arrival. In the meantime, she would pray about whether she should meet the train in Marion and perhaps bring an orphaned child into her home.

"Frau Dyck?"

Herr Elias's call from the dining room jolted Augusta from her pondering. She'd left her guests unattended too long. She entered the room, an apology on her lips, but the other teacher spoke before she had a chance to voice it.

"I had planned to stay and help clean up after dinner, but we visited longer than I realized. I must return to the Langes' and gather up what I'll need for another week in Marion." He held out both hands, and she took hold. "Thank you, Frau Dyck, for the invitation to dinner today. I always enjoy time in your company. I'm sure by next Saturday, I will have more names for your"—he winked—"project. May I bring them to you then?"

She'd told him she wasn't available for dinner on Saturday, which probably meant she shouldn't entertain his company at all on that day. Yet she needed the names so she could compose query letters. "Ja, that would be fine. In the morning, if you are able." Then she would have the afternoon for writing more missives.

"I will do that. And now, since you have other guests, I will see myself out. Guten Tag, Frau Dyck and Herr Rempel." He exited the dining room.

Herr Rempel rose. "I should take my boys home, but please allow me to help clear the table before I go."

"That is kind of you, but unnecessary." Augusta released a short laugh. "Especially since you cleaned all the fish that we ate today. Washing dishes is a much easier task than gutting and skinning catfish."

He'd already made a stack of the plates within his reach. He started gathering up the silverware. "I would have cleaned the fish anyway and then cooked them if not for your offer to do so for all of us. So, please, let me help."

When he asked so kindly, she couldn't refuse. She thanked him and worked alongside him clearing the table. Then, while he scraped the remaining food bits from the plates into the slop bucket, she filled a pot of water to heat on the stove for dishwashing. Although she'd never had a man help with cleanup in her kitchen, she discovered his presence wasn't off-putting. In the years since Hannah's death, he'd seen to the kitchen duties in his own home, so he knew what to do and wasn't shy about doing any of it. But it was more than his knowledge that left her comfortable with him.

He was easygoing, uncomplaining, and sincerely helpful. If he continued as a helper even after remarrying, his new wife would appreciate these things about him. Augusta had already written the letters intended for the half sisters in Marion, but maybe she should rewrite them and include these character traits.

He picked up the slop bucket. "Where would you like this dumped?"

Augusta reached for it. "I will scatter the bits in my garden plot. It makes fine fertilizer."

He held on to the bucket's handle. "I'll do that for you." He headed out the back door before she had a chance to argue. When he returned a few minutes later, all three children trailed him. He put the bucket, which he must have rinsed clean at her outdoor pump, beside the stove where she kept it, then nudged his boys forward. "Tell Frau Dyck thank you."

"Danke, Frau Dyck," the twins chorused, neither smiling.

Augusta couldn't resist pulling them into a hug. "You are welcome, but why are you so glum? Did you eat too many cookies and get a bellyache?"

"Nein." Walden's lower lip poked out. "Pa said we have to leave, but we haven't finished the story. Now we won't know how it ends."

Juliana held up her well-worn copy of *Children's and Household Tales*. She loved the stories compiled by a pair of German brothers named Grimm. "I had just started 'The Dog and the Sparrow.'"

The boys' disappointed faces made Augusta's teacher heart roll over. How could she trample their desire to hear stories read? She kept her hands on their shoulders and beseeched their father with her eyes. "Might you stay a little longer? Let them hear the remainder of the tale?"

Herr Rempel looked at his sons, then Juliana, and finally settled his blue-eyed gaze on Augusta. A rueful chuckle rumbled from his chest. "Ja, well, if Juliana is willing to keep reading, I suppose I should let them listen."

The children whooped, and the boys thundered to Juliana's side. Folker tugged at Juliana's apron skirt. "Let's go back to the tree. I like it out there."

Juliana herded the jabbering boys out of the kitchen. The screen door slammed behind them, and silence fell in the kitchen.

Herr Rempel scuffed a little closer, his expression remorseful.

"They both like books very much. Probably because Hannah read stories to them before bedtime every night. I don't read to them much. I suppose it's something a mother is more prone to do."

His sadness bruised Augusta's heart as much as the twins' disappointment had. She placed her hand on his sleeve. "I will add 'willing to read bedtime stories' to the list of necessary qualifications for your new wife."

His chin rose, and a slight smile creased his face. "Ja, that would be good." Then he glanced at the pot on the stove. "Steam is rising from the water. It should be hot enough now for dishwashing. While Juliana finishes reading the story, I will help you with the dishes. And then we will go and let you have the rest of your day to yourself."

Oddly, in that moment, although she was tired from cooking for and entertaining a houseful of guests, the prospect of having the rest of the day to herself held little appeal. She preferred company. His company.

She gave herself a little shake, discarding the odd feeling, and bunched her apron in her hands to protect them against the pan's heat before lifting it from the stove. "Danke, Herr Rempel. You are a good man." The pleased blush that stole across his face might linger in her memory forever. She quickly turned her attention to the dishes.

They worked in companionable silence, she washing, he drying and stacking the plates and cups on the worktable in her kitchen. As she swept her fingers along the bottom of the basin to ascertain no pieces of cutlery remained, a fear-filled yelp carried from the yard.

Herr Rempel's face jerked toward the sound, his neck popping with the rapid movement. "That was Folker." He darted in the direction of the door, and Augusta hurried after him.

Chapter Twenty

Augusta

Augusta stepped out onto the back porch and then clapped her hand over her mouth. Folker lay on his back beneath Juliana's reading tree, arms flung wide and his face white. Juliana knelt beside him, and Walden paced at Folker's feet, tears raining down his cheeks although he didn't make a sound. Herr Rempel called Folker's name.

Walden turned and stumbled toward his father, who raced toward the children. "Pa, Pa, Folker fell out of the tree!"

Herr Rempel dashed past Walden and went down on one knee beside his still son. Juliana rose and scampered to her mother. Augusta grabbed both Juliana and Walden in an embrace and held them tight while staring at Folker's still form.

"Son? Son?" Herr Rempel patted Folker's cheek, worry carving deep lines across his forehead, his voice calm yet anguished. "Can you hear me? Speak to me if you can hear me."

Folker's eyelids fluttered. A tiny moan escaped his white lips. "Pa . . ."

The boys' father slumped low and sighed out, "Praise the Lord." He cupped Folker's jaw in his broad hands. "Lie very still and tell me where it hurts."

The little boy groaned. "My back. And my head."

"Let me see."

While Herr Rempel rolled Folker onto his side and began running his hands over the boy's head and spine, Augusta ushered Juliana and Walden a few feet away. "Juliana, what happened? Why was Folker in the tree?"

Tears flooded her daughter's eyes. "When I finished the story, I pointed to my reading branch and told the boys that was where I liked to read. Folker asked if he could take my book up there and read a page to us. I said no, he was too small to climb so high."

"But Folker said he could do it." Walden huffed a disgusted snort, clearly an attempt to trample his worry. "He is so stubborn. It wasn't Juliana's fault, Frau Dyck. Folker wouldn't listen."

Augusta wrapped the children in another hug, then turned to Herr Rempel just as the man scooped Folker into his arms and stood. He strode to them, his expression serious but no longer distressed.

"I don't think he's seriously hurt—only scared. He said he fell from the lowest branch. Is that right, Juliana?"

Juliana nodded. "Ja, he didn't climb very far."

"This is good. The thick grass should have provided good cushion. But I am going to take him to Doctor Klaassen for an examination to be safe." He glanced at Walden, and sympathy glimmered in his eyes. "Are you all right, Walden?"

The boy shook his head, burrowing against Augusta's ribs. "When he came down and didn't make any noise, I thought . . . I thought . . ." His chin quivered.

Augusta rubbed his shoulders. "You had a scare, too, Walden. It's all right to be upset." She shifted her attention to Herr Rempel. "Maybe Walden should stay with me while you take Folker to the doctor."

For several seconds, Herr Rempel gazed at Walden, as if uncertain. Then he angled his head slightly. "Walden? Do you want to stay here with Frau Dyck?"

Walden wove his arms around Augusta's waist but didn't say anything.

She stroked his hair. "We'll be fine. You see to Folker, and we will say a prayer he did no real damage in his fall."

Herr Rempel sighed. "Danke. I will come for Walden when we're finished at the doctor's." Then his expression turned firm. "And as soon as I am able, I will come over and build a ladder for Juliana's reading tree. It will be a safer way for her to reach her favorite branch."

Martina

Gerhard slumped in his chair, head back, mouth hanging slack. Martina stood for a few minutes observing him, remembering other days, other times, when he'd lain in that same position. To her knowledge, he hadn't sneaked to the cellar after their quiet dinner. Which should mean he was merely sleeping, not sleeping *off* something. But she couldn't help being suspicious. He'd been sullen and uncommunicative at the dining room table. The depressive behavior too often preceded indulging.

On tiptoe, she moved close and then leaned in. His warm breath hit her face, and she inhaled. Onions. Garlic. Nothing sickeningly sweet. Relieved, she straightened, and as she did, his eyes popped open. His bleary gaze landed on her, and he snuffled and sat up.

"What'd you want?" He slurred the query, something else he did when he indulged, but she believed she could credit it to sleepiness this time.

Thank goodness.

She sank into her chair and reached into the basket beside it for her knitting needles and yarn. "If you want to nap, won't you be more comfortable in bed? Your head hanging to the side that way will make your neck stiff."

He rotated his head, grimacing. "I don't want to nap." His frown turned in her direction. "What are you doing over there?"

She laid the knitted square of dark-blue yarn across her knees. "Working on a sweater for Walden." Such pleasure she found in making the little garment. She could already imagine him wearing it to church over his britches and suspenders, perhaps with a black ribbon tie at his collar. "I want it done for his birthday."

"But his birthday is in September. Why are you working on it now?"

My, he sounded grumpy. So different from last Sunday. But last Sunday, they'd had the pleasure of children at their table. Her heart panged. He would never say with words how much he longed for children, but his attitude screamed its truth. She must be patient with him. Even though she hadn't intended to share her plans, it might cheer him to know everything she was doing with the blue yarn. "I need to finish his so I can then work on yours."

"Mine?" He barked out the simple question.

"Ja. I had several skeins of yarn dyed this dark blue so I could make matching sweaters for you and Walden." She hoped Gerhard and Walden would wear them when they celebrated bringing the boy into their home for good. Surely it would still happen. Surely Frau Dyck wouldn't find the blacksmith a wife who would assume care for the boys. Surely her plans wouldn't all go awry.

Her pulse was pounding, and she took a slow breath to calm her racing thoughts. "He's so fond of his Onkel Gerhard, and he enjoys imitating you. I thought having a sweater like yours to wear would make him feel special."

Gerhard stared at her for several seconds, his expression un-readable. "He imitates me?" The irritation in his voice was gone now, replaced with a sense of wonder.

Martina nodded emphatically. "Do you not notice it? When you two walk from the shop to the house for lunch, he holds his shoulders back and swings his arms the way you do, and he tries to match your stride. At the table, he tucks his napkin into his collar the way you do, and even puts his food on his plate the same way you do, with the meat on the right and vegetables on the left."

Gerhard's mouth dropped open. "I do that?"

Now she couldn't hold back a little laugh. "You have always done that—meat on the right, vegetables on the left, buttered bread balanced at the top of the plate. If your plate were a com-pass, the bread would be north. You are a very orderly man, Ger-hard, and Walden is absorbing all you do." She swallowed the lump that rose in her throat, praying her next words would be taken well. "Your example . . . it matters to him."

Gerhard pushed out of the chair and moved stiffly to the window. Hands locked behind his back, he stared out, his jaw muscles quivering.

Martina set the knitting aside and stood. She crossed behind him and placed her hand on his shoulder. "I upset you."

He shook his head, but his taut shoulders said otherwise.

She gave his shoulder a little squeeze. "Are you sure? I am sorry if I did. I thought it would please you to know how much Walden seems to admire you."

"It . . . it does."

She gathered her courage and asked in a rasping whisper, "Then why do you seem sad?"

Very slowly, he turned his head and looked into her eyes. "Be-cause I am not a man to be admired. I am a fallen man who sets a poor example more often than not."

Was he finally admitting what she'd long needed him to acknowledge? If he finally was willing to speak of it, maybe they could even bring the practice to an end. Hope hummed like a bird's wings in her breast. She pressed her hand firmly. "Gerhard . . ."

He jerked away from her touch and moved to the other side of their parlor. His shoulders held square, his chin still quivering, he glared past her. "Maybe that is why God denied us children. Because He knows I am weak and a poor example. He does not trust me."

The brokenness in his voice and face shattered Martina's heart. She dashed to him and reached to embrace him.

He sidestepped her. "You know what I do." The harshness was in his tone again, but she believed it was aimed at himself and not her this time. "What I've done for years."

Ja, she knew what. And she knew why. The guilt weighed worse than a millstone around her neck. "I'm sorry, Gerhard. I am so very sorry." She placed her hands on her belly, over her useless womb. "I wish . . ." But the words wouldn't form. It hurt so much to hold them. Speaking them would surely destroy her.

"I wish, too," he said so quietly she thought she might have imagined it. Then he gave a jolt and turned toward the kitchen. "I'm going to the cellar. Please don't disturb me." He strode out of the room with his usual proud gait.

Martina staggered to her chair and sank onto its firm cushion. She curled her hands over the armrest and held so tightly her fingers ached. In these last few weeks she'd thought . . . she'd hoped . . . she'd prayed that he'd given up visiting the cellar. Just as in years past she'd thought . . . hoped . . . prayed that she would carry a baby to term and—more recently—thought, hoped, prayed for a child to claim as their own. But what was the use?

No wonder Gerhard drank himself to numbness.

* * *

Gerhard's Sunday melancholy melted away by Monday morning, to Martina's relief. But why should it surprise her? Walden Rempel came and brought sunshine with him. For dinner, she fried a chicken. It was extra work, but it was the boy's favorite. She even laughed when *her men,* as she'd begun thinking of Walden and Gerhard, cleared the entire platter, leaving only one small piece for her.

Before leaving for the shop after lunch, Gerhard took her aside and said, "Herr Rempel wants the boy home before suppertime. Apparently Folker had a little scare over the weekend, so he is feeling extra protective toward both boys. I promised I would take him home right after closing the shop."

Martina's heart caught. "You won't even stop by here on your way?"

"Nein." He gave her upper arm a gentle squeeze. "Why don't you bring our afternoon snack to the shop today? Then you can stay for a little while and talk with him. I know you like time with him, too."

Ja, she did, and she appreciated her husband's understanding. "I will do that."

Midafternoon, she took a basket of applesauce muffins, a tin of milk, and three cups to the shop so she could eat with her men. Gerhard ate quickly and returned to work, but she and Walden sat on a bench outside the door in the sunshine and savored their snack.

Walden swung his feet while he munched. He took a slurp from his cup, then aimed a curious look at Martina. "Do you ever go fishing?"

"I haven't gone fishing since I was a little girl." She used her napkin to remove his milk mustache while answering.

"Did you catch fish from the Cottonwood River?"

She chuckled. "Nein. When I was your age, I lived in Russia, in a village near the Molotschna River. My Vater would take me along sometimes when he and my brothers went fishing at the river even though my Mutter said it was not a suitable pastime for a girl." She enjoyed remembering those carefree days and also sharing them with Walden. "I confess, I didn't catch very many fish, but I enjoyed being at the river with my Vater."

Walden nodded wisely. "I like to go fishing with Pa and Folker even when we don't catch very many. But we went last Saturday and caught so many fish we couldn't eat them all." He took another bite of his muffin and talked with his mouth full. "I wanted to bring some to you so you could cook them for us. I told Pa you're a really good cook."

Her heart warmed.

"But Pa took them to Frau Dyck."

Icy water seemed to flood her veins.

"Then she had us come for Sunday dinner, and we ate the fish. She's a good cook, too." He shoved the last bit of muffin into his mouth and swished his palms together. Crumbs peppered his lap. He grunted and brushed them onto the ground. Then he hopped down from the bench. "Thank you for the muffins, Tante Martina. They were very good. I better go help Onkel Gerhard now." He sauntered off as casually as if he hadn't just stabbed her straight through her middle.

She gathered up the cups and napkins and placed them in her basket. There was a little milk left in the tin, so she poured it into the bowl in the shop for the big orange tabby that chased away the mice for Gerhard. Walden waved to her from his spot next to Gerhard, and she waved in reply. Her hand trembled so badly the action probably resembled a fish flopping on the bank.

She walked the short distance between Gerhard's shop and their home, images of Walden at Augusta Dyck's table filling her mind and tangling her in jealousy. Was it not enough that the teacher had set off on a personal mission to find Herr Rempel a new wife? Did she also have to win the boys' affections? By the time she reached her house, she had built up a full head of steam, and she wouldn't be able to focus on anything until she'd had a chat with Frau Dyck.

Rubbing her aching temples, Martina considered how to approach the situation. The Frauenverein had been in full operation for a month now, yet she and the other officers had only met apart from the group one time. Didn't leaders of most clubs have organizational meetings? It made perfect sense for her to call an officers' meeting. Especially since last week's get-together with the members accomplished little more than bickering. The decision made, she deposited the basket and empty cups in the kitchen, then set off for the Hartmanns' house.

Berta Hartmann seemed surprised to find Martina on her doorstep, but when Martina explained the purpose for coming by, the woman sighed. "I think it's a good idea for us to discuss how to avoid another unpleasant meeting like the last one. When and where would you like to meet?"

Martina had hoped to settle things today, that very hour, but suddenly she realized the foolishness of her impulsive decision. Unlike her, both Berta and Augusta had children at home. They couldn't simply walk away from their responsibilities. "My house is available as a meeting place. As for when . . . before Friday evening, of course. Is there a particular day or time that suits you best?"

"Midmorning seems to be my slowest time of day." Berta's brow puckered in seeming deep thought. "I would prefer to avoid Wednesday as I ready the church for Bible study. But any other day is fine."

"Then let us meet at my house tomorrow morning at nine-thirty." Martina gave a firm nod, setting the day and time in her mind. "I will inform Augusta. Thank you for your willingness to fit this meeting into your week. I believe it will be an important one."

"I do, too, Martina. I'll see you tomorrow."

Even before Berta had clicked the latch on her door, Martina was already hurrying up the street toward the Dycks' house.

Chapter Twenty-One

Augusta

Augusta accepted the cup of tea and slice of some sort of crumbly cake from Martina Krahn. "Danke. This looks delicious."

Berta Hartmann, seated in the middle of a short settee across from Augusta, already balanced a plate on her knee. "I didn't expect refreshments, Martina. You truly didn't need to go to such trouble for our short meeting."

Augusta hoped it would be a short meeting. When Martina showed up unexpectedly on her doorstep yesterday, she was left with the impression that there were several items of importance to discuss. She wasn't worried about Juliana. The girl was responsible enough to be left alone for a few hours. But gardening and other chores awaited her, not to mention the need to transcribe a few more copies of the query letter for potential wives. She fully expected to start receiving responses to the advertisements she'd placed in the Topeka, Wichita, and Kansas City newspapers, and surely Herr Elias would bring more names to her on Saturday. She wanted several copies ready to send.

"I thank you, ladies, for coming." Martina seated herself in the chair next to Augusta. Although she'd seemingly spoken to both women, she turned a firm look solely on Augusta. "I believe we can agree that the purpose of the ladies' society is to help people, bolster camaraderie, and make Alexandertol a stronger community. I believe we also agree that last Friday's meeting was something of a fiasco."

"Ja, it was a very sad meeting." Berta shook her head. "I have done a great deal of thinking and praying about it, and while I still don't understand why things became so unruly, I think I know how it started."

Augusta thought she knew, too, but she wouldn't share her thoughts aloud. She took a bite of the cinnamon-laced cake and silently prayed that if Berta said what Augusta was thinking, Martina wouldn't throw both of them out the door.

Berta took a deep breath. "I think—"

"Frau Dyck's project has created dissension amongst the membership." Martina's statement blasted over Berta's softer voice.

Berta frowned. "Martina, that is not what I was going to say."

"Why not?" Martina's sharp voice made Augusta cringe. "The membership voted not to pursue this matchmaking venture, but she went ahead with it on her own. Now why should we bother to make decisions as a group? Any of the members might take it upon herself to do her own projects. Frau Dyck's choice to ignore the advice of the Frauenverein has undermined the entire organization."

"Martina . . ." Berta gazed at the club's president, dismay evident in her tone and expression. "I truly believe the only reason the women voted not to assist Herr Rempel in his search for a new wife was because of your adamant objection. I like you very much, and I don't mean to hurt your feelings with what I'm about to say, but you must know that you are a very opinionated person. When you voice your opinion, you do so in a way that makes others fearful of speaking an opposing view."

Augusta shrank back, anticipating Martina's explosion. To

her surprise, the woman glared but held her lips in a tight line and remained silent.

Berta went on in her usual kind manner. "I believe we can credit last week's inability to find agreement to an underlying worry that ideas from members don't matter as much as your ideas. Thus, everyone wanted to be heard, and a loud argument ensued."

Augusta had held the same thought and was glad Berta had the courage to speak frankly to Martina. But she also felt sorry for Martina. Every other woman in the community had children or grandchildren to tend, which filled much of their days. Martina, being childless, was left with many empty hours. Augusta understood the pain of empty hours since she lacked a husband to fill her evenings with companionship and her nights with closeness.

Martina smacked her plate onto the little table between the chairs and glared at Berta. "Are you saying you want me to step down as president of the Frauenverein? Do you think more will be accomplished if I am not involved?"

Augusta sat up, nearly tipping her plate. "Frau Krahn, no. That isn't what Berta is saying at all."

Berta nodded, her gaze bouncing from Augusta to Martina. "Your strong personality makes you a good organizer, Martina. We need a good organizer leading the group. I don't wish for you to quit leading. I only ask that, rather than dominating the meetings, you serve as a moderator."

"A moderator . . ." Martina seemed to roll the title on her tongue, as if deciding if its taste suited her. "To be honest, I am not sure how to moderate."

Sympathy wove through Augusta's breast. Of course Martina didn't know. How could she? Augusta leaned forward and placed her fingertips on Martina's knee. "If you'd been raising children or leading a classroom, you would have had much experience in moderating squabbles and solving conflicts. It isn't your fault that—"

Martina bolted from her chair. "You're wrong, Frau Dyck. Very, very wrong."

Augusta drew back in surprise and remorse. She'd meant to commiserate. How had her empathetic words incited such fury?

Berta set her plate aside and stood, reaching for Martina. "I'm sure Augusta didn't intend—"

"It is my fault that I've not spent the last twenty years raising children. My womb!" Martina glared at both of them. She clenched her fists and pressed them against her belly. "It is useless. It expels my babies before they are ready to be born. Six babies in all. So you see, it is my fault that I am without experience in moderating children's disagreements. It is my fault that my husband drinks himself into a stupor when the quietness—" Her eyes went round with horror. She collapsed into her chair and slunk low, hiding her face in her hands.

Unshed tears flooding her eyes, Berta turned to Augusta. Augusta, too, battled weeping. Such a burden this seemingly strong, confident woman carried. What had it cost her to harbor these secrets? Augusta had surmised that Martina Krahn was unable to conceive. To discover she'd lost so many babies was heartbreaking. But even worse was the realization that she blamed herself for her husband's choice to imbibe in alcohol. How had she managed to keep his practice hidden from the community? No wonder she'd always held herself so aloof.

Augusta longed for words of wisdom, of encouragement, of healing to bestow on the other woman. But her mind was too numb from the shock of what she'd just heard.

Berta knelt beside Frau Krahn's chair. She pulled Martina's hands from her face. "Martina, look at me."

Martina turned her head aside, pressing her chin to her shoulder. "Nein. Go away."

Berta shook the woman's hands, her expression kind yet also insistent. "I will not go away until you look at me and listen to me."

Martina's lips nearly disappeared with her scowl, but she jerked her face in Berta's direction.

Berta sighed. "Danke. Now listen. There is no shame in not carrying a baby to term. Sometimes babies go straight to heaven from the mother's womb. It is hurtful, yes, and we mourn the loss, but God alone knows the number of our days. We must trust that He did what was best for your babies."

Although Augusta believed what the minister's wife said was true, she still struggled against the seeming unfairness of it. Why did some babies die too soon? Why did husbands and wives sometimes die at young ages? She wished she could offer some kind of solace to this hurting woman, but how could she explain something she didn't understand herself? Impossible. So she inwardly prayed that the God who'd welcomed Frau Krahn's babies to Him would give their mother comfort and peace.

"As for your husband's way of dealing with your losses, you are not responsible for it."

"Ja, ja . . ." Augusta couldn't stay silent. She might not know why Martina's babies came too early, but she did know that one person was not accountable for another's choices. Herr Krahn alone must bear the weight of using alcohol to comfort himself instead of leaning on the great Comforter. "He is a grown man who makes his own choice."

Martina turned a teary-eyed frown on Augusta. "But he makes his choice in response to my failure to give him the child for whom he longs. Therefore, it is up to me to change his response, to stop him from drinking."

Augusta shook her head. The only One with the power to change was the Lord Almighty, and the one in need of change had to be willing to bend to the Father's will. "Martina, you cannot stop him from drinking any more than you could stop me from helping Herr Rempel."

To her surprise, Martina burst into laughter. "Ja, well, you might be right about that. You have proved more stubborn than I ever thought possible." She sighed deeply, and her head sagged against the high back of the chair. "Since I have already confessed my other ugly secrets, I may as well tell you the third. I did not start the Frauenverein to help the folks of Alexandertol. I did it to help myself."

Berta offered a sympathetic nod. "So you would have something to do since you aren't raising children?"

The woman winced. "In part, perhaps. But mostly to find a child. I thought if we reached out to widows and orphans, we would eventually learn of an orphaned child who needs Gerhard and me as much as we need him. I thought we'd found one, too, except . . . ."

Now Augusta fully understood the woman's fierce opposition to her seeking a wife for Herr Rempel. She sat on the edge of her chair and met Martina's sad gaze. "I understand why you have grown so fond of Walden Rempel. I have been his and his brother's teacher since they started school, and I've known them since they were born because their mother and I were very good friends. They are delightful little boys, personable and quick-witted. But even though their father might find it challenging to raise them on his own, he would never part with them. They are all he has left of Hannah. He loves them. You must realize that even if I don't find him a new helpmeet, he will not give Walden or Folker to someone else to raise."

Tears flooded the older woman's eyes, but she blinked several times and the moisture cleared. She set her jaw at a stubborn angle and sat in silence for a few minutes while the only sound in the room was the steady *tick-tick* of the ornate Kroeger clock hanging on the wall. Then she pushed herself from the chair. Berta rose and moved aside as Martina crossed to the fireplace and rested her hand on the mantel next to a tintype of her and Gerhard. Her focus seemingly fixed on the image, she sighed.

"Ladies, I think it best that I step down as president of the Frauenverein. Berta, you take over leadership. At Friday's meeting, you can elect a new vice president."

Augusta stared at the woman's back, her heart pounding in her chest. She wanted to tell her to reconsider—that the Frauenverein needed her as much as she needed it—but something held her tongue. Oddly, Berta also stood mute.

Still facing away from them, Martina continued in a steady, emotionless voice. "A membership of eleven will insure no vote will be evenly split. This should eliminate future arguments." Abruptly she turned, her unsmiling face aimed in their direction but avoiding eye contact. "If ever I can help with a need that's brought to the committee, please let me know. And now, ladies, as my last act as president, I bring this meeting to a close." She exited via the hallway, and a few seconds later the click of a door latch sealed her away.

Augusta looked at Berta, and Berta looked back. Then in unison they shrugged. Berta sent a glance toward the hallway where Martina had disappeared, then offered Augusta a sad smile.

"Ja, well, I suppose we should go, hm?"

"I suppose we should." Augusta pressed her palms to her aching heart. "I feel guilty leaving her by herself, though, when she's clearly hurting. Isn't there something more we can do for her?"

Berta nodded, her expression grim. "Ja. We can keep her secrets. And we can pray God's healing over both Martina and Gerhard. What you said about Martina not being able to change Gerhard is true. Nor can we change Martina's feelings about why she hasn't borne children. But we can beseech the Great Healer to touch their hearts and bring His change."

Augusta vowed to do as Berta requested and pray for the Krahns. And she would do one thing more. She would pray that God, in His compassion and mercy, would bless them with a child of their own.

Chapter Twenty-Two

Konrad

"I cannot allow you to be unkind to your brother." Konrad sat on the edge of the twins' bed, his palm on Walden's chest. He felt the rise and fall of his son's angry huffs, and sorrow weighted him. He was doing the right thing by disciplining the boy. That didn't mean it was easy. "It gives me no pleasure to send you to your room so early, but if you spend this time by yourself, you will remember to choose a kinder tone and words with him tomorrow."

Walden's lower lip poked out, and his eyes narrowed into slits. "But he's so dumb sometimes, Pa. He doesn't listen. And he never stops talking. He makes me mad."

"'Be ye angry, and sin not . . .'" Konrad quoted from Ephesians 4:26, remembering his Vater teaching it to him. "Getting mad is not the sin, Walden. Letting anger rule your actions . . . that is the sin. There are better ways than yelling and name-calling to let your brother know he is bothering you. What are those better ways?"

Walden rolled his eyes. "Ask him to stop."

Konrad had thought Folker's fall from the tree and Walden's fear-filled response only two days ago would soften him toward Folker's impulsiveness. Apparently, Walden had already forgotten how worried he'd been. Konrad had not forgotten, and he would never set aside his gratitude that Folker suffered only a few bruises in the accident.

Now he drew in a breath to calm his own rush of anger at Walden's insolent tone lest he set a poor example. "*Kindly* ask him to stop. And also try to understand why Folker talks to you so much. He misses you during the day. When he sees you again, he is so happy. He wants to be with you."

Walden scrunched his lips into a scowl. "Sometimes I wish I could just stay with Onkel Gerhard and Tante Martina. Over there, nobody bothers me."

"Ja, well, your home is here, and you are fortunate to have a brother who loves you so much." Konrad snapped out the words more harshly than he'd intended, but Walden's statement stabbed his soul. "I don't expect you to never feel angry with him, but I expect you to behave differently the next time you feel angry. Remember, in this house we treat one another the way we want to be treated. If you don't want Folker telling you to go away, then you shouldn't say it to him."

Walden rolled onto his side. "If he told me to go away, I'd go to Onkel Gerhard."

Konrad came close to yanking his son from the bed and swatting the seat of his pants. But if he did it now, it would be to satisfy his own jealousy and anger rather than change Walden's behavior. Changing behavior should be discipline's purpose. He stood and gazed down at his sullen son for a few moments, until he knew he could speak evenly.

"Stay in your bed and think of the reasons why you are blessed to have Folker as your brother." *And me as your father.* He swallowed hard. "*Schlaf gut.*" After giving his usual nighttime wish for Walden to sleep well, he closed the door behind him and returned to the front room.

Folker sat on the settee with his arms folded and his lower lip sticking out. He looked as disgruntled as Walden had, and Konrad hid a smile as he sat next to him and pulled him close. "I will

tell you what I told your brother. 'Be ye angry, and sin not . . . '"
Then he added the last half of the verse, "'. . . let not the sun go
down upon your wrath.'"

Folker angled his head, looking up at his father. "I'm not
mad, Pa. I'm sad. Saturdays and Sundays, Walden and me are
brothers."

"Folker, you and Walden are always brothers. That will never
change."

"I mean, on Saturdays and Sundays we get along."

Konrad's chuckle rolled. "Well . . . sometimes."

Folker made a sour face. "Most times."

Konrad nodded. "Ja. You do."

"But"—Folker's lips formed a pout—"on the days he goes to
the Krahns' house, we don't get along at all. He doesn't want
anything to do with me. Why is that, Pa?"

Konrad weighed his words. He didn't want to make excuses
for Walden, making it sound as if it was all right for him to be
unkind to his brother. But just as he wanted Walden to understand Folker's feelings, he wanted Folker to understand his
brother's, so they might both grow in compassion. *"Be ye kind
one to another,"* the Bible advised.

"Folker, let me ask you a question. When you are tired, do
you get grumpy?"

Folker shrugged. "Sometimes."

Konrad nudged him, waggling his eyebrows. "Only sometimes?"

A sheepish look crept across his son's face. "Well . . . most
times."

Konrad smiled. "Ja, and you aren't the only one who gets
grumpy when he's tired. Walden works all day at the wheelwright shop. Herr Krahn has him doing things grown men do,
and he's still a boy. Do you think that might wear him out?"

Folker nodded slowly, his blue eyes locked on Konrad's.

"When a person is tired and grumpy, he doesn't always act like he should. When that happens, we have to remind ourselves that it's tiredness talking and not necessarily the person." He spoke to himself as much as to Folker. "This will help us be understanding instead of angry. Does that make sense?"

Folker sat very still, staring up at Konrad for several seconds. Then he nodded again. "It makes sense, but it still hurts my feelings."

Konrad pulled Folker into a hug. "I know, Son." He knew too well. Some of Walden's words had hurt him, too. He planted a kiss on the top of Folker's head and released him. "But Walden's getting some rest now, and when he wakes up"—*please, God*—"he will be ready to be with us again."

Folker wriggled himself beneath Konrad's arm and rested his cheek on his bicep. "I hope so. Because I think he likes it more at the Krahns'. At night, when we're supposed to be sleeping, he tells me how much he likes eating Frau Krahn's food and being with Herr Krahn in his shop. He says"—

Konrad held his breath, wanting to stop Folker from breaking his brother's confidence but also wanting to know what Walden said.

—"Herr Krahn sometimes calls him 'son,' and Frau Krahn calls him her little man. When they do, he pretends he has a pa *and* a ma, and it makes him happy."

Konrad's breath whooshed out. Now he wished he had hushed his son. He'd be happier not knowing how Walden felt about the Krahns. But was it the Krahns that Walden liked so much or only the idea of having a mother again? There was no way to know without asking Walden, and if Konrad asked tonight, he'd probably hear tiredness's reply rather than an honest one. So he would wait.

"Ja, well, here is what makes me happy." He grabbed Folker beneath his arms and heaved him from the settee, roaring like a bear as he did so. Folker's feet met the floor, and he lurched out of his father's grasp, giggling wildly. He spun and grinned at Konrad. "That was fun, Pa."

Konrad stood and ruffled Folker's hair. "Ja, it was, but time for fun is done. It's bedtime."

Folker's countenance immediately drooped. "Do I have to sleep in my bed? My mad's all gone, but Walden's might not be."

Konrad hated to admit it, but Folker was probably right about Walden. His hand on his son's head, Konrad pretended deep thought with his eyes rolled upward. Then he put his hands on his hips. "Just for tonight, you can sleep here on the settee. I'll get you a pillow and a blanket."

Folker whooped and dove onto the settee. He rolled to his back and stretched out, putting his hands under his head and grinning. "My own bed with nobody bumping me. This's going to be good."

Konrad went to fetch the pillow and blanket. Worry trailed him. Both boys seemed to like the idea of being the only one. But they were twins. They'd nestled together in their mother's womb. Shouldn't that bind them? This time of the boys being apart was creating too many problems. If his boys ended up like Jacob and Esau, always at odds with each other, he couldn't bear it. He needed to get married as quickly as possible. Even if it cost money, he should consider asking for help from a matchmaker. Tomorrow, after he took Walden to the Krahns, he would visit Frau Dyck and let her know.

Martina

After a restless night of little sleep, Martina awakened on Wednesday morning with a terrible headache. The only thing that propelled her from bed was the knowledge that she would need to prepare a good dinner for Walden Rempel. If her time with the boy was limited, and according to Augusta Dyck it certainly was, she wouldn't waste a minute of it. But cooking a hearty breakfast for Gerhard was more than she could manage, given the pounding in her head.

She put a pot of water on the stove to boil for coffee, then retrieved from the pantry the pan of cornbread left over from last night's supper. She transferred the mealy squares onto plates—one square for her, three for Gerhard. As she put the plates and a jug of maple syrup on the table, he entered the kitchen. He glanced at his plate, and his eyebrows dipped together. He turned his head and met her gaze, and at once the scowl softened.

"Are you sick?"

The kindness in his voice nearly undid her. She shook her head, touching her fingertips to her throbbing temples. "I think I'm only tired. I did not sleep well."

"I know." He sat in his chair and picked up his napkin. "You were restless."

Had she kept him awake, too? "I'm sorry if I disturbed you."

He shrugged and poured syrup over his cornbread. "I wasn't sleeping much anyway. I was . . . thinking."

She wished the coffee was ready. A cup of strong coffee would do much to bring her to life. She sagged into her chair and fixed her gaze on his somber face. "Thinking about what?"

"What I've been thinking about since Sunday."

The throb in her head increased.

"About those sweaters you're making."

His statement took her by surprise. "The sweaters?" She'd have them finished sooner than she'd originally thought now that she'd given up her leadership of the Frauenverein. "What about them?"

He stabbed his fork into the first chunk of cornbread. The fact that he hadn't prayed first told Martina his thoughts were elsewhere. "Maybe you shouldn't make one for me. I bet Walden would rather match with his brother."

"But—"

"If you make one only for Walden, it will cause hurt feelings for Folker." Gerhard pushed the lump of cornbread around on his plate without lifting it to his mouth. "He's a nice little boy. I don't want us to cause him pain." He glanced across the table at her. "Don't you think it will bother Folker if his brother gets a gift from us and he doesn't?"

Martina hadn't intended to give Walden the gift until he was theirs. Then it wouldn't matter. Or would it? It had all made so much sense before, but now she wondered why she hadn't considered Folker's feelings. She rubbed her temples. "I . . . I suppose it will."

He set his fork down and sighed. "It was a kind gesture, and I would have been proud to wear matching sweaters with the boy, but I think . . . maybe it's best if . . ."

She waited for several seconds, but he didn't finish his sentence. She flicked her fingers at him. "Eat, Gerhard. Walden will be here soon. You can't go to work with an empty stomach." And she couldn't face this day without coffee. She rose and crossed to the stove. Although the water wasn't boiling, steam formed little swirls on the water's surface. It was hot enough to brew coffee.

She readied the ground beans in the little basket and poured the hot water over them. After settling the domed lid in place, she set the pot aside and returned to the table. It would take a little while for the coffee to brew. She should try to eat while she waited. She'd only taken her second bite when the grating sound of wagon wheels filtered through the open kitchen window.

Gerhard stood, yanking his napkin from his collar. "Herr Rempel is here. I will see you at dinnertime."

Martina held out her hand. "But you haven't had any coffee yet."

"I don't need coffee." He rounded the table and gave her a quick kiss—something he hadn't done in more months than she could count. "Why don't you lie down and try to nap? You will likely feel better afterward. Don't cook anything elaborate for our dinner. Sandwiches will fill us." He strode out of the room.

She stared after him. Was it sympathy for her headache that had compelled him to kiss her? Although they shared a bed, she couldn't recall the last time he'd reached for her. She'd thought intimacy was gone, never to be recaptured. But he'd just kissed her. Without prompting, he'd kissed her. Her heart fluttered in her chest—a wondrous feeling.

Although her head still ached, she wouldn't lie down for a nap. She must respond to his tender gesture with one of her own. He'd said not to prepare an elaborate meal, but what else could she do to let him know he'd pleased her? For the past two weeks, she'd planned dinners with Walden's preferences in mind. Today she would prepare foods meant for Gerhard's palate. She knew his favorites. She would need to visit the butcher for a cut of corned beef, but there was a basket of carrots and a crock of pickled cabbage in the cellar.

She retrieved the handled basket she used for shopping and the largest of her nesting crockery bowls from the pantry, then descended the cellar stairs. No lanterns were lit down there, but enough sunlight flowed from the pantry windows down the cellar opening for her to see where she was going. She chose a dozen firm carrots from the basket on a waist-high shelf and laid them in her basket. Then she crouched next to the twenty-gallon crock containing cabbage and carefully removed the lid.

The pungent scent of vinegar and spices filled her nostrils, and her mouth watered. She transferred handfuls of the cabbage to the bowl until it was nearly full. Satisfied there was enough for Gerhard, Walden, and her, she clanked the lid back into place and stood.

As she bent over to pick up the bowl, her gaze slipped past the open shelving to the darker half of the cellar. A prickle of awareness crept up her spine and across her scalp. Something was different. But what? It took a moment for her to realize that a sheet-covered lump no longer hunkered in the corner. The lump beneath was created by Gerhard's wine-making equipment. Where had it gone?

Chapter Twenty-Three

Augusta

Augusta put the clean plate on the shelf and turned to Juliana, who was rinsing soap smears from the wash basin. "When you're finished there, I would appreciate your taking a hoe to the garden. Our little vegetables are poking their heads above the soil, but so are weeds. Will you be able to discern the difference and not chop out the peas and beans?"

Juliana sent a shocked look over her shoulder, then laughed. "Mother, how can I not discern the difference? I planted the seeds in neat rows. Anything growing outside the rows, I will remove."

Juliana's simple response carried Augusta backward in time, to the days of her childhood in Alexanderwohl. Augusta had pilfered a carved, painted spinning top from a vendor cart in the village. Although Mutter was disappointed in Augusta's behavior, she didn't scold. Instead, she took her to the garden plot and showed her the scraps of green growing in the dark, rich soil.

Mutter's wise, tender voice echoed in the back of her mind. "Why do we chop the weeds from our garden, Gussie?"

Augusta remembered her reply. "So the vegetables can grow."

"Ja, you are right. Weeds will prevent the good plants from growing strong and producing fruit." Mutter had taken Augusta's hand and looked fervently into her upturned face. "We must chop sin from our lives the way we chop weeds from the garden rows. Sin keeps us from growing strong in faith and producing fruit for God's kingdom. One weed left to flourish can take over the entire garden. One sin can grow into many that overtake the soul. What you did, my child, by taking something that is not yours, is stealing. God's Holy Book tells us not to steal. Stealing is a sin. What must you do now to make things right again?"

Mutter then knelt with Augusta beside the garden, and Augusta asked God to forgive her for taking the top. Afterward, she visited the cart owner. She apologized and returned the top, but also paid for it. After that day, each time temptation struck, Augusta remembered weeds overtaking a garden—sin overtaking a soul—and strove for holy choices.

Now, in remembrance, Augusta realized Mutter's gentle teaching had impacted her more deeply than harsh punishment would have.

Augusta tucked a loose strand of red-gold hair behind her daughter's ear, then cupped her cheek. "Anything growing outside the row . . . outside the pathway God wants for us . . . we chop out, ja?"

For a moment, Juliana's brow puckered, as if confused by Augusta's statement. Then delight broke on her face. "Ja, I like that, Mother." She rose on tiptoe and kissed Augusta's cheek. "I'll get the hoe now." She scampered out of the kitchen just as someone knocked on the front door.

Augusta hurried to the door, removing her apron as she went, fully expecting to find Berta Hartmann on the porch. They had decided, after the sad meeting at Frau Krahn's house yesterday, to spend some time in prayer together for the Frauenverein but also the Krahns. She swung the door open. "Guten Morgen, Ber—" But she found Herr Rempel there instead.

He held his leather cowboy hat against his thigh. Removing it must have mussed his hair, because tufts stood up above his left ear. Reflexively, her hand rose to smooth the strands into place. Then she realized what she was doing and quickly drew it back. Clasping her hands against her skirt front, she swallowed a nervous titter and smiled at her guest.

"Why, Herr Rempel, what can I do for you this morning?"

"I am sorry to bother you, but there are two things I need to tell you. First, I have gathered the materials to build a ladder and also a small platform for Juliana's reading tree. The platform will not be big enough for her to sit on, but it can hold her book and an apple or two."

Augusta drew back in surprise. "How did you know Juliana takes a snack to the tree?"

A sheepish grin creased his face, giving him a boyish appearance despite the whiskers growing on his cheeks and jaw. "The twins told me."

Of course they had.

"If it is all right with you," he went on, "I will come here after supper on Friday and construct the ladder and platform."

So he would be here working while she was at the Frauenverein meeting. Why did the thought bring a twinge of disappointment? "That is very kind of you, Herr Rempel, but I don't want you to go to too much trouble."

"And I want Juliana to be safe." His determined, concerned tone ended Augusta's argument.

She nodded. "Then I will say danke."

"Bitte. And . . ." He drew a full breath and blew it out. "I want to talk to you about hiring a matchmaker."

He couldn't have surprised her more if he'd flung a cup of cold water in her face. "A matchmaker? But I—" She shook her head, sending away the defensive answer forming on her tongue about the letters she had ready to send. "What made you decide to use a matchmaker?"

He looked aside for a moment, chewing the edge of his mustache, then met her gaze. "I think I must hurry in acquiring a wife. The arrangement I made with Herr Krahn to apprentice Walden isn't working so well."

Not working well? What did he mean? Herr Rempel wasn't one to engage in gossip. He wouldn't tell her if Herr Krahn had been drinking and endangered Walden in some way, but clearly he was troubled about something. Now she was troubled, too. "Then why not just keep Walden at home with you?"

The man grimaced, as if a pain had gripped him. "I can't keep Walden home until someone is there to see to him, or my work will go undone. It goes slowly enough with part of my attention always on Folker." He swung the hat back and forth, creating a gentle *swish-swish* against his trouser fabric. "You said if I use a matchmaker, I could possibly have a wife already by the end of the month. This would be best."

"I've already sent two letters to Marion, to the women Herr Elias had told me about. Maybe one of them will be interested. If so, she would be able to come here more quickly than it will take someone to travel all the way from New York. Would you like to wait and hear back from them before paying a fee to a matchmaker? There's no sense in spending that money unless you have to, ja?"

He tilted his head. "They are good prospects for me?"

Although Augusta knew only the little Herr Elias had told her, she was hopeful one of the sisters would match the list of requirements she'd been given. "I can't say for sure until I hear back from them, but based on what Herr Elias said about them, I think the chances are good."

He stared into her eyes for several seconds, chewing his mustache, then he gave a quick nod. "Ja, I would rather save the money, if possible. I will wait for word from the women in Marion." He slapped his hat over his hair. "Danke, Frau Dyck. You will let me know when replies have come?"

"I will."

"And . . ." He glanced aside, his Adam's apple bobbing in a swallow. "You will contact a matchmaker in New York for me, if need be? You know what to say."

She thought of what she'd written in the stack of letters ready to be sent. Ja, she knew what to say. What woman wouldn't be drawn to the man she'd described in the missives? She nodded and touched his sleeve. "I will continue to help you as much as I can." The worry about what she'd learned regarding Herr Krahn rose in her memory again, and her fingers tightened. "Herr Rempel, my offer to keep the boys with me during the day still stands if you're . . . concerned . . . about Walden being at the Krahns'."

His shoulders rose and fell with a mighty intake and release of breath. "You are a kind woman, and I appreciate your offer. I chose not to leave them with you since you have them all during the school season." He released a rueful chuckle, the outside corners of his eyes crinkling. "I thought you might need a break from them. They are very high-spirited boys."

She lowered her hand and laughed. "Ja, that they are." Then she sobered. "Even so, they're always welcome here. Juliana enjoys their company, as do I. Please know it is not an inconvenience for them to stay with me while you work."

He thanked her again and took a backward step. "I will consider your generous offer and let you know." He turned and trotted to his wagon.

Only then did she notice Folker waiting on the seat. One twin by himself. She'd seen him sitting there alone before when Herr Rempel stopped by, but for some reason today it stung her heart. Maybe because the boy seemed sadder than on previous occasions. She waved farewell to both of them, then walked slowly around the house to check on Juliana. As she went, a prayer formed in her heart.

Lord, whatever is happening at the Krahns', protect Walden. Protect

Frau Krahn. Guide both Herr and Frau Krahn into Your will. Craft for them—the Krahns, Herr Rempel, his new wife, and his boys—a tapestry of Your grace.

Augusta and Juliana walked to town Friday morning. Juliana planned to spend the day with Laura Weber at the general store, and Augusta wanted to check her box at the post office. She'd sent the letters to the pair of half sisters in Marion on Monday. Given the town's proximity to Alexandertol, if either had responded quickly, she might have a response waiting. She hoped so. Each day she'd worried a little more about Walden Rempel spending his days with a man who might be numbing his senses with alcohol and therefore not fully capable of providing good supervision for the boy.

At the mercantile door, Augusta reminded Juliana to be on her best behavior, kissed her good-bye, then crossed the street to the little post office. The door was propped open with a large speckled rock, which allowed her access. Behind the counter, Herr Bauer whistled while sweeping the floor. Augusta stepped up to the counter, and his merry tune ceased.

"Frau Dyck!" He propped the broom in the corner and marched to the row of cubbies hanging on the back wall. "I was hoping you'd come in. You've got a letter waiting. From Marion." He pulled an envelope from Augusta's cubby and slid it across the counter to her.

Augusta picked it up. The return address simply gave the town name—no sender name. She leaned sideways a bit and peered beyond the postal manager to the cubbies. "Are you sure there's only one?"

The man nodded, his bald head shining in the sunlight pouring through the large plate-glass window. "I'm sure. But it's a fat one, Frau Dyck. The woman who sent it must have a lot to say."

Augusta shot the man a sharp look. "What makes you think a woman sent it?"

He laughed. "I might not be a Pinkerton detective, but I can put two and two together." He held up one finger. "In all the years you've lived here, you've never received a letter from Marion before, so you must not have kin or friends living there." He flicked a second finger upward. "You're hunting for a wife for Herr Rempel, and you sent letters to women in Marion earlier this week, so it makes sense this is one of those women responding." He shook his fingers at her, grinning. "Now, if the woman who sent that letter wants to marry Herr Rempel, there will be a real two and two coming together—a man and wife plus two boys, ja?"

Augusta's stomach twisted into a knot. "Herr Bauer, how do you know what those letters I sent were about?"

He shrugged and reached for the broom. "Agnes told me you were helping Herr Rempel find a new wife." He returned to sweeping and whistling.

Augusta stared at him for several seconds, too stunned to speak. She knew Agnes liked to talk. Even Juliana, who was still a child, knew that Agnes liked to talk. Most likely, everyone in Alexandertol exercised caution in what they said to her because she liked to talk. Perhaps it was foolishness on her part to think the woman wouldn't carry home topics shared in Frauenverein meetings. Granted, this wasn't a Frauenverein project, so perhaps Agnes hadn't broken any kind of protocol by telling her husband what Augusta was doing. Still . . .

How she hated confrontation, but this must be said. "Herr Bauer?" He paused and faced her. She looked the man directly in the eyes. "I would appreciate if you would not mention this letter or its purpose to anyone else. Finding a wife is a very personal matter, and Herr Rempel has enough to worry about without being concerned his search is the topic of gossip in town."

Herr Bauer drew back, a little grunt of irritation leaving his throat. "At least the talk has shifted from speculating that he was trying to court you. Now the talk is centered on the truth of the matter instead of supposition. I should think you would appreciate that."

Nein, she did not appreciate it. And even worse, the idea that people no longer suspected him of pursuing a courtship with her left her more offended and jealous than relieved. What was wrong with her?

She snatched up the letter and left the post office. She and Berta had agreed to meet early for tonight's Frauenverein meeting and pray together again before the others arrived. She would talk to the new leader about whether Agnes should be allowed to remain in the club. Ousting someone from a service club didn't rest easily with her, but neither did the worry that confidential matters were not being treated as such.

Martina Krahn had often mentioned the importance of maintaining the integrity of the club. The woman might not be the leader any longer, but her desire for integrity should remain intact.

Chapter Twenty-Four

Martina

Afterwards cleaning up the kitchen on Friday evening, Martina went to the parlor and settled in her chair. The knitting basket was still there, with Walden's partially finished sweater awaiting completion. Even though Gerhard had expressed concern about her making it, and even though Frau Dyck had been adamant Walden Rempel would never live anywhere except with his father, she still felt compelled to finish it. To keep her hands busy? To keep her dream alive? Because she'd been taught to finish what she started? She didn't know for sure which reason took precedence, but she couldn't abandon it—nor the one she intended to make for Gerhard.

He shuffled into the room from the hallway, wearing his robe and slippers over his nightshirt. He drew to a halt and frowned at her. "What are you doing?"

She held up her knitting needles. "Working."

He shook his head. "I meant, what are you doing here? It's Friday. Shouldn't you go to the church for the Frauenverein meeting?"

Martina put the needles to work, their gentle *clack-clack* keeping time with the clock's *tick-tick,* a soothing rhythm. "Nein."

"Why not?"

"Because I resigned from the club."

Gerhard's mouth dropped open. He went to his chair and sat, still gaping at her. "Why would you do such a thing? The club was your idea."

"Ja, it was." Martina put her full focus on her knitting needles and the row of neatly spaced stitches emerging. Ever since Wednesday morning when she'd discovered that his wine-making equipment wasn't in the cellar, she'd wondered where he'd set it up now. She hadn't asked, because she didn't want to ruin the shift in their relationship that had taken place that morning at the breakfast table, when he'd surprised her with his good-bye kiss.

How many kisses had he given her since that morning kiss? One each day after work, another at bedtime, and one on his way out the door in the mornings. Eight in all. More kisses in three days than in the previous three years. How she savored the affection and the connection with him, the absence of which she'd mourned nearly as much as she'd mourned her lost babies. She didn't know why it had returned, but now that it was back, she didn't want to risk losing it again. So the question about the kegs and fruit press and crate of glass bottles remained locked in her mouth.

"Martina?"

Gerhard sounded so sad that she automatically lifted her attention from her knitting to his face.

"Did you quit the club because you fear what I do when I'm home by myself?"

Her hands, still gripping the needles, sagged into her lap. After years of him never speaking of his habit, he'd now brought it up twice. After years of her keeping silent about it, she had no idea now how to speak of it.

"You need not worry about it any longer."

Her entire body jolted, as if she'd been stung by a wasp. "W-what do you mean?"

"I took the equipment to the shop."

Her pulse pounded so fiercely it thundered in her ears.

"I broke it down and put it in the burn barrel."

She stared at him, unsure she'd heard him correctly. "In the . . . burn barrel?"

"Ja. This morning, it"—he swallowed, his eyes closing for a moment, then flicking open and fixing on hers—"all went up in smoke with our other rubbish." He slowly rose and took the single step needed to reach her chair. He perched on the little embroidered footstool she used some evenings when her ankles swelled, and he placed his hands over hers. "When you told me how Walden observes me, imitates me, it . . . broke my heart."

She'd seen it happen, and her heart had broken, too. "That wasn't my intention."

"I know." For a few seconds, he seemed to examine their hands lying on top of the blue yarn, then met her gaze again. "But it made me consider what kind of example I want to leave. Not only for people now, but when I'm gone. When I die, do I want someone to go to the cellar and discover what I'd done in secret? I knew I had to stop. I knew . . ." He shuddered. "What I was doing was a waste for so many reasons. I drank to forget my guilt, but it never went away. It was always within me, and—"

"Your guilt?" The question burst from Martina. "I thought you drank to forget my guilt."

He frowned. "Why would you feel guilty?"

Tears stung her eyes, but she made herself say the words that had haunted her for years. "For not giving you a child."

He hung his head. "Oh, Martina . . ."

Martina shook her hands free. She tossed the partially completed sweater into the basket and then cupped his face. His whiskers were both soft and prickly against her palms, just as this shared moment was both tender and painful. She lifted his head. "Gerhard, for what reason did you feel guilty?"

"For being so selfish and making you with child." He curled his hands lightly around her wrists, then turned his face to and fro, placing kisses on the tender pads at the base of her thumbs.

He linked fingers with her and lowered their joined hands to her lap. "I saw how you suffered when the babies came too soon. I reasoned . . . if I didn't get you with child, you wouldn't suffer. But my needs . . ." He shook his head. "So I drank. Because when I drank, I forgot everything else. And it kept me·from making you suffer again."

She could tell him that holding himself away from her hadn't alleviated her suffering. It had intensified it, making her feel as if he didn't want her. But there'd been enough guilt. Now it was time for grace.

She leaned forward and placed her lips to his. He responded by tipping his head. The pressure increased. His fingers slipped into her hair. She felt the pins bounce off her shoulders, and her hair came loose from its knot. Did she care? Nein.

For several minutes they explored with their lips, their kisses wandering to cheeks and temples and jawlines and even eyelids, as if discovering each other for the first time. When he drew in a quavering breath and sat back, she captured his hands and raised them to her cheek.

"Gerhard, I've missed you. I've missed being with you." The glimmer in his eyes let her know he understood what she was telling him. Her gaze locked on his dark-blue eyes, the same color as the yarn in her basket. "These past few days, your morning and nighttime kisses have ignited something inside of me. I know we don't have children. At our ages, it's unlikely we ever will." Oh, how it hurt to admit it, but at the same time it was somehow freeing to say it out loud. "But we have each other. Can . . . can 'each other' be enough for you?"

He sat for what seemed forever, staring intently into her eyes, his expression unreadable. Then, in one smooth motion, he stood and swept her into his arms. He buried his face in her hair and held her so tightly she could scarcely draw a breath. But oh! How wonderful to be in his strong embrace again. She clung, sending up silent thank-yous to God for this wonderful time of rekindling.

After several wondrous minutes, he loosened his hold and gazed fervently at her. "Martina, I love you. If I am enough to make you happy, then that is all I need for me to be happy." A boyish grin grew on his face, setting her heart into flutters of awareness. He glanced at the basket next to her chair. "Did you need to work on that sweater tonight?"

A girlish giggle built in her chest and escaped. "Walden's birthday isn't until September. The knitting can wait."

"Good." His eyes twinkling, he curved his arm around her waist and turned her toward the hallway. Then he stopped and gave her a sheepish grin. "Oh. Come Christmastime, I might disappoint our neighbors."

A confused laugh trickled out. "You will? Why?"

"I used my fruit press not only for wine, but for cider. The press is gone, so . . ."

She understood his meaning, and a true belly laugh rolled out. She rested her cheek against his chest, the comforting thrum of his heartbeat like music to her ears. "The neighbors will survive without your sweet cider. But I . . ." Dare she say it? She smiled up at him. "I won't survive without your sweet kisses."

He sighed, a sound of contentment. "Ah, my Martina, nor will I. And we won't save them for only at Christmas."

Augusta

Around nine on Saturday morning, Herr Elias came by Augusta's house and delivered a list of names. A short list, only three names. He tapped the middle one and said, "Of the three, I would say this one is most likely to be interested in matrimony.

She's a little older—thirty-one or thirty-two, perhaps—and she's an only child whose parents have passed on. She teaches the youngest grades at the Marion school, which must mean she likes children."

Augusta looked at him in surprise. "You seem to have gathered a great deal of information about . . ." She glanced at the paper again. "Ernestine Gartner."

"Ja, well, I visited with her for quite a while two times this past week when she came to the mercantile. She seemed lonely, and since I am new in town and a little lonely myself, it was easy for us to converse. Most definitely send a query letter to Fräulein Gartner." He slid his hands into his pockets and rocked on his heels, his smile aimed at her. "That is, if one of the women whose names I gave you last week hasn't already laid claim to Herr Rempel. Did either respond to your queries?"

Augusta folded the paper and put it in her apron pocket. "Ja, they each wrote letters in reply"—and saved a stamp by sending them in one envelope, proving their frugality—"but I haven't shared them with Herr Rempel yet. I will do that later today." Would he be as put off by the responses as she had been? Both sisters seemed more interested in the size of Herr Rempel's house and bank account than anything else.

"Are you taking the letters to his house, or is he coming here?"

Did a hint of jealousy enter his tone? His expression remained so friendly that she couldn't be sure. If she told him Herr Rempel had spent yesterday evening at her house constructing a ladder and a small platform in Juliana's reading tree, she might be able to discern his feelings. But if she talked about it, she would think about it. About him effortlessly carrying the lengths of lumber on his broad shoulders, of his faded chambray shirt stretching taut against his muscled back and upper arms as he swung the hammer. He wasn't a large man. Not like Leopold, who'd been very tall and brawny. But Konrad's work at the forge had developed his upper torso until it was shaped like a triangle and seemed as toned as the anvil on which he crafted tools.

And she was thinking too much instead of answering Herr Elias's question. She cleared her throat. "He takes his boys fishing most Saturday afternoons. I expect him to come by here on his way to or from the river."

"I see." He rocked some more, his gaze drifting to the side. "Does he intend to gift you with part of his catch again? I suppose that's a fair enticement to gain your help."

His statement seemed to hold an undercurrent. Was he hinting for another dinner invitation as repayment for helping her gather names? "He brought me fish last week not as a payment, but as a kindness. He and the boys caught more than they could use." Or had he fished until he had enough to share so he could use the fish as a means of bribing her? She'd spent the last weeks questioning Herr Elias's motives in seeking her out. Now he had her questioning Herr Rempel's motives, too. She didn't want to get into a game of one person giving as a means of receiving something in return from someone else. What exactly did Herr Elias want from her? She'd made a mistake by involving him in her pursuit of a wife for Herr Rempel.

It was time to end his participation.

"Herr Elias . . ." She waited until he turned his attention to her. "When we had dinner last Sunday, you mentioned utilizing the services of a matchmaker. If Herr Rempel isn't interested in either of the half sisters who responded this week, he will likely contact a New York matchmaker. Either way, it isn't necessary for you to continue collecting names in Marion."

His eyebrows rose. "He decided to use a matchmaker? So he won't need your help anymore?"

The question unsettled her. Partly because it seemed to communicate his disapproval of her spending time with Herr Rempel, but mostly because she didn't want to give up these snatches of time with Herr Rempel. She pushed the strange pondering aside and focused on her guest. "I will contact the matchmaker for him, just as I promised to contact potential wives. But, I suppose, that arrangement will require much less of my time."

"That is gut, ja?"

Shaded by the porch roof, his expression seemed darker than he likely intended. Even so, her frame convulsed in a little shiver. "It will be good if it results in him finding a suitable wife in an expedient manner." She patted her apron pocket. "Danke for bringing these names. I will let Herr Rempel know about them and let him decide whether or not to contact these women."

Herr Elias nodded. "Remember . . . the most promising name on the list is—"

"Ernestine Gartner, ja, I remember." She'd been rude to interrupt, but suddenly she needed to separate herself from his company. "Guten Tag, Herr Elias." She closed the door. His retreating footsteps brought a rush of relief.

She filled her lungs with air and then let it ease out in increments, releasing with it some of the tension of the last minutes. This shift in his treatment of her, from fellow employee to potential sweetheart, left her on edge around him. At least by disengaging him from her goal to unite Herr Rempel with a new wife, she would eliminate regular contact. Maybe his affections for her would fade as their contact faded. She would pray for it to be so. She didn't dislike the man, but she didn't want to give him wrong ideas, either. And if his affections continued, it would be very difficult to work in the same building with him.

She started for the kitchen, but then the *thud-thud* of feet on the porch came again. She closed her eyes and groaned. Was he back already?

Chapter Twenty-Five

Konrad

When Konrad had pulled up to Frau Dyck's house, the twins noticed Juliana at work in the garden and begged to go say hello to her. He'd intended to leave them in the wagon. He didn't anticipate a lengthy conversation. But since they both requested the same thing—after three disagreements already on what to have for breakfast, which chores to accomplish first, and who would sit where on the seat for the ride to town—he told them to go.

So now he stood on Frau Dyck's porch, as he'd done so many times in the past weeks, with his hat in his hands. And his pulse skipping into double beats. Such a strange internal response, one that had happened on previous visits. Was he nervous? He didn't think so. Frau Dyck was a welcoming, friendly person. There was no reason to be nervous around her. Eager? Maybe. But for what? Her help? Or her presence?

His contemplation ended abruptly as the interior door opened and the subject of his thoughts stood framed behind the screen door. He unconsciously drew back. Welcoming? Friendly? Nein, her firmly set lips and stiff frame spoke the opposite. She must have been busy and he'd disturbed her. He started to apologize and leave, but in the space of a heartbeat her expression changed from frosty and uncertain to warm and . . . pleased.

His pulse raced into a gallop.

"Herr Rempel." She pushed the screen door wide. "You're earlier than I expected. Are you heading to the river already?"

He stood just beyond the threshold, wringing the brim of his hat. "The boys and I did some shopping before we came here, and now we are seeing to other errands. I'll take them to the river this afternoon if they finish all their chores at home without arguing."

Her fine brows dipped. "Arguing? That doesn't sound like the Folker and Walden I know. They're usually pairing up—working with each other, not against each other."

The worry he'd carried about the boys' changes in behavior returned. He wouldn't share those concerns with most people, but she was their teacher. And she'd loved their mother. She would understand. "Ja, that is one of the reasons I let Walden go to the Krahns' to work. The boys were doing more fussing at each other than they'd ever done before. I thought being away from each other for part of the day would help them appreciate each other more. But it hasn't worked very well. Instead, they seem to be growing further apart."

A burst of laughter came from the side yard, and he instinctively looked that way even though he couldn't see around the corner of the house.

She looked, too, and a smile curved her lips. "They sound as if they're getting along well now." Affection laced her tone, which gave him the assurance that he was doing the right thing.

"Ja, they are, and that is why I would like to accept your offer to watch the boys while I am working." He gulped. "Both of them. If that is not too much to ask."

Her lips parted and a little gasp emerged. "It is not too much. Have you spoken to the Krahns yet?" A hint of worry now showed in her hazel eyes.

"Not yet. I wanted to make sure it was all right with you before I told them Walden would not be coming back anymore."

A sigh heaved from her chest, one that seemed to indicate relief. He didn't know her reason for the reaction, but he felt the same way. Separating the twins had not been good for them. He prayed that bringing them back together would fix the rift.

A squeal followed by rollicking laughter reached his ears. Frau Dyck smiled, chuckling, and gestured for him to come inside. "While they're enjoying themselves, come look at the two letters I received from Marion."

The screen door slapped into its frame behind him, and he followed her to a room lined with shelves. Every shelf held books. Dozens—nein, probably hundreds—of books. He hadn't been in this room since before her husband had died. Back then, he and Hannah would sometimes come over for an evening. After Leopold died and while Hannah was still alive, Frau Dyck occasionally came to their house, but she didn't invite them to her house again. In the more than five years since Leopold's death, Konrad had forgotten how many books she owned, and he couldn't hold back a soft *whew* of surprise.

She sent an embarrassed grin in his direction. "I know. It's almost shameful, isn't it, to have so many? But I've always loved reading, as does Juliana. Leopold"—her tone and expression became wistful—"spoiled us." Then she gave a little jerk, as if bringing herself back from somewhere else. "But you aren't interested in all that. Here." She picked up a few sheets of paper from a drop-down desk in one of the shelves and offered them to him. "These were sent by the half sisters I told you about. Read them, and tell me if either of them piques your interest."

He took the letters and sat in one of the chairs in front of the bay window. Each letter was made up of two pages covered in script, both front and back—a lot to read. He read them slowly, pausing now and then to fully consider not only a written phrase but what the statement said about the person who penned it. He waited for some spark, some change in his pulse or other jolt of awareness, but he finished both letters and felt no tug toward either of the senders.

He laid the pages on his knee and lifted his head. Frau Dyck stood beside the desk, her hands linked and resting against her skirt, her patient, heart-shaped face angled in his direction. A bolt of lightning struck his scalp. Or so it seemed, the reaction was so intense. He scratched his head, and the pages fell to the floor. He bent forward and gathered them, and as he sat upright, she moved close enough that he would be able to touch her if he reached out. Another internal zap sent tingles across his scalp and down his spine.

He quickly stood, crushing the pages in his hand. "I am sorry for the trouble you went to, Frau Dyck, but truthfully, neither of these . . . of these . . ." He swallowed. Would she stop looking so intently into his eyes? She was a good reader. Could she read the awareness blooming under his skin? Konrad had no interest in either of these women from Marion, nor in any woman who might be sent from New York to Kansas. Because the one who stood before him fully captured him.

She took the letters and carried them to the desk. She laid them on the slanted surface, smoothed them flat with her hand, then turned to him again. "Since you're being truthful"—

Had he said what he was thinking? He scrambled to remember what he'd said.

—"I will tell you what I thought when I read them." She shook her head, crinkling her nose. "Neither of them are right for you. They're looking for husbands, for sure, but it seems they are more interested in what a man can provide for them than what they can contribute to the relationship."

His ears were ringing. An odd sensation. Maybe he really had been struck by a lightning bolt. He stared at her compassionate yet serious face and struggled to pay attention to her words.

"Hannah was such a loving, giving person. After being married to her, you won't be happy with someone who is self-centered."

Ah, his Hannah. Ja, she'd been loving. Giving. Faithful. And accepting of their simple lifestyle and his physical shortcomings.

"And, frankly, you and the twins deserve someone who will pour herself out on all of you." Her hand slipped into her apron pocket and emerged with a folded piece of paper. "Herr Elias gave me the names of three more women from Marion to query. He mentioned one of them—Fräulein Gartner—is a teacher for young children, without any family of her own, and of an appropriate age for marriage. He believed she could be a good match. If you'd like, I'll send her a letter. Or . . ." She shrugged and set the paper aside. "I can contact an official matchmaker for you. Whatever you deem best for yourself and your sons."

Why did this woman, his sons' teacher and his beloved wife's best friend, suddenly seem like the one deemed best for him? Why hadn't he seen it before he engaged her in this letter-writing mission? How could he have been so blind? Then his vision seemed to expand to the walls of shelves and books. To the grand house in which she lived. Her sweetly worded remembrance—*"Leopold spoiled us"*—whispered in his mind, and reality crashed in around him.

Ja, she was everything he wanted. But he could not be what she wanted. He wasn't wealthy, like Leopold. He wasn't big and bold and unscarred, like Leopold. He had no hearty laugh or teasing nature. Leopold, Hannah often laughingly said, was bigger than life itself, a contrast to his quiet wife. Yet the two had fit together. Frau Dyck had just told him he deserved someone like Hannah. Well, didn't she deserve someone like the husband she had loved?

When he considered the unmarried men in Alexandertol, the only one who came to mind who might match Leopold in height, exuberance, and intelligence was Herr Elias. Jealousy nibbled, but he couldn't deny the two would make a striking couple. They already worked together, and she must like him since she'd invited him to dinner and also had gone to Durham with him if the town gossip was correct. And Herr Elias had no scars. He fit with Frau Dyck so much better than Konrad ever could.

Swallowing a knot of regret, he lowered his head and fixed his gaze on a cabbage rose woven into the patch of carpet centered on the library floor. "I think maybe, ja, you can send a query to the woman Herr Elias recommended. But if she doesn't turn out to be a good match for me"—was there such a thing?—"then we will write to New York."

Martina

Martina worked the soil between the marigolds in the flower bed in front of her porch. The spindly green scraps, transplanted from Agnes Bauer's large backyard garden, would need soft soil in which to spread their roots. Wagons had been passing back and forth all morning, typical for a Saturday when folks came to town to shop, but the sound of one coming to a stop close by captured her attention.

She sat back on her heels and looked over her shoulder. The brim of her bonnet shielded her eyes from the sun, so her vision wasn't hindered, but she blinked several times to be sure she was seeing correctly. Ja, Konrad Rempel and his boys were parked in front of her house on a Saturday.

She pushed to her feet, calling for Gerhard. He had given himself the task of replacing the little basement window, which had gotten cracked and was letting moisture into the cellar. She'd enjoyed listening to him whistle as he worked. Something else that had recently been restored—his old habit of whistling. She liked it.

He rounded the corner of the house, and she crossed to meet him, brushing dirt from her skirt. "The Rempels are here."

"Ja, I see." He took her hand, and together they ambled to the wagon. When they reached its side, he let go of her and reached up. "Guten Morgen, Herr Rempel."

Herr Rempel leaned past Walden, who sat somber and quiet beside him, and shook Gerhard's hand. "Guten Morgen. I hope we are not interrupting your day."

"Nein, you are always welcome to stop by here." Gerhard gave Walden's knee a little bump. "Guten Morgen to you, too, young man."

Walden mumbled a greeting but didn't lift his head. All at once Martina knew why the Rempels were here. She waited for panic or sorrow or even anger to swell. But, to her surprise, no wild emotions filled her breast. Only a calm acceptance. She said, "Herr Rempel, have you brought Walden by to tell us he won't be apprenticing with Gerhard anymore?"

Herr Rempel shot a quick, regretful grimace at his sullen son, then nodded. "Ja. I have appreciated you taking such good care of him, but I must change our arrangement." He put his hand on Walden's knee. "He is sad about not coming back. He has grown very fond of you."

A single tear slid down Walden's cheek, and Martina's heart rolled over. She reached for Gerhard, and he gripped her hand. The assuring pressure of his fingers around hers soothed the ache caused by Walden's unhappiness.

"I hold no ill feelings toward either of you," Herr Rempel went on, "but it has been hard on the boys to be apart. I have prayed about it, and I think it's best for them to be together again."

Folker popped forward and sent a grin past his father's larger frame. "Walden and me are going to stay at Frau Dyck's house while Pa works. Now I won't have to apprentice in the blacksmith shop anymore." He made a face. "It's hot and smelly in there. I'd rather work in the garden or climb Juliana's favorite tree. It's safe now, since Pa built a ladder onto her limb, so he said I can climb it."

Martina smiled at the boy, then angled her head to catch Walden's gaze. "Won't that be fun, Walden, to play all day instead of working?"

He nodded, but his sad eyes said otherwise. "I will miss you, Tante Martina. And Onkel Gerhard, too."

She wished she could give him a hug, but maybe it was best if she didn't. If she took him in her arms, it would be harder to let him go. How could she ease the child's sadness? "We will still see each other. Often, I'm sure. We will see you in town and at church and community gatherings. And, if it's all right with your father, maybe you can come over now and then and visit Onkel Gerhard in his shop."

"Ja, ja," Gerhard boomed out, smiling broadly although she sensed he was putting on a show for the boy's sake. "All of you can come sometimes for Sunday dinner. In fact . . ." He aimed a thoughtful frown at Martina. "Weren't you going to fry chicken tomorrow?" At her nod, he turned to Herr Rempel. "You and your boys come eat with us after church. Even if Walden isn't working here, we can stay friends, can't we?"

Martina expected Herr Rempel to decline the invitation. They'd not been friends before he sent Walden to apprentice with Gerhard. Why would he choose to be now when their help wasn't needed?

"Danke, Herr Krahn."

"Call me Gerhard. It sounds more like friends, ja, Konrad?"

A smile twitched on Herr Rempel's lips. "Ja, it does, Gerhard, and we would be glad to share a meal with you." He looked at Martina. "If you are sure it's not too much work for you."

Martina almost clapped she was so pleased. "It isn't too much." She'd grown accustomed to preparing meals for more than two people. "We will see you tomorrow."

The man released a big sigh, as if a huge weight had rolled from his shoulders. He gave Walden's knee a little shake. "What do you say to the Krahns, Son?"

Walden sat up. "Thank you for letting me come and for being so nice to me." He recited the statement as if he read the words from a book. Then he sent a side-eyed glance at his father, his chin quivering, and he added, "I will always remember you."

Herr Rempel took up the reins. "Thank you for your kindness to my son, both of you. We will enjoy our time with you tomorrow." He flicked the reins, and the horses pulled the wagon up the street.

Gerhard slipped his arm around Martina's waist and they stood together, watching, until Herr Rempel turned the corner. Then Gerhard kissed the top of Martina's head. "Ja, well . . ." He drew in a deep breath. "Back to work now."

He strode off, but Martina remained in place. Walden's sweet yet sad voice repeated in her memory—*"I will always remember you."* She would always remember him, too. He'd brought joy and laughter and life to their home. He wouldn't be with them every day, but the joy, laughter, and life . . . it would remain. Because somehow in the past few weeks, all of those things had been reignited between her and Gerhard. Maybe that was why God had allowed Walden to come. Not for forever, but for a short time, to help them rediscover how much they truly loved each other.

She returned to the flower bed with a grateful smile on her heart.

Chapter Twenty-Six

Augusta

All three children accompanied Augusta to the post office Monday morning shortly after Herr Rempel dropped the twins at her house. After supervising children on the playground for the past several school seasons, she didn't find the excursion taxing, but she did discover she needed to keep a closer watch on Folker and Walden than she did Juliana. Being younger and much more active, they tended to bound from one edge of the sidewalk to the other, sometimes coming dangerously close to the street. Her one scare of them darting into the path of a wagon was enough for her lifetime.

Herr Bauer looked at the address—*Fräulein Ernestine Gartner, Marion, Kansas*—with raised eyebrows, but he didn't say anything as he affixed the postage and put the letter in the outgoing box. However, as she turned to leave, he said, "Frau Dyck, don't you want these letters?" He held aloft three envelopes.

She took them and checked the return addresses. Two from Topeka and one from Wichita, most likely responses to the ads she'd placed in those newspapers. "Danke, Herr Bauer."

He nodded. "Happy reading . . . and good luck."

The postmaster's smirk lingered in Augusta's mind as she herded the children home. Once there, she sent them to the backyard to play, and she took the letters to the library. As she'd suspected, they were brief notes asking for more information about the blacksmith seeking a wife. She would show them to Herr Rempel when he came to retrieve the boys.

Enjoying the sound of the children's happy chatter filter through the open windows, she gathered up sheets, towels, and soiled clothing for washing. Would Herr Rempel change his mind about using a New York matchmaker? He'd wanted to hurry and get a wife to care for his sons. Now that she was seeing to them during the day, the need might not be so urgent in his mind. She hoped this was the case. Choosing a wife shouldn't be rushed. Marriage was forever, and a poor choice could make for a miserable life.

As she'd been doing each time she considered Herr Rempel's situation, she paused and asked God to guide them to the one meant to be Herr Rempel's helpmeet and the boys' new mother. Placing the need in God's hands always eased her worries, and she hummed as she rubbed the sheets from Juliana's bed up and down the washboard.

Midmorning, Walden burst onto the back porch and slid to a stop where Augusta had set up her washtub. "Tante—" He clapped his hand over his mouth and gaped at her for a few seconds. When he dropped his hand, his cheeks were blazing red. "I am sorry, Frau Dyck. I . . . I . . ."

Augusta rose, sudsy water dripping from her hands. "You haven't offended me, Walden. You've been with Tante Martina for several weeks. It is only natural her name would come easily from your lips."

The bright color in his face faded. He nodded. "Ja. I liked having a Tante and Onkel. Onkel Wilhelm and Tante Christina used to come see us sometimes before Mama went to heaven, but that was a long time ago."

Augusta was pleased he remembered his mother's brother since the boys were so young when their mother died. "Tantes and Onkels are important, for sure." She wiped her hands dry on her apron. "Did you need something? You came in so quickly I thought maybe a fox was chasing you."

He laughed. "Nothing was chasing me. I wanted to ask you something. I have a penny in my pocket. Onkel Gerhard gave it to me for doing a good job greasing some wheel hubs. May I walk to the mercantile and buy candy? I will share with Folker and Juliana."

Augusta smoothed the boy's hair into place, smiling. "It's very nice of you to want to treat Juliana and your brother. You may go, but not by yourself. Have Juliana and Folker go with you."

His face crunched into a momentary scowl, but he nodded. "All right. Thank you, Tan—" He rolled his eyes. "Frau Dyck."

Augusta tapped her chin with her finger. "Walden, when we are at school, you'll need to call me Frau Dyck. But here at my house, would you like to call me Tante? My nieces and nephews called me Tante Gussie."

His face lit. "Ja, I like that name. Tante Gussie . . ." He said it slowly, concentration etched into his features. Then he grinned again. "Danke, Tante Gussie. We will stay on the sidewalk and be very careful." He darted out, hollering for Folker and Juliana.

Half an hour later, as Augusta was draping the first of her dresses on the line, the children came around the corner of the house. They were jabbering, their faces flushed, and each had a circle of black decorating their lips. Augusta burst out laughing. "I bet I know what candy you bought."

Folker rubbed his tummy. "Licorice whips were on special, three for a penny. So we each got a whole one all to ourselves." He bopped Walden on the arm and yelled, "Tag!" The pair of boys shot off, laughing.

Augusta raised her eyebrows at Juliana. "Since when do you like black licorice?"

The girl grinned sheepishly and shrugged. "It's not my favorite, but it wasn't my penny, and Walden was buying. I didn't want to complain." She turned her head and watched the two chasing each other. Fondness showed in the soft curve of her lips and the sweetness of her blue eyes. "It's fun having them here, Mother. I'm glad they get to stay with us."

Augusta put her arm around her daughter's shoulders. "I'm glad you feel that way. Because I will likely use your help in keeping them occupied. They are much busier than you ever were."

She giggled. "Ja, but that's what makes it fun. You never know what they'll do next." She aimed a hesitant look upward. "Mother, Walden told Folker they could call you Tante Gussie. Did you tell him that?"

"I did." But maybe she should have asked how Juliana felt about it first. "Does it bother you?"

"Nein." She answered quickly, but Augusta suspected the response wasn't completely truthful.

She gave Juliana's shoulder a squeeze. "Are you sure?"

Her daughter's expression turned introspective. "Ja, I'm sure. It doesn't bother me. It's kind of nice. Especially since I don't have cousins except in Russia and I never see them. Thinking of Folker and Walden as cousins is . . . nice."

Something seemed to be bothering her, though. Augusta shifted and took hold of Juliana's shoulders. "Tell me what you're thinking."

Juliana sighed, the spicy scent of licorice wafting on her breath. "I like being a 'cousin' to the boys, but I'd rather be someone's sister. I'm almost twelve already. Do you think I'll ever have the chance to be someone's sister?"

Herr Elias's comment about the orphans coming by train to Marion played in the back of Augusta's mind. She had no idea if there would be girls on the train. It seemed, from reports of previous deliveries, mostly boys were sent. But she liked the idea of adding to their family. Having a sister to grow up with and share secrets with would be a gift for Juliana and also for the girl they took in. But she couldn't speak of it until she knew if girls were coming.

She kissed Juliana's forehead. "We will pray about it. If God wants you to have a sister, He will see that you get one, ja? For now, would you go check on your 'cousins'? I can't hear them anymore, and sometimes when children are quiet, they are up to mischief."

Juliana's trickling laughter rang. "I will do that and gladly. Playing with the twins is more fun than hanging clothes on the line." She scampered off, and Augusta returned to her laundry.

During the remainder of the day, she closely observed Juliana's interactions with the twins and their interactions with her. Although three years in age separated them and the boys were rowdy compared to Juliana's gentleness, the children got along well. Clearly they enjoyed being together, and it made Augusta think even more seriously about the possibility of adding to her family.

When Herr Rempel arrived late afternoon to retrieve his sons, she escorted him to the library and gave him the letters she'd received. "Read them and let me know with whom you'd like to communicate further. I have missives ready to be sent. It's only a matter of addressing and stamping an envelope."

He pinched the letters between his fingers and bounced them lightly on his opposite palm. "I will let you know tomorrow when I bring the boys." Suddenly his expression turned apprehensive. "If you still want me to bring the boys tomorrow . . ."

She laughed. "Of course I do. They've had a good day, but Juliana is nearly hoarse from reading to them. They sat under the tree in the yard for almost two hours, lost in storybooks."

A smile grew on his face. "That is good. Ja, that is good."

She nodded. Good for the boys, and good for Juliana.

"I was worried Walden might cause you trouble. He liked going to the Krahns so much. He cried yesterday when we left their house after lunch and then pouted all afternoon." He grimaced and slid the letters into his shirt pocket. "Children . . . when they don't get their way, sometimes they don't behave so well. But he was good?"

"Ja, he was very good. He and Folker both." She smiled, various moments of their day together playing in her mind. "This morning, Walden accidentally called me Tante. He was very embarrassed when it happened, so I told him about my nieces and nephews in Russia, that they called me Tante Gussie. Then we decided I could be Tante Gussie to Folker and Walden while they stay with me." Something in his expression sent prickles of apprehension across her flesh. "Is . . . that all right with you? I can ask them to call me Frau Dyck again, if you prefer."

He shook his head, and the strange glimmer—of what? worry? consternation?—cleared. "Nein, Tante Gussie is fine. It is affectionate." One side of his lips tipped upward. "I was only remembering . . . Hannah used to call you Gussie."

Augusta gave a start. How could she have forgotten? Memories of talks and laughter and praying together swept through her. When she and Hannah had teased each other, as good friends did, Hannah shortened her formal name to the childhood nickname. Tears distorted Augusta's vision as loneliness for her dear friend created an ache in the center of her heart. If she missed Hannah, how much more must Herr Rempel, whose relationship with her had been so much deeper and more personal?

She might regret it later, but at that moment it seemed the right thing to do. She said, "Since Hannah called me Gussie, and since the boys are now calling me Tante Gussie, would you like to call me Gussie, too? And I will call you Konrad, as I did when you, Hannah, Leopold, and I were all friends."

He stared at her, unblinking, for several seconds, his frame very still, as if he'd even forgotten to breathe. And then a soft chuckle emerged. He looked down, scuffing the toe of his boot against the floor. When he raised his head again, the twinkle in his eyes lifted her spirits in ways she couldn't describe. "That would be all right with me. We were . . . are . . . friends, ja?"

A worry nibbled. Had she spoken too soon? She'd resisted allowing Herr Elias to call her Augusta in part for propriety's sake. Some in town might find fault with her and Herr Rempel using each other's given names. Especially the nickname. But she and Herr Rempel had been friends in the past. They had a connection in their love for Hannah and for his sons.

What did Mutter used to say about gossipers? *"I do not care if they talk about me. It means they are leaving someone else alone."* Augusta almost laughed, recalling her mother's tart tone as she made the unabashed statement. Augusta could be bold, too, and not care.

She smiled at Herr Rempel—at Konrad—and gave a firm nod. "Ja, we are." She pointed to the letters. "Those coming in tells me the advertisements are working. More responses might arrive. I will check at the post office each delivery day and make sure to give you any new ones that come. Have you given any more thought to hiring a matchmaker?"

"Only if I need to." He spoke with certainty, and she inwardly agreed with his decision. He patted his pocket, but the gesture lacked enthusiasm. "I will read these tonight after I've put the boys to bed and . . . and let you know . . . tomorrow . . . if one appeals." He gulped, his gaze latched on hers.

"And I will pray . . ." A lump filled her throat. The way he was looking at her—and the way she was feeling about him—could she really pray it sincerely? But she must, because she'd promised to help him find a new wife. ". . . that God guides you to your perfect helpmeet." She swallowed and forced a smile. "I'll collect the boys now. I'm sure you're ready to go home." She pinched her skirts and hurried from the room.

Chapter Twenty-Seven

Konrad

G*ussie ... Gussie ...*
Even after Konrad went to bed, even after reading the letters sent by the women in other towns who responded to the advertisements for a wife, even while crickets chirped outside his window and sleepiness weighted him, he could not stop thinking of her. His thoughts tumbled, memories of former days flashing in his mind's eye. Ja, they—him, Hannah, Leopold, Gussie—had all been friends. Such good times they'd had together. They would probably still all be friends if Leopold and Hannah were alive.

He'd agreed that he and Gussie were friends, but were they? Was it even possible? Friendships between men and women were uncommon, maybe because of the temptations that could spring up between them over time. He'd considered Hannah his best friend, but they'd met when they were children. They'd grown from friendship to something more as they left childhood behind. When he looked at Gussie Dyck, he didn't think about engaging her in childish activities like fishing or climbing trees or catching fireflies. Nein, other desires rose in him.

His chest went tight now, worry taking hold of him. "Tante Gussie" his boys now called her with all the affection the title afforded. Just as they both now called Frau Krahn "Tante Martina." On this past Sunday, as he and the boys were leaving the Krahns' house, Gerhard had said, "Konrad, Martina and I would like to have you and your boys join us for dinner the second

Sunday of every month. Write those days on your calendar. This way we can grow our friendship, ja?"

Konrad had thanked him and agreed to the plan. He could be friends with the Krahns because there were two of them—husband and wife. But with Gussie? Could he think of her only as a friend?

Maybe.

After he was married again and these feelings he attached to Gussie were shifted to his new wife.

Maybe.

If his new wife and Gussie formed a friendship the way Hannah and she had.

Maybe . . .

He told himself so again and again, but deep down, he didn't believe it.

Tuesday, when Konrad dropped the boys at Gussie's house, he didn't escort them to the door. He reasoned he could get to work quicker if he didn't take the time to walk with them, and they were old enough to run up there by themselves. But in truth it was meant to erase so many thoughts of Gussie from his mind. Not until he was home again did he remember he was supposed to tell her if he wanted her to send letters to any of the three women who'd responded to his advertisement. In all honesty, none of them sparked any real interest, but he admitted he might be too picky. He should read the letters again before he decided. His second peek while he ate his dinner brought no rush of longing toward any of the women. However, the one from Wichita seemed so eager for a new life that his sympathy went out to her.

When he went to pick the boys up, he told Gussie it was all right to send a letter to the woman from Wichita, and he gave her money for a stamp. She promised to take the letter to the post office in the morning and go again tomorrow afternoon in case Fräulein Gartner from Marion had sent a reply or any others had sent queries in response to the advertisements. Guilt smote him at her kindness. She was working so hard to find him a wife. He prayed long into the night for God to open his heart to the one he was meant to love for the remainder of his days. But Gussie's face continually intruded upon his focus and made him feel as if his prayers were worthless.

Wednesday morning he instructed the boys to watch for his wagon in the afternoon and be ready for him. "Then I won't bother Tante Gussie by knocking on the door. She has other things to do," he told them. They promised to do so, but that afternoon he sat outside her house for nearly five minutes waiting and they didn't come. Finally he gave up and knocked on the door after all, irritation with the boys and with himself— couldn't he look at her as a friend, as she'd requested?—swirling through him like a Kansas twister.

Her bright smile when she opened the door to him nearly undid him. "I checked at the post office, but no letters came on the stage today." Why did her statement bring relief rather than regret? He gritted his teeth and stayed quiet. She invited him to come inside while she fetched Walden and Folker from the kitchen. "Juliana is teaching them to make pots from modeling clay," she said. The activity explained why they hadn't been paying attention, and some of his aggravation melted. But he declined and said to send them to the wagon. She looked puzzled but didn't argue.

On Thursday he reminded them, "Watch for me, boys, and come to the wagon."

"Ja, Pa, we will," they shouted as they ran to the house.

That evening, to his relief, he saw them waiting on the porch when he pulled up. They climbed up beside him and he drove them home without telling Gussie good-bye. He'd thought it would be easier not to see her, but he was wrong. His chest ached all evening, and it was all he could do the next morning not to walk them to the door for the chance to see her pretty face, if only for a minute.

Friday afternoon, the boys again were waiting on the porch when he came to pick them up. But instead of running to the wagon, they entered the house. Moments later, they emerged with Gussie trailing them.

While they clambered into the back and engaged in a game of thumb-wrestling, she moved to the edge of the wagon and gave him a fat envelope. "This came from Marion, from Fräulein Gartner. Although it's addressed to me, I didn't read it. After I opened the ones from the half sisters, I was a little embarrassed. Although I send the queries, the responses really aren't to me. It's best if you open replies."

He was amazed that his trembling fingers could keep hold of it. Maybe he should drop it on purpose, let it blow away. Then he wouldn't have to read it. But what a cowardly act it would be. And unappreciative, considering the trouble Gussie was going to for him. He slid it into his shirt pocket. "Danke."

"If, after reading it, you decide to pursue a relationship with her"—

His pulse skipped a beat, and he gripped the reins hard.

—"please tell me. Or . . ." Her voice quavered. ". . . have the boys tell me."

He closed his eyes for a moment, hating himself for the way he'd held her at bay these past few days. She must be confused and maybe even hurt by his behavior. But he was confused, too, and didn't know how to deal with his feelings. He opened his eyes and forced a quick nod. "Ja. I will let you know."

Her hazel eyes refused to turn aside despite his difficulty in looking at her. She went on sweetly, "Once you've made your choice, I'll send notes to any other women who respond and thank them for their interest but advise them to look elsewhere."

How caring she was to these unknown women, wanting to spare their feelings. And how determined she was to bring love into his life again. There could not be a more giving heart in all of Kansas. "You are too kind to me, Gussie." His voice came out soft, husky.

Her lips quirked into a nervous smile. "It's the least I can do for a f-friend."

The stutter bothered him. She was probably questioning whether he really wanted to be friends with her. He wasn't much acting like a friend, telling his boys to speak for him and holding himself aloof. She deserved better.

He leaned toward her, his elbow digging into his knee. "You've done so much for me and for my boys, and I have done nothing in return."

"You brought me fish."

He almost laughed. "That was nothing. I would like to do something more. Something . . . bigger. I don't want to be selfish, always be the one taking. If you need something—anything—will you tell me?" His conscience could be appeased if she would allow him to favor her somehow.

Her eyebrows lifted, and she drew in a little breath.

He leaned more heavily on his knee, bringing himself closer to her. "There is something. Tell me. What is it?"

"I'm not sure if I'll do it, and I'm not sure when it will be, but . . ."

He watched indecision play over her face as he waited for her to complete her sentence.

"I will need to talk to Herr Elias first. When I know the day, and if I decide to follow through, would you be willing to drive me to Marion?" She finished in a rush. "I'm asking a lot of you, I know. It's a long drive, but I have no other way to get there."

Curiosity writhed in his gut. What did she want there? How was Herr Elias involved? An idea took shape—an idea that left him uncomfortable, one in which he did not want to play a role, given the way his heart was tugging him toward this woman. He waited a few seconds, hoping she would offer further explanation, but she only stood with her hands clasped beneath her chin and her eyes shining with hope. What could he say?

He licked his dry lips and shrugged. "Ja, I will take you when you need to go."

Delight burst on her face. "Danke, Konrad."

How he enjoyed hearing his name from her tongue. He nodded, unable to reply.

She backed away from the wagon, still smiling. She waved. "I will see you tomorrow."

He waited until after the boys went to bed to open the envelope from the Fräulein in Marion. He laid the letter flat on the table and brought the lantern close, then bent over the page and read.

Dear Frau Dyck—

He gave a little jolt. This letter wasn't intended for him after all. He started to fold it back up, but then he reasoned she'd given it to him to read. It concerned his future. He angled the page a little better to catch the light and began again.

Dear Frau Dyck—
  I thank you for your communication. I read your letter several times, nearly memorizing some parts of it. It truly sounds as if

Herr Rempel is a good man, a good provider, and a good father. I was mostly drawn to your description of him as a God-fearing man who is seeking a God-fearing wife. Faith is very important to me. My relationship with Jesus has sustained me through all of life's trials, including the losses of my parents and the tragic death of my beau before we had an opportunity to speak our vows before God. I could not possibly consider a union with a man who did not share my love for and commitment to Jesus.

The description of himself that he found on the page both embarrassed and pleased him. Did Gussie genuinely see him that way? His face warmed, imagining her hand penning such glowing words about him.

The loss of this Fräulein's beau pained him, but it also encouraged him. They'd both suffered the loss of someone they loved, which would help them understand each other. If they built their relationship on a mutual love for Jesus, they might have a chance to grow a strong marriage.

With hope flickering to life deep in his heart, he continued reading.

If I had received your letter a month or perhaps even as little as a week ago, I would have a very different response than the one I am sending. I must decline the opportunity to meet Herr Rempel in person. You see, very recently, I met a man who is new to Marion. My heart is drawn to him and, I dare hope, his is drawn to me. It would be grossly unfair and unkind for me to spend time with Herr Rempel while I pine for the man here in town.

The little spark of hope sputtered and died. He forced himself to finish it.

*I trust you understand, and I will pray that God will bring
to Herr Rempel—and to the little boys you described in such
animated fashion—the wife and mother they need and deserve.*

*Respectfully yours,
Ernestine Gartner*

He sighed and set the letter aside, but a single line from the
letter danced in his mind's eye. *"I met a man who is new to Marion."* Herr Elias was new to Marion. Herr Elias had given Gussie
this woman's name. Was it possible that Ernestine Gartner was
falling in love with the Alexandertol teacher? But what of
Gussie, who asked for Konrad's help in going to Marion for
some kind of secret meeting . . . a meeting he suspected could be
to recite vows at the county courthouse?

He looked again at the Fräulein's letter. *"My heart is drawn to
him and, I dare hope, his is drawn to me."* Was this only wishful
thinking on her part that the other man was drawn to her, or
had he given her reason to believe such a thing? She didn't
sound flighty or whimsical in her letter. If she was speaking of
Herr Elias, then he must be wooing two women at the same
time.

Konrad's pulse pounded in his temples like a mallet on a bass
drum. Did Herr Elias love Gussie, or was she marching toward
a broken heart?

Chapter Twenty-Eight

Augusta

Since Augusta had told Herr Elias not to collect any more names, she didn't expect him to come by her house on Saturday as he'd done the previous weeks. Yet this weekend, she needed to see him. He would surely attend Sunday services, as he always did, but talking in the churchyard, where people could easily overhear or observe and draw their own conclusions, didn't appeal to her. She preferred a private conversation.

He'd walked to town each Saturday morning for as long as she'd known him. The path he took from the Langes' went right by her house. So she put off housecleaning and parked herself on the porch swing. She didn't even allow herself a book to read, fearful she would become lost in it and miss seeing him pass by. After a full week of observing Juliana with the Rempel twins and praying about it each night, she was convinced she was doing the right thing. But she needed his assistance. Again.

Lord, please don't let him read more into my request than I intend. I need his help, but I don't want to stoke the fire of his affection for me.

If she was going to stoke any affection fire, it would be for another man. An ache built in the center of her chest. How could she have known her offer to help Konrad find a new wife would bring so much pain to her heart? Yet she would see it through for the children and man who'd meant the world to her dear friend Hannah . . . and who were becoming more and more important to Augusta by the day.

A cheerful whistle intruded upon her thoughts. She recognized its warble. Craning her neck, she peered around the bushes and waited. Moments later, Herr Elias stepped into her line of view. She bounced from the swing and clattered down the porch steps, calling his name.

He turned, and an easy smile creased his face. He changed direction and came up the walk, meeting her midway to the house. "Why, guten Morgen, Frau Dyck. It's a lovely day, isn't it?"

"Guten Morgen. Ja, it is. Very nice." Her words emerged as breathily as if she'd just run a race. "Are you in a hurry, or may I have a moment of your time?"

"I always have time for you, Frau Dyck."

He'd made similar comments before, and recently they'd left Augusta feeling a bit unsettled. But today he spoke in a light-hearted tone, with no hint of hidden meaning lurking beneath. Relieved, she allowed a genuine smile to pull at her lips. "Danke. You are a good friend. I wondered if I could ask you, as a friend, to do a favor. For me."

He arched a brow. "You've changed your mind and need more names of women from Marion for Herr Rempel?" The jealousy she'd come to expect when speaking of Herr Rempel was also gone. Such a pleasant change.

She shook her head. "Nein, this favor is strictly for me. Well, and for Juliana." She glanced toward the house. She'd told Juliana to attend to dusting, that she needed a private chat with Herr Elias, but curiosity could get the best of her. This scheme, however, needed to remain secret until she knew for sure it would happen.

Seeing no inquisitive face peering out the window, she turned her focus to the tall man. "You said a train of orphans is coming to Marion. On what day will the group arrive?"

He scratched his head, sending his bowler askew. "I believe the poster says June sixth."

Her heart gave a flutter of excitement. Three weeks away. Not too long to wait, but still enough time to prepare. "Is there a photo of the available children on the poster?" Some ads in newspapers listed names, others included grainy photographs. Herr Elias was less likely to have read a list of names, but he might recall faces on an image.

He nodded. "Ja. It looked to be a fairly large group—maybe fifteen or sixteen in all, of various ages."

"Both boys . . . and girls?" She held her breath.

For a moment, his brow pinched. "Mostly boys, but, ja, there were girls, too. I think two, possibly three."

Delight exploded beneath her bodice, and she automatically stacked her palms over her thrumming heart. "Where will people go to meet them?"

"The Presbyterian church." Now his expression turned curious. "Frau Dyck, are you considering—"

"Shhh!" She looked quickly left and right, even though her large yard made it unlikely either of her neighbors could overhear them. "Please, keep this conversation in confidence. If there are only two or three girls, there's no guarantee that I will be fortunate enough to bring one home with me. I don't want Juliana's hopes lifted and then crushed. But, ja, I intend to go to Marion and meet the children."

She sighed, closing her eyes for a moment and sending up a silent prayer for God's favor. "Juliana has expressed her desire for siblings. I cannot provide them for her any other way than adoption. So I am hopeful the train will bring a little girl who will want to come home with me."

A slight scowl pinched his brow. "Do you not think you'll ever remarry? Have more children?"

Two weeks ago she wouldn't have answered his question, not only because the topic was deeply personal, but out of fear he was asking for his own purposes. But she sensed sincere concern in his tone and expression. "I might remarry someday, if

God brings the right man into my life. But even if He did so tomorrow, there is no guarantee our union would be blessed with children. Juliana is growing up alone, and this past week with Walden and Folker has shown her how much she's missed by not having brothers or sisters."

"Ah, Frau Lange told me the boys were with you now instead of apprenticing. I thought she might be mistaken." He grinned. "Did you take the boys in so you could practice having more than one child under your roof?"

She laughed, shaking her head. "Nein, it is only coincidence." Or was it God's way of opening her heart to the idea of providing a home for an orphaned child? "But it has been a joy to see the kind of sister Juliana will be."

"Ja, she is a sweet girl. And you are a good mother. Any child will be fortunate to be part of your family." He placed his hand lightly on her upper arm. "If you like, I will see if there is an extra poster at the mercantile and bring it to you next week. Then you can see the children, start praying about which is meant to be yours, before you go to the church in June."

Such a kind offer. She thanked him with a bright smile. Then she shook her finger. "But remember . . . this is our secret, ja?"

He nodded. "Our secret." Then, again, his brows pinched, but this time it raised a prickle of concern. "Frau Dyck, since you have trusted me with your secret, may I talk to you about something not intended for anyone else?"

During their years of working together, they'd often shared information meant only for the two of them. She nodded without a moment's hesitation.

"Did you send a query to Fräulein Gartner?"

She nodded again. "Ja. I received a reply from her yesterday. I sent it home with Kon—Herr Rempel."

His right eyebrow lifted. "Did you read it first?"

"Nein, I did not." Worry suddenly attacked. "Herr Elias, is there something about the woman that concerns you?"

His head bobbed in a slow, serious nod. "My concern is . . . I happen to know of someone else who holds affection for her. Someone who has been hesitant to allow his feelings for her to grow because of a certain schoolteacher in Alexandertol."

She gave a little start and drew back.

His lips quirked into a sad smile. "Ja, Frau Dyck, I am speaking of you and me. For nearly a year, I have considered pursuing a courtship with you. I'm sure you aren't surprised by this. You're an intelligent woman, and I haven't worked very hard at hiding my intentions."

She'd known. Of course she'd known—and worried over it. "You're a very fine man, but—"

He held up his hand, stilling her words. "What you said a bit ago, *if* God brought someone for you to love . . ." His shoulders rose and fell in a little shrug. "There would have been some sort of spark in your eyes if you were thinking of me. I witnessed no such thing."

She laced her hands together and rested them beneath her chin. "I didn't intend to hurt you."

"You did not. Actually, it was a relief, because I was afraid my attentions may have given you the idea that I would request a courtship and then you would be hurt." He pulled in a full breath, his chest buttons growing tight, then released it in a slow wheeze. "Now I know, and it frees me to explore the possibility of more than friendship with Fräulein Gartner. That is, if she hasn't committed to a courtship with Herr Rempel. In that case, I would not interfere."

He was an honorable man. Her fondness for him rose a notch. She started to tell him how much she admired his ethics, but he spoke first.

"Will Herr Rempel tell you if he and Fräulein Gartner are going to see each other?"

"Ja, he will. Because if she is the one, he will want me to contact the other women who've sent queries and tell them he is . . . taken." Her final word croaked out, as if her throat tried to swallow it.

For several seconds, Herr Elias remained very still and thoughtful, gazing down at her with myriad questions glistening in his eyes. Then a small, sad smile formed on his lips. "Ja, well, then I suppose we will both soon know whether we will be free to share our hearts with the ones we care for."

Augusta slowly moved backward, her gaze locked on his. She should thank him for getting a poster for her. She should thank him for keeping secret her plan to adopt another child. She should ask him to please keep her *other* secret. But to acknowledge it would be to admit its truth. And she wasn't ready to admit it, not even to herself.

She grated out, "Farewell, Herr Elias," then spun and darted into the house.

Martina

Martina sat in her usual spot—fourth bench from the front on the window, not the center aisle, end—and listened to the sermon. Or, rather, she tried to listen. She sent surreptitious glances around the congregation, trying to decide who to ask for Sunday dinner. She was almost giddy. After years of keeping people away, unwilling for them to discover Gerhard's secret, now she could welcome them into her home. Maybe she didn't have children, something she would always wish was different, but she was making friends. First, more deeply with Gerhard, and also with others in the community. Surely her heart was expanding by the minute.

When the service ended, she turned to Edda Schmidt, who sat directly behind her. "Would you and your family like to have dinner at my house today?"

The woman's eyebrows rose so high they nearly disappeared in her fluff of bangs. "Why . . . why, Frau Krahn, that's so unexpected . . . and kind! But I'm afraid I must decline. I left a pork roast in the oven. If we don't go home and eat it, it will be all shriveled."

Martina patted the woman's arm. "No worries at all. Perhaps another time?"

"Ja, ja . . ." Frau Schmidt moved slowly toward the aisle, gazing at Martina with wide eyes. "Another time."

Martina scanned the room, then hurried to Lucinda Klein. "Frau Klein, do you and your husband have dinner planned?"

Lucinda nodded. "Ja, Heinrich brought home a fat goose yesterday and put it in the smoker. The smell was heavenly when we drove away this morning. I—" She looked beyond Martina's shoulder and made a sorry face. "Heinrich is beckoning me. I'd better go." She hurried off.

Disappointed but undeterred—she had prepared enough stew and cornbread for at least eight people—she looked for another likely person to invite. Her gaze drifted out the window and fell on Herr Rempel and Frau Dyck, who were visiting beside his wagon, their children nearby. She hesitated. She still battled jealousy toward Frau Dyck. After all, the woman now enjoyed Walden's company every day. But Martina wanted to rid herself of the negative feelings. God's transforming grace in her relationship with Gerhard should be multiplied until every part of her was permeated by His grace. She could start by inviting the woman to dinner. And the Rempels, too.

Excusing herself as she went, she worked her way past the little clusters of chatting folks and out to the yard. The two were stepping apart from each other, apparently finished with their conversation. They might get away if she didn't hurry. She grabbed her skirts in her fists and broke into a clumsy half walk, half trot. "Augusta! Konrad!" Hearing herself use their given names took her by surprise. She'd never been so informal on the church grounds. Yet it felt right to use them, so she called again, "Augusta and Konrad, please wait a moment. I would have a word with you."

"Tante Martina!"

Walden's joyful cry slowed her feet and brought the sting of tears. Both he and Folker came running and bestowed hugs. She smiled at the pair, then herded them back to their father and teacher. "Augusta, Konrad, would you and your families join Gerhard and me for dinner?" She released a self-deprecating chuckle. "I started peeling turnips and carrots yesterday evening and forgot to stop, so my stew pot is overflowing. You would do me a favor by eating some of it."

The two exchanged uncertain glances. Martina held her breath, holding to hope.

Then Walden yanked on his father's coat sleeve. "Can we, Pa? Please?"

Konrad peeled his son's fingers loose, shaking his head. "Son, we just ate there last week. We're invited for another time in June. We don't want to wear out our welcome."

Martina laughed again. "That cannot happen. Did not Gerhard tell you that you were welcome anytime? He meant it, and I do, too. Please come." She shifted her gaze to include Augusta and her daughter. "We would enjoy the company."

Once again, the pair seemed to seek the other's preference. Observing them, Martina couldn't help but notice how at ease they seemed. If Frau Dyck wasn't working so hard to secure a new wife for the man, Martina might suspect something sizzled between them. She would recognize *sizzling* now that it had sprung to life again between her and Gerhard.

Finally, Konrad turned a smile in Martina's direction. "Danke for the invitation. We will come."

Martina gasped in delight and clapped her palms together. "Fine! Fine! There's no need to be in a hurry. I will need to set the table before we can eat."

"Juliana and I will help with that," Frau Dyck said. "And may I bring the apple-spice cake I baked yesterday?"

Martina had planned to serve canned peaches for dessert, but apple-spice cake would work fine alongside the fruit. "Danke, that would be nice." She inched backward. "But don't worry about helping with the table. It will be set and ready when you come."

She turned and crossed to Gerhard and their buggy as quickly as her full skirts and the thick grass beneath her feet allowed. She couldn't resist calling to him as she came, "We'll have much company today, dear! *Three* children at our table!"

His face lit, and she laughed with joy. Oh, what a blessing!

Chapter Twenty-Nine

Konrad

K onrad drove Gussie to her house to retrieve the cake. She sat on the creaky seat beside him, and the children rode in the back. He couldn't help smiling at the teasing going on in the bed of the wagon. His boys were at ease with Juliana Dyck as if they'd known each other forever. He hadn't realized how different a little girl's giggle was compared to boys' raucous cackles. Together, it was almost musical.

Neither he nor Gussie spoke on the drive. He'd brought the letter from Fräulein Gartner to church and gave it to Gussie after service. It stuck out of her Bible, which lay in her lap with her hands on top of it folded as if in prayer. Although he hadn't told her the letter's contents, he asked her to please notify the other women who'd written that he was no longer seeking a wife.

One of the Fräulein's sentences—*"It would be grossly unfair and unkind for me to spend time with Herr Rempel while I pine for the man here in town"*—had impacted him. He would be unfair and unkind to some unknown woman by inviting her into his life when his feelings for Gussie were so strong. Somehow he and the twins would make do on their own until the Lord had stripped his heart of this infatuation. When he knew he could honestly open himself to love someone else, he would search again. But on his own. He would not put Gussie through such trouble again.

At her house, he helped her down and then waited for her to fetch the cake. While he was waiting, the Lange wagon rumbled by, and Herr Elias called from its bed, "Please stop. I need to get out. I'll walk back from here." Konrad watched Herr Elias clamber over the side of the wagon and then amble up the walkway toward Gussie's porch. Gussie emerged, and the man waylaid her.

Konrad tried not to stare, but it was hard to ignore the two teachers, Herr Elias leaning down to match Gussie's height, both with serious expressions. What were they discussing so quietly? Their conversation only lasted a couple minutes, then he escorted Gussie to the wagon, held the cake plate while Konrad helped her onto the seat, and handed the cake to her.

The man shot a tight smile at Konrad. "Have a pleasant Sunday." He tipped his hat to Gussie, and then he strode up the sidewalk.

Konrad angled a curious look at Gussie. "I thought maybe you would ask him to eat at the Krahns', too."

She shook her head.

"But you will see him later?" Why was he being so pushy? Her relationship with Herr Elias was none of his business. But if Fräulein Gartner was falling in love with Herr Elias, as he suspected, Frau Dyck should know. She could be caught in the middle of something unpleasant. What kind of friend would he be if he didn't give her warning?

She glanced at him, balancing the cake in her lap. "Konrad, we should get to the Krahns' before they think we aren't coming."

He took the hint and brought down the reins. The horses lurched forward, bringing a round of squeals and laughter from the children.

The Krahns were ready for their arrival, and Martina smilingly instructed the children to share the bench, then pointed to two chairs on the opposite side. "Konrad, Augusta, please have a seat."

Konrad wasn't the host and probably should do as he was told, but he wouldn't be able to swallow a bite if he was sitting next to Gussie. He cleared his throat. "I will sit with my boys so I can help them. Frau Dyck, you and Juliana sit across from us." Then he slid onto the end of the bench next to the twins and flopped his napkin into his lap. When he looked up, he realized Gussie had taken the chair directly across from him. This was no better than side by side. In fact, it might be harder to stay focused on his meal with her sweet face in his line of vision. But he couldn't change it now.

They all closed their eyes while Gerhard prayed. Konrad prayed, too, for God's help not to do or say anything that would make his new friends wish they hadn't invited the five of them after all. Martina scooped stew into everyone's bowls, and they passed the platter of cornbread. He was proud of his boys. Neither dribbled stew down his front or chewed with his mouth open. They sat quietly and allowed the grown-ups to talk.

Not that he or Gerhard contributed much. Martina and Augusta did most of the talking, and much of it centered around the Frauenverein's latest project—a friendship quilt that would feature the names of every family in town who chose to contribute a block. They planned to auction it in August to raise funds for benches in the town's little park.

"It's a fine idea, Augusta," Martina said, "not only because of the money it could raise. By involving so many women from town, it will build a sense of community. That is beneficial on many different levels. And, of course, using the funds for something meant to be enjoyed by everyone in town should increase participation."

"Ja, I agree." Gussie took a dainty bite of stew, wiped her

mouth, and then continued. "When Berta first mentioned it, she thought only we in the club would make blocks. To keep things simple. But Frau Zimmerman said it shouldn't be a Frauenverein quilt, it should be an Alexandertol quilt. Everyone, including Berta, voted to approve the idea." She broke off a bit of cornbread with her fork and carried it to her mouth. "If everyone finishes their blocks by mid-July, we should have time to get it quilted and then display it for a few days in the mercantile before bidding opens."

Gerhard paused with his spoon halfway between his bowl and his mouth. "Martina, will you make a square and help with the quilting? You're very handy with a needle and thread."

"Oh, ja, you must make a block, Martina," Gussie said. "After all, the Frauenverein would not have started without you, and this project wouldn't have come about were it not for the ladies coming together and plotting ways to provide benches in the park."

Martina smiled at her husband. "Ja, I will make a block for sure."

"Be sure to embroider your signatures on it," Gussie added. "We want the names of as many townsfolk as possible represented." She sighed. "Years from now, people will be able to look at the squares and see who made this little town their home."

Konrad swallowed a bite of stew and chased it with a drink of water. The quilt wouldn't represent everyone from town. Hannah was gone, so he and his boys would not have a block. Not that it should matter. But somehow it did.

Gussie gave a little start and looked at him. "Konrad, you will want to have your new wi—" She shot a quick, startled look toward Martina, then turned to him again. "I meant to say, you will want to have someone craft a block for your family, too."

Konrad wiped his mouth and laid his napkin beside his plate. "I don't have anyone to ask."

A frown pinched Gussie's face, as if she didn't understand what he'd said.

Martina released a little "uh," almost a grunt. "Of course you do. You can ask me. I have plenty of time to make two blocks now that this rapscallion"—she grinned at Walden—"isn't eating me out of house and home. I would be happy to make a block for you and your children."

And in that moment Walden lost his manners and blurted, "Tante Martina, why don't you have children?"

The woman's face paled. She dabbed her mouth with her napkin and gave a tiny shrug. "Well, Walden, I do—did—have children."

"Where do they live?"

Now her cheeks splotched with pink. "They . . . um . . ."

Konrad reached past Folker and tapped Walden on the shoulder. "Hush."

Gerhard put his hand on Konrad's arm. "Nein, it is all right. The boy asks an honest question, and he deserves an honest answer." Although the man spoke evenly, Konrad glimpsed pain in his eyes. "Walden? Before I answer you, tell me . . . where does your mother live?"

"In heaven," Walden said in his innocent voice, "with God and Jesus and the angels."

Gerhard smiled—a sad smile. "Ja, that is right. Do you know who else she lives with? Mine and Tante Martina's children. They are all in heaven, with—as you said—God and Jesus and the angels."

Folker's mouth fell open. "Your children died?"

Across the table, Gussie lowered her head, but not before Konrad saw tears flood her eyes.

"Ja, they did." Gerhard spoke softly and kindly, his gaze moving back and forth between the boys. "Sometimes people live a long, long time, like Herr Lehrman across the street who turned eighty years old last week. Sometimes people only live a little while, like our children."

"And like our sister." Folker looked up at Konrad. "Right, Pa? She was only a tiny baby when she went to heaven."

Konrad put his arm around his son. "Ja, like your sister."

Gerhard nodded. "Someday, when you go to heaven, you will be with your Mutter and your baby sister again. Forever, you will be together. When we think of the wonderful reunion we will have when we reach heaven's gates, we can be joyful even while we miss the ones who've gone before us."

Silence fell, everyone seemingly lost in their own thoughts. Then Walden said, "Can I ask something else?"

Konrad cleared his throat, bracing himself for whatever his son might say. "Ja, go ahead."

"Is it time for dessert?"

As if choreographed, the adults all gave a jolt and turned startled looks on Walden. Three stunned seconds of absolute quiet followed. Then Gerhard covered a guffaw of laughter behind his hand. His mirth seemed to signal to everyone that they could laugh, too. And laugh they did—for a full minute at least.

Martina stood, shaking her head, her watery eyes dancing with humor. "Ja, well, maybe I should get that cake, hm? Augusta, would you like to cut it while I dish the peaches?"

Both women left the dining room. Juliana rose and began stacking their plates. She arched her brows at the boys. "You can help, you know." The twins giggled, but they slid from the bench and picked up their plates.

While the children cleared the table, Konrad leaned toward Gerhard and said softly, "Thank you for what you said. I don't talk about Hannah and our baby girl because I don't want to make the boys sad. But the way you answered, talking about the joy we can hold even while we mourn, is something they—and I—needed to hear." He swallowed, unaccustomed to sharing his thoughts with anyone besides Hannah. "I am glad we've become friends. You are a good influence in my sons' lives."

Gerhard's eyes went moist. His chin quivered for a moment, then he seemed to set his teeth together and stilled the movement. He swept his hand across his eyes and gave Konrad a firm nod. "Danke. I truly pray I am and will always be."

The women and children returned to the dining room, Martina carrying a tray laden with dessert plates. She circled the table, placing in front of each of them a plate with a thick slice of cake covered with wedges of bright yellow peaches. The boys, their manners apparently restored, waited until she sat before picking up their forks.

Konrad ate with as much enthusiasm as his sons did. The dessert was good, but the fellowship was better. He might not have a wife anymore, but God had given him some good friends who cared about his sons. He glanced across the table to Gussie, and in that moment she looked up and caught his eye. A tiny smile curved her lips before she shifted her attention to her plate. Ja, he'd found some very good friends. And as Gussie's good friend, he needed to be truthful with her.

He would offer to drive her and Juliana home when they left the Krahns. He would send the children off to play, and he would ask to speak with her. By the end of this day, she would know two things—Fräulein Gartner was falling in love with someone besides him, and he was falling in love . . . with Gussie.

Chapter Thirty

Augusta

The Krahns were wonderful hosts, and Augusta enjoyed visiting with Frau Krahn more than she'd expected, but how much longer could she hold her emotions in check? Konrad had told her his search was done. She should be happy, and part of her was. For him. But Herr Elias's reaction to the news riddled her with guilt. She'd found no pleasure in crushing his hopes for pursuing a relationship with Fräulein Gartner. And she didn't dare consider how hard it would be for her to see Konrad with another wife.

They finished their dessert, and Augusta offered to help with cleanup. Martina refused, insisting she and Gerhard would take care of it and everyone should go enjoy their day. Then Konrad said he would drive her and Juliana home. It wasn't a long walk, and Augusta started to say so, but Juliana headed out the door with the twins as if the decision was already made. So Augusta decided to let herself savor a few more minutes in the man's presence before bidding him a final farewell in her heart.

The sun was bright, the day so pleasant it seemed ungracious to harbor melancholy thoughts. She did her best to cast them off during the short drive from the Krahns' home to her own. Once there, she shifted on the seat, intending to thank Konrad for the ride and bid him a good day and happy life with Fräulein Gartner. She pulled in a fortifying breath and opened her mouth.

"Gussie?" He spoke first, his tone serious and his expression fervent. "There's something I must tell you. But"—he flicked a glance into the wagon bed—"not in front of the children."

She nodded. She'd managed to control her feelings thus far, but she wasn't sure how much longer this sadness growing in her chest could stay hidden. The children should not witness an emotional collapse. "Juliana, take Folker and Walden into the house and help them select a book or two to borrow and read this afternoon."

With a whoop, the boys darted from the wagon. Juliana followed more slowly, her thoughtful gaze aimed at her mother.

When the children were all inside, Augusta shifted to the edge of the seat and angled herself to look into Konrad's face. "All right. You can tell me now."

He yanked off his hat and hooked it on his knee. "It is about Fräulein Gartner."

She didn't need to hear the details. What he'd said was already enough. She held up her hand. "You already told me."

His brows came together. "I did?"

"Ja, when you said your search for a wife was done, it told me." She gripped the edges of the crumb-scattered cake plate in her lap the way she might cling to a lifeline. "You've made your choice."

A little huff escaped his throat. He shook his head. "Gussie, you are a very smart woman, very well read, but you read this situation incorrectly. You'll know the truth when you look at her letter. Fräulein Gartner does not wish to meet me. She's already made a choice. Her heart is drawn to someone else. Someone . . . who is new to Marion." He seemed to search her face.

Augusta put the pieces together in her mind, and she drew back. "Are you saying she is attracted to Herr Elias?"

He held his hands wide. "She did not say a name, but I pondered the possibility."

Augusta closed her eyes and groaned. "If this is true, then I made a grave mistake today." She opened her eyes and met his frowning gaze. "I told Herr Elias that your search was done. We both thought that meant you had chosen Fräulein Gartner." She had to get down, to go to the Langes' and tell Herr Elias there was still a chance for him with the young woman in Marion. She placed the cake plate on the seat between them and reached her foot for the wagon wheel.

Konrad grabbed her arm. "What are you doing?"

She sent him an impatient scowl. "Did you not hear me? Herr Elias thinks she is out of reach. I must tell him—" What if there was someone else new in Marion who'd captured the woman's attention? Augusta had already made a supposition about Konrad. She could be wrong about Fräulein Gartner, too. Didn't she inwardly criticize those who formed conclusions without gathering the full truth? She should tell Herr Elias she'd been wrong about Konrad's choice, but she would say nothing about the Fräulein's feelings toward someone else.

Suddenly something else struck her. "If you didn't decide to court Fräulein Gartner, then why are you no longer searching?"

He looked aside. "Because of what the Fräulein said in her letter. She made me realize I could not keep searching. Not . . . not when my heart is entangled with one who is out of reach for me." Very slowly he angled his head until his eyes fixed on hers. "I have fallen in love with my boys' teacher. With the woman who was Hannah's closest friend. With the friend who has worked so hard to find me a helpmeet."

Augusta's hand rose of its own accord and settled over her fluttering heart.

"How can I keep looking," he continued, his deep voice laced with both tenderness and longing, "when I know that someone else could not satisfy my heart? Not while it is so full of you. It would not be fair to her."

Joy exploded beneath Augusta's skin. He was falling in love

with her. He'd said so. How perfect, when she was also falling for him.

"I must first find a way to put to rest these feelings I have for you." His gaze bore into hers, his cornflower-blue eyes sheeny. "I don't know how long it will take. It took more than two years for me to truly lay Hannah to rest. When my heart is open again, then I will ask God to guide me to the right woman."

Confusion riddled her mind. He claimed to love her, yet he wanted to push her away. What kind of love was that? Then she remembered something he'd written on his list of requirements for a new wife—*Without children.*

She sent her attention toward the house, imagining Juliana and the twins in the library together. Ja, the children got along well, but spending a few hours together was different than living together. And she had her heart set on adopting another child, a girl who would be a sister to Juliana. They would want time to grow together before bringing any other people into their family. "To every thing there is a season, and a time to every purpose," her Bible said. Maybe right now wasn't the time for her and Konrad. Maybe these feelings were only meant to show them they were able to love again after losing their spouses. She needed to examine these thoughts in prayer before speaking them to him.

She touched his arm. "Danke for telling me all this, Konrad. You and your boys are very important to me, and I want what is best for all three of you. Just as I have been doing, I will continue to pray and trust God to guide you, in His perfect time and with His perfect grace, to the one who is meant to become your helpmeet and the boys' mother. For now, I must get to the Langes' before Herr Elias leaves for Marion and tell him you and Fräulein Gartner are not pursuing a courtship."

He hopped down and rounded the wagon, then lifted his arms to her. Oh, how difficult to accept this gentlemanly gesture when her heart pined to discover how it felt to be held by him. She squelched her thoughts and took his hands, allowing him to help her down. When her feet met the ground, he kept a light grasp on her hands.

"You stay here with Juliana. The boys and I will drive out to the Langes', and I will tell Herr Elias the whole truth." A sad smile played on the corners of his lips. "You have done enough for me already, Gussie. I will make sure he understands."

Because he could get there faster in the wagon than she could walking and because she desperately needed to separate herself from his presence—he wasn't the only one who had feelings to put to rest—she wouldn't argue with his plan.

"Danke, Konrad." She took a backward step, pulling her hands free. "Would you fetch my cake plate, please? And then I will send the boys out to you."

Konrad

The rhythmic *clop-clop* of the horses' hooves on the ground, the soft whisper of the wind in the tall grasses, and the sweet call of birds created a soothing lullaby. Walden and Folker fell asleep in the back of the wagon, nestled together like a pair of puppies, making for a quiet drive that calmed the frayed edges of Konrad's nerves. The conversation with Gussie, although necessary, had taxed him. At the same time, he would have liked to go on talking with her forever. So very confusing.

As he pulled into the Langes' lane, he spotted Herr Elias swinging into the saddle of the borrowed horse he rode to go back and forth between Marion and Alexandertol each weekend. Konrad blew out a little breath of relief. He'd made it in time.

Herr Elias turned his horse toward the road, and Konrad

waved to capture the man's attention. Herr Elias tapped the horse with his heels and prodded it forward until he came alongside Konrad's wagon. Up close, how odd he looked in the saddle while wearing his fine suit and bowler hat—not like any cowboy Konrad had ever seen. Now, face-to-face with the man, Konrad went tongue-tied. He had been so certain Herr Elias was seeking a courtship with Gussie. They matched each other so well, both with their book knowledge and gentle manners. But Gussie's panic to let Herr Elias know Fräulein Gartner was available for courtship told Konrad he'd been wrong. Of course, what difference did it make if he couldn't claim Gussie for himself?

"Herr Rempel." Herr Elias smiled, but confusion sketched lines across his forehead. "Did you need to see me?"

Konrad cleared his dry throat. "Ja. Guss—I mean, Frau Dyck was worried about you returning to Marion with an incorrect idea about Fräulein Gartner and me." He fiddled with the brim of his best hat, aware of the scorch marks on one side and the little holes where sparks had landed. "Frau Dyck wanted you to know that Fräulein Gartner is not the one I have chosen."

"She's not?"

Konrad didn't know the man well enough to judge for sure if he was pleased or only curious. "Nein."

"But you have chosen someone, ja? She said you were done looking. We presumed that meant—"

"Ja, I already know what you and she presumed, but it isn't true, and now you know the truth." Well, some of the truth. Not all of it. "Frau Dyck wanted to make sure you knew. Since you do, I . . . I will let you go on to Marion now."

"Danke for coming out and telling me. It means a great deal to know this about Fräulein Gartner. Frau Dyck must have told you . . ." The horse shifted a bit, snorting, and Herr Elias patted the animal's sleek neck. When it was calm again, Herr Elias said, "That I like her."

Konrad stared at the man, uncertain who he meant. "You like Frau Dyck?"

"Well, ja, of course I do. But I was speaking of Fräulein Gartner." He blew out a soft breath of relief. "I know I gave her name to Frau Dyck as a potential wife for you, but the more I got to know her, I—" He stopped and shook his head. "I don't know why I'm telling you this. I guess I'm just so thankful to know—" Now he laughed. "I am sorry, Herr Rempel, for taking up so much of your time. You need to return to Alexandertol, and I need to get to Marion. The day is quickly slipping by."

"Ja, it is." Konrad took up the reins. "You have safe travels."

"Danke. Enjoy the rest of your day." Herr Elias lifted his heels as if to prod the horse, but then he drew the reins tight and angled a puzzled look at Konrad. "Herr Rempel, may I ask . . . if not Fräulein Gartner, whom did you choose?"

The sun beamed hot on him, but it seemed as if someone poured cold water over his head. Konrad swallowed. "I did not."

"Pardon?"

Why was his mouth so dry? Talking was painful. He tried swallowing again. "I did not choose. I chose not to choose."

A soft chuckle rumbled. "You're speaking in riddles, sir."

Konrad blurted, "I am not going to marry again. Not right now."

The man leaned back in the saddle and gazed at Konrad for several seconds, his eyes slightly squinted and his face empty of emotion. Then the corners of his lips tipped downward, and he sighed. "I see. That is too bad. I thought maybe . . ." He shrugged. "But I guess it doesn't matter now. And I will be on my way." He chirruped to the horse, tapping his heels. The animal broke into a canter and carried him toward the road.

Konrad turned the wagon around and followed him to the end of the lane, then they went opposite directions. Although he no longer held Herr Elias in his sight, he couldn't help but wonder what the man had meant when he said, *"That is too bad."* Too bad about what . . . or who?

Chapter Thirty-One

Augusta

May slipped by, each day a bit hotter and windier than the one before, absent of the rain farmers prayed would fall and nourish their crops. Each weekday morning, Konrad drove Walden and Folker to Augusta's house. When he dropped them off, she and Konrad exchanged a few words on the porch. Then in the evening when he picked them up, they talked longer. About what book she'd read with the twins, what he had made in his shop, how tall the hardy Turkey Red wheat planted last fall was growing despite the lack of rain. Ordinary things that became somehow extraordinary because it had been so long since she'd enjoyed such daily conversation with a man. If she were a poet, she would call those minutes at the end of the day sweet agony. Sweet in the moment but laden with lonely agony when he departed.

But she found joy in watching Juliana grow and mature, seemingly changing daily in responsibility and patience and compassion. Augusta found joy in lavishing love and attention on Walden and Folker. She considered Frau Krahn's tart comment about becoming too attached to the boys and turning them into teacher's pets, and she tried to temper her heart. But it was too late. She already loved them. Almost as much as she loved their father.

On Saturday, when Augusta and Juliana were beating rugs in the backyard, Herr Elias came by. He waved a rumpled piece of paper as he approached, his grin teasing. "You two are creating such a cloud of dust, people might think you're sending smoke signals."

Augusta lowered her beater, and Juliana did, too. The girl huffed a laugh, then coughed. She waved the cloud away with her hand. "It's embarrassing how much dust is coming out of these rugs. I didn't realize Mother and I tracked in so much dirt."

"Ja, well, it isn't only *your* feet these days, remember. There are yours plus the twins'." He pressed the paper into Augusta's hand and winked. "And maybe soon, even more?"

Augusta's pulse skipped a beat, and she examined the paper with eagerness. The image of sixteen or seventeen children printed on the handbill was grainy and smudged, but to the left of the group were three attired in dresses with big bows in their hair. Her heart caught. She stared hard, trying to make out their features, but the image quality was too poor for such details. But they were girls. Would one soon be Juliana's sister and Augusta's daughter?

Juliana stood nearby, the rug beater still in her hand, watching Augusta, curiosity shining in her blue eyes. Now that Augusta knew for sure girls were coming, she could share her intention with her daughter. But she must exercise caution. There would likely be many people interested in these children. She didn't want to get Juliana's hopes up and then see them dashed if they weren't able to adopt one of these girls.

She lifted her attention to Herr Elias. "Danke for bringing this."

"Bitte." He pointed at the handbill. "I got it from a man at the newspaper office. He said we should hang it here in town somewhere in case others in Alexandertol are interested. If there's a good turnout in Marion for this bunch, the orphanage might make another stop there in the future."

"Oh." Augusta pressed the paper to her apron bib. She'd

hoped to pray over the image, ask God to reveal to her which child was meant to be hers, if any. "So are you taking it with you now?"

Juliana laid aside the rug beater and inched up beside Augusta. Herr Elias glanced at her, and understanding bloomed in his expression. "I can leave it with you. Maybe you could take it by the mercantile or post office later?"

Good choices. Everyone in town visited those places at least once a week. She nodded. "Ja, I will do that."

He glanced at Juliana again, then cleared his throat. "Frau Dyck, could I borrow you from this chore for a minute or two? There's something I'd like to . . ."

Augusta touched Juliana's arm. "Go back to work, wood nymph. I'll be right back." She escorted Herr Elias around the corner of the house. With the rhythmic *whack . . . whack* of Juliana's busy rug beater against a carpet sounding behind them, Augusta looked up at the man and smiled. "What did you need?"

He slipped his hands into his pockets, suddenly seeming shy. Very unlike himself. "I wanted you to be the first to know that I have asked Fräulein Gartner to be my wife, and she has consented."

Augusta gasped. "Oh, Herr Elias, I am so happy for you!"

He beamed. "Danke, I am happy for me, too."

"Have you set a date for your wedding?"

"Ja, we plan to exchange our vows on the eighth of August." He rocked on his heels, as if eager to move into the future. "We aren't yet sure if we will have the wedding in Marion or Alexandertol, though. She has a little house in Marion she inherited from her parents, and we will live there until we are able to find suitable quarters here in Alexandertol. My room at the Langes' is fine for me by myself, but I don't want to live in someone else's home when I'm married."

She understood his reasoning, but something else caught her attention. "She is willing to leave her teaching job in Marion?"

"Ja." Amazement colored the single word. "Ernestine says as much as she loves her job, she loves me more. She wants to become a part of the community I call home and claim it for herself." Pink stole across his clean-shaven cheeks. "She is a wonderful woman, Frau Dyck. God is so good to bring us together."

Augusta laughed. "Who would think that you being shoved from your longtime work at the Schmidts' would result in such a blessing?" She was happy for him, ja, but jealousy also nibbled at her. She pushed the selfish emotion aside and focused on the joy of his announcement. "I will pray that a house will become available for you."

"And maybe a job for her?" His expression turned sheepish. "She says she is so used to working she isn't sure she wants to only keep a house." He leaned forward slightly, his eyes twinkling. "I think she's a bit of a rebel underneath her ladylike exterior. A bit like you, Frau Dyck."

Augusta drew back, shocked. "A rebel? Me?"

"Ja, you." He straightened and peered at her with narrowed eyes. "Most widows remarry quickly, perhaps afraid of being alone, perhaps either unwilling or unable to take care of their property by themselves. If you were like other widows, you would have accepted the attentions of a man by now. Maybe even my attentions. But you'd rather be alone than enter a relationship built on fear or helplessness. You will wait for love."

She considered what he'd said. He was right, and he knew her much better than she'd suspected. She gave a slow nod, her lips pulling into a smile. "I appreciate what you said. And I am so happy that you, too, waited for the love God planned for you. I pray you and your Fräulein Gartner will share many joyful years of blessedness."

"Danke." He pulled one hand free and brushed her upper

arm, a gesture that spoke of friendship and caring. "And I pray you and your sweet daughter will enjoy the blessing of welcoming another child into your home." He tipped his hat. "Guten Tag, Frau Dyck." He strode away, whistling.

Augusta hurried around the house. She must talk to Juliana about her plans, ascertain if her daughter was as excited about the possibility of gaining a sister as Augusta was about gaining another daughter. Then, either way, they would clean themselves up and take this handbill to the mercantile in case others might want to travel to Marion and meet the children.

Konrad

Konrad and Folker waited while Walden took his turn in the barber's chair, Folker wriggling on the bench. Were it not for Folker bumping him with his elbow, Konrad might fall asleep. His days were busy. Full. Exhausting. With no time to just sit. But he wanted it that way. He wanted to be too busy to think. Too busy to feel. Of course, he should already know that busyness did not erase feelings. He hadn't been able to work enough to forget how much he missed Hannah when she'd died, and he couldn't work enough to forget how much he loved Gussie.

When he dropped into his bed at night, no matter how weary his body, his mind refused to rest. It painted images of Gussie behind his closed lids and tormented him. If only he was brawny and boisterous and unscarred, like Leopold. If only he had enough money to spoil her with gifts. If only he could be the kind of man a woman like Gussie deserved. But God had crafted him with a sinewy frame and quiet nature. Life had dealt an unkind blow and marked his face. He was a simple man with a simple lifestyle. These things he could not change. So he did his best to fight his feelings and told himself it would be easier when school started again and he wouldn't have daily contact with the woman who'd captured his heart.

Folker shifted and his knee pressed against his father's. Konrad gently cupped his son's leg and moved it aside a few inches. As he did, he noticed how the boy's pant leg had ridden up, exposing his entire boot and an inch-wide patch of bare skin above the shaft. Apparently Folker hadn't put on stockings. Again.

He gave his son a nudge with his elbow. "Where are your stockings, Folker? You know you're to wear them with your boots."

Folker scrunched his face. "They're too short. They pinch my toes."

"Your stockings or your boots?"

He shrugged. "Both. I'd rather go barefoot."

Konrad sat back and examined his son from the soles of his dusty shoes to the unbuttoned collar of his shirt. Then he shot a startled look at Walden. Only his calves and feet showed beneath the cloth Ben used to protect their clothes from bits of hair, but his pant legs, too, were at least an inch above his boot shafts.

Konrad turned a frown on Folker. "Do you not have any britches, shirts, or stockings that fit?"

The boy shook his head.

"What of your church clothes?"

Folker snorted. "My suit is so tight it cuts into my armpits."

Konrad wanted to hide in shame. How had he not noticed that the twins were growing out of their clothes? If he neglected to see something so obvious, he'd been keeping himself too busy. He sighed. He would rather wait until school started again to buy new clothes, but the boys needed things now. "When we are finished here, we'll go next door to the mercantile and buy you each a set of new clothes to wear to Gussie's each day."

Folker's face lit up. "Danke, Pa!"

Ben snapped the cape from Walden and sent a grin at Folker. "All right. Your turn."

The boys exchanged places, and Konrad picked up a tattered copy of the *Marion Record*, which Ben left lying out for his customers. He unfolded it, and his gaze landed on a sales ad. The Marion mercantile was having a special two-for-one sale on boys' suits through the entire month of June. Marion was pretty far away—a five- or six-hour drive with his team and wagon—but it could be worth the distance to save so much on new suits.

Then he remembered that a while back, Gussie had asked if he would be willing to drive her to Marion. At the time, he presumed it had something to do with Herr Elias. He no longer held those suspicions, and she might not even need to go anymore, but he should find out. If he was going there to buy suits anyway, she could go along.

His stomach turned little flips, its response to thinking about their spending so much time together. Excited flips or nervous flips? He grimaced, pressing his hand to his belly. Probably both.

He paid for their haircuts, then they left the shop. The twins started for the mercantile, but he stopped them. "Hop in the wagon. I need to talk to your Tante Gussie. Let's go over there before we do our shopping."

Walden pointed up the street. "We don't have to go to her house, Pa. Here she comes now."

Konrad adjusted the brim of his hat. Sure enough, there she was with her daughter, coming toward them, each with a shopping basket on her arm. How fetching she appeared in her trim-fitting dress, lace from her bonnet framing her face. The flips changed to cartwheels.

The boys tore off in her direction as if they were in a race. Konrad wished he could run that way, too. Would he be old and gray before he finally released his infatuation with this woman? Or would he ever release it at all?

She gave each of the boys hugs, then turned her hesitant gaze on him. "The boys said you need to talk to me?"

He snatched off his hat. "Ja, I do."

She gave Juliana her basket. "Sweetheart, would you take the boys into the mercantile? Have Frau Weber measure five pounds of flour for us. I'll be with you in a few minutes."

The children scampered off, and she watched after them. The fondness in her eyes, he knew, wasn't reserved for her daughter. How kindly she treated his sons, as if they were her own children. Which only made him love her more.

Then she turned her smile on him. "All right. What do you want to talk about?"

He gestured to the shaded gap between the post office and the apothecary buildings where they'd be out of the sun and also out of sight of other Saturday shoppers. If what he was feeling showed on his face, he would become the topic of conversation at every dinner table in town.

She lifted her skirts a bit and entered the narrow alleyway, then faced him. "I'm listening."

He wrung his hat to keep his hands busy. This secluded spot inspired ideas about drawing this woman into an embrace. Maybe they should have stayed out in the sun. "I wondered . . . you had asked me if I could take you to Marion. Do you still need to go?"

She nodded so eagerly that the lace on her bonnet fluttered. "Ja, I do. I must be at the Presbyterian church by nine-thirty in the morning on the fifth of June."

So early? "Gussie, it's fifteen miles to Marion. To be there by nine-thirty, we would have to leave Alexandertol in the middle of the night. You can't go later in the day?"

"Nein." Her crestfallen expression pierced him. "It will likely all be done by ten-thirty. I won't have a chance at all if I'm not there at nine-thirty."

He chewed his mustache for a moment. He shouldn't ask. Mutter always said not to be nosy. But curiosity got the best of him. "What will you attend at the Presbyterian church that will be done in an hour?"

A look of hopefulness transformed her face. "I hope to adopt a child." She pulled a folded piece of paper from her apron pocket and showed it to him. "Remember when Herr Elias told us a train would bring orphans to Marion? I couldn't stop thinking about it. I've longed for another child, a sister for Juliana. Observing her with Walden and Folker assures me she'll be a good, loving sister. She and I talked about it, and she is as certain about the rightness of bringing a little girl into our family as I am."

Konrad stared at the printed picture of the group of children while Gussie talked. He couldn't lift his eyes from the children's faces. Although it was a very poor image, the somberness in their expressions pierced him. They were children, yet they somehow looked old. They needed joy.

He lifted his head and met Gussie's gaze. "I cannot imagine a better home for any of them than what you would provide." His chest ached at what he must say next. "But for me to take you . . . to not travel at night when it's unsafe . . . we would need to leave the day before. We would need to take a hotel for the night. You and I . . . we . . ." He gulped. "Do you see the problem?"

Her pert chin lifted. "Our children will be with us. We will be in separate rooms. Maybe even on separate floors. No one can find fault with that, can they?"

If they didn't know about it, they couldn't find fault. But if they knew? Many would find fault. Her reputation could be tarnished. Dare he risk it? And—

"And I will pay for the hotel." She spoke with more stubbornness than he'd ever heard from her. "This is my outing, and you are my hired driver. It's only fair that I cover your expenses."

Now his ire rose, driven by pride and a small amount of hurt. "I offered to take you as a favor for a friend. What kind of friend would then take payment for the favor? Nein, I will not allow you to pay my way."

She stared steadily at him for several seconds, her eyebrows pinched into a scowl. Then her brow relaxed. "Konrad?" Her voice had lost its stubborn edge. In its place he heard concern and compassion that squashed his momentary indignation. "Can you afford to pay for a night in a hotel?"

Telling her the truth would shred him of any dignity he possessed, but he wouldn't lie to her. Buying the boys' clothes, even at sale prices, would tax his meager account. He tried to answer, but his vocal cords refused to make a sound. So he shook his head.

"Then I will find another way to get to Marion." She conceded so kindly it stung his heart. She touched his arm. "It's all right. If God wants me to adopt one of these little girls, He will provide transportation for me."

He looked at her slender gloved hand lying against the faded plaid fabric of his shirt. Such a contrast. If he couldn't be burly and handsome and bold, could he not at least be wealthy enough to do her this favor? He wanted to tell her he would pray for God's provision, but his mouth was too dry. So he nodded miserably and escorted her to the mercantile.

Chapter Thirty-Two

Martina

Ordinarily Martina spent Monday bent over her washtub, but at breakfast Gerhard casually mentioned a craving for cinnamon crumb cake. After he left for work, she checked her cupboard and, as she'd suspected, her cinnamon tin was nearly empty. The recipe called for cinnamon in the cake itself as well as several teaspoons in the crumbly topping. She washed their dishes and straightened the kitchen, then set off for town.

A brisk breeze propelled her along, keeping the morning sun from being overly warm. She scanned the sky for clouds, knowing how concerned the farmers were about the length of time between rains, and sent up a prayer for God to send needed moisture. She couldn't help smiling at how easily and automatically prayers formed in her heart these days. After so many years of being angry with God, finding her peace with Him was like starting life fresh and new. How glorious to discover cheerfulness even in her childless state. Perhaps she, like the apostle Paul, had finally learned in whatsoever state she was to be content. The realization lightened her heart and put a little bounce in her step.

At the mercantile, she reached for the door handle. A handbill tucked into the frame of the door's window caught her eye. *WANTED: Homes for Children* was emblazoned at the top. Directly below the heading, the picture of a group of well-dressed but sad-looking children filled the center of the page. She stood with her hand gripping the doorknob, her gaze locked on the children, her pulse pounding with such intensity she feared she might collapse.

Suddenly the door opened from the inside, nearly tugging her off balance. Elsie Weber reached for Martina, and Martina reached back. She clung to the woman's hand, her eyes still fixed on the image. Elsie squeezed Martina's hand. "Frau Krahn, are you all right? You stood out here so long without coming in I was afraid you were ill."

Martina shook her head very slightly, unwilling to turn away from the faces that seemed to beseech her. "I am not ill. I . . ."

Elsie glanced at the handbill. She clucked her tongue on her teeth. "Isn't it sad? So many children without homes. Of course when we were asked, we agreed to post the advertisement even though it has nothing to do with the products we offer in the store. Franz and I are praying that every single one of those unfortunate waifs are taken into homes where they will be loved and brought up in the admonition of the Lord." She gave a little tug, drawing Martina all the way in. She closed the door, removing the handbill from Martina's sight. She patted Martina's hand and then released it. "What brings you to the store this morning?"

Martina blinked at the storekeeper. "What brings me in?" Why had she come? She couldn't remember.

A worried frown creased the storekeeper's face. "Martina, you're as white as newly fallen snow. Do you need to sit down?"

Her legs were quivering, but she didn't want to sit. She wanted to run and dance and sing. Because something she thought she'd been denied might be available after all. And how like God to offer it when she'd found her peace without it. " 'Delight thyself also in the LORD: and he shall give thee the desires of thine heart.' " Psalm 37:4, a scripture she'd memorized as a little girl, spilled from her lips.

Elsie's frown deepened. "Truly, you aren't yourself. Let me take you into our quarters and get you a glass of water."

"Nein, nein." Martina waved her hands. She grasped the doorknob and pulled the door open. She gazed at the image again, her smile growing so wide it pulled at her chapped lips. "I must go now. Danke, Frau Weber."

"Danke?" Elsie shook her head. "I've done nothing for you."

Martina stumbled out onto the boardwalk. The moment her feet met the planked boards, her legs seemed to gain strength. She broke into a trot. She'd never run through town before. People might talk for the next several years about her doing so today, but she didn't care. She had to get to Gerhard now. She had to tell him about the orphans needing homes. She had to find out if he felt the same way she did. She had to know if the desire of her heart was soon to be met.

Augusta

Even though Augusta hadn't yet arranged a ride to Marion, she was compelled to ready Juliana's room to accommodate a second child. The peace she experienced about adding to her family was too real, too telling to ignore. Juliana would have a sister soon. Augusta knew it would happen.

Juliana believed it, too. In the evenings, after Folker and Walden had left with their father and supper was done, Juliana cheerfully helped Augusta rearrange furniture to accommodate her new sister's bed. She made room in her Schrank for her new sister's clothes. She sorted through her many toys and dolls and chose the nicest ones to present to her new sister. Each day, they walked to the mercantile and looked at the handbill, then prayed together for the girl who would be part of their family.

On Friday evening, as Juliana was laying a doll against the fluffed pillows on her new sister's bed, she paused. "Mother, wouldn't it be best to take my new sister to the mercantile and let her choose a few toys? She'll be sleeping in my room, wearing some of my dresses. Won't she feel like she truly matters to us if we buy her new things all her own?"

Pride in her daughter's tender heart swelled so that it brought the sting of tears. Augusta embraced Juliana and kissed her forehead. "Such a kind, wise idea. Ja, we will do that after we've brought her home." Then she cupped Juliana's face in her hands. "Part of being in a family is sharing. You already know this and you're showing it by being willing to share your room and belongings. Please don't be offended if your new sister doesn't want to share right away. If she's lived a long time in an orphanage where everything must be shared with several children, she might want to be selfish with her things for a while until she understands they won't be taken away."

Juliana gazed thoughtfully at Augusta for several seconds. "We are very excited to have her here, but she might be shy. I hadn't thought of that. I will be patient with her and give her a chance to grow to love me as much as I already love her."

When Augusta went to bed that night, although she had many things about which to pray, she first thanked the Lord for Juliana's openness to others. How many children raised all alone and blessed with nearly everything their hearts desired would be willing to share it all with a child they'd never met? Not many, she wagered. Juliana was special. The new daughter would need lots of love and affection to help her feel at home here, but Augusta reminded herself not to neglect Juliana in the process. Just before falling asleep, she reminded the Lord she still needed a way to get to Marion if she was to bring home the daughter He had selected for her. Secure that He would meet the need, she slept well.

The last Saturday in May, Augusta awakened to the thought that in only one more week, her life would change mightily with the addition of another child. It could take weeks for the new child to settle in and feel at ease, which would limit any socializing. She'd intended to invite the Krahns to Sunday dinner in return for their kind invitation two weeks ago, but busyness had intruded upon intention. If she was going to have them over in a timely manner, it needed to be tomorrow.

After breakfast, she gave Juliana her list of chores, kissed her on the cheek, and promised to be home soon. Then, with a quart jar of home-canned pickled beets tucked into the curve of her arm, she set off for the Krahns'. She couldn't help but remember how her stomach used to churn when she knew she would see Frau Krahn. Today, however, she experienced no such nervousness. The woman had changed so much since her breakdown in front of Augusta and Berta Hartmann. Maybe confessing her secrets had crumbled her walls. Whatever the reason, Augusta appreciated the changes. She even considered the woman a friend now—a welcome idea.

She knocked on the Krahns' front door, and Martina answered. Although she wore an apron over her dress and her hair was hidden by a knotted towel, the signs of someone who was hard at work, she smiled brightly and invited Augusta in.

Augusta stepped over the threshold and held out the jar. "I wanted to give you this as a belated thank-you gift for your kind invitation to Sunday dinner two weeks ago."

Martina took the jar, delight blooming on her round, flushed face. "Pickled beets?"

"Ja, from my Mutter's recipe, with lots of cloves."

The woman licked her lips, then hugged the jar, laughing. "Oh, my, we will enjoy these. Danke sehr."

Augusta couldn't hold back a huge smile in reply. Would she have ever imagined stern Frau Krahn acting so lighthearted?

"Bitte. And"—she pulled in a big breath, anticipating an argument—"I would like to invite you and Gerhard to have dinner tomorrow at my house with Juliana and me."

Martina's mouth fell open. She clapped one hand to her cheek. "Invite . . . Gerhard and me . . ."

Her astonishment made Augusta's chest ache. Had no one ever invited the couple to Sunday dinner? Were there others in town who were similarly overlooked? She needed to talk to the Frauenverein about becoming aware of those who might simply need a friendly gesture.

Martina shook her head. "Are you sure? I know how busy you are all week, caring for the Rempel twins and your own dear daughter, seeing to your household responsibilities all on your own, not to mention so dutifully serving on the Frauenverein." She lowered her hand and placed it on Augusta's shoulder. "I wouldn't wish to burden you."

Augusta grasped Martina's hand and gave it a squeeze. "I am very sure. Please come. We want to get to know you better."

Tears flooded Martina's eyes. "We will come, and I will bring the dessert this time, ja?"

Augusta smiled. "Perfect."

Augusta enjoyed a relaxed meal with the Krahns, and when they were finished eating, she hated to see them leave. So she brought out the coffeepot and poured everyone fresh cups, then settled into her chair in the hopes of more conversation.

. Juliana sat across the table, polite and uncomplaining, but Augusta sensed she'd rather take a book to her favorite tree or go to her room and draw on her sketch pad. She caught her daughter's eyes. "Would you mind clearing the dishes for us, dear? Then you may be excused."

The girl rose without a moment's pause and circled the table, stacking plates in the careful way Augusta had taught her.

Herr Krahn watched her over the rim of his coffee cup, and he gave a nod that showed approval. "You're a very good helper for your mother, Juliana. I am sure she is very proud of you."

Juliana blushed prettily. "Danke, sir." Her eyes sparkled. "And just think, Mother, after next week, you will have two helpers."

Augusta hadn't expressly forbidden Juliana from speaking of their desire to bring home an orphaned child. They'd spoken of Juliana's *new sister* so many times she probably hadn't even thought before mentioning it. But once the words were out, the pink staining her cheeks changed to dark crimson. She gaped at Augusta in mute horror.

Gerhard and Martina exchanged a glance, and Martina turned a speculative look on Augusta. "Two helpers? Are you planning to remarry?"

Juliana hurried out of the room, abandoning Augusta to tie up the thread she had left dangling. "Nein, I am not. But I suppose it's all right for you to know what Juliana was talking about. After all, if it works out, the whole town will know soon enough." She cradled the cup between her palms and sighed airily. "I have decided to adopt another child. A girl."

Martina clattered her cup onto the table. "From the group of orphans coming to Marion?"

"How did you—" Then Augusta inwardly mocked herself. Why should she be surprised that Martina would already know about the upcoming arrival of orphans? Even if she hadn't seen the handbill at the mercantile herself, Agnes Bauer lived right next door to her. Agnes knew everything and was willing to share it.

Augusta nodded. "Ja. Juliana is very excited about having a sister with whom to giggle and play games and talk late into the night . . . and share chores." She laughed lightly. "We've both prayed about it, and we believe we are doing the right thing by bringing an orphaned child into our home. Isn't that what the Frauenverein encourages—meeting the needs of the fatherless?"

Martina's mouth flapped open and closed, like a fish gulping for air. Augusta had no idea her decision would bring such a reaction. She hoped her new friend wouldn't have an attack of apoplexy.

Gerhard put his hand over Martina's but looked at Augusta. "Martina is stunned, no doubt, because your decision is also our decision. We plan to go to Marion on Saturday, too, and see about adopting a boy." He turned to his wife. "Or a pair of brothers, ja?"

Martina's mouth snapped closed. She nodded hard. "I am so happy to know your plans, Augusta. If you bring home a girl and we bring a boy"—

"Or two," Gerhard said.

—"or two," Martina echoed, "from the same orphan's home, it will be nice for the children. They'll already know someone else in the community. Shouldn't it make them feel more at ease?"

Augusta hadn't considered it before, but she agreed. "I wonder if we're the only ones in Alexandertol who plan to go to Marion and meet the children. Have you heard of anyone else?"

"Nein." Gerhard picked up his coffee cup and took a noisy draw. "Martina and I will drive there on Friday. I wired to Marion and arranged a room at the hotel. We want to be at the church on time so we have a chance to meet all the children."

Martina smiled at Gerhard. "And we trust that God will guide us to the ones we're meant to raise as our own."

"Ja," he said. The two exchanged a tender look.

Observing them, Augusta missed the days when she and Leopold communicated with a look. Wishing to set aside pining over what she no longer had, she pondered aloud, "I wonder if I should wire ahead about a room."

They both shifted their attention to her. Gerhard angled a worried frown at her. "May I ask how you plan to get to Marion? You aren't driving yourself, are you?"

Augusta smiled at his concern. "I sold our wagon and team after Leopold died, so I don't have the means to drive myself. Initially, a friend was going to take me, but . . ." She swallowed, still sad about the uncomfortable position in which she'd placed Konrad. She shrugged. "That's no longer a possibility. You said you are trusting God to guide you to your new child. I'm doing the same, and part of that is trusting Him to provide a ride to Marion."

The pair looked at each other again. A slow smile grew on Gerhard's lips, and then Martina laughed. "Augusta, Augusta . . ." She shook her head, her eyes merry. "We had planned to keep secret our excursion and then surprise everyone by arriving at church with our new son—"

"Or sons."

Augusta hid a smile. Gerhard was set on a large family. She prayed, after all their losses, that God would bless them with more than one child.

Martina crinkled her nose at her husband. "Sons. But Juliana's little faux pas concerning your plans has exposed ours, and it's all for the best." She sat upright and assumed the authoritative pose with which Augusta was very familiar. "We will pick you up in our buggy at noon on Friday and take you to Marion with us. If we're both successful in adopting children, the ride home will be crowded, but that will just give us the opportunity to become quickly acquainted, ja?"

Chapter Thirty-Three

Augusta

Juliana held so tightly to Augusta's hand that it hurt, but Augusta refused to pull away. Juliana was probably feeling as overwhelmed as Augusta was, and a child's emotions ran deeper. Augusta hadn't expected such a sad spectacle. In her mind, she'd envisioned a type of social gathering, with potential parents sitting next to a child and getting acquainted. The reality was much less relaxed.

The children were lined up on the church dais in a stiff, unsmiling row. A tall, slender woman had introduced herself as Miss Genevieve Wallace, a representative of Gentle Shepherd Orphan's Asylum. Her dour appearance made Martina Krahn's former countenance seem sunny. She delivered several instructions for those who'd come to see the children, then she began calling names one by one.

When his or her name was called, the child stepped forward. Those seated in the pews examined the child the way buyers might examine a horse or a cow. Then interested parents moved to the front and engaged in short conversations with the child. Sometimes the child left the stage with the parents, other times they returned to the line. Augusta found the entire process demeaning. What happened to the children who weren't selected? Did they go through this again and again? Her heart ached at the humiliation the children must be experiencing.

She had told Juliana to squeeze her hand if she felt the Spirit's nudge about any of the girls. Of course, as tightly as she held on, Augusta might not recognize a squeeze. But she would know her own reaction. Each time a girl stepped forward, she waited for some indication in her heart—a flutter, a spark, even a settling—that meant she was the one. But although she felt compassion toward each child, she didn't feel drawn. Not like a mother should to her child.

The third of the three girls moved to the front of the stage without any convicting prick in Augusta's spirit to claim her. Juliana released her hand and looked up at her, tears swimming in her blue eyes. Augusta read the same questions in her daughter's eyes that filled her heart. Why had God opened her to the idea of adoption and made it possible for her to be here if she wasn't meant to take one of these girls home? She couldn't make sense of it, either.

They stayed in the pew until the remaining children, a pair of brothers named Titus and Amos, ages nine and eleven, moved hand in hand to the stage's edge. In one accord, Gerhard and Martina rose and went forward. A few minutes later, the pair of slender, dark-headed boys trailed the Krahns to the table where the attendees had been instructed to complete paperwork for transfer of responsibility from the orphanage to the adoptive parents.

Augusta silently rejoiced for the Krahns even while confusion riddled her mind. She put her arm around Juliana and sighed. "Ja, well, I suppose our girl wasn't in this group. There was such a good turnout, though, I'm sure more will come this way. We will be patient and—"

An unearthly screech echoed from the rafters of the church. Augusta jerked her attention in the direction of the sound, and she gasped in shock. A woman was dragging a little girl onto the dais. The child had her arms locked around a wooden stick of some sort, and the woman used it as a makeshift leash to pull the child behind her. The little girl expressed her outrage in shrill shrieks.

Juliana grabbed hold of Augusta's arm and squeezed, her face alight. "Mother! She's the one!"

Augusta gaped at her daughter. "What?"

Before Juliana could respond, Miss Wallace shouted over the child's tantrum.

"This is Helena Maria, age seven. She is of Caucasian parentage and healthy, without blemishes, deformities, or abnormalities." The description continued while the girl and the woman on stage seemed to engage in a wrestling match. How could such a small child be so fierce? Something must be wrong with her.

Juliana pushed at Augusta. "Mother, go quickly before someone else takes my new sister."

A glance over her shoulder confirmed Augusta's thinking. No one was going forward to claim this child. Augusta's heart. rolled over, and tears stung her eyes.

Juliana stood, yanking on Augusta's arm. "Mother, please!"

Augusta stood and hurried to Miss Wallace. "Excuse me? Is this child truly from your orphanage? She wasn't in the photograph on the handbill."

The woman's thin lips pressed into a firm line. "Of course she wasn't. She wouldn't stand in line with the other children without her broom."

Augusta shot a look at the stick. Now that she was closer, she spotted ratty bristles tied at the upper end of the stick.

"We couldn't put her and that . . . that broom in the photo. What would people think?" The woman huffed. "We'll likely never place her. She's incorrigible. The only appropriate placement is an insane asylum."

Something in the center of Augusta's soul squeezed and held.

She observed the child for several seconds. Her little face, beet red, seemed more panicked than angry. Fear seemed to pulsate from her little frame. She was the tiniest seven-year-old Augusta had ever seen, smaller than any of the first-year students who'd entered her classroom, and many of them were only five when they started school. Augusta's hands instinctively stretched toward the little girl.

The child threw her head back and screamed, "Nooooo! Miiiiiine!"

Augusta withdrew her hands, but her heart continued to ache. "Why does she have a broom?" she heard herself ask.

Miss Wallace folded her arms. "Her mother sold brooms on a street corner to earn enough money for bread. There was only one broom left in the woman's stash when officers found her last February, frozen solid on the street. They were shocked to discover a child cuddled beneath her, still alive." No compassion warmed the woman's icy glare as she watched Helena Maria fight with the worker for full control of the broom. "She grabbed the broom when the officers carried her away. We haven't been able to separate her from it since. So when we put her on the train, it came, too." Derision curled her lips. "She even sleeps with it, or I'd have burned it weeks ago."

Augusta couldn't take another moment of this woman's apathy. She moved to the edge of the stage and snapped her fingers. "You there!" She waited until the worker noticed her. "Let go of her."

The worker sought Miss Wallace's gaze. Miss Wallace shrugged, and the worker let go. The child fell on her bottom, then curled herself around the broom and glowered at the woman.

"Helena Maria?" Augusta used her teacher voice—soft, firm, expectant. "Helena Maria, look at me, please."

The little girl turned her face to Augusta, and her heart rolled over. Heart shaped, with a button nose and pink rosebud lips. Her blonde hair frizzed around her head in uncombed curls, but she was as exquisite as a china doll.

A smile formed on Augusta's face without effort. "I promise not to take your broom." She put her hands behind her back. "See? I don't want your broom. I only want to talk to you. Come here, please."

For what seemed like hours, Helena Maria stared at Augusta, her sweet face expressionless. Then, as slowly as an inchworm's progress, she pulled with her heels and slid on her bottom until she was only a yard or so from Augusta.

Augusta rewarded her with a nod. "Danke—thank you."

"Bitte," the child said.

A little gasp came from behind Augusta, and Juliana stepped forward. "Helena Maria?" Juliana's voice quavered in excitement. *"Sprechen Sie Deutsch?"*

Wonder bloomed on the little girl's face. She struggled to her feet, still clinging to the broom the way a bear cub held to a tree trunk. *"Ich spreche Deutsch."* She began jabbering in German, sentences spilling one on top of the other like a spring bubbling from the ground at winter's end. With each word, she inched forward until the toes of her button-up shoes met the edge of the stage. Her voice fell silent, and she peered down at Augusta and Juliana with something Augusta could only define as hope glimmering in her pale blue-green eyes.

Juliana slowly reached up and put her hand on Helena Maria's elbow. *"Willst du meine neue Schwester sein?"*

Augusta held her breath, waiting for Helena Maria's answer to Juliana's sweetly uttered query—*"Will you be my new sister?"*

A smile broke on the child's face. "Ja, bitte."

Juliana beamed at Augusta. "Yes, please!"

Augusta looked from her precious child to the precious child on the stage holding a broom as if her life depended on it. Such love filled her breast she could hardly contain it. Later she would be Helena Maria's mother, but she sensed having a sister was what the little girl would respond to most right now. Someone closer to her age and size, on whom she could depend and learn to trust. In time, Helena Maria would realize that being Juliana's sister meant being Augusta's daughter. Augusta would give her time to grow into that role. In the meantime, she would simply love her.

Augusta turned to Miss Wallace. "Would you ready the paperwork for transfer of responsibility, please? Helena Maria will be going home with us."

Konrad

"Are we almost there, Pa?" Walden asked.

At the same time, Folker whined, "How much farther, Pa?"

Konrad gritted his teeth and inwardly prayed for patience. "Another hour, maybe hour and a half to go yet. So, ja, we are almost there."

The pair groaned in unison, and Konrad decided to ignore the wordless complaint. He wasn't any happier than the boys about sitting in the wagon for so long, but the lure of two suits for $3.75 in Marion compared to $4.00 apiece in his local mercantile proved too hard to resist.

Before setting out for Marion Saturday morning, he had packed the back of the wagon with jugs of water and a basket of food, a stack of tarps and blankets in case it got too late for travel and they were forced to camp by the road, and a fat storybook out of which the twins could take turns reading aloud. Now it was roughly noon according to the sun's placement in the sky. The food was half gone. The twins had made a rumpled nest of the once neatly folded blankets in the wagon bed. And they were tired of reading. Konrad was tired of listening to them grumble.

He glanced over his shoulder at their sullen faces. "Come sit on the seat with me where you can see better. One on either side of me."

Mutters rumbled, but the pair climbed over the seat back and settled next to him, Folker on his right and Walden, wearing his newsboy cap, on his left.

He bounced his elbows outward, giving them each a nudge. "Look for crows on your side of the wagon and count them. Whoever finds the most by the time we reach Marion will get a penny's worth of gumdrops."

The boys craned their necks, searching the brush, the ground, and the sky and calling out numbers. Konrad silently congratulated himself for finding a means of entertaining them. He stared at the winding road beyond the horses' bobbing heads and hoped for glimpses of Marion over the next rise.

He spotted something, but it wasn't a house or store. A buggy was coming toward them, right down the middle of the dirt roadway carved from the prairie. Then he gave a start. That was the Krahns' buggy. As it drew nearer, he realized several people were riding in it—three for sure in the front seat, and more in the second.

Gerhard must have recognized Konrad, because he stuck his hand out the side and waggled it.

Walden pointed ahead, bouncing on the seat. "Pa! It's Onkel Gerhard and Tante Martina! And . . ." A puzzled scowl creased his freckled face. "Somebody else."

Konrad tugged the reins, urging the horses to move a bit to the right, then he drew the team to a stop. Gerhard pulled his buggy alongside the wagon, and Konrad got a good look into the conveyance. A dark-haired boy around the twins' age sat between the Krahns. A second boy, a little older, sat behind Gerhard in the second seat. In the middle, Juliana Dyck held a little blonde-haired girl who was clutching, of all things, a broom. Gussie sat behind Martina.

So she'd found her ride. He was torn between gratitude and envy.

Gerhard beamed at Konrad. "What are you folks doing so far from home?"

"Pa is buying us new suits at the mercantile in Marion," Folker answered, his voice as chipper as a spring sparrow. "Our old ones are too small."

Gerhard chuckled. "I'm not surprised. You boys are growing as fast as the wheat. It's nice to encounter you. This way some of our best friends get to be the first to meet our newly adopted sons. Titus, Amos . . ." He angled a smile at the boys by turn. "Please meet Herr Rempel and his sons, Walden and Folker. That's Walden wearing the cap. Can you say hello?"

"Hello," the boys said in unison, reminding Konrad of the twins.

"Hello," Konrad said. Walden and Folker stared, as quiet as Konrad had ever seen them.

Gerhard leaned sideways a bit. "I don't know if you can see behind me, but Frau Dyck and Juliana were blessed, too. Little Helena Maria is coming to live with them."

Konrad bent low and peeked past the others' heads to Gussie. She looked straight back at him, her eyes reflecting peace and . . . something more. There was much Konrad wanted to say, but not with the Krahns listening in. So he said, "That is wonderful. Congratulations, Guss—Frau Dyck."

"Danke," came her soft voice.

"Danke," the little girl said.

Gerhard chuckled. "Ja, well, it is a long ride and we should be

going on. Enjoy your shopping trip. I look forward to seeing the
boys wear their new suits. Guten Tag, Rempel family." He flicked
the reins, and the buggy rolled away, carrying the Krahns and
the Dycks away with it.

"Pa?" Folker tugged at his sleeve. "Onkel Gerhard said a little
girl was going to live with Tante Gussie now. Does that mean
she is Juliana's sister?"

"Ja, Son, that is exactly what it means."

Folker sighed. "Juliana is lucky. She gets a new sister."

Walden leaned forward and looked past Konrad to his
brother. "And did you hear? Onkel Gerhard and Tante Martina
get new sons."

"Ja." Folker's lower lip poked out. "But we don't get anything."

"You're getting new suits." Konrad gave Folker a teasing
bump with his elbow. "What more do you think you need? Another brother? A sister?"

He hung his head. "A mother."

Konrad clenched the reins in his fists. He wasn't the most
educated man in the world, not even the most educated man in
the small town of Alexandertol, but he knew this much. The
Rempel family should be more than Konrad and two small
boys. It should also include a wife and one—nein, two now—
blonde-haired girls.

They were so close to Marion, but he smacked the reins on
the horses' rumps and called, "Haw! Haw!" The horses snorted,
but they turned the wagon around.

Walden clung to the rocking seat. "Pa, what are we doing?"

"Going back to Alexandertol."

A little squawk left Folker's throat. "But what about our
suits?"

"We'll buy them at our own mercantile." It would cost more,

ja, but what cost even more—what cost too much—was denying these feelings. He couldn't go on fighting with himself. Even if she rejected him, even if she laughed in his face, he wouldn't be able to go another day without asking Gussie to join him in holy matrimony.

Chapter Thirty-Four

Augusta

"Mister? Someone is following us." Amos, the older of the two boys adopted by the Krahns, leaned sideways and peered behind the buggy. "I think it's the driver you met on the road. The one you said was Herr Rempel."

Augusta gave a jolt. She sat up as high as possible and peeked out the little window in the leather canopy, her hair catching on the ragged bristles of Helena Maria's broom. He was right. But why were the Rempels returning to town?

Martina turned backward in her seat and aimed a worried look at Augusta. "I hope nothing is wrong. The boys seemed so excited about shopping in Marion. They haven't had time to do that yet."

"Maybe one of them got sick." Juliana shifted Helena Maria a bit, grimacing. Her legs were probably tired from supporting the child's weight.

"Oh, I hope not." Martina worried her lip between her teeth. "Gerhard, stop and let them catch up. I need to be sure Walden and Folker are all right."

"Whoa . . ." The horses responded to Gerhard's command and came to a stop.

They sat quietly, waiting, the wind gently rocking the buggy and Helena Maria softly humming as she toyed with the bristles of her broom. Finally the crunch of wagon wheels on the ground reached their ears, and Konrad brought his wagon up beside Gerhard's.

He searched the interior, and his gaze landed on Augusta's. "Gussie, I have to talk to you."

"Now?" The word squeaked from her throat.

He nodded. "Juliana and Helena Maria can come, too. There are blankets in the wagon bed. The children can stretch out, be more comfortable. I brought sandwiches and dried apples, too. They can have a . . . a wagon picnic."

The twins whooped and climbed into the back.

His gaze did not waver from her face. "Will you please ride with me? So we can talk?"

Augusta didn't move. Why, she couldn't explain. Hadn't she longed for his company? Hadn't she counted the minutes of conversation they shared and wished for more? Another four hours of driving stretched before them. They would be on the prairie with no curious eyes save their own children's. They could talk to their hearts' content. So why didn't she get out?

Martina reached across the seat and patted Augusta's knee. "If you don't want to go, you don't have to. But he seems to have something important on his mind. If you don't let him say it, it will fester between you two." She glanced at Gerhard over Titus's head, and he nodded. She gave Augusta's knee one more pat. "Take my parasol from beneath the seat to keep the sun off your face, but go, Augusta. You'll regret it if you don't."

Never would Augusta have thought she would take advice from Martina Krahn, but she did as the woman suggested. She climbed down from the buggy, helped Juliana and Helena Maria out, and rounded the back of the vehicle. Konrad was already at the side of the wagon, his face reflecting both apprehension and joy.

"Here, Helena Maria. You first." He caught the little girl under her arms and swung her over the side into the back. The child giggled and peeked at Augusta and Juliana over the side. "Now you, Juliana." He made a sling with his hands. She stepped into it, and he raised her high enough to clamber over in a somewhat ladylike fashion. She sank down, and Helena Maria's little face disappeared, too. Only the tip of the broom handle stuck up above the box's side.

Then he turned to Augusta. "Ready?"

Her pulse thrummed, but she nodded. He made no sling of his hands nor lifted her beneath her arms. Nein, he put his hands on her waist and boosted her up. And then he smiled at her so shyly that her face flamed. She snapped the parasol open and angled it over her head while he went around the horses and climbed up on his side.

Gerhard waved, then flicked the reins. The buggy rolled past with Amos lounging by himself in the second seat. Konrad glanced at her. "I'll wait until they're far ahead. Then the wind won't toss the dust from their wheels in our faces."

She nodded. Always solicitous. When the Krahns' buggy had crossed a small rise about a half mile ahead, he chirruped to the horses, and they obediently strained forward. They rode without talking until his wagon had topped that same rise, and then Augusta shifted slightly to face him. "What did you want to talk about?"

He stared straight ahead. "I wanted to tell you . . . I know I am nothing like Leopold. Hannah called him a rowdy man, and she always said it with a laugh, as if just the thought of him brought happiness. I am a quiet man, Gussie. He was strong and handsome. I am strong—I have to be to mold the iron. But handsome? Nein, I am not."

He'd seated her on his right, and she had a view of his profile and the pinkish ripples flowing from the lobe of his ear down his neck and disappearing beneath his collar. Maybe he was quiet because he thought his scars made him unattractive. Although it might be considered a personal topic, she decided it should be said. "Hannah never thought you were unattractive. Nor do I."

He shot a quick, astounded glance at her, then zipped his gaze forward again. "Ja, well, danke for saying so, but I have mirrors in my house. So I know. I cannot compete with Leopold in appearance. Nor in wealth."

She shook her head, confused. "Konrad, why do you think you need to compete with Leopold?"

"Because you love him, and because I love you."

Augusta peeked into the back of the wagon. The children were seated in a circle around a basket, happily munching. They seemed completely unaware of the emotionally charged words being spoken by the man holding the reins.

She faced him again and kept her voice low. "Konrad, when a man tells a woman he loves her, he should be looking her in the eyes, not staring at the backside of horses."

He snorted a chortle. He planted his fists on his knees, the reins trailing down his calves, and turned his head fully until he was gazing directly into her eyes. "I love you, Gussie."

She smiled and kept her eyes pinned on his. "I love you, too."

His eyebrows shot up. "You do?"

"Ja, I do. I have for a long time. But I didn't tell you, because I know I am not what you're seeking."

He frowned. "What makes you think that?"

She gestured to the wagon bed. "I had Juliana. Now I have Helena Maria, too. The first requirement on the list you gave me for your new wife said no children. Remember? You were worried she wouldn't be able to love your children if she had her own. And you . . ." She swallowed, worry nibbling. "You said you weren't sure you'd be able to love someone else's children as much as you love Folker and Walden."

He turned forward again and gave the reins some gentle pulls that brought the horses back to the center of the wagon wheels–carved road. "Ja, I did say all that."

"And did you mean it?" If he meant it, then all hope was lost for them. True, Juliana was growing up fast and wouldn't live at home many more years, but Helena Maria was young. She would be under Augusta's roof for a good long while. She couldn't possibly marry someone who would not be able to love her children.

Very slowly, his head bobbed in a nod. "Ja. At the time I said it, I meant it. I feared it. But you see, Gussie, I wasn't considering grace." He chewed the corner of his mustache, the muscles in his jaw twitching. Then he sighed. "I wish I was a learned man so I could say things better, but these past weeks you have shown me that it is possible to love children who were not born to you. You love Walden and Folker. I can see it."

She sent a smile over her shoulder at the boys, even though they weren't paying any attention to her. "Ja. I do."

"My boys love you, and they love Juliana. You should hear how they talk about her, always like she is the most wonderful person. The things they say make me love her, too, because she is so good to them, so kind and patient." He flicked a side-eyed look at her. "Like her mother."

Augusta's face heated again, but she didn't mind. She enjoyed hearing shy Konrad Rempel sing her praises. Now it was time to sing his.

"Konrad, as much as I love my daughter and your sons, the favorite minutes of my day for the past month have been the ones shared with you on my porch when you come to pick up your boys." She set her hand on his sleeve. His muscles beneath the fabric of his shirt, as taut as rope, proved how hard he worked. "I've seen your kindness, your faithfulness, your helpfulness. Every day, after I tell you and the twins good-bye, I go inside and mourn because it will be twenty-four hours until I can enjoy your company again. You don't have to be a learned man to know what that means. Tell me what it means, Konrad."

He angled his face toward her. His eyes glowed with gratitude and wonder and more love than she thought she would experience again in this lifetime. "It means you feel for me what I feel for you. And I would be a fool not to ask you to be my helpmeet, my wife, my lover, my joy, my—"

She placed a kiss on his lips that cut off whatever else he planned to say. Forward? Ja, but she had to show him how much she wanted to be everything he was asking her to be.

He pulled the reins, drawing the wagon to a stop, set the brake, then draped the reins over his knees and cupped her face in his gloved hands. The borrowed parasol slid sideways, shielding them from the children's view. He delivered a sweet, lingering kiss that assured her his words were sincere. Then he pulled back, adjusted the parasol, and smiled at her. "We will not do that again until we stand in front of a preacher and commit our lives to each other, but that won't be much longer." He tipped his head, his expression teasing. "Will it?"

She would exchange vows with him tomorrow were it not for the little girl holding a broom in the back of the wagon. "As soon as we can work everything out, the answer is bitte—yes, please."

He laughed, the sound filled with joy.

The remainder of the drive they talked about important things—the reason Helena Maria held to her broom, whether Helena Maria would be ready to attend school with the other children in the fall given her shaky start to life and her attachment to a broom that represented her mother, where they should live, how to combine their belongings and bank accounts without denting Konrad's pride or being unfair to Augusta. They also talked about incidental things—her favorite flowers, his favorite desserts, whether they'd rather play checkers or dominoes, favorite childhood memories, traditions they wished to pass on to their children, and so much more.

Augusta's throat was hoarse by the time they reached Alexandertol, but she wasn't finished talking with this man. She didn't want to tell him good-bye. Not even for a day. He parked the wagon in front of her house and helped the girls down. Juliana took Helena Maria by the hand and led her up the walkway. Konrad and Augusta followed more slowly, their arms around each other's waists.

At the base of the stairs, he turned and took her hands. "Will you come to church tomorrow, or is it too soon to take Helena Maria into the community?"

"I will be there. Church is important to our family." How she loved saying *our family*. Now it meant Juliana and her. Eventually it would include all of them. "Helena Maria is part of the family, so she will learn to go."

He nodded. Then he dropped his head back and groaned.

Alarmed, she tugged his hand. "What is it?"

"The mercantile is surely closed by now. Folker and Walden didn't get their new suits in Marion. So they'll have to wear their old ones, and Folker says his coat cuts him under the arms."

He looked so forlorn that she shouldn't laugh, but she couldn't resist. "A suit doesn't matter. Take the boys in their best shirts and britches. Then bring the suits to me on Monday. If I cannot modify them to fit better, I'll go to the mercantile and buy fabric and make some."

His eyebrows shot high. "You can do that?"

"Ja, I can do that." She decided to tease him a little bit. "I can cook, and sew, and garden, and I love children, and—"

His laughter ended her list. "Ja, ja, I see what you're doing here. Proving to me that you are the helpmeet I wanted all along. Well . . ." He leaned forward until their foreheads touched.

"The most important thing on the list is *loves the Lord*. He shines in you, Gussie, and I am a blessed man to spend the rest of my life with you."

If he didn't want any more kisses until their wedding, he needed to leave now. She stepped free of his light hold. "You and the twins come for dinner tomorrow. We need to get used to sitting around the table, all of us together. Because together, bonded through God's amazing grace, we are going to weave a life tapestry of joy and commitment."

He lifted his hand and gently slid his knuckles along her jaw. In a tender voice, he said, "Amen."

Epilogue

Augusta

"Ja, well, that is the last of it." Konrad rested his hand on the top of the packed crate and smiled at Augusta. "Now all that is left is saying auf Wiedersehen."

Augusta drew in a full breath of the early fall air and released it by increments, savoring each moment of this sweet farewell. Sweet, because it all was so right. She leaned against her husband's sturdy frame and relished his arms closing around her. For a full week she'd had the joy of stepping into his embrace whenever she pleased. She would always treasure this man's stalwart presence.

His cheek rested on her head. "Maybe it is too late to ask since we've already packed your belongings, but are you sure you don't want us to live in your house?"

The concern in his tone brought her head up. "I am sure, Konrad. We've talked about it, and it's best for us to make your house our home."

He sent a slow look from the peak of the roof to the porch where the two of them had spent so many pleasant evenings in the past months. "But this house, Gussie . . . it is so much nicer than—"

"No more comparisons." She put her finger on his lips and smiled. "I want to be close by the blacksmith shop, where I can come out and talk to you whenever I please. I want the children to grow up witnessing how hard their father works to provide for them and learning from your example to be hard workers themselves." She shrugged and picked at a splinter caught in the fabric of his shirt. "Besides, the Eliases are moving in later this week. Where will they go if I change my mind? Nein, we have it all worked out, and we will keep our word to them."

Dean and Ernestine, which was how Augusta now thought of the couple, would take excellent care of the house Leopold had built. They were renting it. Augusta hadn't felt right about selling the house, and Konrad agreed that it should belong to Juliana someday. If, when Juliana was grown, she decided to sell it, Augusta wouldn't stand in her way. But deep down, she hoped her daughter would choose to live in it so she would be close enough to visit. The thought of not having her eldest child under her roof was hard to consider.

She dropped the tiny sliver of wood onto the ground. "I pray Dean and Ernestine will build as many happy memories here as I did."

Konrad chuckled, gazing down at her from beneath the brim of his familiar leather cowboy hat. "Frau Elias will be cooking in your kitchen and also sitting in your desk at the schoolhouse. I hope she realizes what big shoes she has to fill." Then he sobered. "Gussie, you have given up so much to become my wife. I hope you won't regret it someday."

Augusta gaped at him. "Regret it? Konrad . . ." She shook her head. "What I am gaining is so much more than what I leave behind. Will I miss this house? Ja, but home is where the people you love reside, so *home* is now with you. Will I miss teaching the children? I know I will, but my teaching days are not done. Watching Helena Maria grasp the meaning of words and numbers, seeing her grow in knowledge brings me so much joy."

Pride filled Augusta as she considered how eagerly the little girl responded to her tutelage. "As fast as she's learning, in another year she will be caught up and ready to join the children at the school. For now, though, staying home with me will let us bond as mother and daughter."

His expression turned contemplative. "Do you think she will be able to leave the broom at home when she goes to the school-house?"

Although Helena Maria was still attached to the broom, after three months of living with Augusta, she no longer hugged it to her side both day and night. She dragged it with her, let it lay nearby while she played, or propped it against the table at meal-times. Juliana reported that it spent more nights resting against the headboard of the bed than in the bed with the girls. The pixie-like child had made tremendous progress in so many ways.

"Ja, I think she will. But if she doesn't, it will be a lesson in compassion for the other children." Augusta wagged her finger. "Learning compassion is always a good thing."

He kissed her forehead. "Helena Maria is lucky to have a teacher-mother who lavishes compassion on her. The two of you are a match made in heaven."

Augusta's heart swelled. "As are we, my dear husband."

Right there on the street under the early September sunshine, he delivered a sweet kiss on her willing lips. Then he drew back and tipped his head. His brows came together in a thoughtful frown. "What did you read from the poetry book last night? 'Grow old . . .'"

"'Grow old along with me! The best is yet to be,'" she quoted.

His eyes crinkled in a tender smile. "Ja, well, let us go home to our children and get started on that 'yet to be.'"

She rose on tiptoe and pecked a kiss on his lips. "Let's go."

Readers Guide

1. The characters in this story are based on Mennonites from Germany who settled in Russia in the late 1700s at Catherine the Great's invitation, wooed by the promise of practicing Christianity and pacifism without government interference. Many of these "Russian Mennonites" then left Russia for America in the late 1800s when the promises were broken by the new leaders. Religious freedom was so important to them that they left their familiar country and, in some cases, family members in order to freely worship God. Have you ever had to give up something important or comfortable for the sake of Christianity? How did the sacrifice affect your life?

2. Martina organized the Frauenverein (which, by the way, was an actual organization founded by German immigrants in New York in the early 1800s and spread all across the United States in communities with a strong German presence) for a selfish reason: She wanted to find an orphaned child to bring into her home. Although her motivation was selfish, the end result proved positive for many members of Alexandertol. This reminds me of God making beauty from ashes. When in your life have you seen God use what could be deemed a negative circumstance to make beauty from ashes?

3. Despite being a widow, Augusta lived a comfortable existence and seemed content with her life. In this time period, being without a husband was a "bigger deal" than it seems today. Why do you think she didn't remarry after Leopold died?

4. Due to a childhood accident, Konrad carried scars on his face and also on his soul. In what ways did his scars affect him, physically and emotionally? What advice would you have given Konrad when he compares himself unfavorably to Leopold?

5. Dean Elias viewed losing his summer job in Alexandertol as a hardship, but taking the job in Marion turned out to be a blessing. Recall a time when something "bad" turned out to be "good" for you. Take the time to thank God for His mysterious ways.

6. Augusta set out to find a new wife for Konrad. Why is this pursuit so important to her? Have you ever been determined to do something special for someone you know? Did you accomplish your goal? How did the effort affect you as well as your friend?

7. Gerhard secretly used alcohol to numb his feelings. Why was this an ineffective practice? What are some helpful ways to deal with sadness or disappointment?

8. Even though Augusta was widowed, she decided to bring another child into her house so Juliana would have a sibling. Both she and Juliana prayed for God to guide them to the child she was meant to adopt, and God introduced them to Helena Maria (and her broom). Why was this child

a good "fit" for Augusta and Juliana? Have you ever considered adopting a child? What do you think are the benefits of adoption? The challenges?

9. Initially Konrad didn't want to marry a woman who was already a mother. Could you understand his reasoning? What changed his mind? Are you or is someone you know part of a blended family? How did you/they meld into one? What words of wisdom might you give to someone who is trying to blend two families into one?

10. Early in the story, Augusta mused that to consistently grow in God's grace was the most important thing Juliana could learn. Do you agree or disagree with her assessment? Why or why not?

11. Martina and Gerhard eventually found contentment in their childless state. Then God provided the means for them to adopt children. Martina contemplated Psalm 37:4 when considering the timing of the children's arrival. What does it mean to delight yourself in the Lord? How does He shape the desires of our hearts? What desire are you harboring that hasn't yet been met? How will you find your contentment while you wait?

Acknowledgments

I always thank family first, so deep appreciation expressed to my wonderful parents, *Ralph* and *Helen Vogel*. They taught me to love and serve Jesus, to love books and learning, and to appreciate the sacrifice of the previous generations who left their countries for America, thereby giving me the opportunity to grow up in freedom. Thank you to my husband, *Don,* for dedicating decades of his life in the service of this country. Thank you to my daughters, *Kristian, Kaitlyn,* and *Kamryn,* for being all-around terrific people and for giving me ten precious granddarlings. And thank you to those granddarlings for carrying our faith and patriotism into the next generation.

Major shout-out to my wonderful agent, *Tamela Hancock Murray.* The past twenty years have flown, and she has guided my career so well. I am ever grateful God chose her as my publishing expert and advocate.

Since I'm speaking of publishing, thank you to the fantastic *team at WaterBrook* who puts the stories of my heart into the hands of readers. And to *Julee Schwarzburg,* editor extraordinaire, bless you for your recommendations—you know your stuff!

Finally, and most importantly, heartfelt gratitude to my *Father God.* He has met my every need and blessed me with the desires of my heart. I cannot imagine navigating life without His presence, guidance, and grace. May any praise or glory be reflected directly to Him.

About the Author

Kim Vogel Sawyer is a highly acclaimed, bestselling author with more than 1.5 million books in print in seven different languages. Her titles have earned numerous accolades, including the ACFW Carol Award, the Inspirational Readers Choice Award, and the Gayle Wilson Award of Excellence. Kim and her retired military husband, Don, live in central Kansas, where she continues to write gentle stories of hope. She enjoys spending time with her three daughters and her grandchildren.

An Essential Historical Fiction Collection by Bestselling Author
Kim Vogel Sawyer

Find more titles at kimvogelsawyer.com